Praise for *Underneath It All* by Margo Candela!

"Page turner? Check. Laugh-out-loud funn[illegible] voice
with a new take on life for mode[illegible] you
how glad I am that Margo Ca[illegible] great
big reason to prune my toes [illegible]'t
put this fun, ve[illegible]
—Alisa Val[illegible]
New York Times b[illegible] author of
The Dirty Girls Social Club

"Fresh, vibrant, and fast-paced, *Underneath It All* takes you from laughing out loud to screaming, "You go, girl!" Jacqueline Sanchez is as real as they come, a woman trying to make the most out of life in spite of her meddling family, boring ex-husband, hottie Mayor boss (and his ex-soap star wife), troubled friends . . . oh, and her therapist. Don't miss the chance to experience Margo Candela's captivating debut!"

—Kelley St. John, author of
Real Women Don't Wear Size 2
National Reader's Choice Award winner 2006

"Margo Candela balances wit as sharp as a tack with engaging humor and a voice as fresh as spring rain . . . An engaging, sexy read about friends, family and career choices—all of which seem to be taking modern career woman Jacqueline Sanchez down a circuitous and sometimes near impossible path in life. Definitely a book to save for an afternoon of guilty pleasures."

—Caridad Piñeiro, author of
More Than a Mission and
Sex and the South Beach Chicas

"Witty, fast-paced and full of memorable characters, this is one book you won't be able to toss aside until you've read every delicious word. Jacqs will be your new best friend!"

—Berta Platas, author of *Cinderella Lopez*

Please turn the page for more praise!

"Margo Candela and her new novel, *Underneath It All*, are refreshing. Anyone whose life has veered off track will relate to her heroine, Jacqueline Sanchez, who bears the weight of an impossible boss, needy friends, and questionable romances with comedic wit and self-deprecating humor. You'll fall in love with Jacqs and *Underneath It All*."

—Patrick Sanchez, author of
Tight and *The Way It Is*

"A sweet and funny debut about a woman defying family expectations and coming into her own. *Underneath It All* is tops!"

—Stephanie Lehman, author of
The Art of Undressing and
Thoughts While Having Sex

"Get ready for a witty, cleverly humorous treat! The main character Jacqs, is so charmingly human, she'll make you smile throughout the entire book. I could not put *Underneath It All* down. Loved It! Loved It! Loved It!"

—Lara Rios, author of
Becoming Latina in 10 Easy Steps and
Becoming Americana

"By turns, uproariously dysfunctional, touching, and melancholy. Margo Candela nails it all in her fabulous debut . . . Jacqs' trials and tribulations are so familiar and relatable, you'll find yourself both laughing and cringing, often at the same time. Straight-up, straight ahead, and straight on 'til morning, because trust me, you will stay up all night to find out what lies *Underneath It All*."

—Caridad Ferrer, author of *Adious to My Old Life*

"Take one recently divorced woman with a dead-end job, add an over-the-top boss, a collection of friends-with-issues, a platonic "boyfriend" getting in touch with his inner Donald Trump, and a hilariously dysfunctional family, and you end up with one fresh, funny, fabulous read. Jacqs Sanchez is a vibrant and complex character who practically leaps off the page."

—Tracy Montoya, author of
Shadow Guardian and *Finding His Family*

Underneath It All

MARGO CANDELA

KENSINGTON BOOKS
http://www.kensingtonbooks.com

KENSINGTON BOOKS are published by

Kensington Publishing Corp.
850 Third Avenue
New York, NY 10022

All Kensington titles, imprints and distributed lines are available at special quantity discounts for bulk purchases for sales promotion, premiums, fund-raising, educational or institutional use.

Special book excerpts or customized printings can also be created to fit specific needs. For details, write or phone the office of the Kensington Special Sales Manager: Kensington Publishing Corp., 850 Third Avenue, New York, NY 10022. Attn. Special Sales Department. Phone: 1-800-221-2647.

ISBN 0-7582-1570-3

First Kensington Trade Paperback Printing: January 2007
10 9 8 7 6 5 4 3 2 1

Printed in the United States of America

Acknowledgments

First and foremost I'd like to thank cell phones and insomnia. Without the two working together, this book may have never happened, or at least not as happily. Thanks to my cell phone's memory I was able to retrieve the number for my agent, Jenoyne Adams, and call her in the hopes she was still interested in my writing. Luckily for me she was. Within the same 24-hour period my wonderful editor at Kensington, Sulay Hernandez, was suffering a bout of insomnia that had her searching the Web for modern Latina-centered fiction. The Internet gods led her to my web page and I woke up to a request to submit. She read the manuscript in one sitting and with the guidance of her able boss, Kate Duffy, it ultimately became *Underneath It All*.

I'd also like to thank my friend Laura for her keen eyes and patience. I owe thanks to my mother-in-law, Melanie, for practicing her hypnosis on me, which uncovered the nut of the idea somewhere deep inside me. A big thanks to my husband, Jeremy, not for always being patient but for at least being there and also not being there when I needed my space. And to my family: Mom, Dad, Martha, Laura, Monica, Alfredo, Justin and Andrew, for all the angst, anxiety and good times that have made me who I am today. And, of course, to Elias. If it hadn't been for his arrival, I would never have lost my job and I might still be toiling at some failing Web site. Thanks, kid!

1

Mamá and Papá

I'm not looking forward to this but it has to be done. I've put it off long enough.

I clear my throat and lean forward, the sticky plastic covers on my mother's prized living room furniture squeaking under my sweating thighs.

"*¿Necesitas algo, mija?*" My mother half-rises from her chair, closest to the kitchen and with a clear view of the front window and door, always at the ready to take care of someone else's needs.

"No. *No gracias.* Uh, I'm fine, great, everything is . . ." I trail off as my mother looks over at me and smiles expectantly. I have no choice but to bury my face behind my glass of limeade, made fresh from the limes my father grows in the side yard.

I'm home on a Saturday night, sitting with my parents watching "*Sabado Gigante*" (a raunchy Mexican variety show that seems to have been on before television was born) while my mother folds my laundry and my father hogs the remote. This is completely typical, except I don't live here anymore, my mother laundered clean clothes straight out of my suitcase and there are no batteries in the remote my father has a death grip on. (My brother Noel has been dispatched to the store to get some, conveniently leaving me alone to make my announcements in some privacy.)

It can go one of two ways. Either my parents will be upset but reasonable, and offer me their unconditional love, or they'll react the same way they did when I announced almost a decade ago that I was leaving our tidy home in Los Angeles to go all the way to Berkeley for college.

My dad just grunted and said I shouldn't expect him to pay for it. He thought it was just another one of my indulgences—like braces and driving lessons. My mother took to her bed for three days. The neighborhood priest had to be called over, even though my parents have never attended church on a regular basis, to coax her back to the land of the living. But I left and I made it! And now I'm back home asking for their permission, their blessing, their . . . something, for what I've done now.

I look at my watch. If my brother takes his time (and I know he will) I can break the news and have things well on their way to being sorted out before he gets back. (My brother is the only one in the Sanchez family who doesn't like to fight.)

I think I'll get some more limeade.

"Jacquelyn, did I tell you Yvette *dio luz a su bebé?*" my mother calls after me. "A boy! He's beautiful."

"Yes, *Mamá*, you did."

From the moment she picked me up at Burbank Airport from my flight in from San Francisco, my mother has been dropping names of old friends and distant cousins who have gotten married or given birth, some even in that order.

"If Yvette could see you now she'd never recognize you!" This is her way of expressing disapproval that I don't live around the corner, if not at home, as do the rest of my brothers and sisters. "I told her you look so different every time I get to see you."

"When she knew me I was a *gordita* with a bad haircut."

"You weren't *gorda*, Jacquelyn," my mother says, dismissing what may have been the most formative experience of my teenage years. "You just weren't tall enough for your *peso*."

I double over the sink, laughing. Not only from what she said, but that I'm now doing my parents' dishes. It's only costing me my last free weekend and the $350 I spent for my last-minute full-fare plane tickets.

After I'm done I walk back into the living room and catch sight of Noel lurking in the bushes. I wave him off. He retreats back to the driveway to smoke a cigarette.

It's now or never . . . I'll just wait for the next commercial. Much too soon Don Francisco, sweaty after judging the impressive posteriors of the dancing ladies, screams us all into my less-jiggy reality.

"*Mamá*, *Papá*, I have something to tell you guys." My mother stills her hands, my father glances away from the TV. "Nate and I are getting a divorce."

Technically we're already divorced and he's moved out, but I don't think it's necessary to burden them with those details.

"And," I blurt out before they can say anything, "I've got a great new job! I'm going to work for the mayor of San Francisco! Actually, his wife, but it'll make it easier for me to get a job on his staff. I'll finally get to work in politics like I've always wanted. Isn't this great?"

My mother sits there, blinks for a few seconds and then unleashes her tears. My father shakes his head and tries to change the channel with the useless remote.

"Noel!" my father barks, causing me to jump, "*las baterías!*"

"Don't cry, Mom! It's totally OK. *De verdad*, really. It's all been sorted out. *Cuidé todo*," I add before my father can make some comment that I've come home so my parents can clean up my mess. "Everything is settled and taken care of."

"*¿Otro trabajo*, Jacquelyn? You left how many jobs this year?" I know I'm not meant to answer so I keep quiet while my father gets warmed up "*Es un* commitment, *un compromiso*. You just can't walk out of it because you are bored or it's hard. What will people say? *Personas hablarán*."

"People will talk about my job history or my divorce?"

This makes my mother cry harder. I can only assume she thought I flew home out of the blue to tell her to expect another grandbaby. Poor woman.

"*¿Qué dice*, Nate?" my mother asks through her sobs. "He agreed?"

"Nate?" I knew she'd take his side. Righteous anger fills my chest and I think it's time my mother got a realistic view of her adored Nate. "It's as much his divorce as it is mine. It's both of our *culpas,* not just mine, Mother."

"Don't talk to your *madre en ese tono de voz,* Jacquelyn. This is my house, you will respect us." My father looks angry, but then again he always looks slightly pissed off. "This is our *casa, hable con respeto.*"

"Or what? Move out?" I snort under my breath. If they want respect, shouldn't they respect my decisions, too?

My mother's crying continues and my father turns his face away from me. This just makes me angrier and bolder.

Over the years, I've composed a speech in which I declare my independence from following the unwritten Mexican-American handbook that seems to dictate our lives. This seems like a good time to give it. It's not like I can get in any more trouble than I am in now.

"*Mamá. Papá.* I know you don't understand, but I have to do what is best for me. Whether it's leaving a job or a *husband.* I am not a bad girl, I mean, *person* . . . I just . . ."

The phone rings. Noel creeps into the living room sheepishly and tosses the batteries at my father before fleeing once more. My mother answers the phone and bursts into a fresh bout of tears, news of my divorce out of her mouth before she says hello. My father jams the batteries in the remote and turns back to the TV.

I think it's best to save my announcement about entering therapy for another time.

2

Myra

"Never, NEVER let Anita or Lei answer the door. That's rule number one." Myra, wearing old jeans, a peasant blouse and Teva sandals, leads me at top speed up a grand staircase into the inner sanctum, as she calls it.

"Aren't they the housekeepers?" I was under the impression it was one of the benefits of having them around. It's my first day on the job and clearly I wore heels that are too high for all this sprinting.

"Security announces everyone on this cell. It's your job to figure out if they are to come to the front door, garden or back through the kitchen if they park in the garage. She answers the door for her friends and guests. She likes to keep things informal but controlled."

"Do they use the front or back door?" So far I have two other cell phones I need to keep track of: one for her appointments and another for her personal use. "Is there a difference other than, uh, location?"

Myra pushes open a pair of double doors and rushes inside. I glance around nervously, but avoid looking at the huge, picture-perfect bed that dominates one side of the master bedroom. Without looking back she leads me through another doorway into a walk-in closet of epic proportions. It's as big as my living room/dining room/kitchen and filled with a dizzying array of clothes, shoes and handbags.

"She absolutely covets these black thong panty liners. Buy them in bulk when they're on sale. It'll make your life a lot easier." Myra shoves a velvet case in my hands. "To her jeweler, number is on the desk, the clasp is broken again."

"Holy crap!" Inside is a collar of diamonds. My working-class family didn't have much, but we would never have let a virtual stranger come into our house and start going through our possessions. "Should I be fingerprinted or something? Or, I don't know, meet her?"

"I hope you like to read." Myra hands me a stack of magazines, journals and newspaper clippings. "When she asks for a new magazine or newspaper, always subscribe for two—one for you, one for her. She expects a summary of every interesting article, news event and other topical stuff, divided by subject, articles photocopied onto acid-free paper and in the ivory folders. The red are for event backgrounds. Blue are for family and friends. Birthdays, current job, rehab stints, eating disorders, divorces. Usual stuff."

"She keeps files on her friends and family?"

"She doesn't. You do. Everything else is pretty self-explanatory." Myra finally stops moving and turns around to give me a hug. "Don't look so worried. This job is a piece of cake! You're perfect for it."

"Can I call you if I have, you know, questions?"

"I'll be in Tibet and India, Jacqs."

"Can I come with you?"

3

Mrs. Mayor

"Katherine?" Nothing. Not even a courtesy flicker in my direction. "Katherine?"

My boss, Katherine Bishop-Baxter, née Kate Bishop, aka Mrs. Mayor when she's not in earshot, scrutinizes every inch of her perfect exterior while she keeps the City of San Francisco waiting.

In the year I've worked for her she's never been on time, much less early, for any of these things. You'd think I'd be used to it by now.

Behind me her makeup artist, Natasha, a six-foot-four-inch former college football player wearing tiger-print pants and a halter top, bites into her fist as she watches Mrs. Mayor pick up a lipstick brush.

"Katherine, the Mayor would like to know if you'll be much longer," I say, trying to sound neither intimidated nor frustrated. To show any sign of either just encourages her to further debate lip liner and gloss versus just gloss on her collagen-enhanced lips.

"You couldn't look more luminous," Natasha adds in hopes his, er, her canvass won't go from masterpiece to velvet painting with one unnecessary stroke.

"Is he waiting?" Clear blue eyes blink back at me innocently.

She knows he's waiting. He's always waiting for her. We're all always waiting for her.

"Do something, Jacqs," Natasha hisses into my ear as she swoops in on her custom-made Lucite kitten heels and begins to smooth out Mrs. Mayor's already perfectly coifed hair. "You couldn't look more perfect, Katherine. So classic."

"Thank you, Natasha." She doesn't put down the lip brush.

Since she rather suddenly ascended, by virtue of a fabulous marriage, into one of the most established and prominent social and political families in America, Mrs. Mayor has totally transformed herself. From her hair to the color of her toes, all is engineered to convey an image of a refined Wasp. But something is missing. Something so elusive Mrs. Mayor has made it her life's goal to steal it, buy it or fake it—class.

"Don't you agree, Jacqs?" Natasha digs her favorite hairbrush into my side.

"I completely agree." I do and I don't, but now is not the time to quibble about the shade of eye shadow and the way Natasha applied it.

"I just think I look so . . . bland?" Many of Mrs. Mayor's sentences end in a question even when she's making a demand.

"Bland!" Natasha gasps. "I don't do bland, Katherine. I am not a bland person. It goes against my nature."

"I don't think Katherine means bland, Natasha. More like refined and classic." I quickly step in between Natasha and Mrs. Mayor.

"I don't know?" With some difficulty Mrs. Mayor squints at her reflection. Her most recent round of Botox has left her skin smooth and expression-free.

"You'll photograph well, Katherine." This usually gets the process moving along, but today Mrs. Mayor is extra-doubtful.

"Don't you think I look a little too like I'm playing the part of the first lady? That part of my life is over. I want people to accept me in my new role, not in my old one."

Mrs. Mayor's insecurity about her soap-star past isn't helped by the fact that the Baxter clan thinks she's a bit déclassé. Not that there is anything wrong with being a former soap opera actress, but a former soap opera actress who posed for *Playboy* . . . that kind of muddies the waters.

"Do you have any plans today, Jacquelyn?" Mrs. Mayor continues to hold the brush centimeters from her cupid's bow. Natasha emits a low-pitched wail.

The new stylist, a small, birdlike woman who, in the week I've known her, has worn a variation of the same black pants and turtlenecks with a changing array of chunky jewelry, pokes her head out of Mrs. Mayor's walk-in closet. "Is everything OK?"

We all ignore her.

"Besides this coffee thing with you and the Mayor this morning?" I've officially been on the clock since 5, she slept in until 6:30. We're supposed to be there at 7:30 which is like . . . now. "I have a couple of midday meetings to resolve about that, um, issue with your steam shower and then, um, I'm coordinating your schedule for next week, after you and the Mayor get back from your weekend in Napa."

"And the dry cleaning? I want to wear my Narciso Rodriguez and they promised they could get the awful cigar-smoke smell out of it." Label-speak is Mrs. Mayor's second language. A dress is not a dress but a (insert designer name here).

"Of course, top of my list. I'll pick it up right after this thing that we're supposed to be at now."

When I started working for Mrs. Mayor, I thought my dreams of hobnobbing with San Francisco's political elite and working to make the city a better place for everyone were a little closer to coming true. Instead my days are full of meetings with personal shoppers, aestheticians, fitness trainers, private chefs and dieticians. I don't have time to figure out solutions to the homeless issue, turning around bad schools and how to keep potholes filled. I have enough on my hands with making sure the Mayor's wife looks and sounds good so he can do his job.

"Busy girl, Jacquelyn." She fluffs her hair and moves one golden highlight from the left to the right side. And, just like that, she's gone from sophisticated first lady to aging LA party girl.

Natasha throws up her hands in defeat and starts to alphabetize her huge makeup case.

"Yes, busy." What I really plan to do is meet a couple of friends for lunch and go to a doctor's appointment.

"Sounds like fun. I wish I could putter around like a normal person. It must be nice," Katherine says sincerely as she continues to stare blankly at her reflection. "What kind of mascara are you wearing, Jacquelyn?"

"I'm not wearing any, Katherine." I want to add that it's not even 8 in the morning and I haven't had a chance to have my first cup of coffee of the day, much less sweep on a coat of mascara.

Mrs. Mayor, on the other hand, has two people (Natasha and her stylist) dedicated to the sole task of getting her ready for a burnt coffee and sticky-donut meet-and-greet at a neighborhood recreation center in Chinatown. Downstairs, a house staff of three takes care of all the other essential tasks like cleaning, cooking and opening the car door. And then there's me, her personal assistant. I take care of everyone and oversee everything Mrs. Mayor.

"No mascara? Lucky you." She gives me the once-over and it makes me stand up straighter. "I think Keiko overdid the highlights . . . Who does your color, Jacquelyn?"

"Um, I don't color my hair, Katherine. It's pretty dark. Naturally." My hair *is* great, glossy and thick, thanks to my mom and her weekly mayonnaise treatments. Sure, now I can't stand the smell, look or existence of mayonnaise, but I credit it for one of the reasons Mrs. Mayor would trade in her all-American ice-princess looks for my exotic Latina beauty. At least, this is what I like to think as I eat my dry sandwiches. I'm allergic to mustard.

"Oh." More staring. It's like she's drunk on her own reflection.

My hands tighten into fists and then I count to ten. What do I care if she's late? She's always late. Reporters have taken to calling her the Late First Lady of San Francisco. Why can't she hurry the fuck up!

"I just don't know about this scarf . . ." She pinches the pink silk Hermès scarf between her fingers.

"It sort of bunches up at the neckline," I eagerly agree. She got it yesterday after her weekly three-hour spa visit. I had to make do with a nap in an empty treatment room.

"Here, you take it, Jacquelyn. It's more of a brunette thing." It's not a compliment to me or the scarf.

"Thanks." My fists relax. Slightly.

The stuff she tosses aside without a second thought is in a whole other league from my older sisters' Sassoon jeans hand-me-downs. The first time Mrs. Mayor offered me stuff from her closet, I said no thank you, just as I had been taught, and watched as Danny (Mr. Mayor's driver and resident letch) carted off a garbage bag full of Marc Jacobs, Gucci and Prada to the Goodwill. Some of the stuff still had tags on it.

After a designated time, enough to keep Mr. Mayor waiting, but not enough to truly piss him off or give me an aneurysm, she stands up from her vanity table and sashays toward the door, only to stop short.

We all hold our breaths waiting for what comes next.

Mrs. Mayor may be retired from the biz, as she fondly calls it, but still manages to live her own soap opera in real life, with me and everyone else here as bit characters. No matter how trivial the matter, Mrs. Mayor will milk it for every ounce she's worth.

"Do you think this dress makes me look puffy?"

"No. Nope. Not at all." Even if it does, it's my job to get her downstairs, on his arm and out the door as soon as possible. I watch her turn this way and that way until loyalty forces me to say something mildly negative, but easily remedied. "Well . . . Maybe there is a *hint* of a panty line."

"Hmmm. Maybe you're right . . ." Mrs. Mayor twirls around like a dog chasing its tail and after a few turns she reaches up under her dress and yanks off her panties. With a completely straight face she hands them to me. "Do something with those, will you, Jacquelyn?"

4

Anita and Lei

I rush past Mrs. Mayor as she stops to take one last look at the complete package in the full-length mirror by her dressing room door.

"Danny, ready in ten to twelve minutes." I whisper into the phone/walkie-talkie units I've outfitted us with. "Stand by with the car. I'll call Vivian in five."

I head down to the kitchen where Lei and Anita are waiting with a glass of freshly pressed carrot and parsley juice and Mrs. Mayor's coat and purse.

"Good morning, Anita, Lei. How long ago was this made?" I hate to ask but I know Mrs. Mayor will. Silently, Anita hands it to me and begins to feed carrots into the commercial-grade juicer. I gulp it down while inspecting the contents of Mrs. Mayor's handbag.

"The stylist told me to prepare that bag," Lei says as she smooths a lint brush over Mrs. Mayor's coat.

It's a clutch. Six is *so* fired. As this woman is the sixth stylist in as many months, we don't bother to memorize their names anymore—they are either One, Two and so on and so forth. Mrs. Mayor blames them for all her bad press, bad moods, bad weather . . . She complains to me and I give them the heave-ho, along with a generous bonus and a promise of a glowing written recommendation signed by me in Mrs. Mayor's name. Then it's on to the next one.

"She can't take a lizard-skin clutch to a coffee and donut meet-and-greet. Reporters will be all over her ass and then she'll be all over mine." I take a peek inside at the label and groan, it's Dolce & Gabana lizard. Six obviously didn't get the memo on our (my) plan to make Mrs. Mayor seem more down-to-earth. Like carrying a purse she got on sale at Nordstrom, not one with a six-month waiting list—only bypassed after a fax on official City of San Francisco Mayor letterhead.

I dump out the purse's contents into mine. All she really needs to carry are lip gloss and a compact of pressed powder. I'm the one who carries around the PDA, phones, sewing kit, cash, credit cards, keys, panty liners and nipple petals to keep the headlight action to a minimum. (Mrs. Mayor's nipples refuse to be anything but erect and her doctor refuses to inject them with Botox. Something about possibly impairing her future ability to breast-feed. Yeah, like I won't be the one who ends up doing that for her, too.) And the gum, can't forget the gum. The one time I did she invoked the holy name of Saint Myra. Since her departure to an ashram in India, Myra has become the measure of all that's good and holy in the realm of personal assisting.

In cases where I screw up, like forgetting the gum, Mrs. Mayor will say, "Myra would never have let this happen. Myra always made sure I didn't have to worry about things like this."

Anita hands me today's paper so I can quickly page through, looking for anything Mrs. Mayor shouldn't see before me, like Emilio Cortez's *San Francisco Times*'s column and his latest jab at Mrs. Mayor. Where he gets his info is beyond me, but I have my suspicions.

Emilio Cortez, Pulitzer Prize–winning reporter and Mr. Mayor's archenemy. For fun, he likes to write withering Op-Ed pieces on all things Katherine and Kit Baxter—the Barbie and Ken of politics, as he's dubbed them. He's also raising some (valid) questions about a few pet bills of the Mayor's. I don't know which annoys Mr. Mayor more, the fact that Cortez published a link to some saucy Mrs. Mayor pics or that he exposed a slight problem with nepotism in the Mayor's administration.

As self-righteous as San Franciscans can be, they love juicy gossip, and their ingrained contempt for anything SoCal has made Cortez the man to read every weekday morning and on Sunday.

And there it is buried in his musings about the state of San Francisco: "First Lady or Washed-Up Soap Star?" I tear the whole thing out.

"She hates that picture. Put it on my desk, Anita. Thanks. I'll deal with it when we get back."

Mrs. Mayor likes to read all about herself, especially the bad stuff. So I indulge in a little creative freedom with dossiers I present to her in the specially ordered pale-lavender folders. Pictures are swapped, names are highlighted, and stories that will make her sad are kept to a bare minimum. What makes her most sad, though, is when her name isn't in the press.

"Your phone," Anita says curtly. She doesn't like me much and I've learned not to care.

"Which one?" I dig through my bag, a roomy leather hobo I got on sale at Banana Republic. It dwarfs Mrs. Mayor's silly clutch. I wonder if she'll notice if I borrow it. "Hello, this is Jacquelyn."

"Jacqs! I need her ass down here ASAP! Kit is stalling a building full of people waiting for Her Majesty. Reporters are foaming at the mouth!" It's Vivian Martin, Mr. Mayor's va va voom, highly competent and newly married press secretary. "She better know what this thing is for. Make her write it down on her hand or whatever it is you do to make her seem lucid. Last thing we need is a repeat of last week."

"She's been thoroughly prepped. Not to worry. She was just a little off that day. Cramps, bad ones."

As long as Mrs. Mayor sticks to the script, she comes off as an intelligent and charming woman. But if someone throws her a curve ball, or she's dipped into her stash of Xanax, things can get ugly fast, like asking the president of the Korean-American Association if his mother has any sushi secrets she'd like to pass on.

"Prepped or not, where the hell is she?" Vivian doesn't like Mrs. Mayor much and Mrs. Mayor likes her even less. But when they deal with each other in person you'd think they were long-lost sisters.

"On our way, Vivian. In the car. Traffic. Call you in five." I don't like lying to Vivian, but I have no choice. It's not like I can climb the stairs and physically carry Mrs. Mayor to the car.

"Jacqs, where do you think you're going?" Natasha plunks down her makeup case on the counter and takes my face into her hands. "She's taking a pee. We have two minutes, tops."

"Now that she's not wearing panties, she'll save all sorts of time urinating." I try to stand still as Natasha works her magic on me in overdrive.

"Next time use a straw to drink that stuff. You look like you went down on E.T."

"Thanks for the tip." I stop and listen to the sound of $600 shoes on the mahogany staircase. I reach for my cell phone just as Natasha finishes applying my lipstick, walking along with me as I try to get to the foyer without breaking into a run. My life would be lots easier if I could wear Rollerblades. "OK. We're a go. Danny, we're a go. Mrs. Mayor is at the foot of the stairs."

She stands there looking impatient. Anita helps her slip on her coat while Lei stands by with a glass of the funky-colored juice.

"I don't have time for breakfast." Mrs. Mayor allows Natasha to give her one final polish. The (fired) stylist pulls out a lint brush and flutters around, picking off imaginary lint until Mrs. Mayor clears her throat. We all automatically take a few steps back. "I'll just have some gum."

I hand her a piece with the same hand she put her panties in.

5

Bina

"Guess what, Jacqs?" Bina asks, her nut-butter brown skin looking flushed and dewy. We're sitting at the sporadically open Casa Sanchez Mexican Taqueria near San Francisco General Hospital where she works erratic hours as an intern.

The place is swarming with people flashing their Casa Sanchez (no relation) logo tattoos (a kid in a sombrero riding a giant ear of corn) and claiming their free lunch at the counter. You get a tattoo and as promised they produce a free lunch—for the rest of your life or for as long as you have the tattoo.

During my lean days, right out of college, I actually considered getting one. My plan was to make a difference, a good one, in the world. Instead I took a job at some lame dot-com and after a while began to believe I deserved a raise every three months for enjoying the various perks each subsequent company offered to get me to work there. That I had even considered taking a minimum-wage job as a public television intern was never mentioned by anyone, least of all me.

Sometimes I wonder how my life would have turned out if I'd gotten the tattoo and lived up to my own expectations. But why torture myself with ifs? It's all water under the bridge and saved interest on student loans I was able to pay off early.

"Hurry! Guess!" There are only a couple of ways to get the glow she has. I know she's not pregnant, since our periods are weirdly synchronized.

"You won the lotto." Both of us buy a weekly joint ticket but I know she buys one of her own on the sly . . . at least I hope she does, because I do.

"Jacqs! Be serious," Bina says, ignoring the guy next to her who is buttoning up his shirt after exposing way too much of himself for a medium *hortacha*, side salad and superburrito. "Try and guess!"

"You got crabs again." Bina and I have always shown our affection for each other by casually hinting at various imaginary afflictions and diseases. STDs are always a favorite and a way for both of us to declare independence from our sex-phobic rearing.

"I'm getting married!" Bina beams, radiates, fairly oozes bride-to-be stupidity.

"To who?" I know the answer but I can't help myself.

A couple of months ago, Bina went to a friend's housewarming party I had to skip because Mrs. Mayor needed me to hold her head still, post-Botox. While Bina was commiserating about her stressful job, Sanjay Gupta, hotshot tax attorney, walked in. They talked for about fifteen minutes, and since then it's been a non-stop Sanjay Gupta lovefest.

"Married," she says just to hammer it in, making me flinch, "to Sanjay, of course!"

"You're joking." She may be lying but her complexion isn't.

"Look!" she gushes, and I recoil when she shoves her enormous rock under my nose. "See!"

"You. Are. Not," I sputter, almost collapsing face-first into the guacamole bowl. "You don't even know this person!"

"I know. A woman knows," Bina says, patting my hand sympathetically so her ring catches the light and temporarily blinds me. "My parents and Sanjay's parents have agreed that it is a good match."

"They've what, and when did this happen?" I stare hard into her eyes to see any signs of madness or that this is her idea of a joke. A sick one. How could I have left her unsupervised? I am a bad, bad best friend.

"Agreed that it's a good match!" she giggles a bit hysterically. Usually Bina is a no-nonsense kind of gal, with her stylish yet conservative inky bobbed hair, skin devoid of almost all makeup except eyeliner, but right now it looks like she's been dredged in fairy dust. "He asked me last night. OK, he actually asked me a couple of nights ago but there was an issue with the ring."

"Are you crazy?" I ask with sincerity. She must be crazy. Then I remember what I did for love so who am I to call her crazy. But still. "Fucking crazy, Bina."

This woman—a doctor and homeowner, who I've seen drink many an overgrown frat boy under the table, happily flash a cheering crowd of men at Mardi Gras and swim nude on our last trip to Hawaii—is allowing her parents to essentially arrange her marriage to a man she's known only a few weeks? If my mother hears about this she'll pester me until I give in to an arranged marriage myself. *No gracias*, sincerely.

"Aren't you happy for me?" she asks, her smile still plastered to her face.

"Don't try to change the subject. What do parents have to do with this, this thing!" I'd never even consider dating a man who had my parents' seal of approval. And something about Sanjay Gupta just doesn't sit right with me. He's too perfect.

"You just don't understand, Jacqs. Indians are a very traditional people," says the woman who has watched every season of *Friends*, every *Melrose Place* rerun twice and eaten enough Americanized Mexican food with me to qualify as anything but a traditional Indian girl.

"Traditional? And Mexican-American Catholics aren't?" Has she learned nothing from me?

"I'm getting married, Jacqs!" Bina's caramel-colored eyes are shiny with happy tears. If Mrs. Mayor envies my eyelashes, she needs to get a load of Bina's. They're so long and thick, they're pornographic. "Married! Can you believe it!"

"Which part?"

6

George

"Sorry I'm late. Traffic." I sit down and stare up at the pleasantly weathered face of George as he helps me with my chair. His face has the kind of sun damage that comes from lounging on the deck of a boat over an extended vacation in the Mediterranean, not from working outdoors like my dad got his premelanoma tan.

Attractive sun damage or no, George is just a friend. (An older, sophisticated, rich and in-the-process-of-separating-from-his-wife type of friend.) We met a month ago in the art history section of a bookstore I wandered into, looking for the latest issue of *Cosmo* while Mrs. Mayor was visiting her spiritual consultant. We've only met for lunch and dinner. It's perfectly innocent and expensively delicious—financially for him and morally for me.

"Never apologize for keeping a man waiting. It ruins the anticipation, Jacquelyn." He signals for the waiter to pour the wine.

"Then I'm not sorry I'm late." I cross my legs, tightly. From the waist up I assume my nonchalant pose: head cocked slightly to the side, arms loosely crossed and showing my manicure to its best benefit.

"I'm so glad you could meet me today. I was craving their lobster pot pie," he says as if lunch at Aqua was a trip to a Fisherman's Wharf crab stand. "You don't mind seafood, Jacquelyn? I should have asked before I had my assistant make the reservation."

"This is fine, I guess." I'm teasing, but I'm really not. I'm not hungry, already slightly tipsy and I should be stone-cold sober for my appointment after my second lunch of the day. I take a generous sip of wine and then another.

"That's what I love about you, Jacquelyn. You're always willing to try new things on the spur of the moment." George leans forward and his tanned hand reaches out and tucks a strand of hair behind my ear. His fingers give my ear a little tickle and I feel myself blush, which just makes George smile wider.

"So what do I owe the occasion to, besides your craving for lobster pot pie?" I ask, not a little bit flustered.

"You look beautiful, as usual, Jacquelyn," he says. From under the table he brings up a good-sized box from Neiman Marcus, sets it on the table and with one strong finger pushes it toward me.

"George!" Panic, excitement and embarrassment rise from the very core of my traditional Catholic upbringing (that so far I've been able to mostly ignore).

"Don't say you can't accept it. It's bought and paid for and I've torn up the receipt. If you don't want it, we'll have to give it to the hostess." He rests his jaw on his palm and grins at me. I could never treat money the way he does, even on a good day. Even on a good day when I was really drunk and felt like shopping.

"George. Really. What will people think?" I'm sure my shrink would think the George thing has its deep roots in the distant relationship I have with my father. I don't want to know what my parents and Bina would think of me "dating" a gift-giving man who is still legally and spiritually married. I don't think it's an issue for anyone but George's wife, who he doesn't seem to think much of.

"No more stalling, Jacquelyn. Open it. Just take a look. What could be the harm in that?"

"You ever heard of Pandora's Box, George?" I open the box and, snug in layers of white tissue, is a chocolate tote bag that puts my Banana Republic bag to shame. I momentarily lose my composure. "Oh, wow!"

"You like?" George asks, looking very pleased with my reaction. He knows I don't like it, I lust it. "The saleswoman told me it's crocodile."

"Crocodile!" Oh, crap, it must have cost at least . . . a lot. "George I can't—"

"It would be very rude for you to not accept it, Jacquelyn. What would your mother say about your manners if she found out you refused a heartfelt gift from a friend?"

"I can think of a few things she'd say," I say, not looking up, right before she hauled me off by the hair to a convent. I could always donate it. Or I could keep it; no one would ever have to know where it came from. I could store it away in my closet, way back in my closet if, on the odd chance, my parents would ever come visit me from Los Angeles. Unannounced visits are a big thing with Latinos.

"Tell me the truth, do you love it?"

I tuck the bag carefully back into the box, carefully, so as not to crease the tissue paper. If I'm going to hell, at least I'm going in a (crocodile) handbasket. "I don't hate it."

7

Dr. N

"Jacquelyn, how long have you been coming here?"

"Um?" I made my first appointment with Dr. N the day after I signed the divorce papers that ended my brief marriage to Nate, my college everything. "A while."

"And?"

"Uh, it's been very interesting?" I'm a lot past tipsy now. I sip my tub of coffee in hopes of sobering up before I head back to work. "And enlightening, of course. I've got such a better perspective on myself and my family and, uh, stuff."

"Have you found your parents to be more supportive of your decisions in life because of our work together?"

"Supportive?"

If my family ever found out I was seeing a shrink they'd freak. In their view, one of the worst things a child can do is talk about family secrets and problems to a complete stranger who is not sitting on the other side of a darkened confessional screen. With all I've already put my family through, the last thing they need to hear is that my psychiatrist thinks they are codependent, antisocial, closed-minded traditionalists.

"As an adult you have a right to make decisions based on your needs. There is nothing wrong with that, Jacquelyn. It's part of growing up and having your own life."

"Of course! I completely agree."

It's my fault Dr. N has this impression of my family. If only I had been more selective about what I shared with her. Then she'd be able to see the good and other stuff I'm sure is relatively normal about them. Not that I think they're crazy or bad people, they're just—

"Jacquelyn?" My shrink, whom I'm paying $150 a minute to listen to me, sounds annoyed that I've drifted off.

"Sorry." I take a swig of coffee and try to concentrate on what she wants me to say. "I've made a lot of progress, uh, with my family. I think."

"Your communication with your parents and family is much more open?"

"You bet. We communicate so much more openly now." I guess I've told them to get over it and accept me for who I am. Just not so directly, disrespectfully and definitely not in so many words.

"And how about your other issue?" Dr. N asks, arching a fuzzy eyebrow.

"Ah . . . my inability to, uh . . ." I should know this by now. I should be able to recite it backward and forward.

"Take responsibility for your own actions, assume control of your life and improve your chances for establishing a long-lasting, fulfilling relationship."

"Yeah, that!"

I don't mean to make Dr. N work for her fee, but I have lots on my mind. The last thing I need is to spend an hour in therapy.

"So do you think you've made progress toward those goals?"

"Well, sure. I can relate to my parents as an adult. I'm so over my divorce, and I'm not falling apart because Bina totally blind-sided me with her getting married. I really feel as if my life is coming together. I might even be ready to start dating again. Soon."

See? Calm, cool and collected. Dr. N nods and smiles. Good answer!

"And how about the issue of your work life encroaching on your private life?"

"Oh, that. Ha, I've managed to work out a balance." One time, for lack of anything else to bitch about and forty minutes of therapy to fill, I talked about Mrs. Mayor and what I do all day, night and morning. Nothing major, nothing out of the ordinary, I just went through a normal 23-hour day on the job. Somehow she got the idea that I'm hiding behind my work and now it's an issue, one of my many issues, as she puts it.

"I was hoping you'd say that. We seem to have gotten you to a good place in your life."

"Absolutely." Not.

"We should really evaluate where you want to go with your therapy." Dr. N looks at me and smiles slightly. "At this point, I think we've come to a good place to think about scaling back or even stopping your sessions."

"I think that's a good idea." Is Dr. N dumping me? If I've ever needed a therapist, it's now. "Umm, but I think scaling back would be better for me. You know, to kind of wean me off. Like the patch when I quit smoking."

I took up smoking for about a week after a messy breakup from a rebound jerk and stayed on the patch for six months. How was I supposed to know I had an addictive personality?

"I agree. So, instead of meeting once a week, let's go to one session every other week and then go from there." Dr. N makes a series of checks and scribbles on my chart. "I think we can safely say you'll be out of therapy soon, Jacquelyn. Isn't that great news?"

"Great. Great news. Thanks!" I never know if I should thank Dr. N; I mean, I *am* paying her for her time, and it's not as if she's doing me a favor, but I can't seem to not thank her. "OK. See you next week. Thanks."

"Very good. Good-bye, Jacquelyn." Dr. N nods slightly, the corners of her mouth twitch into a smile, and she looks down at her notepad.

"Bye, thanks again."

8

Yolie

Though I know my mother will still love me if she doesn't hear from me this very moment, guilt outweighs my duty to both the woman who puts bread on my plate and to San Francisco's traffic laws. Not by much, but still. I hate calling her after seeing my shrink. Even with the physical distance between us, I always feel she can sense when I've been up to no good, therapeutic or not.

It's not like I didn't try the church route, in fact my shrink sessions are essentially sanctioned by the pope. Shortly before my divorce, when things were looking very bleak, I went to confession and after twenty minutes the priest suggested I consider talking to a professional. If I told this to my mom she'd only want to know what scandalous things I said to the poor priest.

"Hello? Hello?" The phone gives one more watery ring. I make an illegal right turn onto Market Street and am soundly beeped by at least five other drivers.

"*¿Hola?*" I freeze. It's my sister Yolie, the last person on earth I want to talk to. Ever. "*Hola!*"

"Oh, hey, Yolie. It's me." I check my watch, a Cartier Panther Mrs. Mayor gave me. It's yet another hand-me-down, but real. I made sure to inquire, discreetly, when I went in to get the battery changed the day after she gave it to me to make up for almost getting me arrested at Saks.

"Me?" Yolie's mouth twists around the word. She knows who it is. Who else would be presumptuous enough to assume that she would know it was me except for me?

"Your sister, Jacquelyn." I roll my eyes and run a red light. "Is Mom around?"

"*Mom* isn't here. *Mamá* is running errands," Yolie says. All of a sudden I am reminded how wonderful life can be when you're not her.

"Whatever. Tell her I called."

"Sure." Click.

"Hello?" I make sure we're disconnected. "Talk to you soon, you miserable bitch."

9

Mr. Mayor

I pull into the Mayors's cavernous garage, behind Mr. Mayor's new silver Audi, but leave the Neiman Marcus box in my car, underneath some of my own dry cleaning, as if trying to suffocate the poor, innocent bag for my guilt at not having the will to decline it. I try to do this casually. This place is wired tighter than the White House and I never know who's watching or from where.

Last week, I was casually checking out the Audi and noticed it was open so I slid into the driver's seat. I put my hands on the steering wheel and imagined I was driving up to Bodega Bay wearing sunglasses and wrapped in that luxurious cashmere coat Mrs. Mayor had me pick up from Neiman Marcus last week (where I spied the bag that I mentioned to George, which is now in my trunk). I was about to trail my hand out the window, letting the cool Pacific wind slip through my fingers when Danny sprang up behind me, cackling like a madman. I almost peed all over the buttery leather seats.

I hurry up the stairs and into the Kitchen. And this is a Kitchen with a capital *K.* Miles of polished concrete floors and marble counters and rich wood everywhere. Even the fridge has wood doors. Julia Childs could be interred in this Kitchen.

My parents' kitchen back home on Idell Street is all about bleached linoleum and scuffed Formica. I thought that my flat's kitchen, with its tile floor and Corian countertops, was pretty spiffy. But now I know better. I have seen the light gleaming off polished marble. It turns out a kitchen can be more than just where you cook and store food. It can be a place you want to hang out in, not one you avoid at all costs because your father will yell at you to wash the dishes because you happen to be dumb enough to get caught grabbing a Pepsi out of the fridge.

The Mayors's Kitchen gets used only when they throw a dinner party or when Mr. Mayor pours his morning bowl of sugared oats. Mrs. Mayor doesn't cook, big surprise, but has all her meals scientifically prepared for optimal nutrition and minimal fat by her diet guru, who delivers them several times a week. When they do throw a party, a caterer brings in the food already cooked. Seems a shame to waste such a beautiful space. Don't even get me started on the master suite.

I can go to the suite one of two ways: through the foyer, past the library and up the main staircase, or up what Mrs. Mayor calls the butler's stairs, which are right off the Kitchen and past Danny's room.

I shift thousands of dollars of chiffon and silk onto my other shoulder and head out to the foyer. I'm in no mood to tangle with Danny right now. I hurry past the closed library door, trying to silence the clicking of my heels on the vast marble floor that covers the foyer leading to the upstairs staircase.

"Jacquelyn?" Mr. Mayor is standing in the open door, wearing his tuxedo with his bow tie undone. I almost let the miles of silk fall to the floor and puddle around my suddenly sweating feet.

"Yes, Mr. Mayor?" I ask with my stomach in my throat and flakey mascara on my cheeks.

"Can I trouble you for a moment?" he asks in his clipped, prep-school tone. He's a weird but intoxicating mixture of Mel Gibson (pre-pre-pre-*Passion of the Christ*), with the suaveness of Jude Law and a dash of a young Robert Redford all rolled into one hunky man package with a brain the size of Minnesota.

"Sure. No trouble. What's the matter?" Please let it be your loveless marriage and the lack of me in your life.

"Can you help me with this?" He gestures to his bow tie.

"Um. Well . . ." I couldn't be more shocked if he had gestured to his zipper.

"My wife is holed upstairs with a small army of people putting her face on. Please, Jacquelyn. I'm sorry, but I never could manage a decent knot."

This is true. Many a time I've seen Mrs. Mayor undo his tie right at the front door and do it over again. I don't know about any zipper action. That's the one thing Mrs. Mayor is completely mum about: their sex life.

"Um, OK." Why not? It's just a tie.

"You're a lifesaver." Mr. Mayor's long legs stride over to me and he takes the heaps of clothes out of my suddenly weak arms. God, he smells *so* good. Clean and powerful. He piles them onto a very expensive side chair as if it was a Pottery Barn floor sample and the clothes were Old Navy sweatpants. He stands straight up in front of me, his arms at his sides. "I'm all yours."

"Yeah! Ha! Um. OK. Lift your chin?" He does. Like this is totally normal. I quickly tie his bow tie and step back. I can't help but reach over and straighten it. "There! All done!"

"Many thanks, Jackie." He casually checks himself out in the huge gilded mirror.

"Actually?" He looks over at me, straight into my eyes for the first time. I lick my lips and work up my courage. "Actually, Mr. Mayor, it's Jacqs."

I rush past him, gather up his wife's dry cleaning and try not to fall face-first on the stairs.

10

Mrs. Mayor

I try to tiptoe past Mrs. Mayor, hoping that she can't see me through the cloud of face powder and hairspray. I get as far as her closet before she stops me cold.

"Jacquelyn, I hope you didn't forget to pick up my studs?" Mrs. Mayor leans back so Natasha can apply false lashes with her huge but deft hands. "Reynold promised he'd have them ready today."

"Uh . . ." She never mentioned anything about any studs, but that's not her fault. "Actually, I talked to Reynold about what you might be wearing and he suggested something else."

"He did? And what does Reynold think I should be wearing?" She arches a brow and tilts her head.

"Yeah. Something new. They haven't even been on display or in the catalog yet. He said he'd be happy to loan them to you for tonight."

"That Reynold." Mrs. Mayor tosses back her head and gives a throaty laugh. "Well, let me see them."

"Uh, OK. Let me just go put these down."

"I hope it's nothing too garish," Mrs. Mayor warns.

"No, no. Very classic," I call over my shoulder as I scamper into her walk-in closet and hang up the dry-cleaned gowns with the other dry-cleaned gowns.

Trying to look like the picture of innocence (and it's getting more difficult these days) I drop a pair of two-pairs-for-$10 earrings I picked up at Clair's into Mrs. Mayor's freshly manicured hand.

"Oh! So delicate. Who's the designer?" Mrs. Mayor must be in a good mood. Usually she sits in stony silence as if she's enduring a Pap smear and not getting pampered by a team of people who want only to make her happy.

"I, uh, Sanjay Gupta. He's a new designer. Very new. These, in fact, are one of a kind." This is all sort of true, if it weren't a total lie.

"Is he ethnic? Oh, that should make Martin happy." Mrs. Mayor doesn't like Vivian. With her shampoo-commercial red curls and perfect peaches-and-cream complexion, she's naturally beautiful, while Mrs. Mayor's beauty is the work of modern science. "Make sure she knows, will you, Jacquelyn?"

"I'll call her right now." I actually think Vivian is really nice and competent but distractingly attractive, and therefore usually regarded with suspicion by her own gender. Especially by Mrs. Mayor, who doesn't trust anyone who could be considered a smidgen better-looking than she is. Hey, what does that say about my looks?

In a beauty contest I think I'd come in a solid third. And that's because Vivian was an actual Midwestern beauty pageant queen and Mrs. Mayor has spent so much money on her looks that she can't help but look frightfully good. I'd come in first if the contest was based on raw potential.

"Oh, and Jacquelyn, can you also ask her to make sure the reporters keep their distance during the event?"

Mrs. Mayor pretends to ask, but we all know it's an order. She once told me she hasn't forgotten what it's like to be at the bottom. She was a waitress for a whole month before landing the role of Leslie Dumont, sexy nanny and eventually sexy brain surgeon on the long-running soap *Love and Lies.*

I actually remember Mrs. Mayor's first day on the show. I was fifteen years old and at home for a long, boring summer. *Love and*

Lies was my favorite soap. I was in love with wild Colt Holmes, twenty-four-year-old widower with an infant daughter to care for. I had read about a new character being introduced but hadn't paid much attention. Mrs. Mayor came on in the role of the baby's nanny.

"I'm so . . . so sorry . . . Colt . . . but I . . . can't." Katherine/Leslie batted her eyelashes between each pause for effect. "You can't . . . We . . . can't."

"Leslie, I've never met a woman like you. When I look into your eyes I feel like I could drown." Colt (I don't remember his real name) was shirtless for some reason. Actually, as I remember, he spent most of his time on screen shirtless or in the process of taking off his shirt.

"Like your . . . late wife . . . drowned?" She stared up at him, letting each word drip like honey from her lips.

"Yes, but in a good way." He growled and pulled her into a meaty embrace and then they sucked face. It didn't get much better than that.

I was sure she would be one of those bit characters who'd be around for a while and then disappear. And she did, sort of. Her character turned out to be way more scheming and soon dyed her hair blonde and got bigger lips and boobs, and so a star was born/manufactured. Colt Holmes was eventually killed off, and Mrs. Mayor went on to become one of the most hated and beloved soap opera actresses of her time. And now I work for her. How weird is that?

"Jacquelyn?" Mrs. Mayor never calls me Jacqs, and I never call her anything but Katherine (to her face). I accidentally called her Leslie and she laughed it off, but her look told me I'd get away with it only once. "What do you think?"

She waves her hands toward a selection of dresses spread out on the bed. (None of which is the gown she specifically had me pick up from the dry cleaner for this event.) I run my eyes quickly over the dresses and, as if I'm pulled by a magnet, my eyes land on a pink gown with spaghetti straps, plunging neckline and delicate beading. It's the kind of dress I wouldn't mind being buried in.

I pick it up, imagining myself slipping it on and then having Mr. Mayor come up behind me, putting his big, warm hands on my shoulders and slowly turning me around . . .

"Mr. Mayor . . . we can't. Please . . ." Naturally long and lush lashes sweep against my flushed cheeks.

"We can and we will. Jacqs, I've never wanted a woman more than I've wanted you." His hands undo the impossibly long row of tiny buttons with deft fingers. "Oh, and by the way, call me Mr. Baxter."

"O . . . K . . ." My toned arms entwine around—

"Didn't I tell you, Natasha? I knew she'd pick that one. It's like I can read her mind."

Mrs. Mayor laughs. Natasha giggles, and from the dressing room the new stylist chortles well after the moment.

"Yeah, like you can read my mind, ha!" I busy myself with smoothing out the dress.

"Did you see the latest?" Mrs. Mayor gestures to the Post-it-thick issue of *Home & Garden* where one of the many Baxter residences and its fabulous furniture is anonymously featured in a ten-page spread.

The Mayors are décor poor since his mother emptied the Mansion of every stick of family furniture when her son stuck to his guns and married his soap star. Now it's furnished and decorated nicely, very nicely even. Way beyond Pottery Barn, but not heirloom quality. I don't care how old-timey Restoration Hardware tries to be, it's not Chippendale and never will be. This much I've learned from all my Mrs. Mayor-required reading.

"Make sure to file it with the others after you input the particulars into the computer. Thank you, Jacquelyn."

"Of course," I say, not hinting at the sheer paranoia and pettiness of one of my many Mrs. Mayor tasks.

Part of my job is to sit and listen to Mrs. Mayor talk about the Baxter family sideboards that came over on the second or third ship after the *Mayflower*. The Chippendale chairs presidents have sat on, and the many houses, sorry, estates, where all this stuff resides safely out of her reach since invitations have been few and far between. I have turned all of this information into a complex spreadsheet, which she studies with the intensity of a federal prosecutor on her first big case.

Before she married Mr. Mayor she lived in a two-bedroom condo in Studio City.

"About this event tonight, what can you tell me? I need some interesting insights." She looks over at me or, actually, above my head.

"Um . . ." I wrote up her crib sheet, as usual, and I know she read it, so why is she asking for more information? "What kind of insights, Katherine?"

"Your family is from Mexico, right? This is a benefit for the Mexican Art Museum, correct?" Mrs. Mayor is getting annoyed, and I'm too flabbergasted to be offended.

"Yeah, at some point my family came from Mexico and before that over the Bering Strait, but that's debatable. I, uh, I didn't major in art in college, Katherine. I took Art 101 and, of course, we covered Diego Rivera, Frida Kahlo, just the basics, and I've put those in your memo. As for interesting insights, I'm afraid I'm as clueless as you are," I say before realizing I've called Mrs. Mayor clueless to her face.

Natasha pretends to cough, but her face is red and her eyes are bulging out from holding back laughter.

"Can you let the Mayor know I'll be down shortly?" That means at least another half hour. And, yes, she calls her own husband the Mayor.

"Of course." Last thing I want to do is face Mr. Mayor again after my "Actually, it's Jacqs" incident.

Christ, I'll never live that down in my own mind.

11

Danny

Dismissed with little more than a withering look, I head out of the master suite, down the butler's stairs and stop at Danny's room. He might make my skin crawl, but he'll do just about anything I ask him to.

I press my ear to the door and try to listen for any suspicious sounds. I always imagine that he's whacking off. It grosses me out to even think about it, but I can't help it. Silence, normal silence, at least. It must be safe. I drum my fingers on the door and step way back just in case.

Danny opens the door slowly and peeks out. He must have been doing something nasty after all. When he sees me, his chest puffs out and a huge grin covers his face, as if I showed up at his door with a six-pack and one of Mrs. Mayor's needlepoint pillows with the inspirational sayings her kooky friend from LA insists on sending and Mrs. Mayor insists on displaying.

"Jacquelyn. Fancy meeting you here." He leans up against the doorjamb, crossing his hairy arms over his dingy undershirt. I see he's developing a bit of a beer belly. "Or should I call you Jacqs?"

"No. Danny, do me a huge favor—"

"Huge? I think I can handle that."

"Uh, right, Danny, you pig. Can you skip over to the library and let Mr. Mayor know that Mrs. Mayor will be down in forty-five minutes?"

"Sure. But what will you give me?"

"Nothing, Danny, as usual." I check the polish on my fingers.

"Not good enough. I need some incentive, if you know what I mean." He wiggles his eyebrows at me.

"OK. I won't tell Mr. Mayor that you keep a rolled-up porn mag underneath your seat in the car, if you know what I mean."

"Let me put on my shirt." Danny shuts the door in my face.

"Thanks, Danny, you're a peach."

12

Anita and Lei

I wander into the Kitchen as Anita and Lei, the two-woman cleaning machine, polish and wipe. Since they wear jeans and T-shirts, not the traditional maid uniform Mrs. Mayor believes more appropriate to a mayor's mansion, she insists Danny or I answer the door. She answers only when she wants to seem down-to-earth and she knows it's friendly press or one of her stray Hollywood friends dropping in on their way to Napa.

"Hi, guys. How's everything going?" I try to sound as if I'm asking them not because I'm supervising them but because I myself am being supervised.

"Very good, Jacquelyn," Lei answers cheerfully. She's mopping the Kitchen floor and Anita is scrubbing the counters. Everything looks dust-free and polished. Like a house in a magazine. Exactly the way Mrs. Mayor likes it and Mr. Mayor expects it.

Lei is from China, and how she hooked up with Anita, who's from Honduras, I don't know. Anyway, they've been cleaning the Mansion as a team for years. I don't think they ever exchange more than two words to each other about anything except cleaning while at the Mansion.

Anita hardly ever talks. When I first met her, I asked her something in Spanish, only she gave me a curt reply in accented but perfect English. Lei serves as the de facto head housekeeper. She takes care of all the nitty-gritty details, such as making sure that there's always a large supply of toilet paper and that the mail makes it from the mailbox to my desk for sorting after Danny makes sure it's bomb-free. She also deals with the other people the Mayors employ to keep their house looking good and running smoothly.

The Mayors have a professional landscape service take care of the yard. Bert, the owner, comes along to supervise an ever-changing parade of Latino and Asian men who never come in the house. Not even to ask to use the bathroom. I think they're under orders from Bert to hold it until they're done. Or else they're peeing in the bougainvillea.

Midway through their work, Lei will have Bert in for a cup of coffee in the Kitchen, where they'll talk about the state of the plants and flowers. If Mrs. Mayor wants new plants or whatever, she tells me, and I tell Lei, and Lei tells Bert. While this is going on, Anita goes outside with water and snacks for the crew.

There is a very set hierarchy but sometimes I don't quite know where I fit in. I know Anita thinks I'm privileged, and she treats me with the same polite detachment she treats Mrs. Mayor with. She's a bit warmer toward Mr. Mayor and babies him a bit, which he seems to like. Danny she hates outright. She thinks he's lazy and immoral. She found his porn stash while cleaning his room, and Lei asked me to tell him to keep it somewhere else on days they clean his room.

Lei is friendly with me the same way my bikini wax woman is. She's privy to a lot of the intimate details of my and everyone else's life, but she's so matter-of-fact about what she sees, hears and knows, it doesn't seem to make anyone uncomfortable. Lei does treat me as her superior, though, even when she merely comes to me for confirmation of something she knows needs to be done and has probably already done.

"Would you like some coffee or tea?" Lei asks. Anita pauses. It's her job to make the coffee or tea that Lei offers.

"No thanks. I have some work to do in my office."

13

Natasha

I head through the Kitchen and into my office, the former maid's room, where I spend most of my time when I'm not attending Mrs. Mayor's needs. She had a decorator come in and do it up for me based on my chakras. They don't have a live-in maid since it would be very un-PC. Anita and Lei, who keep this place shiny, have to trek across the city by bus six days a week with the Fast Passes that Mrs. Mayor has me purchase for them. Just because she trusts them with her panties doesn't mean they won't take the $35 and buy crack, or costume jewelry on QVC.

Around my office I've scattered some scented candles along with the tall plain white candles in thick glass containers I got at the botanica around the corner from my flat. When I'm feeling especially superstitious or desperate, I group them all on a table and burn a little sage. This is something I picked up from a wanna-be hippie roommate while at Berkeley. Up until then I thought you had to haul your ass to church to ask for what you wanted.

My parents are lackadaisical Catholics and, aside from an odd cross or two, religion was relegated to church, appropriate holidays and moral occasions where they could use Catholicism to bend me to their will. But my college roommate, a white girl from Connecticut, had a whole shrine set up in her room and it seemed to work for her, so what the hell? There is nothing wrong with lighting a few candles and burning a tad of dried sage during times of crises or indecision. Right?

At least I don't dive for the Xanax like Mrs. Mayor does, which then makes my life all the more difficult. It's hard to present her as the caring and articulate First Lady of San Francisco when she's higher than a cloud and couldn't care less about anything except waving her fingers in front of her face.

"Jacqs, honey, you decent?" Natasha pokes her head in. Without waiting for an answer, she lugs her makeup case over to my bathroom vanity. "We gotta make this quick. Mrs. Mayor will want a touch-up after she's done getting dressed. You're looking a little peaked, darling."

"I have jaundice." For all I know I might.

"Honey, what you need is a vacation and some sex. That'll perk your complexion right up. Always does mine." Natasha takes my chin into her huge paw and begins to paint on foundation.

"Sex? Vacation? I don't think either is in my job description." But I could use more sleep. When I sleep I can enjoy both in my head, don't have to go anywhere and don't have to explain to my mother why I went on a real vacation (and probably had sex, lots of it) instead of coming home for a visit like the obedient nonsex-having-three-times-a-week-calling daughter she thinks she's raised me to be.

"Just tell her you need a long weekend to get laid. She'll understand that." Natasha flicks an extra coat of mascara on my lashes.

"Oh, sure, and afterward we could braid each other's hair and eat s'mores while I tell her all about it." Mrs. Mayor loves gossip. So do I, but this woman thrives off it, especially when it's about her.

"I doubt that woman has ever had a true woman friend. She even finds me threatening." Natasha rubs, tickles and smears with singular concentration.

"Natasha, honey, you're more woman than most biological women can ever aspire to."

Natasha executes a graceful curtsey and then comes at me with a lip brush. In a matter of minutes I look like I've had a week of sun and sex. Or at least some fresh air.

"The 'Isla Bonita' look . . ." Natasha caps her favorite red lipstick.

"Natasha, I hate to break it to you, but you are aware that Madonna is Italian, not a Latina or Indian or whatever she's into this month."

"She's Jewish now, I think." Natasha worships at the altar of the Material Girl, who can do no wrong in Natasha's eyes. All her makeup looks are based on the different phases of Madonna's career. Last week she sent me out Madonna circa "Like A Prayer" and Mrs. Mayor looking like a Waspy version of "Justify My Love."

"So is she pissed at me?" Last thing I want is for Mrs. Mayor to hold a grudge. It'll just grow over the weekend, and I don't want to face an angry wannabe socialite on Monday morning.

"Pissed? Maybe a little high. She *is* clueless. She asked me, *me,* for blow job tips." Natasha puts a hand to her padded breast. "Me of all people."

"She did not!" Mrs. Mayor might have no problem with culturally insensitive questions and assumptions or inspecting my guinea-pig bikini waxes, but she's never gotten *that* personal. "What did you tell her?"

"I told her I was a good Catholic girl saving myself for marriage." Natasha purses her lips and gets back to work on my face.

"You and me both, sister . . . Still, where does she get off asking me about Mexican art? I've never implied I know anything about art, Mexican or otherwise."

"Honey, don't you know yet? We're here to function as emissaries and the tellers of secret wisdoms from our respective tribes. If you were black, she'd ask you how to pick a good watermelon." She shrugs her massive shoulders nonchalantly.

"Natasha!" I'm shocked that she has the guts to say what I've always thought, but never wanted to admit to. No matter how easily I can move between my personas of Jacqs and Jacquelyn, I'm still an anomaly, and the most innocuous events will remind me of that. "It still doesn't make it right."

"No, it doesn't, but that's the way it is. If you want to dance with the piper, you gotta dance to his—or, in this case, her—tune."

"Speaking of which, how's your man doing?" Natasha's husband is a dancer with some elaborate gay revue.

"Doing everyone within dick range, from what I can tell." Natasha fusses with my hair. "You've got great hair, honey. Thank your mother for me. I found some blond pubes in his Calvin Klein. And not my shade of blond."

"What are you doing inspecting his underwear?" I pull my head away. Sure I had my share of suspicions about boyfriends and my ex-husband but I never resorted to digging through the hamper for evidence.

"Jacqs, for such a smart girl you are a stupid woman," she says as she plants a kiss on the top of my head.

"Maybe they just got there by accident." Yep, I think those seven words pretty much confirm my stupidity.

"Yeah, he accidentally rubbed his crotch against some skinnier, younger, more energetic version of me." She checks herself out in the mirror and sighs.

"Jesus wouldn't do that." I swear that's his name and his bit involves a white robe and golden halo. He goes by the Spanish pronunciation of his name, as in HeySeuss, but it doesn't make anything he does any less shocking to his mostly Anglo audience. "He loves you."

"How can he not? I'm fabulous," Natasha says without her normal verve. "This marriage thing is a bitch. No wonder you bailed."

"My circumstances were a little more boring than yours." To say the least.

"Boring, that's me! I'm a boring, old, fat married lady." With one final sweep of the brush, Natasha steps back. "I've never been happier or more miserable."

"Have you considered therapy?" I like Jesus. I just wish he wasn't such a slut.

"Therapy, feng shui, acupuncture, couples massage. You name it, we've done it." She leans in and hugs me hard, all 200-plus pounds of her. "You're the last romantic, Jacqs."

"That's me, a romantic."

14

Nate

I lock my office door and click open a web browser to an anonymizer site. Never can be too careful when one is slightly stalking an ex-husband over the Internet.

Nate is a creature of habit and it's made it very easy to keep track of him, though he did smarten up and change his e-mail passwords shortly after he rightly suspected I was peeking into his accounts. I don't know why he bothered; he lays his whole life out in his blog for the world to read. Why anybody besides me would read it is beyond me, but Nate always thought very highly of himself.

Mostly his entries deal with his job, traveling for his job, movies he's seen and food he's eaten. He also frequents a handful of message boards that I don't bother to search more than once or twice a month. There's only so much personal stuff I can glean from vmware.for-linux.configuration and comp.dcom.sys.cisco postings, other than he's still as big a geek as the day I divorced him.

I find it all sort of comforting; knowing that Nate's life is as boring as I told him it would be if he lost me. The proof is here right in front of me on my monitor.

We met on a wild spring break in Palm Springs, when he saved me from a marauding group of frat boys intent on dousing me and my T-shirt with stale beer. True, I did "spill" the first one down my front, but it rapidly got out of hand. Nate was a party boy, majoring in nothing in particular at UC San Diego, and I was in debt up to my then-unpierced ears as an earnest Berkeley poly-sci major with definite plans to continue on to law school and fight the good fight. Friends said it would never work out, but they were wrong. At least until we split up.

We wound up living together, much to my mother's horror and my father's denial, when Nate came up to San Francisco after graduation to make his millions at some dot-com. After a year Nate proposed—or rather, was strongly encouraged to propose by me right before a rare visit from both of my parents. I couldn't ask Nate to move out of our flat and there was no question that my parents would stay with me, I mean, us. I had to figure out a way to show my parents I was an independent grown woman, without getting in trouble for it. I decided the best way to do it was over the phone.

It all went wrong somewhere and I somehow gave my parents the impression that Nate had something *very* important to ask my father. After that lie, all it took were three solid days and nights of intense conversation (mostly on my part) to get Nate to march off to Tiffany's.

A Tiffany engagement ring! Not that I didn't have real goals and aspirations (I had taken my LSATs and did well), but getting a ring from Tiffany's was something I had never even dared to imagine, though somehow I always knew I wouldn't accept less.

The appearance of the ring on my finger changed everything. My parents were happy, his parents were happy, even Nate seemed happy. And I felt like a fraud, but it didn't stop me from accumulating a small library of wedding guides, books and magazines.

Despite all my reading on having the perfect wedding, we ended up eloping. Bina was there, teary-eyed, and some other friends, but no family. We always planned to do something formal, something real, but never got around to it.

Whatever, by that time I was so over it, Tiffany or no Tiffany. I still dream about the ring, though. It was so sparkly and pretty. It wasn't the ring's fault that it symbolized my unrealized dreams of a nice wedding surrounded by our happy families instead of the hasty elopement I suggested only to spare both of our families from having to meet each other. Secretly, I think everyone was relieved. A Nate-and-Jacqs wedding ceremony and reception was just too much trouble for everyone, including Nate and Jacqs, to deal with.

There was nothing romantic or fuzzy feeling about the whole ordeal. I felt cheated, and it was my own fault. I didn't let things progress naturally and so I got an unnatural result—a forced proposal, an impersonal marriage ceremony and a nagging sense that things weren't exactly the way they should be when two people get married.

Nate, on the other hand, settled into married life, *really* settled. I realized this one rare night when we were getting frisky on the couch, instead of staring glassy-eyed at the TV as we usually did when we found ourselves home together after a long day at work.

"Hold on. What the hell . . ." I flipped on the light and, to my horror, found a solid chunk of flesh in my hand where Nate's formerly trim body used to be.

"Let go, Jacqs." Nate moved my hand lower. "Come on, I have to get up early tomorrow."

"Come here!" I grabbed his hand, pulled him into the bathroom and on the scale. "Holy crap, Nate! You've gained . . . what? . . . thirty pounds?"

"Yeah? So?" Nate shrugged. "Listen, baby, this isn't doing much to get me in the mood."

The sight of a shirtless Nate in bright fluorescent light didn't do a thing for me either, but it wasn't the time to be petty. "Nate, this is serious. You have to start going to the gym and especially stop eating fast food."

"I don't have time to go to the gym. Come on, are we going to do it or not?" Nate tugged on my hand and flipped off the light.

"Do it? *It?* We used to make love, Nate. Now we just do it and we don't do it that often. I'm serious. You need balance in your life. It's all work, work, work. All we talk about is your job or what's on TV or where we're going to eat. It's boring, Nate."

"Maybe your little job gives you time to go to the gym, read magazines or whatever it is you do with all your free time, but I have real responsibilities." Nate reached into the medicine cabinet for the dental floss.

"Don't make fun of my job, asshole." But how could he not? I'd been at my fourth dot-com for three months and still didn't have my own desk. I spent most of my day rotating amongst other people's computers or reading magazines in the reception area. For this I was earning $65,000 and I'd already gotten a raise and a promotion, but no desk. Not even a hollow-core door balanced on two filing cabinets. "I'm looking for another job, I told you this yesterday."

"Whatever. I have a real job that I can't set aside just because I feel like going shoe shopping or whatever. How do you think we can afford to live the way we do?" Nate snapped.

"Honey, you don't make nearly enough money to get away with being this fat."

And that was the beginning of the end. No one was surprised when we announced we were splitting up. My mother, of course, but she tends to get upset over every minor and major life event, from cutting bangs in to my hair when I was twelve to shacking up with Nate, to my elopement with Nate, to my failure to stay married to Nate. What did she expect? We were both pretty immature and he was really fat.

Nate's family, an amalgamation of a long legacy of divorces and remarriages, saw this one as an unpleasant but somewhat necessary family initiation ritual. Because of this, I ended up confiding to his mother more than to my own. She was actually very pleasant throughout the whole thing and gave me some good advice, which resulted in my gaining custody of our flat and he taking the ring back and moving out of the country.

The ring was the only perfect thing about the whole thing.

15

Bina

I pull out my cell phone and speed dial the one person who will be brutally honest and tell me when I'm being a selfish pig wallowing in my not so wallow-worthy past.

"Bina?" I check my watch. Less than half an hour to go until liftoff. "It's me."

"Jacqs? Is that you?" I can hear hospital noises in the background. "It couldn't be my long-lost friend Jacquelyn, could it? Twice in one day. It's a miracle."

"Funny, Bina. You should talk. Who is it that flaked on me last weekend to make kissy faces with . . . with that man you say you're going to marry."

"Sanjay, that jerk."

"What's his problem?" I ask smoothly, no accusations, no name-calling, just a subtle reinforcement of what she's already thinking.

"The wedding this, the wedding that. I'm ready to tear my hair out. Where are you? And don't say work."

"I'm getting ready to go to a swanky fund-raiser for the Mexican Art Museum, as a matter of fact," I say smartly.

"With a real-live date? Is he marriage material?" Bina has only marriage on the brain. It's a sickness, really.

"*¿Mamá?* Is that you? Going with the Mayors." I smear some lotion on my legs one-handed, careful to avoid the hem of my dress. A put-together woman, like Mrs. Mayor, would put lotion on *before* getting dressed. I'm still learning.

"I thought so."

Bina hates my job, aside from the perks she seems only too happy to partake in. I think she's jealous of all the time I spend with Mrs. Mayor. Maybe that's why she's marrying Sanjay—a convoluted form of girlfriend revenge. I'll have to ask Dr. N.

"You should let me set you up, Jacqs. I know a very handsome, brilliant surgeon. He just divorced."

"That's always a plus." The George thing and keeping up with Nate's Internet activities just don't leave me with the time or energy for an actual, real date that may or may not lead to a lifelong fulfilling relationship. Just thinking about it makes me want to take a nap. "I don't know if I want to be set up. Too awkward."

"So is dying alone in your flat and not being discovered for weeks or months," Bina says sensibly. As a doctor, she sees all sorts of stuff. Like the single mother who had to drive herself to the hospital to give birth and the many unattached people who go unvisited during their stays in the hospital. "Jacqs, life is all about little decisions, and if you never decide to do anything, nothing will ever happen."

"God, Bina, I'm going to rush off and embroider that on a pillow right this second."

"He was married to another doctor. She's also very brilliant. She used to model," Bina continues, as if I hadn't said anything.

"A brilliant doctor divorced from another brilliant doctor who used to be a model. Gee, that sort of raises the bar a bit." I flick on another coat of lip gloss, hoping I don't overdo Natasha's handiwork.

"I think he wants to meet someone normal. So you would just have to pretend that you're normal."

"I'd have to up my medication. So are we on tomorrow?" I ask. We've had a standing Saturday afternoon matinee date for years now, and I'm not letting her fiancé get in the way of that. Mrs. Mayor is a whole other story.

"I should ask you." Definitely some sort of best-friend abandonment issues.

"Don't be that way, Bina. Anyway, the Mayors are going out of town this weekend, and even if they don't, I'll turn off my cell phone." Or at least put it on vibrate. It's one sure way to have a cheap tickle once an hour or so.

"You promise? Because if you don't . . ."

"I swear. I promise. See you tomorrow." Perfect. We'll watch a cotton-candy movie, stuff ourselves full of popcorn, and then wander around window-shopping while we talk about nothing and everything. Just like before that Sanjay Gupta or this job came along.

Now all I have to do is get through tonight and I'm free for two whole days.

16

Mrs. Mayor

I join Danny in the foyer to wait for the Mayors to make their entrances. He from the library, she down the staircase from their bedroom.

"I see you're wearing a shirt, Danny, how nice of you." I smirk at him. It's kind of like teasing a male cousin who's big on hugs but you know he's really just trying to cop a feel and deep down in the reptilian part of your brain you like it.

"What's keeping your boobies from popping out?" Danny leans in, too close. I back away. Just because I tease him doesn't mean he's allowed to react.

"Wouldn't you like to know?" It's actually toupee tape, courtesy of Natasha, but he doesn't need to know. It would probably give him fodder for hours of masturbation fun and lead to a nasty duct tape incident and emergency room visit like the one Bina recounted to me last week. "As a matter of fact . . ."

Just then Mr. Mayor authoritatively throws open the huge walnut doors of his office and strides in, adjusting his cuff links, putting an end to my smack talk with Danny.

"Danny. Jac—Jacquelyn. Is my wife ready?"

"Any second now, Mr. Mayor." My heart beats junior-high fast. I must commit this to memory so tomorrow I can share it in excruciating detail with Bina.

We all check our watches and wait. And wait and wait.

"I'll go check on her status. Excuse me, Mr. Mayor." I climb the stairs, knowing I have two sets of eyes on my ass.

I press my ear to the door and listen for any suspicious sounds like purging, or other bathroom noises I don't want to know about. Silence. I knock softly and push open the door. Mrs. Mayor, alone now, sits on the edge of her bed looking very unhappy. The straps of her gown droop on her shoulders, all of her droops—except her boobs, which are incapable of it.

"Katherine? The Mayor is downstairs . . ." I've seen her looking glum but not this theatrically sad. Mrs. Mayor heaves an enormous sigh and continues to sit. I furtively check myself out in the huge antique mirror that is propped against one wall. Its angle makes you look taller and thinner. I could stand here for hours . . . "Is everything OK?"

"No, Jacquelyn, everything is decidedly not OK." She sounds annoyed that it took me so long to ask. Well, *pardon me,* am I supposed to go blind just because she's having some sort of issue?

"Um, anything I can do?" I guess it is, after all, my job to make her life easier.

"Yes, can you tell me who my husband is screwing? Because it's certainly not me!" No quiver in her voice, just a firm and dramatic declaration of fact. This is where the harpy music would swell up and we'd fade into a commercial for toilet cleaner.

"Pardon me, Katherine?" I take a few stiff steps forward and sit on the bed next to her, but not too close. Mr. Mayor is screwing around? And not with me? That's so unfair!

"My husband is having an affair," she declares, straightening up and dabbing gently at the corner of her eyes. She turns to face me. I have no choice but to look at her. "He's cheating on me. On *me!*"

I sit there and feel a lame smile twitching at the corners of my mouth. Maybe if I don't acknowledge her announcement we can pretend she didn't say it and then my life won't be any more complicated than it is. I would never before admit it, but, yeah, I was harboring more than fantasies about me and Mr. Mayor. It's one thing for him to be unfaithful to his wife, people cheat all the time, but to cheat on me!

Mrs. Mayor looks at me hard, indicating it's my turn to speak.

"Really? I mean, are you sure?" I have no idea how I'm supposed to react to this, but details would help me work through it.

"A woman knows." Mrs. Mayor admires herself in the mirror. Tragic and beautiful and, as always, camera ready.

"Sorry, Katherine, but that's a little . . . vague." I need more than a gut feeling to go on, especially after Bina pulled that same "a woman knows" crap on me. Although usually I put a lot of stock into a woman's intuition, you can't just weird someone out like that and then not have pictures or video to back it up. Especially when we are talking about a well-known public figure I've dreamed of having a meaningful affair, if not a full-fledged relationship, with.

"You've been married before, Jacquelyn." She says this as if it should explain everything.

She's got nothing, *nothing!* My heart skips a beat and I start to relax. This is just another Mrs. Mayor freak-out, like the time she was positive his mother had bugged the entire Mansion. She had me flipping over pictures and unscrewing lamp finials for days before she moved on to the next conspiracy plot.

"Yes. Yes, I was." The story of my marriage and why we divorced is exactly not what Mrs. Mayor needs to hear right now. It didn't have anything to do with infidelity and I don't want to have to make something up. When Nate and I were on the rocks my mom suggested that I should cook for him more to make him feel wanted. Cook? For my husband? I told her I was too busy watching him get fat to cook anything.

"Do you think Mr. Mayor still finds me attractive?" she asks the mirror.

It's a good thing Mrs. Mayor is conceited and self-centered or else I'd have to commiserate with her on the trials and tribulations of my marriage and instead of on her obvious stunning good looks.

"How could he possibly not!" How could I possibly be having

this conversation? Should I fake a seizure so she'll stop talking? Little chance of that, when Mrs. Mayor is on a roll she can go for hours. I cut right to the heart of the matter and tell Mrs. Mayor what she wants to know. "You're a very attractive and intelligent woman. He'd be crazy to see someone else. Insane, beyond insane."

"So why *is* he seeing someone else? Maybe I should leave the bastard? Oh, that would throw a kink into his plans to run for governor." Mrs. Mayor reaches inside her dress and adjusts her cleavage to make sure her nipples line up with each other.

"I'm sure he's not. Having an affair, I mean. Wow. Governor. How exciting," I ramble. I had no idea Mr. Mayor was even interested in running for governor this soon. If you ask me, he needs to at least finish this term as mayor. His advisors are jumping the gun big time. Mrs. Mayor gives me an annoyed look. Guess it's time to talk about what *she* wants to talk about. "What makes you think he's, uh, you know, having an affair?"

"He's . . . He just hasn't been here for me lately." She dabs at her eyes again even though they look dry to me.

"He has been a bit busy with all this, you know, mayor stuff, but I'm sure once the city council—"

"By here I don't mean here. I mean here, *here*."

"Oh. Oh!" Yuck. I reach over and awkwardly pat her bare shoulder a couple of times and then fold my hands tightly in my lap. There. All done. Let's go!

"When we first got married he couldn't keep his hands off of me. Now . . ." She manages to make her eyes all bright and shiny, but not too much to ruin her eye makeup.

"It's just the stress and soon things will calm down and he'll, uh, be all over you again." We have less than ten minutes to get to Fort Mason and since the Mayors are hosting the gala, I'm thinking Mrs. Mayor should get up and haul ass.

"Why does he hate me so much?" She's perfected the act of sobbing without the tears.

"He doesn't hate you, Katherine." Maybe he does, but what does she want me to do about it?

"Yes, he does. See!" She reaches in the beside table and hands me Emilio Cortez's column. Crap. Someone screwed up and let her see an intact edition of the paper.

"Oh, him . . . He's just trying to sell papers, Katherine. He does say something nice . . . Here. 'Katherine Baxter may have left Hollywood behind but she's doing her part to make San Francisco phony friendly.' See, he says you're like an ambassador or something." Even I don't believe the bullshit I'm shoveling.

"Will you talk to him? Ask him why he hates me. Please."

She clutches at my hands, crumpling the piece of newspaper. Now we'll both have to wash our hands.

"I'll talk to him." Emilio Cortez is going to write what he's going to write. "What should I tell the Mayor?"

"Tell him I'll be down shortly. And thank you for . . . for being such a good friend, Jacquelyn," Mrs. Mayor says to the mirror, her eyes getting round and bright with tears again.

I get out of there as quickly as I can. It is one thing for your boss to tell you she thinks her husband is having an affair, but quite another for her to refer to you as her friend.

That's just wrong.

17

Mr. Mayor

"She'll be right down," I say to Mr. Mayor. I resume my place next to Danny and smile lamely down at the polished marble floor, unable to meet their eyes.

"I'll be in my office." Mr. Mayor strides toward the huge double doors.

We watch him go. Danny wiggles his eyebrows at me and nudges me toward Mr. Mayor. He handled the last "incident," as we call them, and he's making sure I take my turn at bat. There goes my weekend. As far as I know, Danny's life revolves around 24/7 peep shows and cable sports so his antisocial calendar is a bit more flexible than mine is.

"Darling, I hope I didn't keep you waiting." Mrs. Mayor stands at the head of the stairs, ready to make her frothy descent.

"No, of course not, sweetheart, but we really must rush. We're late." This is about as blunt as Mr. Mayor gets with Mrs. Mayor. He's pissed, but not so pissed that he will hold it against her longer than it takes him to pass gas.

"Yes, I understand." Mrs. Mayor is pissed and I know she'll hold it against him forever and then some.

In my bag I can feel my cell phone vibrate, making a tinny sound as it hits the box of mints Mrs. Mayor makes me carry around for her. That would be Vivian wondering where the hell we are.

Danny clears his throat. I freeze. Now is not the time you want to draw attention to yourself. I try to fade into the background.

"Well, let's go, then." Mrs. Mayor stalks down the rest of the stairs and yanks open the front door.

Danny follows at a quick trot so she doesn't have to open the car door herself.

"Jacquelyn, is there something the matter with my wife that I should know about?"

"I, uh, really couldn't say, Mr. Mayor." I surreptitiously reach for my cell phone to stop its constant vibrating. For a second my bag is filled with the sound of Vivian's pissed-off voice.

"We're supposed to go away this weekend, but I don't know if it's such a good idea now." He rubs his hand across his chin.

That's his signature move. Most TV spots and many a photo have captured him in it. I never get tired of watching him do it.

"Yes, you should! I mean, yeah, she's been, you know . . . It's not easy for her to . . . not that she can't handle her duties, you know, but I know she's really been looking forward to your weekend. You should really go. Really."

Yesterday, I spent three hours supervising Six as she packed Mrs. Mayor's faux jodhpurs, coordinating cashmere sweater sets in between sheets of tissue paper and multiple pairs of loafers in individual silk bags, only to have Mrs. Mayor tell me to repack the suitcases with a "romantic theme, but not slutty."

Four hours later, her case was stuffed with gauzy dresses, lacy lingerie and more high heels than she could possibly wear in two days. Now her request makes perfect sense to me. She's hoping to win back Mr. Mayor with frilly and romantic, as opposed to reinforcing her shaky image as a younger version of his own mother.

She's off to a rocky start if her own husband is afraid to go away with her. She should have gone for slutty. If she thinks that her man is bailing someone else's hay, a little Frederick's of Hollywood might keep his pitchfork at home. But Mrs. Mayor is too studiously refined for that now, maybe in her soap days she would have thrown on a pair of crotchless panties, but not now. Instead she has a drawer full of La Perla lingerie: beautiful, expensive and somehow off-putting. La Perla and body fluids just don't mix.

"She hasn't mentioned anything to you?" Mr. Mayor nervously twists his cuff link.

"No." I can feel my eyes widen like they do whenever I am lying. "Not a thing. Except . . ."

"Except what?"

Mr. Mayor smells so good. I can't help but enjoy his undivided attention even though we are talking about his wife who suspects he's cheating on her and, therefore, me.

"Except she's really looking forward to leaving. I mean, going away. This weekend. With you."

"I guess you're right, Jacqs. Some time away would do us both some good." He runs his hand through his hair, making it look even better. He walks to the door and holds it open for me. "We should get to the car before people start talking."

I desperately want him to tell me what these people would start talking about, even though I know exactly what he means.

I slide into the front passenger seat before Danny can make a big show of helping me in, and fold my hands in my lap. I can feel the tension radiating from the backseat. Mr. Mayor clears his throat and Mrs. Mayor shifts around.

Danny gets in and pulls into the street. Behind us an unmarked police car follows at a discreet distance. The protection is mostly for Mrs. Mayor due to some overenthusiastic fan, or "fucking nut case," as she calls him. The press has been hounding the Mayors to pay for the detail themselves since it's not strictly a city responsibility to protect a former soap opera actress, even if she is the mayor's wife.

"What is that noise?" Mrs. Mayor's voice cuts through the silence.

I see Danny flinch out of the corner of my eye.

"It's my phone." I hate my phone. I hate Vivian for dialing my phone.

"Answer it then, Jacquelyn," Mrs. Mayor snaps.

"Yes, sorry." I dig it out of my bag and press it to my ear, wishing I could disappear inside of it. "Hello?"

"Where the hell are you! I have a dozen reporters here waiting!" Vivian screams into my ear.

"Oh, hi. Everything is great. We are on our way, see you in . . ." I glance over at Danny and he throws up his hands. "In a little bit. Bye!"

"Was that Vivian?" Mr. Mayor leans forward and I can feel his breath near my neck.

I turn around and am face-to-face with him. Mrs. Mayor stares stonily out her window. Neither he nor Mrs. Mayor carries a cell phone. That's what their employees are for.

"Do you want to talk to her?" I hand Mr. Mayor my phone, my finger already pressing speed dial. I don't feel like a Judas because I'm convinced Mr. Mayor could never have an affair with his press secretary. Too cliché. His mother may have given him a pass on marrying an actress, but an affair with an employee, a city employee, would be too gauche for her to stomach.

Mr. Mayor doesn't notice that his wife has exiled him to marital Siberia and speaks into my phone as if this was just another day at the office.

"Vivian. Yes, we are on our way. Please double-check about that . . . OK. You're a lifesaver, Vivvy. See you in about ten minutes."

"Oh, is *Vivvy* getting impatient? We wouldn't want to keep *Viv* waiting."

"Thanks, Jacqs." Mr. Mayor leans forward and hands me back my phone. "I'm not in the mood for this, Katherine. Not tonight."

Danny speeds up.

18

Vivian

As soon as we pull up to the curb, Vivian yanks open my door. She ushers me to the sidelines where generally we spend most of our time when working. From the corner of my eye I see Danny hunch down in his seat and drive away as soon as the last car door is closed.

"Jacqs, how could you let this happen?" she hisses in my ear through her toothy smile. Her green eyes sweep the perimeter, scouting for rogue reporters and their pesky ears.

"Hello to you, too, Vivian." I smile back. We can have complete conversations without actually moving our mouths, like two ventriloquists playing the dummies.

We both stand back and watch the Mayors go through the motions. The bright TV lights shine in their faces and flashbulbs pop like crazy. Both are all smiles and Mr. Mayor sort of has his arm sort of around her waist. It's times like these that I realize how gullible people want to be, myself included.

"How bad is it?" Vivian nods assuredly to a couple of reporters.

Vivian has a tougher job than I do since she's accountable to the People, City and County of San Francisco. Vivian has to deal with an aggressive press, irate citizens, and sleazy lobbyists and other politicos. Not that handling fawning celeb journalists, overenthusiastic fans and temperamental manicurists isn't hard, but it's not quite in the same league.

"On a scale of one to ten? I'd give this one about a billion." I don't know how much I should share with Vivian out on the sidewalk while we are surrounded by reporters and society gossips.

"Oh, Christ. What is it this time?" Her cat eyes flicker off to her right and left, as if she's watching a tennis match and not her boss and mine pantomiming a happy marriage.

"Listen, have you, uh, noticed Mr. Mayor, um . . ." What can I say? . . . Vivian, have you noticed Mr. Mayor banging someone other than his wife during his lunch hour? "Has he seemed *distracted* to you?"

"No more than usual. Despite what your boss thinks, being mayor of San Francisco is a full-time job and then some." Vivian tilts her head toward mine and we both smile as a photographer points his camera at us.

"Yeah, but she feels he's a little too *preoccupied*." I lean in to her so that she gets the importance of what I'm saying. Vivian works with politicians and nosy journalists; you'd think she'd be a little more astute.

"He's a busy man, she should know that," Vivian says dismissively.

Her own husband is a busy man and, from what she's confided in me, a tad inattentive.

"It's just, you know, I think she may think he's a little too *busy*."

"You tell her she has nothing to worry about." Her mouth is set in a tight line.

Oh. My. God. Vivian is having an affair with the Mayor. It's so obvious! She's sexy. He's sexy. They spend hours and hours together. Vivian has known him longer than Mrs. Mayor has. Vivian can finish his sentences. She is the yin to his yang. How could they not eventually have sex?

"Let's go. They're finally moving inside." Vivian grabs my elbow and leads me like a dairy cow inside.

After some more handshaking (him) and air kisses (her), the Mayors finally make their way inside and take seats in front of an impromptu stage. We've held up the performance, and the press will have a field day with that. At some point, Vivian and I need to coordinate our stories so they don't find out the real reason we were late.

Dancers in traditional *folclórico* costumes assume poses on-stage and wait for the mariachis to begin playing. I feel butterflies in my stomach, watching the familiar dances and listening to the music of my youth. Who would have thought I'd be watching this at a $1,000-a-plate benefit in San Francisco? Not me, that's for sure.

Vivian taps me on the shoulder and I know that's as much of the performance as I'm going to get to see. We make our way to the one sure place we're not going to run into anyone: the maintenance closet.

"OK. This is what I think we should say." Vivian pulls out a notepad. "You guys were late because Mr. Mayor got held up on a conference call."

"To who?"

"Um, how about with Cortez?"

"No dice. Remember Cortez said he wouldn't talk to the Mayor unless it was in an open forum? And he's here and could easily blow a hole in that story."

"Damn him. Where does he get off being so freaking ethical? Just makes my job harder." Vivian looks tired. More tired than I've ever seen her. She needs this weekend off more than I do.

"How about we hint that they got tied up having a quiet dinner at home?" I suggest. I listen through the door as the music ends and the crowd applauds enthusiastically.

"Together?"

"Of course together! Give it a little Camelot spin. They'll eat that up." Hopefully.

"Thanks, Jacqs. Listen, I'll take care of this and why don't you catch some of the performance. I know you've been looking forward to it."

19

Emilio

We slip out of the closet and I watch as Vivian makes her way over to the bar where a couple of reporters just happen to be hanging out. Reporters always congregate around the food and drinks, especially when it's free. Reminds me of my dot-com salad days. I make my way outside to get some fresh air.

"*Señorita Sanchez, buenas noches.*"

"Cortez." My heart thumps in my chest, and not just because he startled me. Emilio Cortez is exactly the kind of man my mother warned me about. The kind who will show you a good time, keep life interesting and ultimately break your heart. That's why I've made the choice to go with the total opposite: the safe guy, the unavailable guy. My ex-husband, Mr. Mayor, George. Gee, thanks, *Mamá*.

"Call me Emilio. Or call me whatever else you want." Cortez is more Mr. Mayor than Mr. Mayor is—more vocal, more liberal, taller, darker and, if possible, even more handsome.

"Call me Jacquelyn." When he's not upsetting Mr. Mayor's political applecart, he's romancing most of the eligible women in the Bay Area. Black, white, Asian, Latina, you name it, he's banged it, or at least rumored to have. He's definitely not a one-woman man, but if I was ever to have a *ménage à trois* I wouldn't mind him being on one side of a me sandwich. With Mr. Mayor bringing up the rear.

"Jacquelyn, *bueno*. How is the lovely Katherine tonight?" Emilio leans against the railing with his arms crossed over his chest.

His focus is completely on me, but I can't help but notice the growing buzz from the actual guests who don't appreciate my monopolizing his time.

"Fine." Each time I've spoken to Cortez I've needed a fresh pair of undies. The extra laundry and loyalty to my boss and Mr. Mayor are why I avoid him at parties, functions and events. Both the Mayors are really paranoid about him, with good reason. "*Muchas gracias* for asking."

"Truce, Jacquelyn. I'm not working. I'm here as a lover of art. Just like your boss. I'm sure the two of you can spend hours talking about the merits of Mexican art. You can offer her so many . . . insights."

"What did you say?"

"I wonder how a woman as smart as you could end up working for her." (Oh, and he has the annoying habit of probing questions. I already pay someone to poke around in my psyche so I don't appreciate it from him.)

"What do you mean?" I play dumb. Something I'm sure he can understand. It's much easier to get the advantage when the people you work with (and for) underestimate you.

"I hear that you did well, very well, at Berkeley." Emilio leans into me, and I'm tempted to push him away with my finger, knowing it will drive him crazy. He likes the chase, or so I've heard. "You can't tell me it's your life's ambition to run errands for the queen of San Francisco's consumer class?"

"Consumer class?"

"She consumes therefore she thinks she has class. The *chisme* is you got accepted to law school but got . . . distracted." He smiles at me.

Distracted? Me? Yes, I did get distracted but I don't know if he means by the easy dot-com money or my ex-husband's all-American penis. I stare at him blankly like I do when I'm facing a particularly thorny question from Dr. N.

"Law school is still there, Cortez. I'm exploring my options."

"Your boss will be supportive of whatever you choose to do. Just like with Mrs. Mayor's other assistant. Myra? The rumor is little Myra had an attack of the nerves and is now resting comfortably in a group home in Humboldt. All paid for by your boss and her husband, of course. You can tell me, Jacquelyn, I promise I won't tell anyone," he prods, but not the way I want him to.

"Gossip is gossip. You of all people should know not to take it to heart. Or print it. But, then again, you wouldn't have much of a job, would you?" I wonder what Cortez will do when Mr. Mayor leaves for Sacramento? They're a political Cain and Abel. I doubt they could exist without each other. I wonder what I'll do? "And I do a lot more than run errands. But thank you for your concern."

"You may find this surprising, but my humble goal is to speak for the common people of San Francisco."

"And the common people of San Francisco really need to know how much my boss spends at Neiman Marcus every month?"

"She's an outsider, worse, she's from Los Angeles. You can't blame people for being a little suspicious, Jacquelyn."

"It just makes my job all the more difficult," I mutter underneath my breath.

"The job market is tight, but you could have done better, Jacquelyn." He leans forward and looks serious. Too serious. "Things are changing in San Francisco, Jacquelyn, but slowly. Look around. You and I are the only Latinos here not carrying a tray or playing a guitar. You could do better for yourself and your community."

"Are you offering me a job, Emilio? Does your *esposa* need someone to pick up her dry cleaning? Oh, wait, you're not married." People have started to press in on us, trying to get his attention. Relieved, I take a step away from him. I'm not ready to deal with the implications of being an underachieving Latina. Not tonight, at least, when I had sort of convinced myself I was doing pretty well for myself.

"Don't get mad at me, Jacquelyn. I'm just trying to give you some advice."

"Fine, thanks." We stare at each other, neither of us angry, just resigned to our respective roles. "Lay off Katherine for a while. Find someone else to pick on."

"I'll try, but she makes it so difficult. Time to feed the sharks," he sighs. He pulls out a card from his shirt pocket and hands it to me. "We should have coffee sometime and talk when you're ready to do some good and help *la raza*."

"I think *la raza* can do fine without me, Cortez, but thanks for thinking of me in a bilingual way." I blush at my audacity (twice in one day!) but he merely smiles and turns around.

20

George

I back away, watching him work his magic with the money people, and bump into someone. "Pardon me!"

"Not a problem." She's well preserved and ageless, like most rich women tend to be. She could be in her late thirties, or older, I can't tell because of all the work she's had done. It's not very obvious, expensively so, but normal people aren't as smooth and lineless.

"Sorry again!" I say when I realize I've been staring.

"I'm waiting for my husband." She coils a very expensive-looking strand of pearls around her finger like it was one of those candy necklaces I used to buy from the ice-cream truck when I was a kid. "He forgot something in the car and has been gone forever."

"I can get someone to check if you want." I'm in at-your-service mode. Mrs. Mayor thinks nothing of asking me to march into the men's room to retrieve Mr. Mayor when she thinks he's been gone too long.

"Oh, no thanks! I just hate waiting here. Makes me feel like people are thinking I've been stood up or something," she says with a smile as she starts to twist around the very-impressive, emerald-cut diamond ring on her finger.

From the way she talks she has to be under forty. Maybe thirty-five? No, older, but not by much.

"Nice night, huh?" I ask, trying to make conversation.

"Hey, sorry. I don't want to keep you!" She puts a hand on my arm and then pulls it away quickly.

"Nah, don't worry about it. I'm actually here for work." I wait for her to ask me who I work for when a familiar figure strides up the steps.

"George!" we both call out in unison. She turns to look at me and I pretend to sneeze.

"Pardon me." I dig through my bag for nonexistent tissue. She hands me one from her own bag. I make a big show of blowing my nose while George, my married boyfriend, looks stunned for a moment and then slides over to his wife. His estranged wife, or so I thought.

"Sorry to keep you waiting, darling." He plants a perfunctory kiss on her cheek.

"We missed the dancers, George. Thank you. I have to visit the ladies' room. Wait here." All of a sudden she seems older and very sophisticated—a woman who would never maltreat her jewelry in nervousness. She turns expertly on one heel and calls over her shoulder to me, "You have a good night."

I nod and nod, my eyes close to bursting out of my skull as if she just caught me with my hand in her husband's cookie jar.

"You look ravishing, Jacquelyn, as usual," he says after the door swings shut on his wife.

"What are you doing here, George?" What are you doing here with your wife is what I really want to ask.

"She loves this kind of shindig. It's the least I could do, that and write a huge check for the new building." The least he could do is stop taking me out and buying me gifts. Gifts that I really, really like. I'm sure if his wife knew about that she'd less than love it. "I left a message on your machine. I guess this is why you didn't pick up your phone."

"Obviously! I was out here having a pleasant conversation with a woman who turns out to be your wife." This is so wrong. I was never supposed to meet her. Not that George and I have technically done anything wrong. Sharing long, expensive meals, some innocent flirting and one-sided gift-giving aren't grounds for me to be sent to hell as an adulterer. Are they? "I have to get back to my seat."

"Jacquelyn, don't be angry. I'm sure you go out with other men and it's totally innocent."

"Maybe it is, maybe it isn't." Truth is George is the closest I've come to getting any in a while. And, yeah, I know he's not divorced, but I didn't want to know that he and his wife still do married-people things. Now I wonder what other kind of things they do together. Do they go to the supermarket and squeeze produce? Shop for toilet paper and hand soap? Do they have sex?

Now that would be a kick in the ass. My married boyfriend is having sex with his wife and I haven't gotten laid since . . . a really long time.

"So, George, are you and your wife on the mend?" I can't help but feel a little peeved. I mean, all he's ever said is how cold she is and how they have nothing in common, blah, blah, blah. "Or do you really love art this much?"

"Lunch next week?" he asks with a smile.

You have to hand it to George. His wife (third wife) is pulling up her pantyhose not 20 feet away and he still has the balls to make a date with me. From the corner of my eye I watch Emilio shake hands and smile at the people who hold his political future in their hands.

"Lunch? You can't be serious," I say, trying to resist temptation.

"Just lunch, Jacquelyn."

"I'm sure that's what you tell all the girls."

George leans in for a chaste kiss on my cheek and I let him.

21

Bina

There is nothing in the world that can get me out of my bed. Not a raise, not a slightly used Prada bag, not Mr. Mayor begging me to quit my job and become the new Mrs. Mayor. Nothing. Not even my mother's plaintive voice from my answering machine. Nope. Nothing. *Nada*.

I open one eye and check to see if I have any messages on my cell or answering machine. No message, not even a hang-up call from Mrs. Mayor. She usually has at least one last-minute crisis for me to take care of before a trip, appointment or engagement. Maybe I should call her to make sure everything is OK? No, that would be a sign that something is really lacking in my life. Like a life.

I could call my mom but the chance of getting another earful of Yolie is enough to make me roll over and close my eyes again.

At 8:15 AM I give up on sleeping. I know it's too early to call Bina, who works the late shift at the hospital on Friday nights. I should let her sleep. I bet that Sanjay Gupta isn't as considerate. I bet he calls her first thing in the morning and asks her to drop off his dry cleaning on her way to work where she saves lives.

I could clean up my flat, read a good book, give myself a pedicure or do something equally useful. Or I could call my mom. I opt for TV.

I grab a glass of orange juice and a box of granola and settle on my couch for some serious ingesting of mass culture. Of course, since I don't have cable at home my choices are limited to cartoons and shopping channels.

After a few hours of watching cartoons and commercials, I now know why kids are ultraviolent and/or shallow and materialistic. The stuff they put on TV is just garbage. And it's nothing short of disgusting how many calories a fistful of granola has.

It's almost noon so I pick up the phone to call Bina. It rings ten times before she picks up.

"Hello?" Bina sounds sleepy.

"Are you still asleep? It's almost noon."

"It's . . . it's 10:30! Jacqs, you wretched, wretched girl!" Bina covers the phone with her hand and I can hear muffled talking.

"Hey! Hey, who are you talking to?" I press my ear tighter to the phone.

"It's Sanjay, you dope."

"Oh. My. God. What is he doing in your bedroom? I thought you told me it was Indian custom to wait until you got married to let him have a bit of your curry and you were going to do it all by the book. Which book is that, huh, Bina? The *Kama Sutra?*"

I had slept with other guys before Nate and I'm sure my parents knew, but they were shocked when I fessed up that Nate and I were living together. My mother even gave me the cow-and-the-*gratis*-milk speech. Ugh, like that's what I really needed to hear. I told her Nate was lactose intolerant and she hit me over the head with a dishrag.

"What would your parents say? Hmmm, Bina?" I continue, knowing she'll have no good answer to that one. It's not that I'm surprised Bina is sleeping with the man she says she's going to marry, if anything, if she wasn't sleeping with him I'd think she was crazy. But why does it have to be him? "After all the trouble you went through to convince them to let you live on your own and now you do this? Tsk, tsk, tsk."

"Yes, well, I'm American, too, you know."

Bina sounds more awake now. Good. That means we'll make

the first show and have plenty of time to talk and shop before she has to run back to that Sanjay.

"American when it comes to premarital sex? Indian when it comes to letting your parents arrange your marriage? Isn't that convenient?" I turn on the water in my shower. I hear Bina flush the toilet.

"I have the best of both worlds. Give me half an hour. Kiss, kiss."

"Yeah, kiss, kiss to you, too, you hypocrite slut." I toss the phone on a pile of towels and I step into the shower.

"So? Tell me the latest." Bina's ass hasn't even touched the passenger seat before she asks. She knows my weakness is gossip. At least, it's one of my weaknesses and one I'm all too happy to share with her.

"Oh, not much." I sniff. I need to punish her for letting Sanjay in her bed. She could have least warned me.

"Oh, this has to be good." Bina rubs her hands together.

"You are so evil, Bina. OK, but you have to swear not to tell anyone. Not even Sanjay. Especially not Sanjay."

Bina crosses her heart. I know she won't tell anyone but it makes me feel better to make her promise. And it makes me feel even better to know that I have a bond with Bina that Sanjay will never have.

"First, it looks like he's going to run for governor." I wait for Bina's response. She likes people gossip but not political gossip. I can't get enough of either. Other people look forward to the Oscars or the Olympics, I live for election nights, even when it's obvious who's going to win and what is and isn't going to pass. "Did you hear what I said?"

"*Pfft.* It's so obvious that man has a fifteen-year plan. First become mayor, then governor, then run for president. He's very American." All of a sudden Bina has been pointing out how very American things are that don't meet with her approval.

"Don't call him that. He's brilliant. And supercute. What's wrong with having a plan? I have a plan."

"You do?" She looks at me doubtfully.

"Shut up. I do. I'm in the process of sort of reworking it."

"Don't make any plans for the third week of April. You are coming to India. My parents and Sanjay's parents insist we have a ceremony in India."

"You are so kidding? India? Your parents haven't been to India in ages. And you haven't been back since you moved here, like, what, twenty years ago? From *England*, for Christ's sake!"

"Yes, but it's very important to share this with our relatives and continue our traditions."

"I thought most of your relatives live in Union City?" I feel snarky, but I know Bina can handle it. Maybe I'm jealous because she's had sex in the last twelve hours and I've only thought about it in the last twelve months.

"Don't get cheeky with me, Jacqs. And don't think I haven't noticed that you are keeping the best gossip from me."

"You have a one-track mind. OK. Promise—" I say, dragging it out deliciously.

"I promise! Tell me," Bina snaps.

"Mrs. Mayor thinks Mr. Mayor is having an affair."

Bina gasps, actually gasps. One thing I know she has always taken seriously is marital fidelity. That's why I can't share my George stories with her even though technically we haven't *done* anything. But I've entertained the thought and that's close enough. Plus, now there is the matter of the one-sided gift-giving. A bouquet of flowers? Even she and my mom would let me get away with that. They might even think it's sweet, if I neglected to mention his marital status and why, after seeing him for almost two months, I've never mentioned him. But an expensive purse from a man who I wasn't either in the process of marrying or married to? I may as well sew a scarlet letter *S* for slut over my left boob.

"No!" She clutches my arm. Bina, despite her numerous ex-boyfriends, is very into monogamy. She always made sure to dump one before she moved on to another.

"Yes. And she called me her *friend* after she told me." Why does that creep me out so much? A year ago if someone would have told me I'd be *friends* with the idolized soap star of my teen years I would have wet my pants with glee. Now all I want to do is scrub the memory from my brain.

"What are you going to do, Jacqs?" Bina sounds genuinely concerned. Before, most of my Mrs. Mayor gossip had to do with plastic surgery, double-sided tape and hair-removal stories. Nothing malicious but it was trippy having access to the most intimate moments of a celebrity's life, although I never imagined they'd be this intimate.

"Me? Nothing. At least, that was my plan. What should I do? Spy on Mr. Mayor for her? Confront him? I don't know. I don't want to know."

"Do you think he's cheating on her?"

Bina checks her phone for messages. I pretend not to notice.

"Who knows?" Vivian would know, that's who, but after my last attempt to broach the subject, I don't think I want to know what she may know. "I mean, yeah, they fight and are icy toward each other, but, you know, I thought that's the way it was with all rich-and-powerful couples."

"I don't envy them. What good is money and power when you can't be happy with the person you are married to? That is so very Western."

"Puhleez, Bina. Are you saying the only good marriage is an arranged marriage? How about all those stories on the news about women seeking political asylum to escape an arranged marriage? Or killing themselves because they can't get out of marrying some village creep?"

"Yes, but that's beside the point. So are you coming to India or not? And let me stress that *not* is not an option."

"India? I don't know how Mrs. Mayor will take that. Remember, Myra abandoned her to wander around India. She still mentions it when she's unhappy with something I've done or not done. And if my mom finds out I'm going to India for any sort of religious reason she'll get on my case for not making an effort to drop in on the pope at the Vatican."

"That woman is manipulative," Bina says as she expertly lines her eyes with the extradark liner she buys at the drugstore.

"Which? My mother or my boss?" I ask, even though I know the answer.

"Both. No offense to your mother." Bina was also raised to revere her elders but it's never stopped her from talking smack about them.

"Yeah, but don't you think we all are? To a point, of course." I know I am. There is nothing wrong with conscientious manipulation. Done correctly it is both an art and a virtue.

"A mother can't help making you feel guilty. They do it because they love us. Women have different ways of getting things done, but that doesn't make it OK . . ." she says self-righteously. "Mrs. Mayor is outright manipulative. A very unattractive trait in a woman."

"Oh, really?" I give Bina a look and gesture toward the impressive engagement ring on her finger.

"In *some* cases it is essential to finesse a man's opinion," Bina concedes.

The first ring Sanjay presented her with was pitiful, but a Gupta family heirloom. It took some fancy and covert emotional footwork but Sanjay soon realized that his modern bride needed a 2-carat pear-shaped diamond with baguettes flanking either side. The heirloom is now relegated to Bina's right hand, where it will make appearances only at occasions where Sanjay's family will be around.

"She's a pro, that's for sure. She and the Mayor had a fight last night, not a yelling-and-throwing-the-family-crystal kind, but it was pretty tense. By the end of the night she let me know to pack for Carmel *and* Santa Barbara."

Mr. Mayor is attending to some family business in Carmel and then on to some politico conference in Santa Barbara. He made it clear that it was not a pleasure trip and, as a (very bad) example, he pointed out that Vivian was going with him. All work and no play, he swore. Now Mrs. Mayor is going along to make sure that's just what happens.

"You mean, he's taking her?" Bina nods her head. "OK, she's manipulative, but she does get what she wants."

"Isn't that the whole point? And I get to go, even if I do have to go as her assistant."

"This is exactly why you need to come to India, so you can anchor yourself. You are morally adrift and your soul is hungry for nourishment. Oh, there's a sale at Club Monaco, let's stop by after the movie."

"I like your version of spirituality, Bina. It's so . . . so very Western."

22

George

By the time I'm done primping for a date with George, I feel like a present that begs to be unwrapped, which is stupid because even though I think about being naked with George, a lot, I know I could never go through with it. Plus, George has never hinted that he wants to have sex with me or watch me have sex with someone else, which I wouldn't put past any man.

During our first few lunches at Globe I was on the edge of my seat, waiting for him to suggest we get a room. I had planned on smiling gently but firmly stating that I didn't like him that way and I understood if he didn't want to get together anymore. But it never happened. I finally worked up my courage and asked him why the hell he hadn't tried to get into my pants. By this point I was sort of offended. Who wouldn't be?

"Jacquelyn, we have such a great time together, why complicate it? And, you know, I'm still technically married. I couldn't see myself cheating with someone I like so much. You have to have a bite of my dessert . . . Delicious? I knew you'd like it."

Knowing that George likes me so much that he doesn't want to ruin our relationship by having sex makes me feel better and a little less guilty about the whole thing. Aside from the fact that George is married, a couple of decades my senior and not sexually or emotionally available, I think we have an ideal relationship.

What everyone else thinks about it is immaterial. But just to make sure this never materializes is why no one knows about George.

After my divorce I did try to date men in my mating range, but I would eventually realize they were stand-ins for Nate. It wasn't at all fair to them and didn't make much sense to me. If I had gone through all the trouble to get rid of Nate why would I get involved with someone who was a poor copy of him?

I never bothered mentioning any of them to my mom. I didn't want to get her hopes up that I had finally maybe found *he* of the elusive qualities and culturally correct background. After a while, I just stopped dating or even hoping that there was a guy out there for me. It was too much work, and even I was confused about my expectations. Did I just want to have fun, or was I looking for a husband so I'd make my parents happy?

Not even Dr. N has helped me figure that one out. Not that I've shared this dilemma with her, or anyone else. There are some things that are even too personal to share with my doctor, who thinks I'm cured, my mother, who'd marry me off to the Devil if he proposed, and even Bina, especially since she's crossed over to the bride side.

This is why the George thing is perfect. He is so unlike Nate or any of the other men I've been involved with.

And if I skip a wax now and then, I don't have to worry because I'm sure George won't see me in or out of my panties and, if he did, he came of age (the eighties, seventies?) when women sported full bushes.

23

Mamá

I glance up and catch sight of the wall calendar my mother gave me, the kind she sends me every year at Christmas. She fills in the date boxes under the pictures of kittens or national monuments, or whatever that year's theme is, with family birthdays, anniversaries, and any and all possible occasions where I either must be there, send a card or gift, or at least make a phone call.

To her handiwork I have added another regular reminder: a phone call to her once every three days without fail. It's the minimum I can get away with. If she doesn't hear from me she begins to suspect that I've been kidnapped, am delirious with fever and malnutrition, or happy and therefore doing things I'm not supposed to. To make things even more convoluted, she'll call me in between my calls, but only when she knows she'll get my machine. And she'll leave a message, saying that I must be at work and that whatever she had to tell me can wait until my next phone call. These are the rituals that occupy my mother's time. So, all in all, I hear my mom's voice about five to seven days a week, whether we have a real conversation or not.

Lately, my mother has begun all her conversations with a list of her aches and pains. That's when I realized she was getting old. Only old people think varicose veins and creaky joints are interesting topics of conversation. It made me pretty sad at first, but my mother really seems to get off on talking about how miserable she is and now that she has medical proof she can point to, she's happier than ever.

I'm not in the mood, but prefer to call her before my date with George rather than after. If I call her now I won't have any of that post-lunch taint on me that only a mother can sense. Plus, after a phone call with my mom there is the possibility I could call George, cancel and be my mother's good little girl. Not that I intend to, but I could, and that I actually entertained the thought of doing the right thing is enough to keep me sleeping peacefully at night.

To prepare I take a few deep breaths and I close my closet door, even though the crocodile bag, still in the box, is shoved so far back I'll need a pickax and a flashlight to dig it out. I pick up the phone, dial and count the rings. They don't have a working answering machine and even then I don't think it would help because they'd never plug it in. After six rings she picks up. I note this on the calendar. Last week it was two. A sign of something, no doubt.

"*¿Hola?*" She sounds tired.

"Hi, *Mamá*. It's Jacquelyn!" I hope that if I sound chipper enough she'll get the hint that today is a happy day and a good mother wouldn't burden her beloved daughter with her concerns. "Your favorite *hija*."

"Jacquelyn! *¿Cómo estas?* I was going to call you." She always says this.

"How is everything?" I take a deep breath and brace myself for the onslaught of ailments. "*Llamé*. Did Yolie tell you?"

"Yes. She drove me to the doctor for that blood work." This lets me know I should have called back Friday afternoon or at the latest on Saturday to inquire if my mother was dying of cancer or not. The doctor suspected she was anemic, but my mother figured she may as well prepare herself and her kids for the worst. The first few times she predicted her death, I got all worked up. I even flew home, only to find out it was wax buildup in her ear, not brain cancer, that was causing her to lose her balance. I feel guilty just thinking about getting annoyed with her. She's still my mother, after all.

"And what happened?" She'll tell me anyway, but I have to ask to show I care. My mother has been complaining of feeling tired and unmotivated. I suggested depression but Mexican-American Catholics don't get depressed, they get cancer.

"Oh, he said everything was fine. That I should try and *relajar.*" Relax is not a word in my mother's vocabulary. For my mother relaxation comes in the form of a constant, low-grade worry. If something doesn't seem wrong, then something even worse is possible.

"You should do that," I say, staring out the window trying to gauge the weather. "You should go to that spa again. *Yo pago*. No problem, I'll get you that same spa deal. It wasn't so expensive."

A few Mother's Days ago I booked her a full day of pampering. Afterward she raved on and on about it and I've offered to send her again, but she's always vague about committing to a date—too busy, she claims. It was like she had a glimpse of heaven but is content to live in her own, private purgatory, knowing that someday she may experience it again. Maybe.

"Oh, someday. It's your *padre* who should pay." My mother—a martyr without a pedicure.

"That's right!" I try to encourage my mother's feeble attempts at living the lessons she learns on *Oprah*. So far it's been all talk, but that's more than I thought she'd ever get the courage to do.

Not that my dad is an ogre. He's OK, but I always made sure my boyfriends were as unlike him as possible. Unfortunately they all shared one same trait: they were men. And I was disappointed to find out that no matter how liberal, open-minded or sensitive they claimed to be, all of them still wanted what only a mother could give them—absolute adulation of their very existence. And sex, of course, but only when *they* were in the mood.

"Last week, on *Oprah*, she had a show of *esposas* who leave their husbands and how they can have better *vidas* and find new, better relationships." My mother has never pressured me directly to hurry up and get married (again) but I know she worries about it. The worst fate my mother can imagine is her children winding up unattached and therefore uncared for. We could be drowning in a loveless marriage, but at least we'd have someone to hold our head underwater. "*¿Lo viste?*"

"Must have missed that one."

My mother was never one to give advice outright and now her *consejos* are cloaked in *Oprah* show recaps. The closest she ever came to imparting a life's lesson was to tell me to always look my best for a job interview, doctor's appointment or haircut so I'd be taken more seriously and/or get better service. To this day I can't help following it. Other than that she just told me what to do (go to church, do you homework, be a good girl) until I got old enough to where her admonishing me to not have sex, drink too much and never sleep in my makeup kind of went in one ear and out the other since I was doing all those things and more.

"It just makes me think that maybe you weren't so wrong in, you know"—she lowers her voice—"divorcing Nate." She pronounces his name Nayet.

My mother has never really brought up my divorce, not directly, at least. It's one of those things she just prefers to pretend never happened, like my brother Noel with the shoplifting and later, a stint at county jail for vandalizing a neighbor's car. I've done my best to play along that my marriage and divorce were no big deals. I still think going to jail is a bit more serious, but people in glass houses can't throw stones. And knowing my mother, she'd probably get in the way with a roll of paper towels and a bottle of Windex.

Once she got over the shock she reassured me the marriage didn't count because it hadn't taken place in a church in front of God, my family or the neighbors. My father just grunted and told me not to tell my ailing grandmother. She had been under the impression that I was making plans to join a convent, an impression she got from my father. Something about the youngest daughter being turned over to God for the honor of the family or some crap like that.

"I, well, we did what we thought was best for both of us." I keep my tone light, but firm. To betray any emotion will lead my mother to blame herself for my current state as a used-up, childless spinster. "*Qué era, era*. Right, *Mamá?*"

"Oprah has never been married, *tampoco*," she says, ignoring the fact that I *have* been married and Oprah has been living in sin with some guy for years.

"So are you feeling better?" I ask, already knowing the answer. I look at my watch.

"Oh, *sí*. Just tired." She's never just happy. How hard can that be? I'm almost tempted to ask, but I know it'd make her cry that she's failed me in some way. (And deep down, I secretly think she has.) "Always *cansada.*"

"Get some rest. Take a nap. You deserve it. I'm going to be late, *Mamá*. My boss is going to Carmel and Santa Barbara in a few days so I need to make some arrangements."

"How exciting." My mother doesn't ask if I'm going to go. Either she assumes I am and would rather not have to worry about me or she thinks I'm not important enough to warrant an invitation to go along.

"Yeah, just more *trabajo* for me." I hope this assures my mother that I have enough work to keep me employed and for her not to worry about me. Second on her list of worries is my employment status. Getting married would null those two. Popping out a kid exactly nine months from my wedding night would take care of the third.

"Did I tell you your cousin Kiki is in Atlanta now? *Con su marido*. He got transferred and Kiki went with him. Your *Tía* Carmen is heartbroken." She lowers her voice just in case someone should walk in and catch her midgossip. "What did she expect? For Kiki to let her husband move to Atlanta *solo?*"

"That's too bad," I say blandly. Too bad for my aunt, who I've *never* liked, won't have poor Kiki at her beck and call anymore. Now my mousy cousin Lina will have to bear the brunt of Hurricane Carmen. That woman is maternal poison, but my father's older sister so I can't show any disrespect. At least not outright.

"Now she can't say to me that all I do is cry about my kids who have moved far from home. She's doing it now, too."

Ouch.

"Yeah. Hey, maybe I can visit for a few days. We're practically going to be in LA anyway. I'm sure she'll give me the days off. This always happens. Guilt, guilt, guilt. All of Dr. N's very logical reassurances about making my own life away from my family come to nothing when I'm on the phone with my mother.

"We could have a party! Just for *la familia*." For the first time she sounds full of energy.

My mother loves parties. She always complained that her own mother could never manage to get one together so she and her brothers and sisters grew up dreading birthdays and other special occasions. Once my mother had her own children our parties became her way of getting back at her mother without actually confronting her.

"Let me know when you will be here. I have to go. Your father is grumpy for his *café*."

"OK." I really do love her, but, shit, couldn't she cut me some slack? This much reality so early in the morning makes me realize how contrived and shallow my life is and how very, very much I like it that way.

I slump over on my bed feeling totally deflated.

24

Mrs. Mayor

"Katherine, I was wondering if I could take some time off after this trip to visit my parents in LA?" I ask as I install her in their king-sized bed with a stack of glossy magazines and herbal tea that I'm sure she'll supplement with the Xanax she keeps squirreled away in her nightstand.

After public engagements where Mrs. Mayor has to play Mrs. Mayor full time she's so exhausted she spends a day or two recuperating—not the most vote-getting pastime for a political wife. If we don't give her time to "unwind," I have to lead her around like some impeccably dressed, drugged monkey.

"Sure, sure. You deserve some time off. Right? I have so many friends in LA. Good friends. I don't care what Kit says about them. Don't you think, Jacquelyn?"

"Yeah. Is there anything else I can get you, Katherine?" I look at my watch. It's not even 10 AM but my workday is effectively over. "Anita and Lei are downstairs if you need more tea or maybe something to eat."

"I'll be fine. I just need some sleep and quiet time to think."

She is demanding, nosy, pushy and needy, but a real hands-off boss who doesn't mind letting me wander off on my own while she's enjoying a drug-induced mental vacation. After my morning phone flagellation with my mother, it's almost a relief to be around a woman whose main interest in life is herself.

"I'm off to run some errands and stuff." I smooth out the cashmere throw, which is her security blanket on these (frequent) occasions.

"Good night, Jacquelyn." Her eyes are droopy and her voice is slurred.

"Good night, Katherine."

25

George

George is waiting on the sidewalk in front of Globe, our usual lunch spot. When he sees me he smiles. I smile. We smile at each other.

To passersby we may look like a successful businessman and his sexy and equally as accomplished colleague getting together for a legitimate lunch. Or it may seem what it really is. Either way, I don't really care, but I keep my sunglasses on until we get inside.

The restaurant staff surely knows, and maybe they're used to an older man out for an expensive lunch with his much younger girlfriend. And I'm sure they speculate about what happens after lunch, even though we always make a point to part in front of the restaurant and walk off in different directions.

If I was them, I'd assume the worst, too. Why else would George be with me if not for confidence-building sex? What they don't know is that we both share a love of old movies (in George's case, movies from his youth), art, good food and wine. And this is what we mainly talk about—not politics, not my job and certainly not his wife or my ex-husband. (George doesn't even know I've been married.)

"Jacquelyn, you look beautiful, as always." George gives me a peck on the cheek and at the same time slips something into my hand. It doesn't feel like flesh so I don't freak out. My mother instilled in me that men are always after only one thing. And even though I've encouraged this in many a man, I still feel I'm obligated to feel a bit apprehensive.

"What's this?" My heart beats fast. It's a Cartier box. This is definitely something I should *not* accept. I should slip it back in his pocket and shake his hand, walk away and never look back.

"Open it and find out." George takes my elbow and leads me into the restaurant. Like a lot of men from his generation, George automatically holds open doors, half-rises from his seat when you get up to go to the bathroom and takes your elbow whenever you walk next to him, and it never feels condescending. It's so charming and old-fashioned, kind of like a Cary Grant movie. George reminds me a lot of Cary Grant: same dark hair, tanned skin and wolfish smile. I'd never tell him this. He'd only find it amusing that I know who Cary Grant is.

George pulls out my seat, waits for me to sit and gives my chair a gentle push toward the table. I make sure to cross my legs tightly and angle them toward the exit.

"George, this . . . I really can't." I could, but I really, really shouldn't.

"Don't make up your mind until you see it, Jacquelyn."

The hostess hovers, eager to catch a glimpse. George ignores her and concentrates on me.

"OK. But I'm not making any promises."

I hope George understands I mean more than just keeping the gift. He's not some thirtysomething ex-jock with a hard-on and a case of beer who is invoking the third-date rule. I open the box and gasp. So does the hostess, who hurries away after George gives her a dirty look.

"I can't accept this. It's just too . . . too perfect." It's the bracelet I'd admired when I went in to get my watch battery changed at Cartier a few months ago. The sales guy even insisted I try it on while he gave me the spiel. I had forgotten all about it, but I guess the sales guy made a note in hopes that my sugar daddy would wander in one day in the mood to buy his girlfriend a shiny bauble. Now it was in my hand, staring me in the face, daring me to put it on. All I have to do is slip it on my wrist, have George fasten it, and it will be mine. All mine for the eternity I would spend in hell impeccably accessorized.

"You don't like it?" George looks confused.

"It's beautiful, George, really." I really, really want to put it on. To prove how much stronger I am than temptation in the form of platinum and diamonds, I push the box away from me a few centimeters.

"Put it on," he smiles coaxingly, "just to see how it looks."

"I can't." But even I know that means I won't. Up until this point the most important piece of jewelry I ever received was my engagement ring from Nate. That was totally legit, even though he gave it to me under duress and while we were already living together in the Biblical sense. "You don't understand. I can't."

"Jacquelyn, it's just my way of saying that I appreciate you for giving an old man a reason to get dressed in the morning." George's voice is like a caress.

"George, you aren't that old," I tease to break the sentimental moment.

Nice lunches and fancy dinners are one thing. An expensive handbag, maybe something a little more. But accepting a luxury piece of jewelry?

His offering it to me says more about me and how far I've strayed than about George. He's just a married man plying a young woman with gifts to . . . what? Impress me? Amuse himself? Get in my pants?

"What would your wife say?"

"My wife's lawyers have finally convinced her not to fight our prenup, my divorce is just a formality at this point."

"I'm sorry." Hell, not really! Not that I want to marry George. It hasn't really crossed my mind. Much.

"Please, just try it on. For me, Jacquelyn. It would make me happy after such a sad day," he says. I hold out my wrist and George takes the bracelet out of the velvet box and snaps it on my wrist. Purely for the purposes of trying it on to make him happy, of course.

"It's beautiful, George. Really." Better to graciously accept it now and decide later if I should keep it. Yes, later I'll be in better shape to deeply examine my conscience and morals. I'm sure I have them written on a slip of paper somewhere in the bag George gave me.

"Now, tell me what you thought of the benefit." George signals for the waiter to pour the wine.

"It was interesting." The bracelet glints as I lift my glass to my lips.

26

Mrs. Mayor

People and luggage are aboard three double-parked shiny-black Mercedes SUVs, but no one is going anywhere until Mr. and Mrs. Mayor finish their fight in the foyer. Somehow I have to make time stand still or get Mrs. Mayor moving before Vivian starts bleeding from her ears.

"Does he think I'm stupid or something?" Mrs. Mayor, wrapped in cashmere, her sunglasses perched on top of her head, shoves her overstuffed tote bag toward me. I guess it's hard to notice I already have my hands full with her other tote bag and large non-fat latte. "Well, does he?"

Realizing it was not a rhetorical question I answer as diplomatically as I possibly can. "I don't think so."

Natasha solemnly primps Mrs. Mayor, her mood as blue as her eye shadow. Jesus didn't come home until this morning and wasn't in the mood to talk about the state of their union. She's inconsolable, but still did a fabulous job on Mrs. Mayor, Vivian and me.

"His mother is behind this." Mrs. Mayor raises her chin so Natasha can dust the underside with the shimmer powder she'd dunk her whole body into if we let her. "Don't you think so, Jacquelyn? Don't you think she's behind all of this?"

"I . . . I couldn't say, Katherine." Not if I want to keep my job.

Mrs. Mayor generally assumes anything that doesn't go her way is her mother-in-law's fault. This time she happens to be right. The proof—actual, physical proof, for once—is in the fax Vivian showed me before she put it through the shredder (per Mr. Mayor's instructions).

In very lawyerly language Mr. Mayor's mother, the venerable Gail R. Wadsworth Baxter, chastised her son for inviting three unexpected guests (one who happens to be his wife) without sufficient notice and advised him to advise his wife to make arrangements for her staff to stay in a nearby motel. Attached to the fax were a string of newspaper clippings documenting the ups and downs of Mrs. Mayor's hemlines and necklines. She had penned a huge, sad face next to each of them.

"I'm not going to let some old witch intimidate me. I kept Faye Dunaway from cutting in line at The Ivy. And this woman thinks she can treat me like this? She's off her priceless antique rocker. I'm Mrs. Baxter now, not her."

"I . . . well . . . Oh, here's your latte! Would you like anything else?"

I'd give my firstborn to be able to retreat into the Kitchen with Anita and Lei who are lucky enough to be staying behind. Even Mrs. Mayor couldn't justify bringing her two housekeepers along with me and Natasha. Mr. Mayor also nixed the idea of bringing their monogrammed 1,000-thread-count sheets when he found out they'd need to rent another SUV just to transport them.

Normally I wouldn't take issue, but those sheets make getting into bed like stepping into a vat of butter, in a good way. I got a set cheap on eBay and since then I—

"Jacquelyn?"

"Sorry?" I snap out of my stupor.

"His family treats our home like their private hotel. And she expects me to put my assistant and my makeup artist in a motel, a *motel*, three miles away? How it could be possible she doesn't have room for all of us? Not even a pull-out couch for my assistant when they have a room for her." Mrs. Mayor tosses her head in Vivian's direction. "It's bad enough I have to leave the stylist here. I mean, I'm traveling light. It's not like I'm bringing an entourage."

I nod, but not too enthusiastically. I don't want to encourage her or let on that I just fired stylist number six, and number seven isn't due to start until after we get back from LA and until then Mrs. Mayor is styleless. Not that she'll notice number seven is not number six or five or four. To Mrs. Mayor they've all become interchangeable, like coordinating bra-and-panties sets. And, for some reason, these people are still lining up to work for her even though they know they won't last. It's become a stylist's version of climbing Everest and they want to be the first to reach the peak. From what I understand, a San Francisco stylist is not worth his or her salt until I fire them on Mrs. Mayor's behalf. I knew these people were a little off—who really cares that much about accessories?—but the whole thing sort of creeps me out.

"We could always double up with Vivian. I'm sure she wouldn't mind." Vivian has scored a guest house (an actual *house*), after being hastily bumped from the main residence once it was confirmed Mrs. Mayor would be accompanying her husband despite the fact that she wasn't invited.

"There is no way in hell I'm letting her shortchange me, Jacquelyn. Who do they think I am? I'm his wife for fuck's sake. I deserve a room for my assistant."

"Uh, thanks?" I don't want to stay in a broom closet just so she can make a point.

"You either stay near me or I'm not going." Mrs. Mayor slams her sunglasses down over her eyes and cinches the belt tighter on her trench coat.

Natasha rolls her eyes, showing the first signs of life this morning. We all know it's an empty threat, even she does. There is nothing in the world that could keep Mrs. Mayor from getting her stilettos into one of the doors of a yet-uncataloged Baxter residence. She bought me a new digital camera just so I could "document" the furniture at the Baxter Family Carmel retreat and add the photos to correspond to the spreadsheets.

"Katherine, I don't think—"

"This is ridiculous. Where's my coffee?"

27

Vivian

Natasha, wearing earplugs and a nightshade, snorts on her heated leather seat. I pat her thigh and she settles down again, looking sad even in her tiny, pink pill–induced sleep. I shift closer to Vivian. I should bring up some important local matter and help her see it from a different perspective, which she can then pass on to the Mayor and give me credit for it and then just like that—tah-dah!—a job on the Mayor's staff.

"Hey, Vivian?"

"What?" She doesn't look up from her laptop. How she's not carsick is beyond me. Normally she would ride with Mr. Mayor, but since he's traveling with his wife she's been exiled to a staff car with me and Natasha.

"Where did you stay the last time you visited Carmel with Mr. Mayor?"

"I stayed up at the house." Vivian takes off her glasses and puts them in her purse. I wait for her to elaborate, but she doesn't.

"Oh, is it nice?" I can't help but ask.

"Nice? It's beyond nice. It's . . . well mannered. You almost want to apologize to the furniture for using it. You'll see. If they offer you something to drink, just ask for a glass of water. They always offer and it just makes things easier."

"OK." That doesn't seem so different from my parents' house. My mother is forever offering visitors something to drink or eat.

Even the time my brother got picked up for shoplifting she offered lemonade to the cops who drove him home (in handcuffs).

"If you don't take them up on it, they'll think you're intimidated by them. But make sure to only ask for water. If you ask for anything more complicated they'll think you're imposing."

"OK." Now this was a little more involved than I would have expected, but it seemed simple enough. Just ask for a glass of water, no big deal.

"I'm not trying to freak you out, Jacqs."

"I'm not freaked out." I am beginning to get really freaked out.

"They're just like normal people," Vivian says sarcastically.

"Sure, just normal people." With a lot more money, power and privilege, but just people who are sort of famous. Not even sort of famous, somewhat well known. Mostly by people who follow politics and are interested in minor-league US history.

"They have an awful tendency to give nicknames." Vivian warms up to her subject. "You'll never guess what the Mayors have been dubbed. Go ahead, guess. I dare you."

"Um . . . Um . . ." Nicknames? What, like Muffy and Binks?

"Kit and Kat. Get it? KitKat? Like the candy? Christ, these people." Vivian rolls her eyes. "Don't worry about it. We'll be out of there by tomorrow morning and on our way to Santa Barbara before they can slap one on you."

"You got one?" I can't help but ask.

"Vivvy, and I consider myself lucky."

"That's not too bad." Mr. Mayor calls her Vivvy sometimes. I always thought it was cute.

"I guess it could have been worse"—she looks back down at her laptop—"but don't call me Vivvy."

"So, um, will this Santa Barbara thing be any fun?" Must be a lack of oxygen to the brain (Natasha won't let us crack open a window or turn on the air conditioner—bad for her sinuses), usually I'm a lot more, uh, relevant?

"I don't plan to find out. My goal is to hole up in my room, get very drunk on overpriced minibar liquor and not answer my phone. You?"

"Weird. That was my plan, too. And maybe get a massage." Since I don't have anything better to do, I quickly switch gears into full-on friend mode. "Is everything OK with you and Curtis?"

"Don't get me started . . . Jacqs, you've been married before, right?" Vivian shuts her laptop closed with a click and gives a wary look over in Natasha's direction. Her pill must have kicked in because she's softly snoring, the only indication that she's still alive.

"Yeah." Oh, crap, here we go again. Doesn't anyone within a mile radius of me have a normal sort of happy relationship and why do I seem to be the doppelganger for marital success?

"I don't mean to pry . . ." Vivian twists her wedding ring around her finger. When she moves it up to her knuckle I can see she has a slight rash.

"No, go ahead. Ask me anything." I settle in my seat and get into Dr. N mode.

"This whole marriage thing. It's a lot harder than I thought. I mean, I love Curtis, but . . ."

"You hate his guts and can't stand the sight of him chewing or brushing his teeth?"

"Exactly! That's exactly it! He's almost repellant to me. All we seem to do is argue about the stupidest things. Like this morning, I don't even remember what set us off." Vivian's face flushes attractively. She must have been holding this in for a while. "Is that normal, Jacqs?"

"What's normal? I didn't have sex with my husband for six of the fourteen months we were married," I say with not a small amount of pride.

"Oh, my God. How did you manage to hold out?"

"I just watched him get dressed for bed at night and it pretty much took care of any sexual feelings I had." I also bought my very first vibrator around that time. I sent away for it and for a whole week left work early to make sure I intercepted the mailman. When it did finally come, well, so did I.

"Did you hate him?" Vivian's forehead creases. I make a mental note to slip her Mrs. Mayor's Botox doctor's card. She gives discounts for referrals.

"Sure, but we didn't part on bad terms. We actually had a lot of fun toward the end. Once we decided to split up, that is. I guess you can say we found out things were still pretty special."

"Really?"

"Not special enough to stay married, but it's not like I'd mow him down with my car if I saw him crossing the street. We both knew divorce was our best option, but we are still friends." I'm really on a roll now. "He's been traveling around doing computer stuff. He's down in LA, actually."

I didn't mention to Bina that Nate and I would be in the same time zone, if not zip code. I am under strict orders not to bring up Nate's name around Bina. I sort of almost drove her crazy with all my Nate talk. I talked about him when we met, more when we dated, even more when we lived together, I had plenty more to say about him while we were married and I sort of exhausted the subject after our divorce.

Hence, Dr. N, who I have to pay to listen to me talk about Nate. It's been very therapeutic and expensive, but Bina and I are closer than ever. Now that I've added Vivian to my tree phone of Nate I get that familiar thrill of discovering a fresh set of ears.

"Are you going to meet up with him?" Vivian perks up. I had no idea she was an incurable romantic. Maybe that's her problem with marriage? "You have to see him!"

"Uh . . ." How can I break it to Vivian that my relationship with Nate is one-sided and electronic?

"Maybe. Mrs. Mayor keeps me on a short leash."

"Not this weekend, Jacqs. She'll be too busy trying to impress the family." Vivian has always had a jaundiced but accurate view of Mrs. Mayor. "They'll play kissie face with her and then tear her apart behind her back. And then she'll come home with her tail between her legs and work even harder at polishing her image as the ideal wife of a rising politician."

"Well, yeah." I feel it's my duty as her employee to defend her. "Yeah, well."

"So are you with me for a wild weekend in Carmel with all the other well-preserved geriatrics and then for some wild orgy sex with young and willing political aides in Santa Barbara?"

This is a tricky spot I'm in. On the one hand, I know Vivian is in need of a good time to forget about her problems with her husband and on the other, I don't know if it's a good idea if I encourage her to have a good time to forget her husband, which may cause more problems.

Best to err on the side of caution. "Sure. What about your husband?"

A nonjudgmental acceptance of her desire to have a "wild weekend" but, like any good friend, I've acknowledged that a "wild weekend" and "husband" may not mix. Dr. N would be proud. I think.

"Who?" Vivian lowers her eyes and frowns. "I hate arguing with him. I can never win."

"Maybe you should just call Curtis and talk it out, not let things fester." Not to be callous, but a year of therapy has proven to me that it's best to get it all out and move on to another problem because there is always another problem and another . . .

"I guess. I don't know. Maybe." She twists her hair around her finger.

I heave a huge sigh. "Yeah."

Vivian gives me a quizzical look. "Something wrong?"

"Nope. Just thinking about all the baggage I brought with me."

I stand aside as a beefy, good-looking man unloads the suitcases from the back of the SUVs. All I am required to do is point out the bags and he'll lift them. This is great! I've never had someone actually do my dirty work. I can see how a person could get used to this.

He didn't introduce himself and I'm not sure what the protocol is on these things. Can I tell him what to do or should I just ignore him like everyone else is? He must have lots of information, and information is vital to my job. Mrs. Mayor will expect me to give her a full report of any of my dealings with the "staff," and pass on any relevant and not-so-relevant gossip to add to her arsenal. Nothing beats inside information and from what I've noticed, rich people tend to forget that their staff have eyes, ears and, most importantly for me, mouths.

Mr. Mayor and Vivian are huddled in the corner going over schedules. Mrs. Mayor has yet to emerge from the backseat of the first car where Natasha disappeared the instant we stopped. We're all in a holding pattern until she comes out.

"I'm Gus. You need anything call me. You staying in the main house, guest house or the staff quarters?"

"I'm not sure."

"Place is packed this week. Big powwow with all the heads of the family."

You couldn't get away with saying powwow in San Francisco. Junta maybe, but definitely not powwow.

Mrs. Mayor, looking stunning, gracefully steps out of the car, as if she's about to walk the red carpet, and minces her way over to Mr. Mayor. Gus whistles under his breath.

"She's a looker, your boss. Sorry."

"No, she is. Very beautiful." I don't know why I feel a stab of pride. And stab is right. Working for such an attractive person always reminds me I work for an attractive person. I count the bags and regain my composure. "That's it!"

"I'll call you girls and your, uh, friend, a golf cart. Unless you gals brought your hiking shoes and a compass."

"Is this place really that big?" The house looks impressive, from what I can see of it in the fog but, sheesh, how much space can one family need for a rarely used weekend home?

"Rumor is Mr. Baxter isn't dead. He went for a walk and is still trying to find his way to the pool after all these years."

"A golf cart would be great."

Vivian extracts herself from Mr. Mayor and walks over to me, passing Gus, who is carrying about 300 pounds of Mrs. Mayor's luggage. She nods at him curtly and walks on. Even under the strain of Mrs. Mayor's Louis Vuitton, he still manages to give her the once-over.

"Have they called us a golf cart? No way am I trekking to the other side of this national park in these heels." Vivian grunts as she shoulders her tote bag and laptop case, and extends the handle on her suitcase.

I notice she's packed less than I have. I guess she really doesn't plan on doing much besides drinking in her room.

"Yeah, he said this place is pretty big."

"Don't look so scared, Jacqs. Just think of this place as your everyday sixth or seventh rarely used family home and frequently photographed family retreat."

"I'm not at all scared," I say, sounding scared. I have no choice but to distract her and me. "Are you going to call Curtis?"

"He knows my number. He can call me." Vivian smiles but looks worried. We both know he won't call. He's probably over it by now, but she'll never know because she won't call him and it would never occur to him to call her.

Mr. and Mrs. Mayor arrange themselves to look like a happy couple and start their ascent up the grand stone stairway just as the huge doors are thrown open and a flood of jocular-looking relatives spill out to greet them. They are all holding drinks in their hands.

"Smell that, Jacqs?" Vivian asks, chucking her suitcase into the back of a pristine-looking golf cart.

I tentatively inhale and shake my head. "What should I be sniffing for?"

"The avalanche of bullshit heading your way."

28

Gail

"Hello, I'm Jacquelyn Sanchez, Katherine's assistant. Pleased to meet you, Mrs.—"

"Call me Gail, dear." Gail, dear, Mr. Mayor's mom and the official matriarch of the Baxter clan, is asking me to call her by her first name. I watch helplessly as Vivian rushes up the grand staircase after Mr. Mayor to take an emergency conference call upstairs. It is, of course, Emilio Cortez-related. "May I call you Jacquelyn?"

"Sure," I squeak out and nod.

"Why don't we wait in my private sitting room?" Gail takes my elbow in her birdlike grip and steers me toward a pair of huge closed doors. "How long have you worked for Kat, dear?"

"About a year or so." God, has it already been that long? A whole year of assisting Mrs. Mayor with the sole act of being Mrs. Mayor.

Gail somehow manages to push open two 12-foot solid-oak doors and I come face-to-face with perfection, filthy-rich perfection. Next to this room the Mayors's Mansion looks like a starter home in Chico. No wonder Mrs. Mayor is bitter. Who wouldn't be?

"I'm sure Kat keeps you very busy. We were so surprised when Kit called and said she'd be coming along. She always seems to be so busy jetting off to Los Angeles to visit her actor friends." Gail settles her bones on the couch and gives me what I think she thinks is a reassuring smile. "Must be very interesting, too, working for Kat and so close to Kit."

"Um, it's . . ." Unlikely that she really cares, or does she? If she does, I can guess it's not for the right reasons. "It really is a pleasure working for *Katherine.*"

There's no way in hell I'm calling Mrs. Mayor *Kat.* I can tell it's not a nickname that's been bestowed on her with love and affection. Neither is the name Mrs. Mayor, of course, but I work for the woman and have a right to be bitchy.

"Dear, would you care for something to drink?" Gail reaches over and presses a tiny button. Seconds later I hear muffled footsteps behind me.

"Water would be great, thanks."

"Mineral, flat, flavored?"

"Uh . . . regular water?" Vivian never mentioned there would be subcategories to choose from.

"Are you sure, dear? It's no trouble." Gail gives me a tight smile and tilts her coiffed head slightly. This must be the test part.

"Thanks, but just plain old water will be perfect. Thank you."

"Mayleen, will you bring us some water, please." She doesn't bother to look at Mayleen as she asks. Instead, Gail leans over and nudges the geometrically perfect arrangement of magazines into further submission. I pretend to cough instead of giggle.

In a rare moment of humanness, Mrs. Mayor and I shared a laugh when she told me her mother-in-law demands that the maids Windex the covers of the magazines at regular intervals.

"I really shouldn't impose, I'm sure I should check in on Katherine." I half-make to rise knowing that Gail, dear has me firmly in her gentle tentacles.

"Vivian will be back in a jiffy. Kit promised to keep work at a minimum. We are having the staff do all the unpacking, and Kit and Kat are getting settled. Kat is upstairs with her, uh, wardrobe assistant . . ."

"Natasha. She's a makeup artist. She's just pitching in until we find a new stylist. The last one didn't work out," I ramble stupidly. This woman doesn't care.

"Of course. We're playing a round of golf at Clint's."

"Katherine loves golf." Mrs. Mayor said nothing about golf or packing for golflike activities. I have no idea what kind of outfit Natasha can come up with to pass the muster of Clint Eastwood and his golf course. At least, I think that's the Clint that Gail, dear is referring too. Could there be any other?

"Tell me . . . Oh, thank you, Mayleen." Gail stiffens and we both watch as Mayleen sets down a tray with two glasses, a pitcher of water and lemon wedges on a small crystal dish on the side. Gail pours water into the glasses and gestures to the lemon wedges. I nod. She extends a glass of water toward me. "Tell me about yourself, dear."

"Me?" I stop midreach.

"Yes, dear, you." Gail smiles again, causing the sides of her mouth to crease but not showing any teeth.

"Me?" Not that I don't think I'm interesting, but I can't imagine why Gail would even care what my name is.

"Oh, aren't you a delight. Kit mentioned you had a sense of humor. I'm sure it comes in handy with Kat. She has such a unique sense of humor."

"Yes, I guess. It helps to have a sense of humor." Mr. Mayor has talked about me to his *mother*. Sorry, but instead of feeling a thrill, it kind of creeps me out.

"Kit has nothing but praise for you, dear. He says Kat would be lost without you."

"Uh, thanks?" Praise for my job performance at the expense of my boss. I'm not sure how I should take it.

"Tell me, how do you find that our Kat is adjusting?"

"Fine."

"Fine?" Gail raises an eyebrow and purses her mouth.

"She enjoys her duties, I mean, she likes to cut ribbons and go to functions and stuff like that. She likes kids. She really does well at functions where kids are involved." This is not quite true. She always makes me carry hand sanitizer and vitamin C whenever we have to drop in on after-school programs or library readings.

"Yes, but I'm sure you know there is more to being the wife of a politician than looking pretty for pictures. She is now representing the Baxter family."

It's no secret that the Baxter family is the poor person's version of the Kennedy clan and, despite being Presbyterian, lacks that *oomph* to fill books and inspire a miniseries or two. This lasting stain on the good family name is something that has irked Gail, dear to no end, and she's spent her entire life trying to redeem the family legacy.

"I think she's doing OK." And I really do just mean OK. Not bad, not spectacular, just OK. I know this won't cut the mustard with Gail, dear. "At least, I think so."

"What can you tell me about this reporter Emilio Cortez?"

"Not much." Especially, not that he's trying to tempt me to spill my guts or go work for him. I'm not sure which would be considered a worse betrayal in this family.

"He seems to have ears in places where he shouldn't." Gail's hands are loosely clasped on her lap, making them look like talons.

"I've discussed it with Katherine. And I, uh, mentioned it to him, Emilio Cortez. I'm not sure what I can do about it. We're all very discreet, of course. If someone is talking, it's not me."

"It's the Baxter-family image that is being damaged and as her assistant it's your job to make sure she upholds those standards."

If this woman knew how much I'd sacrificed for the sake of keeping her son and his wife looking halfway happy she'd be kissing my ass instead of trying to grill it. I take a deep breath and then another one. I'm pissed.

"Is there an issue with my performance?" And if there is, shouldn't it be the Mayors who should bring it up?

"Of course not, dear. What would ever give you that idea? I just want you to know that if there is ever any situation where you think you need a little help I want you to make sure to call my assistant and we'll be there for you. And for Kat, of course."

"Of course." I watch Gail's eyes focus on something behind me, for an instant they narrow in annoyance.

"Jacqs?" Vivian calls from the foyer.

"Here!" I clear my throat and stand up. "Here. In here, Vivian."

"Hello?" Vivian enters cautiously. I almost cry with relief when I see she's carrying our coats. "Hello, Mrs. Baxter. Are you ready to go, Jacquelyn? We're all done here."

"Leaving so soon? Are you sure you wouldn't care for something to drink?" Gail is forced to ask, but clearly the arrival of Vivian has ruined the momentum of her polite interrogation of me.

"No, thank you, Mrs. Baxter," Vivian says, "We have some urgent business to attend to for the Mayor and Katherine." Vivian entwines my arm with hers. "If you would excuse us."

"Thank you for the water," I say, not wanting to piss off Gail any more than I may already have.

"My pleasure," Gail, dear says, shooting Vivian a stony smile in return, to my relief. "Dinner is promptly at 7, cocktails at 6."

"Bye!" Not a chance in hell I'm setting foot in that place again. Even if I didn't get a look at the rest of it.

29

Vivian and Natasha

Around us stilted conversation and uncomfortable laughter abound. This could be a family gathering or a wake. Small groups and couples dot the ballroom-sized terrace while uniform clad wait staff hired for the evening circulate with mixed drinks on silver trays. The perfect summer scene, except it's February and freezing.

Mrs. Baxter says we are to socialize, assistants and mayoral staff included, for exactly twenty-five more minutes before we are let in for dinner. I think I have about fifteen minutes until hypothermia sets in but I'm too intimidated to retreat inside.

"What's up with Natasha and those little pills and where can I get some?" Vivian asks as she waves over a waiter.

"I'm not sure." I shrug. But I'm not sure I don't want to know. She's been popping them like crazy, each color changing her energy level and mood. "Look, they've finally moved!"

I grab Vivian's hand and charge toward the sole heat lamp Mrs. Baxter has allowed on the terrace. Vivian's lips are turning slightly blue underneath her peachy lip gloss.

"Is it her slut husband?" Vivian rolls her eyes.

"You know about Jesus?" I'm hurt. I thought this was just between me and Natasha, something she could only confide in me.

We both look to where Natasha is sitting, enveloped in a faux fur coat, having an animated conversation with seventy-five-year-old Clarence W. Baxter, retired CEO of some Baxter conglomerate or another. Whatever tales Natasha is regaling him with have left him doubled over with laughter.

At least they seem to be having a good time, unlike Mrs. Mayor in her painfully tasteful Chanel suit who is (unsuccessfully) trying to blend in. She can play witty, but this crowd demands razor wit. I almost feel sorry for her.

"What's the deal? They breaking up?" Vivian just won't let the subject drop.

"I don't think so." I should be asking Vivian the same question. Right before "cocktail hour" Vivian called Curtis and gave him a tongue-lashing and he returned the favor. Even though she retreated to the bathroom, Natasha and I could make out every cringe-inducing word. They went from spat to separation in one phone call.

"You can tell me, Jacqs." Vivian pokes me in the ribs.

"She's hinted that life with him has been less than rosy." I'll indulge her, she needs the distraction.

"Welcome to the club, sister." Vivian rewraps herself in a flimsy shawl.

"I, for one, am a happy ex-member, thank you very much. Honestly, why bother? Men and relationships just seem to be too much trouble and a waste of energy. Where are the benefits?" The more time that passes between the now me and the married me, the more that seems clear. I think it's a breakthrough of sorts. I'll have to make sure to mention this to Dr. N.

"You're just fooling yourself, Jacqs. You're in love with Mr. Mayor."

"I am not!" Not love, but definitely a huge, throbbing crush.

"You've just confirmed it for me! Ha!" Vivian is getting loud. I take her empty glass out of her hand and shoo away the waiter when he offers to bring a fresh one. Vivian inclines her head toward where Natasha is being summarily dismissed. "Looks like Mrs. Stick-Up-Her-Ass has reclaimed her hubby before he can experience any more joy in life."

"These people, man, they have the best manners but manage to be rude at the same time." After my trial-by-Gail, I've been reluctant to engage any of them in conversation, much less make eye contact. I tried to get out of dinner but was informed that this would not be acceptable.

"It's called breeding, my dear. They can't help themselves. Their nannies never really loved them." Vivian snorts. People look over at us.

"Hi, gals, what's shaking?" Natasha bats her Twiggy eyelashes at us innocently.

"Making friends, I see." I entwine my arm through hers for warmth and to keep her out of trouble.

"Oh, Clarence? He's a hoot. There is some gay in that old dog."

"I'm sure his wife would be thrilled to find that out." Vivian takes Natasha's other arm.

I am exhausted from standing up so straight and minding my manners. Not that anyone has bothered to test me, but I must remain vigilant. "We just have to make it through this dinner and then we can leave tomorrow for Santa Barbara."

Instead of a constipated bunch of uptight Wasps, I can relax around a swarm of backstabbing gossipmongers who talk policy the way these people talk horses. Suddenly a trip home amongst my family, who drive me crazy but aren't phonies, sounds like just what I need.

"About dinner, Jacqs, these things usually have assigned seating," Vivian says with the slightest of slurs. "Where you sit says a lot as to how important you are in the Baxter universe."

"We can't sit together?" Panic rises in my chest. I already have spied at least four people I don't want to sit next to or even share oxygen with. Not that I'm flattering myself; they look like they'd crush me like a bug just for the entertainment. Now I have to worry about this being a popularity contest?

"Oh, goody, I hope they sit me next to that Clarence. That old coot is a hoot," Natasha says a bit too loudly. Vivian pats her arm.

"They're all coots." Vivian and Natasha laugh for a bit longer than they should. "It'll be OK, Jacqs. Like you said, just this dinner and we're out of here."

"Is it too late to get appendicitis and bail?"

"That wouldn't be polite," Vivian and Natasha answer simultaneously.

30

Scooter

"Scooter Baxter." The young, prematurely bald guy on my left offers me his right hand to shake. A firm three pumps and he snakes it back to his side and I'm left wanting more.

"Hi, Jacquelyn Sanchez." I'm a bit drunk, but I think I'm hiding it rather well. I turn to my right to greet the other side of the sandwich. "Hello?"

She's an ancient woman and I'm guessing will get her meal pumped through one of the bags suspended from her IV pole.

"Never mind Martha. She's as old as the hills my family strip-mined to make its fortune," Scooter says to me, then leans over and calls loudly, "AREN'T YOU, AUNTY MARTY!"

Aunty Marty lists from side to side and mumbles. I notice there is a nurse sitting right behind her. I smile at her, she ignores me. Fine. Whatever. Bitch.

"Are you a friend of the family or . . ." Scooter lets the question trail off onto less unpleasant paths.

"I'm Katherine's personal assistant so I guess that makes me an 'or.'"

"Do you like that line of work, the personal assistant racket?" Scooter asks earnestly, very conscious of his whiteness, which, I'm sure, he's tried to compensate for by reading and rereading *One-Hundred Years of Solitude* and making an effort to get to know the "help" as real people. "You must get such a unique opportunity to get to know people on such different levels."

"It's just a job. I never thought I'd be doing this, you know. I thought I'd do something way more, I don't know, significant with my life . . . oh, well!" Did I just say that out loud? That old biddy Baxter must have slipped some truth serum into my third or fourth Tom Collins. Lucky for me, Scooter can feel my pain.

"I'm the poster boy for bad Baxter behavior this month. I was in law school, but I said to myself, 'Is this what I really want? To be yet another Baxter lawyer?' So I quit and that's why I'm here."

"Oh." I carefully arranged my napkin in my lap.

"Lucky for me your boss still hasn't fallen in line. It's a small scandal for the family, you know."

"How so?" I ask, playing dumb.

Even Aunty Marty must know Mrs. Mayor is on the outs and is dragging her hubby down with her. He's been bumped from the head of the table, sitting two seats down on his mother's left. Katherine is way on the other side, sandwiched between two stony-faced women who won't look at her. I almost feel sorry for her, trying so hard in her brand-new suit. Maybe she'll blame the Chanel for her failure to win over the Baxter bitches and give it to me.

"Kit is in a bit of hot water with Aunt Gail, but I'm sure the golden boy will set things right. He always does." I detect a slight snarl in Scooter's voice.

"Yup." I nod. I've been to some tense family events, but this takes the cake. "So is Scooter your nickname?"

"I can't stand my nickname." Scooter leans in close and whispers, "It's Herbert."

"I'm sorry." On both counts.

"How do you like Carmel?" Scooter picks up a spoon and starts on his soup. I do the same. I can be as bland as the next person . . . maybe not as much as Aunt Marty but Scooter has nothing on me.

"Fine. Great. So beautiful." I spent most of the day on the phone frantically tracking down the perfect pair of faux pearls to complete Mrs. Mayor's ensemble. She insisted they had to be faux in keeping with the "Chanel spirit."

"Is your family in San Francisco?" An ambiguous-enough question, yet I don't trust Scooter's motives.

"No." That should take care of this line of questioning.

"Ah, where does your family live?" Scooter asks, his eyes trained on the sensibly low centerpiece in the middle of the table.

"Los Angeles." I take a closer look at it, just in case I'm missing something.

"I prefer New York. You get back to Los Angeles much?"

"I visit my parents all the time," I say, eyeing him warily. He goes from asking about scenery to my family? This guy is working all the angles.

"Where are your parents from?" He swivels around to face me.

"Los Angeles," I sigh. And so are my grandparents, and their parents and the parents before them, but I don't think this will impress Scooter.

"Ah, originally?" Scooter doesn't bother to hide his disappointment.

"Originally they're from outer space, but I'm not supposed to talk about that."

"Oh." Scooter looks momentarily perplexed, but recovers suavely. "Oh! You are funny."

"Are *your* parents here?" I don't really care, but I hope if I get him talking about his family, he'll leave mine alone.

"I'm afraid my mother and Aunt Gail are on the outs at the moment," Scooter says, nodding solemnly.

"That must make life difficult." I'm prepared to be sympathetic. At least, a sympathetic drunk, which is more than I can say for most of the people around this table.

"I hardly ever see or speak to either of them," Scooter continues on as if this is the most normal thing to reveal to a complete stranger. "My dad is currently in Bridgeport, that's in Connecticut, and Mother is resting at a spa in upstate New York."

"I love spas." Finally, something I can talk about.

"It's not that kind of spa," Scooter says with a snort.

"Oh."

"How about your family?" he asks, tilting his head in a way

that I assume is supposed to melt my heart and loosen my tongue.

"My family? Well, there are seven of us. Nine if you count my parents," I say and brace myself for the usual gasp. The Kennedy family has kennels of kids, but they're Catholic, so what else would you expect.

"Big family," Scooter says, looking at me and, yes, nodding.

"Two are twins," I say a bit defensively. "So really it's only five. There's my older sister, who works in a hospital counting bedpans or something. A job that totally suits her personality. There are my two brothers, who are the sons in Sanchez and Sons Electricians. Then there are the twins, who are moms. Then there is my other brother, I'm not sure what he's doing at the moment. Maybe time, maybe nothing. And then there is me. Me, me, me. Me!"

"I would have thought you were an only child."

"You know, you're not the first person to say that," I snicker.

"Over there is Meems." Scooter nods his head toward a skinny, horse-faced girl with overprocessed blonde hair and an aggressive tan.

We all smile at each other politely until I'm on the verge of tears. I finally resort to a fake sneeze to bring an end to the staring match.

"She's in banking and graduated from Harvard with honors." This has been going on all night with everyone I've been introduced to: current job, past job if it was better than current job, university of graduation (accolades, if any) and sometimes an interesting hobby (if it's unique).

"Wow. Honors."

"And next to her is Maxfield. He's in technology, the black sheep of the family. He started at Penn, but transferred to Harvard, thank God."

"Harvard is my favorite." I take a huge swallow of wine. Liquor seems to be its own food group for the Baxters.

"So do you speak Spanish?"

I guess he thinks we're best chums now and it's OK to delve a little deeper into my ethnicity. I nod and wait for Scooter to ask me to say something in Spanish but, perhaps thinking it would be like asking a monkey to perform a trick, he conscientiously resists the urge to have me prove my Latinaness.

"I speak French." Scooter leans back and casually drapes an arm on the seat back behind me. "I've always wanted to learn Spanish. Or Italian."

"They're practically the same thing!" I say a little too loudly and startle Aunty Marty out of her stupor. The nurse quickly adjusts the dials on her pole, calming the old gal down.

Scooter nods and smiles. I nod and smile. Guessing this is the perfect segue he asks, "So, you want to hook up after dinner?"

I stop smiling.

31

Mrs. Mayor

"You want me to what?"

"It'll be fun, trust me, Myles always shows me a good time when I'm in LA. Won't that be great?"

Mrs. Mayor grabs my hand, almost making me lose my grip on the plushy white robe I threw on just before she charged in. Steam is still rising off my head from my shower. The water pressure in this place is amazing and I was thoroughly enjoying my last shower here before we head out to Santa Barbara in a couple of hours.

"Hold on, I must have water in my ears." I shake my head, careful not to get any drops on Mrs. Mayor.

She's wearing a pair of khaki short-shorts, a snug polo shirt with all the buttons open and Coach sneakers. She topped off the ensemble with a logo baseball cap, set at a jaunty angle over her impeccable hair and makeup. She could feasibly be on her way out for a round of golf or to shoot a porno film on a golf course.

"Hurry, Jacquelyn, Clint's waiting." She looks genuinely happy. It can't be the prospect of golf. She's allergic to most types of grass and pollen, and generally hates being outdoors. "He's such a sweetheart, letting me and Gail . . . or is it Gail and I?"

"One issue at a time, Katherine. You want me to go down to LA and hang out with—"

"He's the producer I told you about. A major player."

"—your good friend the major producer Myles while you stay here?"

This guy Myles wants her to "star" in his next action movie. Her role would mainly consist of running around without a bra and screaming at appropriate moments. She's actually considering it.

"Gail and I are going to spend some time together, just the two of us, so we can bond. Isn't that great?" Mrs. Mayor is beaming. Poor lamb.

"What about Santa Barbara and the conference? Are you still going to that?"

"God, no! Those conference things bore me to death, you know? Remind me of high school." Mrs. Mayor adjusts her cleavage.

"Um, what about Mr. Mayor?"

"He's still going." Her expression darkens a smidge.

"OK . . . I thought you were, you know, worried about how much he's been working lately?" Not to rub salt in her imagined wound, but one of us has to be realistic.

"You go in my place and keep Vivian company." Meaning: make sure Vivian doesn't keep company with her husband. "Kit is going to pick me up on his way back. So, see? It all works out for everyone. You can go visit your family, hang out with Myles and get into that political stuff you like so much, without having to worry about little old me."

"And Mrs. Baxter, she's OK with all this? Just the two of you here in this huge house. By yourselves?" Aside from the dozen or so faceless staff, of course.

"She's the one who suggested it! Can you believe it?"

"Yes, I can."

32

Emilio

Kit Baxter, great hope of the Democratic Party and mainstay of my sweaty fantasies, just gave me a warm hug and kiss on the cheek in the lobby of the Santa Barbara Four Seasons. In front of a small army of reporters, political groupies and party officials.

Since my room, which I'm sharing with Natasha, isn't ready, I have no choice but to nonchalantly make my way to a club chair and flip through a magazine as I struggle to keep my face intelligently blank.

"Nice day," a warm voice says. I look up. Sitting opposite me is Emilio Cortez.

"Holy crap! What are you doing here?" I yelp. I glance around to make sure I haven't attracted more unwanted attention.

"I am a loyal Democrat, Jacquelyn, despite what you might have heard. I am just as concerned with the direction our party is taking as our very friendly mayor is." Cortez looks gorgeous and, as usual, is smiling at me. "There is plenty of news, it seems, for me to report on already."

I can't help but blush, mostly because I know he knows I was enjoying the afterglow of my mayoral kiss. Mr. Mayor's purely political kiss.

"You're out of luck. Katherine didn't come so I'm afraid you're going to have to write about some real news, not what my boss is wearing or what she spends at the hotel boutique."

"Gloves off, Jacquelyn. Like your boss's husband, I'm in Santa Barbara to make nice with the big men in charge or, as we used to say in my old neighborhood, *chingarnos el hefe*." Cortez laughs at his own joke.

"Oh . . . Here?" I can't imagine a reporter, whose politics are so far to the left he makes Mr. Mayor look like a Republican, would be staying at as fancy a hotel as the Four Seasons.

"A friend of mine is staying here, Jacquelyn. I'm not stalking you. It's not my style."

"Yeah, you're a real gentleman, Cortez."

Yesterday's column had a lengthy diatribe on how Mrs. Mayor was trying to make San Francisco into Hollywood North. And, for good measure, he outed the Mayors as a nonrecycling/non-composting household.

"I report what the City of San Francisco wants to know. Needs to know." Emilio stresses the last part. Even he must realize how petty it's all become.

"Why do you have it in for Katherine? She's harmless." She's only a danger to herself, but he already knows that.

He leans back in his chair, regarding me closely. "San Francisco is a unique animal, Jacquelyn. Very open in arms, but closed in mentality. The right kind of weirdo can go far, but someone like your boss . . . She will never be a true San Franciscan."

"How about me? I wasn't born there, but I don't get hate mail or dragged through the mud by the press for every silly, innocent mistake."

"That's true, but, then again, *mi amore*, you aren't involved with the mayor of San Francisco." Emilio raises an eyebrow and leans toward me. "Or are you?"

"Of course not!" I say too loudly, sounding guilty even to my own ears. Cortez smiles at me. "Well, I'm not!"

33

Scooter

"There are a million reasons why I won't sleep with you, Scooter." I should be tired of this cat-and-mouse game, but I'm not. It's kept my mind off my encounters with Mr. Mayor and Emilio Cortez, both of which were too close for comfort.

I try to find a comfortable position on my stiff, standard-issue hotel dining chair as I look for Vivian and Natasha. Over Scooter's head, a writhing mass of bodies get down to the sounds of a cheesy cover band. After a day of fetching coffee, practicing their nascent networking skills and collating paper, the young Democrat aides and interns have been set free on the hotel parquet dance floor while their elders watch from a dignified distance.

"Just one, I don't think my ego can stand a million," Scooter says next to my ear. I shove him away with my shoulder.

Scooter has been pawned off on Mr. Mayor in hopes that he will see the error of his ways and return to law school. Mr. Mayor promptly pawned him off on me, with a kiss and a hug to seal the deal. I suppose he wants Scooter to see what happens to people who don't put their educations to proper use.

The only ambition Scooter has expressed so far is getting me in bed. I've had fantasies of banging a Baxter, but definitely not this Baxter.

"Fine. Reason number one is I have a boyfriend." That's settled, maybe now we can talk about something interesting. Like Baxter family gossip and scandal that doesn't involve Mrs. Mayor.

"Is he here?" I foolishly shake my head. "I won't tell if you don't tell."

"Oh, I'll tell." I told Vivian that Scooter has been humping my leg and she thinks I should throw the boy a bone and make a real man of him. Seems Scooter has been labeled the Loser Baxter. I don't know how sleeping with me will nudge him into the winner category.

"You are a cruel and heartless woman, Jacquelyn," Scooter says with obvious delight.

Masochist. Looks like I temporarily have another Danny on my hands.

"Thank you. Go try your twisted Ivy League psychology on the interns. I'm sure you can swing a threesome as soon as you mention who you're related to."

People have been fawning over Mr. Mayor, and Vivian has had her work cut out beating them off, especially the women. The Baxter name is golden in these circles and Kit Baxter is a future ticket to a job near the Oval Office.

"Jackie, I love a challenge."

"Would you love my elbow in your throat?" I ask, removing Scooter's hand from my thigh. "Call me Jackie again and I'll knock your toupee off."

"Who is this boyfriend?" Scooter tries to casually pat his rug without looking like he is. "Kit said you were single."

"Oh, did he?" A thrill rushes through me, or maybe it's the cheap red wine we had with dinner that's killing my brain cells. "What else did he say?"

"He said you were smart and single. I'm smart, single and attractive . . . so?"

"No. I have a boyfriend. George. We've been together for a while now." George will never find out that I'm using him as my beard.

"It's not like you're going to marry this guy, right?" Scooter asks, pouring himself more cheap wine.

"You never know." I even sound confused and unsure to my own ears. Would I marry George? I've never even kissed him. And there's still the little matter of his current marital status.

"Here she comes," Scooter says, straightening up and bracing himself against his chair.

"Who comes?" I ask nervously. I don't think I can stomach another drunk idealist with a resume in one hand and a knife in the other. "Which she? All these girls look alike to me."

"Pamela Richards Barstow. The Florida Barstows, not the New York Barstows, but the Maine Richards, so it evens out, barely. Brown alum, worked in fashion for a while but is now an aide for Senator Cullman of Connecticut. Pammy! You look beautiful, as always," Scooter says with such sincerity that I now can't help but doubt his attraction to me.

"Scooter!" She air-kisses him and checks me out at the same time. "Where have you been hiding? And with whom?"

"This is Jacquelyn. She's visiting from San Francisco. She works for Kat," Scooter adds dismissively. I almost want to interject that I graduated summa cum laud from Berkeley and am currently at work on a novel, but don't. I don't think she'd be much impressed even if it was true.

"Who?" Pammy looks over at me a bit more closely. Her eyes are too closely set together, her hair is overprocessed and someone should explain the principal behind bronzing powder.

"Kat, Katie, Kate Bishop, she was on *Love and Lies*." Scooter openly appraises Pammy's neckline.

"Oh, her? Is she here? These things attract such second-rate celebrities." It's obvious she knows who Scooter is talking about.

"She goes by Katherine Baxter now." Scooter crosses his arms over his chest waiting for the inevitable.

"Oh, Kit! Where is that scrumptious thing?" Pammy exclaims, continuing to ignore me. "I can't believe how gorgeous that man is. Tell me, Scooter, I heard he's hung like a horse. So where is he?"

"He's hard at work trying to save the world," I say. I can't help myself, but I hate her. Tonight, I hate everyone who pretends I'm not here when clearly I am. Or, like Scooter, lavishes attention on me and acts like everything I say is significant and rife with hidden meaning.

"How boring. Oh, Scooter, look, it's Veronica. Veronica!" Pammy raises her glass and sloshes her drink on the table, and me, waving over another horse-faced girl, this one also tanned and even skinnier but with a huge rack on her. Fake, of course.

"Veronica is also a Brown alum. She worked in publishing, now she's a legislative aide in Washington to some feminist congresswoman or something. She, we, used to go out," Scooter confesses in my ear.

Pammy stares at us. I can tell she's trying to size me up to see what kind of hold I might have on Scooter. I throw my arm around him and sit closer. Scooter grins stupidly.

"I'm so sorry for you," I say loud enough for Pammy to hear me over the music.

Scooter laughs, causing Pammy to narrow her eyes at him.

"Veronica, you bitch. Where have you been?" Pammy says to her carbon copy as they exchange kisses and some good-natured faux-lesbian fondling.

"I was in my room recuperating from a bikini wax. Scooter, darling." Veronica leans over me and plants a huge, wet kiss on his mouth. I get a face full of fake tits. "Who is your little friend?"

"I'm Jacquelyn. We're not really friends. I'm just here because my boss decided to stay in Carmel and take inventory of the furniture so when her mother-in-law finally keels over she won't get screwed out of her fair share of the loot."

Veronica and Pammy laugh, making me feel stupid and petty just like Veronica and Pammy.

Vivian strides over, her arm linked with Natasha's. She's past tipsy and is now gloriously drunk. Seeing her approach, Veronica and Pammy stand up simultaneously.

"Call me, Scooter, when you're not so busy." Veronica takes Pammy's hand and they walk off, out of arm's reach but close enough to give Vivian dirty looks.

"What was that, a bulimic convention?" Vivian asks with a broad smile on her face.

Pammy and Veronica look outraged and edge back closer to the table, like suicidal moths to a homicidal flame.

"Come on, ladies, not tonight." Natasha throws an arm around Vivian and looks around for any roving reporters and photographers. They're all drunk and dancing, having long ago abandoned their journalistic duty to document the important goings-on of democracy in action.

"Not tonight *what?*" I demand, my pulse kicking up a notch, just as it did right before junior-high cat fights. I'm fully prepared to back Vivian up.

"Vivian and Veronica don't see eye to eye," Scooter whispers excitedly in my ear. I guess Scooter has a thing for women wrestling in front of him. Hell, who doesn't?

"Is it because Vivian didn't go to Brown?" I ask, exasperated at Scooter's infinitesimal attention span.

"No, it's . . . oh, hee hee." Scooter laughs, his eyes on Vivian and Veronica, ready for the inevitable confrontation. "There was a . . . well, an incident at a fund-raising party for Kit at Aunt Gail's. Veronica got a little too enthusiastic with her, um, support for his, you know, campaign."

"And?" I prod. Scooter needs a lot of prodding to stay on track. We've known each other only a few hours and I already feel I've been married to him for fifty mostly senile years.

"And Vivian sort of poured red wine down the front of Veronica's white dress," Scooter says, not taking his eyes off the impending action.

Veronica, with Pammy closely in tow, passes our table, purposely bumping into Vivian. Vivian turns around and grabs a handful of Veronica's straw hair and yanks. Hard.

"Ouch, my hair!" Veronica takes a wide slap at Vivian, catching her under the jaw.

Natasha and Scooter pull Vivian and Veronica apart, right before a couple of burly security guards show up. It all happens so fast I don't have a chance to spring over the table and tackle Pammy.

"Seems these ladies have had a little too much to drink."

Natasha gestures to Veronica and Pammy, hiding Vivian behind her bulk.

"She hit me first!" Vivian screams.

"Veronica would never hit anyone! She's a vegan!" yells Pammy.

"Then someone should let her know that her tits are totally artificial," Vivian says, rubbing her jaw.

"Come on, ladies. Night's over for you two," one of the guards says, as he and his partner step over to Veronica and Pammy, firmly grasp their boney arms and prepare to escort them toward the exit.

"OK, I think I'll call it a night, too." I get up and hand Vivian her purse. "Scooter, thanks for the conversation. It was . . . Natasha, you ready to go?"

"Since yesterday, honey." She tips her head at Scooter and walks us out, holding Vivian firmly by the upper arm.

"It's cool. I'll catch you later. Call me!" Scooter calls after us.

As we wade through the crowd for the door, I watch Scooter flow into a cluster of people and, like an amoeba, is seamlessly absorbed.

34

Vivian

In the hallway, Vivian looks completely calm, as if nothing had happened, but whatever did sobered her up.

"I can't believe that fucker hasn't called me." There is a slight slur to her voice, but she sounds lucid enough. "What should I do, Jacqs?"

"What do you want to do?" From my experience, at this stage Vivian doesn't want advice, she wants reassurance.

"I should leave his ass, is what I should do."

"Vivian, you've only been married a few months. Maybe it's just, you know, growing pains." As a formerly married woman who has been through her fair share of therapy, I have to be rational and logical. Something I never really was when I was married to Nate.

"Growing pains! I caught him in bed with another *woman!*"

"For Christ's sake!" Natasha jerks to a stop, causing us to run into her. "Pigs. Men are pigs."

"Amen, brother," Vivian sings out, sounding drunk again, "amen!"

"I'm so sorry, Vivian. Really."

Cheating. I can't really take the moral high ground on that one since my boyfriend is slightly married. Wait, is he even my boyfriend? He must be, since I turned down an invitation to have sex with a man I find reasonably attractive.

"It's not what you think," Vivian grumbles.

"It's not?" Natasha and I say at the same time.

"OK, they weren't actually in bed," Vivian admits.

"Vivian"—I cup her face in my hands so she has to look me directly in the eyes—"is Curtis sleeping with another woman or not?"

"Technically, not," Vivian says, looking down. "As far as I know!"

Natasha rolls her eyes. "So which is it? Because it's pretty obvious when you walk in on your man banging some slut."

"Is it another man?" I don't ask only because we live in San Francisco, but because I'm an open-minded person and I've always had my suspicions about Curtis—either that, or he's into heavy bondage. Natasha's eyebrows shoot up and she looks a lot more sympathetic.

"No!" Vivian looks horrified.

Ouch. I guess, a little late, it never entered her mind that her husband might be gay or, at least, bisexual. Thanks to me, it's now firmly rooted there. I'll pat myself on the back later.

"So who? If you don't mind me asking." She shouldn't, since she's the one who brought it up, after all.

"I listened to his messages." Vivian blushes like it's the first time she's done this. "On his cell phone."

"Uh-huh." This I did know about Vivian. Suspicious, manipulative and sneaky, but in a good way. These are skills she's honed on the job and techniques she's been happy to pass on to me.

"And . . ." Vivian's eyes are watering.

"And what?" Natasha asks with all the expectation I feel. This is going to be good.

"There was a message from a woman. Saying to meet him for lunch. And when I asked him he said it was *work* related." She wipes her nose with the back of her hand.

Curtis is the publisher of an edgy magazine and has to deal with unconventional models, literary types and people who are too cool for their own good. With her milk-and-honey beauty-pageant looks, above average but pedestrian intellect, Vivian is at a great disadvantage. At a party Curtis once complained to me that she wasn't esoteric. I drunkenly suggested he try wine, soft music and lube before he broached that kind of action again.

"Maybe it was. You know he works with all types of people." I am willing to give Curtis the benefit of the doubt. I'd put my money on him having an affair, all right, but with a guy, not a woman. Having an affair with a woman is boring, unless she happens to be a lesbian. "Did he go to the lunch?"

"Well, no. We had a huge fight and he sort of missed it because I sort of flattened all his tires," Vivian says between sobs. Natasha hands her a handkerchief.

"Vivian! You did not!" I knew Vivian had a temper; all redheads are a little off, if you ask me, but I never imagined she'd resort to something so physical and destructive. That's pretty impressive.

"I did and he hasn't spoken to me since," Vivian hiccups between sobs.

"Maybe that's why he hasn't called?" asks Natasha.

Vivian sobs louder.

"Thanks, Natasha. Vivian, listen to me." I'm about to impart some sage advice and I want to make sure she's listening. She looks sober but wobbly on her stilettos.

"What?" She dabs at her eyes, mascara everywhere.

"You've got to apologize to him."

"And buy him some new tires," adds Natasha.

"I don't want to!" she cries, and then blows her nose.

I send Natasha a sympathetic look. She likes Vivian, I can tell, but I doubt she'll want a snot-covered handkerchief back.

"Listen, is it really worth it? All this grief over a lunch date, a *work* lunch date he didn't even go to?" I am sort of enjoying me the grown-up. Usually it's Vivian who's organized within an inch of her life—this explains why she's finally snapped.

"I guess not." Vivian covers her face, resentment giving way to the realization that her husband is not talking to her and is alone in their ultramodern San Francisco loft where he can have another woman (or man) for breakfast, lunch and dinner.

"Trust me, it isn't. We'll call him when we get to your room. *After* you've had some coffee." I pat her back and she leans heavily into me.

"Thanks, Jacqs. Really. Natasha, thanks."

"No problem. That's what we are here for," I say, bracing myself under her weight. Natasha takes her other elbow as we carefully make our way to the bank of elevators.

"Yeah, I'll give him a call and everything will be great. Just . . ." With that, Vivian passes out.

I smile lamely at the small crowd of onlookers. Out of nowhere a bellhop appears with a wheelchair, and Natasha and the bellhop settle her boneless form into it. I try to push her knees together but have little success.

I can feel the crowd staring at us as I maneuver the wheelchair through the doors, holding my head up high and not making eye contact.

35

London

I wake up with the sun in my eyes. Natasha snores softly in the double bed next to me. I immediately check my cell phone to see if Mrs. Mayor has left me any messages. It's not even 7:30 but Mrs. Mayor likes to get an early start on making her presence known to the world at large.

Nothing. I don't know if I should feel relieved or prepare for the inevitable storm. Mrs. Mayor's "happy phase" usually lasts about three days to a week. And then it's either a period of frantic activity: 6 AM workouts, marathon spa treatments, visits to her therapist, mentor, and spiritual guide—or crushing inertia where she "works" from bed and I have to perch myself beside her, speak in soft, soothing tones and pretend I like Crystal Light because that's all she'll drink and fat-free Fig Newtons because that's all she'll eat.

I pick up the phone and dial the number she left for me. It's picked up precisely at one-and-a-half rings.

"Hello, London speaking."

"Pardon me?" I thought I was calling Carmel. I clear my throat. "Is this the Baxter residence?"

"Would this be Jacquelyn?" She doesn't seem to have an English accent, but she does sound uptight.

"Yes, as a matter of fact it is." My brain is too fuzzy to be as freaked out as I should be. "I'm looking—"

"Yes, I'm London, Gail's assistant. Mrs. Baxter. Or, rather, the original Mrs. Baxter. I'm helping out the mayor's wife while she's staying here."

"Hi . . . London. I was hoping to speak to Katherine." I nudge myself up onto my elbow, feeling a bit at a disadvantage wearing my ratty T-shirt and boxer shorts while London is probably wearing a wool suit and real pearls at this hour of the morning.

"Of course, you can leave a message with me and I'll make sure she gets it." Clipped, precise and disapproving—exactly what you want in a personal assistant.

"That's great, but I was hoping to speak to her directly." I yawn and don't bother to hide it.

"Is this a *personal* matter?" London perks up.

I guess she's hoping I'll ask her to pass on that the doctor said it was just a yeast infection and Mrs. Mayor shouldn't worry.

"*Yes,* it is, actually."

"You can have *complete* confidence in my discretion, Jacquelyn."

Oh, so now we're discretionary friends, are we?

"I'm *sure* I can."

Normally I would enjoy a good game of tease the staff, but I have to rouse both Vivian and Natasha so we can start our drive to Los Angeles. Last night Mr. Mayor took me aside and asked me to take Vivian along with me. He seems to think she could use a couple days away from San Francisco.

"I just wanted to check in with Katherine and see how's she's doing."

"Oh. Is that it?" She sounds disappointed that the drama wasn't a drama at all.

"Thanks for all your help, London. It was an experience." I hang up and collapse back into bed.

36

Emilio

After that, there is no hope of going back to sleep. I shower and dress quietly so as not to wake Natasha, my head full of all my shortcomings and faults.

I pick at my breakfast in the hotel restaurant and try and keep from letting my chin sink into my chest.

I can start anew. Dr. N was right, after all. I am capable of whatever she said it was I could do and change about me and my life. I think I might need to double up on my appointments again. I don't know how Dr. N is going to take it. I hope she doesn't get mad that all the progress she'd thought I made went right down the toilet with my ego in one night. Maybe she'll see this as a breakthrough of sorts?

I scheduled an appointment for the day after I get back from visiting my family, which serves two purposes: I have a solid excuse as to why I have to leave, and I'll need to decompress after visiting my family.

I make myself sit up straight. I will allow myself to wallow in misery up until I get to Los Angeles and then after that I will make myself snap out of it. If my family gets a hint that I'm not ecstatically happy with my life, I'll spend my whole visit warding off their questions and suggestions about how my life went all wrong, starting with my choice of junior-high boyfriends.

"*Señorita* Sanchez." Emilio slides into the seat opposite mine and signals to the waiter.

"You again." I'm not in the mood. He laughs. I guess he likes it rough. "What are you doing here? Meeting another friend?"

"I heard this place makes the best waffles in Santa Barbara," he says as he plucks a strawberry off my plate. "I just had to come try them. The Hilton has good room service, but I'm a sucker for waffles."

"Waffles at the Four Seasons. Cortez, what would your readers say?"

"What they don't know won't hurt them."

"How very, very political of you, Emilio, you sound like you're running for office," I say, but I begin to relax. It feels good not to have to put on an act for anyone. Even though we don't know each other very well, I don't see the point of keeping up my façade. He can see right through me.

"You called me Emilio. I was beginning to think you didn't like me."

"Whatever would give you that idea," I say sweetly but laced with what I hope is enough sarcasm to let him know I'm no pushover. "Sometimes I even read your column because it's informative."

"That's good to know. You are a *mujer* full of surprises." He leans back and rubs his eyes. He looks tired.

"Long night?" I try to defrost. It's not his fault I'm in a crappy mood.

"Too many meetings. Too many people. You'll be happy to hear that most of the party looks favorably on your little boss. They all say she is very well versed on the issues of the day."

"I should hope so. I work hard enough at it," I say and immediately feel guilty. All the prep work that goes into turning Katherine Bishop into Mrs. Kit Baxter, wife of the mayor of San Francisco, is none of Emilio Cortez's business.

"You're wasting your talents, Jacquelyn." He states this simply and smiles up at the waiter as a plateful of delicious-looking waffles is placed in front of him. "Don't tell my mother you saw me eating this. She still thinks her *machaca* is my favorite food in the world."

"Trust me. I'm good at keeping those kinds of secrets."

37

Vivian

The halls are wide and quiet with a few maids' carts dotted here and there. I can't help but peek into the open doors of rooms, comparing layouts, furniture quality, and what its occupants have left strewn all over the floor for the nameless maids to pick up.

I get to Vivian's door. The DO NOT DISTURB sign is still on the knob, right where I left it the night before.

"Vivian, it's me. Jacqs." I knock softly and press my ear to the thick door.

"Jacqs?" Vivian croaks. "Save me."

After a few minutes, Vivian drags herself to the door and opens it. She looks like crap and doesn't smell much better. She sinks back into bed, wrapped in a bedsheet.

"Have you had any water, lots of water?" I go over and pour her a glass. She takes it in shaky hands. "What did you drink last night?"

"I don't remember. Why aren't you hungover?" She takes small sips, pausing to see if any of it will come back up.

"I was afraid that Scooter would ask me about the history of chimichangas and I'd be too drunk to give him a satisfying answer."

"Don't make me laugh." Vivian holds her head and peeks at me with one eye. She moans as the sound ricochets off the walls and back to her head. "Did I get here last night with my wallet and wearing my own underwear?"

"What are friends for?" I ask and hold up her bag and point to her crumpled pair of underpants.

"To keep you from getting shit-faced and calling your husband at 3 AM and accusing him of screwing other women *and* men?"

"No! You didn't." This is not something I'd put past a drunk or sober Vivian, but I feel I need to act shocked for her benefit. No one likes their friends to assume they are capable of truly embarrassing behavior.

"I think I did." Vivian hangs her head and shuffles toward the bathroom wearing only her earrings from last night.

"Lucky for you I had the front desk put a lock on your phone. You must have given an earful to some poor guy at the front desk."

"You're the best, Jacqs. Really." Vivian stops and gives me a hug.

Peaking out from underneath her bed is a torn condom wrapper.

"I know I am." I pat her naked back.

38

Natasha

I turn in our room keys while Vivian takes care of some last-minute Mr. Mayor details. Natasha lurks in the corner wearing huge dark sunglasses, a black scarf (hiding her platinum-blonde hair) and a leopard-print trench coat. It still doesn't distract from how sad she looks.

She hasn't been able to reach Jesus for the last few days and fears the worst. So do I, but I want so much for this thing between them to work out that I've been psychotically positive about the whole thing. I'm sure I'm wearing thin on Natasha's nerves, but she knows I mean well.

"Is this your secret-agent look?" I hope to lighten the mood.

"I'm hiding out from Jesus." She looks around as if he could actually materialize in front of us at the sound of his name.

"You can't hide from Jesus." Another lame attempt. She frowns at me. "Are you sure you don't want to come down to LA with me and Vivian? We're staying at the Beverly Wilshire, courtesy of our favorite soap star. It'll be fun. Just us gals, no work and all play . . . until I have to ditch you guys to go to my parents."

I know I'm wasting my breath, but I feel bad abandoning Natasha. She shouldn't have to face this alone. Plus, Vivian already has made it clear I'm on my own with Myles, and I could use the company. His assistant has already called and confirmed early dinner and some vague party I'll be attending with him.

I've yet to speak to the man personally, but his assistant sounds lovely.

"Honey, I'm about as likely to have a good time as I am to vote Republican in the next election," Natasha sighs. "Just drop my butt at the airport."

"Airport? I thought you were taking the train back up to San Francisco—to have time to, um, think?" This is what she tearfully told me last night, at least.

"I love him so much!" She begins to cry. Now I see why she's wearing the glasses. I scoot into her bulk and drape my arms around her.

"What do you want to do?"

"Nothing. I had the locks changed before I left. It's over."

"Dang. Just like that?" I expected this to be drawn out a couple more months, if not until the end of the year.

"He cheated on me! He lies to me. He steals from me!" She pauses to take a breath to continue.

"I get the picture," I say before she can get started again.

"I'm going on a long vacation, to visit some friends in New York. I'm leaving tonight."

"Tonight?" What about Mrs. Mayor?

"Here is my key." She hands me her key chain, a pair of tiny, fuzzy pink dice. "Will you water my plants until I get back?"

"If you could just wait a few days, I can leave my parents' house early . . ."

"Don't use me as an excuse to avoid your family. I'll be fine, honey. I have your number and my little pills." She begins to weep again. "I love you, Jacqs."

"I love you, Natasha." We stand there holding each other, ignoring everyone. I smile lamely up at her, realizing how truly useless I am. "I'm so sorry."

"Me, too, honey. *C'est la vie* or whatever it is you Latins say."

"That's exactly what we say. Or, as Doris Day used to sing, 'Kay Sir Ah, Sir Ah . . .' "

It wasn't until I saw the song title scroll up on one of those commercials for record compilations that I realized all these years poor Doris had been singing in Spanish.

Natasha drops her head onto my shoulder. "Don't make fun of me; I'm in a sensitive state."

"I know you are, honey." I pat her back and feel my eyes well up with tears and once again find myself taking Jesus's name in vain.

39

Myles

"I'm working on a project right now that you should be interested in."

Myles and I (or is it me and Myles?) are sitting at a patio table at The Ivy. Yeah, that Ivy. Two tables away I can see the back of Teri Hatcher's head. I'm almost certain I took a pee in the stall next to Brittany Murphy a few minutes ago.

"It's Hispanic," he adds for clarification.

"I'm an expert on all things *Hispanic.*" I've quickly realized I have to hit Myles over the head with sarcasm to get him to register anything I say.

"Asians had their day with the martial arts stuff, but now the forecast is all about Hispanics. Hispanics are hot right now." Myles is tanned, faux tanned, his intense blue eyes never stop moving. "Looks like Keanu is in the house. Keanu, dude! Call me."

I shrug, but my heart revs up. Bina is going to die when I tell her. I've lost count as to how many times he's interrupted himself or me to point out someone or another.

"Yeah, anyway, Hispanics are hot. All of them."

Myles fiddles with his phone. I made the mistake of asking him about it and for the entire car ride over he bitched about how awful it was, but it was the "cool" phone to have.

"I'm so relieved." I can't help but feel this is part of the reason he's taken me under his wing and has volunteered to be my guide to West LA. Not that I'd ever tell him, but it *is* a hell of a lot different from Northeast LA.

"It's about this guy who travels to the Amazon. He's a doctor, trying to get away from his past in the big city. He's on a quest, or some shit like that, and he winds up living with a tribe. He helps them fight off the ranchers who want to burn down the tribes' land for grazing land. Colin Farrell is hot for it, but I'm thinking we'll go American. Christian Bale is hot right now."

"He's English. And Colin Farrell is Irish."

"Close enough. These people live like it's the turn of the century."

"Really." I'm not sure if he's talking about tribes in the Amazon or Colin Farrell/Christian Bale. "Which century?"

"Anyway, this project, it's really opened my eyes to how the rest of the world lives," Myles says and looks like he enjoys saying at every opportunity. I can imagine it's got him laid a bunch of times. Myles shuffles his cell phone and PDA as if they were playing cards. "The way they live is unreal."

"I bet." Unreal to a man who just moved into a 5,000 square foot home in the Hollywood Hills because he wants to "scale down."

"These places haven't been touched, ruined, really, by technology. No roads, nothing. Just the fucking jungle as far as you can see. People live in, like, these shacks and shit. You have to get your water from rivers and fight off mosquitoes the size of pigeons. You wouldn't believe it if I told you. It's like a whole other world out there."

"Good thing I can look forward to the movie."

"Exactly." Myles straightens up and looks attentive. "Maybe we'll make the première a benefit or some shit like that. To raise awareness that places like these need to be preserved."

"I'm sure the folks there in the Amazon would really appreciate it." Who needs things like roads and clean water when a Hollywood genius appreciates the harsh beauty of the Amazon? Instead of saying this I take a sip of my jasmine-infused ice tea.

"Maybe I should approach Russell . . . you know, Russell Crowe. He could use some good publicity." Myles furiously pecks out a memo on his Blackberry.

"He's Australian, but same difference. So are you going to show these lucky folks your movie once it's done?" I've picked up Myles's habit of scanning the crowd. And I'm not disappointed as Teri Hatcher catches my eye. I smile and look quickly away.

"Which folks?" Myles doesn't look up.

"The people who Russell or Christian or Colin are going to save from extinction?" Tonight I'll dream of the Amazon, complete with Myles in a loincloth aiming a poisoned dart at my heart.

"They don't do English. And even if we subtitled it, they couldn't read it." He puts down his Blackberry and then picks up his cell phone. He has to keep at least one electronic thing in his hand to feel grounded.

"Plus, even if they could *do English*, they wouldn't have electricity to see it." I sit back and wait for Myles not to be shocked.

"Exactly." Myles lights up a cigarette. A woman at the table next to us throws him a dirty look. "They're herbal, lady. Someone should really do something about that. Everyone should have access to a decent movie theater."

"I'll get right on it." I snort.

"We can't shoot it in the real Amazon, too fucking expensive. We're thinking Mexico." Myles does another crowd scan.

"Same difference." I push my plate away from me and wait for Myles's inevitable answer.

"Exactly!"

A few hours later, after cooling my heels in Myles's sleek office penthouse and gazing at his impressive collection of modern art and accepting endless cups of tea from one of his three assistants, we arrive at the party. Myles fastens a yellow hospital-type band around my left wrist, but instead of my name and insurance info it has a series of black stars on it. He doesn't bother to take one from the hostess for himself. Then he puts a hand on the small of my back to steer me through the crowd of people. I find myself feeling insecure about how I look just because everyone seems to be checking me out and I can't help checking myself out to see where I stand. It's a vicious cycle. I miss San Francisco.

"Do I look OK?" I cringe as I hear myself asking Myles for his approval.

"You look fucking hot." In Myles-speak that's very good.

"Thanks." Sincerely. This is like the first day of seventh grade in so many ways. Everyone is wearing the right jeans, the right shoes and has their hair tousled just so. No wonder Vivian refused to come. "So, what's the deal with this party?"

"I'll introduce you to people, you don't say any more than you have to and along the way I'll set you up with some crazy free shit." Myles waves and nods at people but doesn't stop to talk to them.

"You're kidding, right?"

"Just follow my lead . . . Roth, hey Roth! Mike Roth is head of development at Sony, make nice." For once he doesn't ignore the shocked looked on my face. "Please."

"Myles, you fuck. Why aren't you returning my calls?"

Mike Roth, heavyset guy in a designer suit and ponytail, so wrong on so many levels. Even though this place is air-conditioned to the point of being frosty, he has a fine sheen of sweat on his forehead and upper lip and a case of Orbit gum under his arm.

"I was going to ask you the same thing. This is Jacquelyn Sanchez." Myles proudly presents me.

"Hi, nice to meet you." I look over to Myles to make sure I haven't said more than I should.

"You an actress?" Mike checks me out, not unlike the women around here do. I guess it's a bad habit that crosses the gender line. Maybe it's not considered rude to stare? What do I know? "Myles has a thing for actresses."

"No." I've faked my fair share of orgasms but I don't think that counts as acting. "I'm definitely not an actress."

"Too bad. Latinas are hot right now." Mike Roth may be a

condescending jerk, but at least he has enough sense to use the preferred terminology.

"Thank you." Myles and I answer at the same time.

Once again I feel Myles's firm hand on my back steering me toward another Hollywood type as he calls over his shoulder, "Roth, we'll do breakfast next week, talk about getting a package together."

An hour later my yellow wristband (and Myles) has scored me two iPods, a Nokia cell phone I don't need or want, two Armani clutches, a $200 gift certificate for La Prairie skin care products, enough gum to keep Mrs. Mayor chewing for the rest of the decade and the promise of a free dress at some Montana Ave. boutique, along with other assorted goodies Myles had some waiter schlep out to his Mercedes. All the while he's kept up the chatter so I know who's in, who's on the way out, who's phony, a drunk, gay or all three, and who'll slit my throat in a second if they think it could get them a meeting with him. After he imparts these nuggets he greets them like old friends, insults them and we move on to the next person.

I'm starting to like Myles and I know it's a bad, bad thing. This place is filled up with so much empty, I'm starting to feel faint and grossed out. People can't actually live this way, can they? This is not the Los Angeles I grew up in, even though we're less than twenty miles from where my parents still live.

"I need to sit down, Myles. My head is spinning."

"Let's grab a table. I need to text my assistant." Myles waves off yet another person hoping for a second of his time to pitch something or someone.

"It's pretty late. Won't she be asleep?" I ask as he pulls out a pink Lucite chair for me to sit on. I hate when Mrs. Mayor calls me late at night or early in the morning just to remind me of something that could have clearly waited.

"She's right over there at the bar." Myles jerks his head in that direction but doesn't look up, even though his assistant (wearing a tiny pleated skirt and tube top) waves at us. I smile and wave back.

"Of course." I notice he hasn't bothered to score her a yellow band. She has a blue one, which most of the people here do. "Listen, about all this stuff . . . I really can't accept any of it."

"If you don't take it someone else will." Myles shrugs philosophically. "So why shouldn't you have it?"

"There are a million reasons." I struggle to think of one that will mean something to Myles.

"Don't give yourself a headache. This is the way things are done around here, Jacquelyn. Katie furnished her condo for free by letting *InTouch* magazine do a spread." He tucks away his Blackberry and takes a swig of his low-sodium seltzer water.

"Really?" Mrs. Mayor always goes on and on about how she's had to work for every single thing she's ever gotten in her life. "So it's not, um, wrong to take four pairs of shoes just because the person behind the table offers them to me?"

"Steve Madden is lucky to have a chance for his shoes to be on your feet." Myles pats my arm kindly. I think he actually means it.

"I guess . . . What about the free dress from that boutique? There is no way that's OK." I don't need a dress, even a free one from some ultrachic boutique I've read about in Mrs. Mayor's *Vogue*, *Harper's Bazaar* and *Elle* magazines. Before I started working for her I was more of a *Marie Claire* type of gal, where I got my fashion tips and my outrage over women's lives in developing countries in the same issue.

"So they think you're going to wear it to a première." Myles hails a waiter by waving his empty glass in the air. "Let them think what they want and you get the dress. Everyone is happy."

"They only think I'm going to wear it to a première because you told them I would be!" That has to be a sin, to let people think they're going to get free publicity at a big Hollywood event when there is no hope because Myles hasn't invited me to any première.

"Don't sweat it. They'll never know. They think you're the next Eva Longoria, who was the next Jennifer Lopez. But Jessica Alba and Eva Mendes are the next Eva Longoria, you heard it here first." Myles looks tired for the first time tonight. "Hispanics are hot right now. Live it up, baby, next month it might be Albanians."

"I can't compete with Albanians."

"I'm going to call it a night. I have a 4 AM call into Australia tomorrow to suck Russell's cock over a satellite to get him to read this script." Myles must be able to sense impending neediness.

"OK." There is a catch in my voice.

"Listen, just go down there, get a dress and go out for a nice dinner." Myles looks at me intensely, not leaving any room for anything but honesty.

"Why are you being this way to me? You don't even know me. I just work for Katherine. She's my boss." I want to add that I'm no one special, but I know it would just piss Myles off. I would be insulting his judgment on who is and isn't worthy of his time.

"I like you, Jacquelyn. I don't want to fuck you. I don't want to make you a star. And I know you don't want anything from me either. In this town, that's a rare quality." Myles summarizes our six-hour friendship with a casual flick of his French cuffs. "Look me up when you're in LA next time. We'll do it again."

"Promise?"

40

Nate

It's been a long time since I've had sex with another person and Nate looks as likely a candidate as anyone. I have absolutely no qualms with the idea, and eventual reality, of having sex with my ex-husband, whom I have spent the last year in therapy getting over. Technically my marriage and divorce were the catalysts that drove me to therapy. Nate was incidental yet essential.

The next morning, while Vivian enjoys a half day spa retreat I scored last night, I unfold the list of spots I want to check out in my miniquest to find my ex-husband while making it seem like it is pure chance that has thrown us together once more. From his blog I know he gets his caffeine at the Olympic and Bundy Coffee Bean and Tea Leaf.

Nate cannot function in the morning without his jumbo mug of coffee. And even though I don't drink it, somehow it became my responsibility to keep the supply of Pete's Viennese blend ground for a gold filter in ready supply. I figure in my absence he's grown too lazy to stock his own coffee and he should stop by between 8:30 and 9:45. No later because he never liked sleeping in, even on a Sunday, something that I considered my right as a tax-paying American citizen.

With my pot of green tea, I'm about to start highlighting stories I've downloaded from *The New York Times, The Los Angeles Times, The Washington Post, The Wall Street Journal*, etc., when Nate walks in. I grip my chubby fluorescent highlighter in my hand and almost cough up a mouthful of lukewarm green tea.

Suddenly, the desperation and idiocy of what I'm doing hits me. My heart pounds as I debate making a dash for the door, sliding under my table or holding an *Atlantic Monthly* up to my face and peering around it so I can watch him.

I do nothing and just sit there and stare. Totally out in the open, just begging to be caught.

"Hey," I want to whisper to the woman sitting at the table closest to mine, "that's my ex-husband. We've seen each other naked. (It bends slightly to the left, by the way.) I got to keep our two-bedroom flat in San Francisco and he took possession of my mucho-expensive engagement-slash-wedding ring. (An almost-2-carat diamond with a platinum band from Tiffany's.) I'm here spying on him to make sure he's getting coffee *alone.*"

And if I whisper this to her, I know she'll nod, provide some cover and even offer up some info on him if she knows anything. It's a universal need to know what happens to the person whom you once loved with all your heart but let go for your own good, only to wonder what he's having for breakfast every morning.

As I expected he orders the largest size of coffee they have, and then leans groggily against the counter, staring off into space. From my profile view of him, I can see that his six-months'-pregnant man belly is gone. He's not overly muscled but not scrawny either. His hair is short, too short, I always preferred longer.

He's wearing a shirt I forced him to buy in the early days of our marriage. It looks like it's gone through too many washings. Should I take this as a sign that he's clinging to this shirt because of its connection to me? Or should I just assume that, like any guy, Nate wakes up, sees shirt, smells shirt, puts on shirt, comes home, takes off shirt, gathers up all shirts and drops off at laundry service?

Nate shifts and catches sight of me. I freeze. He squints. I shrink into my seat. Recognition floods his face. So now the moment of truth has arrived and I'm so ill-prepared for the real thing, even though I've acted it out in my mind countless times.

I'm caught, but no way am I going to let him get the upper hand so quickly. I straighten up, lean forward and try to make my face look attractively befuddled and my voice unsure but welcoming. "Nate? Is that you?"

"Jacqs? Jacqs! Jesus Christ! What are you doing here?" He looks surprised, happy and really confused. I get up and rush over to him and give him a friendly hug. He squeezes me tight and then holds me at arm's length. "It is you! This is unbelievable. What are you doing here, Jacqs? Are you here with your parents?"

Here come the questions. Here come the lies.

"I'm in town for work and got the day off and decided to come see a friend of mine for coffee." A friend of mine should tell him it's not a mutual friend so there is no way he can check out my story.

"Wow. She show up yet?" Nate runs his hands up and down my arms. I knew I should have gotten an arm wax, but it's been so chilly in San Francisco that I haven't needed to bare my arms. I'm the only woman in my family whose forearms are (usually) hair-free and though they comment on how nice my arms look, no one has been bold enough to ask me how I've suddenly become selectively bald. Just another thing for them to whisper about when I'm not there.

"He." So like Nate to assume I'm meeting a female friend.

"Oh, he show up yet?" The slight hiccup in Nate's voice tells me he's registered the fact (or the fiction) that my friend is a man and this bothers him for reasons he'll never understand without tons of therapy.

"As a matter of fact, he just called and canceled on me. A raging case of strep throat." I know how Nate feels about strep throat. He doesn't fear anything more than strep throat except sharks. I once teased him that with his luck he'd run into a shark with strep. He didn't think it was funny.

"That sucks." He guides me back to my table and takes a seat across from me. "God, it's great to see you. How are your parents? How is Noel?"

"Fine, fine, everyone is fine." They have no idea I'm this close to them because I haven't told them. "This is so weird. Small world, huh?" Thanks to the Internet!

"Reading much?" He gestures to my stack of magazines and newspaper printouts.

"Oh, you know me. How about you? What are you doing lately?" Like I don't already know.

"Working and working. The usual. Man, this is so surreal." Nate is satisfactorily knocked off balance, giving me the advantage.

"What? Are you going to tell me you were just thinking of me the other day and now here I am?" I ask coyly.

"No, no," he says offhandedly, not realizing the impact of his words. I try not to let my face look as crushed as I feel inside.

"That's good. Well . . ." I look at my watch. I can't let him think that I find him appealing enough to spend any more time catching up with him. "I've got a busy day today."

"Maybe we can get together before you go back to San Francisco and catch up?" Nate offers.

"Well, maybe . . ." I'm sweating from the effort to let him believe this is his own original, spur-of-the-moment idea.

"Come on, it'll be fun! Just like old times."

I don't want to seem too eager, after all, eagerness is what got me into our relationship in the first place. "I'm really booked. What about lunch on Monday?"

"Fuck! I'm leaving for Chicago tomorrow night." Nate runs his hand through his hair.

Crap! My plan has backfired. By seeming to be too busy I might have talked myself out of a lunch date and a trip to check out his apartment. Only to look for more clues into his life post-me, of course.

"Well, wait, um, I was supposed to have dinner with my friend, but since he's really, really sick . . ." Get the hint, Nate. Don't make me ask.

"That sucks." Nate is the kind of man whom you have to spell things out for. Nuances of human behavior throw him for a loop.

This is why he is so great with computers. You push a series of keys and get a predetermined response. With some time and effort I could coax the correct response out of him, but why bother? I'm here, he's here (alone) and he's leaving town tomorrow.

"Nate, would you like to get some dinner with me tonight?" I feel that familiar annoyance creep into my voice. Nate doesn't pick up on it. Some things never change.

41

Vivian

After a few pots of tea for me—and some double-strength Tylenol for Vivian and some more bitching and moaning about Curtis, marriage and life—Vivian feels up for some shopping. As we head out in a cab she starts to get excited for me and insists we look for the perfect dress for my "date."

"There is nothing more satisfying than looking drop-dead gorgeous for your ex-husband," Vivian says as we crawl through traffic in the back of a taxi.

"I looked pretty good this morning," I say defensively.

"That doesn't count," Vivian says with a dismissive wave of her hand.

"It doesn't? Why not?" I put a lot of effort into that look. More than I'd ever admit to.

"Because no matter how much you try, having coffee in the morning is a sporty, casual affair. Even in LA." Vivian, like Mrs. Mayor, does only high-drama casual. "Men say they like natural sporty girls, but they're lying."

"True." After a year of waiting for this sexual showdown, I should go all-out. "I guess I'll go for the jugular."

"Or the zipper," Vivian adds sagely.

"What's the difference?" We laugh in an evil, throaty way that causes the driver to turn around and give us a worried look.

"Anyways, who knows what could happen? You guys might

get back together!" Vivian gushes with more enthusiasm than she's been able to dredge up in a while.

I give Vivian a doubtful look, then I remember the vicarious pleasure I've taken in another person's blooming romance when my chances were in the toilet. And what could be more romantic than a tightly engineered encounter between a woman and her ex-husband who currently reside in different cities? But since I'm trying to be neutral I think it's best if I inject a little reality into our excursion.

"Are you going to call Curtis?" I ask cautiously. I don't want her to jump down my throat.

"No. Maybe. Yes. I am not sure. What would you do?" Vivian bites her slightly chapped lip.

"I'd call him or not. It depends what *you* want. He might not have even noticed you haven't called. You know how guys are." I reach into her bag and hand her a tube of lip balm.

"I hate that about men. Just, ugh, makes me so mad!"

"Yeah, that's why I got divorced. And that's why I'm going shopping for a new dress I don't need that I'll wear at dinner with my ex. It's a vicious cycle."

The driver leaves us off in front of Maxine on Montana. Suddenly I feel unsure of myself and my motives. Plus, I haven't exactly explained to Vivian why we're at this specific store.

"I don't know, Vivian. I was just going to browse, not exactly buy." That's sort of the truth. Well, isn't it?

"Oh, come on! Live a little. You deserve it—a night out in a gorgeous dress to cock tease your ex-husband is the least you deserve."

"I guess so." The taxi is only a few feet away . . .

This could all end tomorrow if Mrs. Mayor decides to give me the (Manolo) boot. The free clothes and accessories, the travel, the discounts on haircuts and bikini waxes—poof! I'd be back to working for some dead-end company and having only an entrée and splitting dessert with friends. Plus, I'd have no choice but to get a real life again and that costs money, too.

Vivian links her arm through mine and we stride in. "So what kind of look are you going for? Ice queen? Sophisticated? Unavailable but approachable?"

"How about 'Out of your league, but willing to consider it'?" I want to look great but I don't want to look so good that I'll totally intimidate him out of trying to have ex-sex with me.

"Sounds good to me."

"But nothing black. He'll expect me to wear black and I want him to know that I'm a much more confident and daring person since we got divorced." My hands are sweaty and my heart is palpitating as I catch the eye of the woman who offered the dress last night. She waves and indicates that she'll be off the phone in a minute.

"Relax, Jacqs. Who cares if it costs hundreds of dollars? It's just money." Vivian sniffs as she goes through the racks of silky dresses in a riot of jewel tones.

"Yeah, just money." And my soul, which I've practically sold. "OK. I'll do it and I won't regret it. Right?"

"Darling, we all deserve something special. At least once in our lives," Vivian says, doing a perfect imitation of Natasha.

I try not to look at the prices as we go through the carefully tended racks. I feel a rush of euphoria when I glance at myself in a mirror holding a dazzling dress in front of myself. I have that rosy look Mrs. Mayor gets when she goes shopping. So this is what it feels like to put oneself above all others, starving illiterate children included. Damn, it feels good.

"Jacquelyn! You look beautiful, I love those jeans. Juicy?" Andie is just as hopped up as she was last night. In fact I think she's wearing last night's mascara. It looks rock 'n' roll chic.

"This is my friend Vivian," I say as I extract myself from Andie's anorexic bear hug.

"I love your hair. Natural?" She embraces Vivian and presses her cheek to hers, both sides.

"Natural," Vivian says, looking totally off balance. This much affection from a stranger has to be a little shocking from someone who, despite five years on the West Coast, is still solidly Midwestern.

"Love, love, love it. I was thinking of going red." Andie fingers Vivian's hair. Vivian cowers next to me. "OK! Jacquelyn. Myles just called and he told me you were being shy! You're so cute!"

"I, uh . . ." I look over at Vivian, who is looking at me intensely, and smile feebly at her.

"Jacquelyn is having dinner with her ex tonight so we have to make sure he regrets every shitty thing he ever did to her while they were together." Vivian chooses to take the 'what-I-don't-know-won't-lower-my opinion-of-you' route. Bless her.

"I love, love, love it! You came to the right place. *InStyle* just rated us the sexist dress shop on the West Coast. Let's get this party started!"

"Let's," Vivian and I say at the same time. Andie doesn't notice we are making fun of her.

I retreat to a dressing room, gently holding two skirts and two dresses. I figure I can pair either of the skirts with my cashmere mock turtle I have back at the hotel. It is black but the skirts are otherworldly shades: one a soft, shiny steel lilac, the other a gunmetal blue. I slip on the blue skirt first and step out to show Vivian.

"What do you think?" The material feels better than sex against my skin. I'm on the verge of happy tears just wearing it in the dressing room.

"Oh, nice. Very nice, but I thought you really wanted to knock his socks off!" Vivian says as she struggles to pull a complicated halter top over her head.

"True . . ."

"Honey, go all out." She points with her free elbow. "Try one of those dresses on."

I pull the curtain shut and shed my top and carefully hang up the skirt. I slip on a champagne-colored dress with skinny straps. I could die in this dress. I stand there for a moment feeling weak and I haven't even seen the price yet. I step outside and wait to be admired.

"Holy crap, Jacquelyn. That dress looks . . ."

"I love it!" Andie gushes. "Love it!"

"Thanks." I run my hand down and smooth the hips. It skims my body wonderfully, like water. When I move the hem floats around my knees, tickling me.

"How much is it?" I ask but I really don't want to know.

"You're so funny! Myles was right!" Andie laughs loudly. Vivian joins in for a second. I almost pass out when I check out the price tag: $987.

"Try the other one on before you pass out. Remember, no regret," Vivian, my enabler, says.

I sleepwalk back into the dressing room and shake my head to wake myself up. I slip the other dress off the padded hanger. From the instant I saw it I knew it was the dress I was always meant to have. That's why I saved it for last.

It's a luminescent, whipped-cream silk with slightly thicker straps, a simple V-neckline and delicate darts down the sides to give it some shape before it falls into petals of material that sensuously undulate below my knees.

I could get married in this dress. I should have gotten married in this dress! Instead I wore my best Bebe interview skirt and Banana Republic sweater set. But then again, all those (couple of) years ago, I could never have imagined even considering trying on such a dress, let alone buying it just because I wanted it.

Back then, my life would have dictated my most expensive and special dress to be the dress I got married in, once. Not a dress that is so beautiful and perfect that it is wasted on not only me but on my ex-husband, who will probably comment that I'm wearing a nightgown to dinner. This is a dress that shows just how far I've really come yet how closely I'm still living in my past. I'm living in a fantasyland, but now fully prepared to pretend that I'm going to put it on my American Express card.

"I think this is it," I say as I step out. Vivian and Andie gasp. "Yup, I think it is."

42

Papá

Dress, coiffed and painted. Now I have twenty excruciating minutes to kill before I meet Nate in the lobby. I've retreated to the bathroom to give Vivian some privacy as she makes another attempt to reach Curtis in San Francisco.

A voice in the back of my head keeps telling me to take off my dress just in case I get a spontaneous nosebleed or something. But I won't let it own me.

This is my dress, and if I want to loll around on my hotel bed and carelessly freshen up my lipstick, I'll do it. Maybe I'll have a *huge* glass of red wine. I don't care what my mother would say.

So I call her. I use my cell phone because technically she thinks I'm still either in Carmel or Santa Barbara and not in an exclusive hotel on Sunset Blvd. The only reason I can get away with this lie is my parents (my whole family, really) rarely venture to the other side of Dodger Stadium.

The phone rings and rings. Usually I give it ten rings before I give up. On the seventh it's picked up and my father grunts into my ear.

"*Hola.*" He sounds annoyed, but, then again, I've never heard him sound any other way.

"Hi! *Papá*, it's Jacquelyn!" My voice comes out squeaky from the sheer surprise of him actually answering the phone for once.

"Your *madre* isn't here." He's a charmer, really he is.

"Oh. OK . . . How are you doing?" I try my usual method, wondering if it will unleash a torrent of conversation the way it does with my mother.

"Noel drove her to the supermarket."

"Oh. Wow." Silence. I can hear some sort of sports match in the background. "Oh. OK . . . I'm still in Santa Barbara."

"Yeah." Not a question, just a declaration. I could have said I was on the moon and I bet I would have gotten the same response.

"OK. Tell her I called. Bye, *Papá!*" No use dragging this out.

"OK." Click. Now I see where Yolie gets her phone etiquette from.

43

Vivian

Moving on.

I sit at the very edge of the tub and try to center myself. Not going to happen. I press my ear to the door to see if I can hear Vivian. Nothing.

"You want me to come out and show off?" I call out. I think I look great, but a second opinion can't hurt.

"Please! I'm going stir-crazy here. I'm waiting for room service."

Room service! I love room service. I love everything about hotels, actually. A vacation is not a vacation unless you are booked in a hotel. Nate and I once spent a horrible week in a friend's cabin in Tahoe. We had to do all our own cleaning and cooking. I was so miserable. It wasn't a vacation, it was an ordeal. Nate didn't even notice how unhappy I was.

He was too preoccupied with keeping the woodpile stocked. Every fifteen minutes he'd ask me if I was cold, and whether I was or was not, he'd head outside with the stupid ax. I'm sure if I had said I had a hankering for venison he would have taken the antique shotgun down from over the fireplace and tried to hunt down Bambi's mother himself.

I sweep open the door, almost hitting Vivian as she stands there holding a covered dish and shooing away the waiter.

"Holy crap. Your ex doesn't stand a chance!"

"I almost feel sorry for the poor bastard. Speaking of which, you call your husband?"

"Yes! I left a message on his cell and nothing! That's why I've ordered half the room-service menu. If I get fat, it's all his fault." She sits on the bed and tries to balance a huge plate of steaming pasta on her left and a slab of chocolate cake on her right.

"Yeah, but room service here is great." I gingerly lift the lids that cover the surface of the cart.

"True. Are you sure you don't want to stay here with me and enjoy this spread and some soft core, pay-per-view porn?"

"As tempting as it sounds, no. This might be my only chance to have sex this year and I can't pass it up." Though I haven't ruled out sex with George, I'm sure his wife has.

"I hear that, sister." Vivian raises a chocolatey fork at me.

"I should go downstairs so I can strategically arrange myself in the lobby." I look at my watch and sigh. I look at the room-service cart and sigh again.

"Hap ah umg pim, Japs."

"I will." Like all sexually frustrated women, I speak chocolate.

44

Nate

"So where are you flying off to tomorrow?" One way to get Nate to open up is to ask him about work. Another way is to mention *Star Trek*, or "Star Track," as I insisted on calling it throughout our relationship.

"Chicago, then India," he mutters, looking distracted as the waiter clears away our salads.

"India! Wow. That's exciting. Bina, you remember my friend Bina?" How could he not? We were inseparable, but Nate never really registered Bina. He seemed intimidated by her drive and success. "She's going to India."

"Oh, yeah? How's she doing?"

"Great. Getting married. She's having a ceremony in India. I'm invited, of course. Maybe I'll see you there," I say as I climb into the car. Nate hands the valet a tip.

"Maybe. India is a big country."

"Is it?" I ask sarcastically. Nate always complained I had no sense of direction.

"Yeah. Really big." Nate climbs in next to me and we zoom off.

"I'll keep that in mind. Where else have you been?" As if I don't already know.

"Australia, Czech Republic, Greece and, now, India."

"All that traveling must be hell on your complexion."

"Huh?" Nate looks confused.

He never gave a second thought to his pores and thought slapping on some sunscreen was the ultimate in skin care. No point in veering the conversation into a dead end this early on in the evening.

"Wow." I'll give Nate a pass for now. And empty flattery about his world travels is sure to boost his ego. It's not like he flew the plane himself, but I don't need to point that out. I want to make nice so we can make nasty later. "All that traveling must be so exciting."

"It's OK. Kind of lonely." He gives me a sheepish smile.

"I can imagine." Oh, yes I can!

"Yeah, you just run into the same people working on the same projects. It's tough to have a real relationship, much less a life. When I first came back, after we . . . you know . . . I dated a dancer."

Nate has always had a hard spot for dancers. Ballerinas especially.

"Pole dancer?" I ask in what I hope is a jokey voice.

"No!" From his tone, I can tell she did some pole dancing. His pole probably.

"Uh-huh."

"She was way too LA for me."

"What does that mean?" I'm from LA. OK, not this LA but Los Angeles all the same.

"She just wasn't what I expected. Not at all like you." He smiles at me again. I smile and look out the window, feeling pretty fucking hot.

Back and forth we go and things are humming along nicely right up until we dig into our entrées.

"What do you think of the food? Every time I eat here, I think of you," Nate says earnestly as we sit at a fancy Latin American fusion restaurant, *Teatro de Antojos*. The food has Spanish names (names I know), but what comes out of the kitchen is not like anything I've ever seen.

"It's, um, good. It's not really traditional Mexican food or even any kind of Latin American food, you do know that, right?" I don't think many people south of the border sit down to $12 starter salads on a regular basis.

"What do you mean? Your parents always gave us jicama salad when we went to visit."

"Yes, jicama, but not as a salad; it was more of a snack." My dad would hack it into chunks and drown it in lime juice with a little salt and hot sauce. This jicama had been julienned with carrots and lightly sprinkled with a white vinegar dressing. "Just because they throw cilantro on something doesn't make it Mexican food, Nate."

"You don't like it?" Nate seems genuinely disappointed. "I was sure you'd get it." I wonder where he would have taken me to eat if I was Asian? Nobu, perhaps, and gone on about how the $20 sushi roll reminded him of my mom's.

"Sure. It's good . . . but different." And so is the crowd. Though the restaurant claims to specialize in traditional Mexican cuisine, I can't imagine a real Mexican family coming here for a Sunday dinner. "I guess it's just a different interpretation of what, you know, Latin American food is. Whatever that means."

"Trust me, this place has the best flan in the city," Nate assures me.

I guess he's forgotten that I'm not much of a flan person. Now, a vanilla crème brûlée from Moose's in North Beach, *that* I could imagine him remembering me by. Especially since I made a point of ordering it for dessert every time we went out to eat, which had been a lot.

"So you've had lots of short relationships?" Circling the subject hasn't yielded much so far. No point in being subtle. I don't have time for subtle. I'm reluctant to turn up the heat before we receive our entrées of puréed yucca root over goat cheese and persimmon-stuffed, roasted poblano peppers. The menu called them *chilies rellenos,* and I'm almost embarrassed I ordered them. I felt stupid ordering my food in proper Spanish, as if I was putting on a big act for the waiter.

"Yeah. Hey! Remember the last time we went out for a nice dinner?" Nate leans forward.

I guess he's got food on the brain.

"No." Of course I do.

Our last fancy dinner together was for our fuckiversary, commemorating the day/night we first had sex. This was the only special date either of us could be counted on to remember. We were a few months short of our first wedding anniversary, and even though things were turning sour, we both felt, or at least I did, compelled to give it a try and do something special. So for our fuckiversary we were sitting in this high-priced restaurant—and both of us knew we were in no mood to end our evening with a bang.

We ate in virtual silence, exchanging only a few stilted words. It was all just so sad and made even more so by the fact that we both knew it was over, even though neither of us was ready to call it quits.

"Yeah, you do. It was at that place that did only fish. Man, that was a great meal." Obviously Nate was on a different planet that night. "One of the best dinners ever."

"Pardon me?" I sputter. It was a horrible night. I can't remember what was on the plate in front of me. I might as well have been eating glass. I felt physically hurt after it. It was the first thing I talked to Dr. N about.

"Yeah, I had that fish." Nate gets a dreamy look on his face. "I hate fish, but that fish was so good. I wish I could remember the name of it."

"You mean you actually look back on that night *fondly?*" I ask incredulously.

"Sure. One of the best meals of my life. You ate everything on your plate and dessert, too."

It wasn't flan, I'll tell you that right now.

"We hardly said a word to each other the whole night! We didn't even bother to have *sex* when we got home!" This is unbelievable. Just more evidence that men live in a parallel universe.

"We didn't?"

"No. We. Didn't." I spit. How could he forget our failure to even attempt to consummate our fuckiversary? As soon as we got back to our flat, I headed for the bathroom, put on my rattiest pajamas and my retainers (a sure sign that I wasn't considering sex), and when I came out, I found him in front of the TV fiddling with the surround-sound system. He didn't even try to talk me out of my retainers. All he did was kiss me on the cheek and tell me he'd come to bed in a minute. The last time I looked at the clock before I finally fell asleep it was 1:30, and he was still in the living room calibrating the damn speakers.

"Oh, well, it was still a great piece of fish." Nate smiles stupidly at me as if his revelation is nothing more than reminiscing.

"I'm happy for you and your fish. I hope you find each other one day and live happily ever-fucking after, Nate." One year in therapy and a good portion of it dedicated to discussing Nate, when all I had to do was throw a good piece of fish at him. Unbelievable.

"Hey, Jacqs, don't get mad. What's in the past is in the past."

"For some of us, obviously." I feel stupid. I've held on this long and now the person I thought I had some nominal hold on has just told me to get over it.

"What do you want me to say? That every day I die a little because I was an asshole and I wasn't the perfect husband to you?"

"That's a start." I do think I deserve an apology. Especially after all I've been through and am currently going through sitting right in front of him.

"Please. What about what you did to me?" Nate knocks back his drink and signals the waiter for another one.

"What did I do?" I am shocked, truly shocked, but I'm trying to keep my voice low. I don't like airing dirty laundry in public, but I hate losing an argument.

"What did you do? I moved to San Francisco for you. I left all my friends—"

"Who all ended up moving to San Francisco anyway." He can't

blame me for that. It's really unfair, considering it was his job that took over our lives.

"Whatever. All I'm saying is that you weren't the perfect wife either."

"Perfect wife? What did you expect? You were hardly ever home and when you were, you were in front of the TV or your computer."

"Where were you, Jacqs? Out with your friends or at some party or another. Or holed up in the bathroom."

This is technically true, but only because he was at work so much I had to find other things to keep me occupied. So I turned to friends, an endless stream of launch parties Nate had no interest in going to and long baths while reading cheap romances. That is what became of my life as a married woman and I didn't like it.

Even though I sort of do the same things now, at least I'm not married and by myself. I'm single and independent—a huge difference. If I want to spend an hour in the tub, it's my right, I'm not hiding out from anyone.

"What was I supposed to do, Nate? Sit around and keep the pot roast warm in the oven until you showed up?"

"What's wrong with that?" Nate scoffs, but I know it's closer to the truth than he'll ever admit. "Every time we visited your parents, you were always so nice to me."

"What do you mean, nice?" I know what he's talking about, and I knew it'd come back to bite me in the ass.

"I used to joke that those visits were the only times you'd ever, you know, wait on me. Not wait on me, exactly, but take care of me. Like your mom does your dad."

"Nate, I did that only to keep you out of my mother's kitchen. And I wasn't waiting on you!" I hiss.

But I had waited on him, to a lesser degree than the other men had been waited upon by their wives, daughters and girlfriends. But still, while Nate sat in the living room, I had fetched an odd beer or three. OK, fine, and I filled a plate and presented it to him and made sure he had access to warm tortillas. But I only did it to keep my family from giving me that look of shock and disapproval because I didn't wait on my husband hand and foot. I only did it to be a courteous hostess, not to wait on him.

"Your mom always made sure I had a cold beer or something to eat before we even got in the front door. At home you never even turned on the stove. It wasn't until she came to visit that someone actually used the oven."

"You didn't want a wife, Nate, you wanted your mother." I sit back and cross my arms. That effectively ends his side of the argument.

"What's wrong with that?" Nate asks.

He's either very secure with himself or doesn't realize how creepy it is to hear from a man that you slept with that he wants to marry his mother. Or rather, my mother.

"Oh, I see. When we were together I got the feeling that you liked me, *loved* me, because I'm me. Faults and all. That's what you told me," I remind him. Nate doesn't bother to look contrite or even slightly upset. "So now you're telling me you fell out of love with me because I didn't turn into someone like your mother? Or my mother?"

"We just wanted different things." Nate shrugs.

It's like water rolling off his back. What I'm saying doesn't penetrate, or even scratch the surface of Nate's untouched psyche. Time to be blunt.

"Yeah, I wanted a sex life. And you wanted your mommy." Bitter, bitter, bitter. I already knew this; it had come up in therapy, but to have him confirm it makes me so angry and a little sad. I didn't expect him to declare his still-smoldering love and passion for me, pull out my ring and ask me, beg me, to marry him again. (This time the right way—in a church, with a dress and with all our family looking on.) Still, a girl likes to be asked.

"Whatever . . . What's in the past is in the past. I've moved on. So should you."

Nate's pearls of wisdom, offered up without a thought to how useless they are.

"What does that mean?" I've moved on! I'm wearing white. I have a new job (which he hasn't asked me about!), I have a (married) boyfriend and tons of other things going on in my life. My life is a hundred times better now than it was with him. If it wasn't I wouldn't have invited him out to dinner so he could find out.

"Listen, Jacqs, I didn't want to tell you like this, but I'm getting married." Nate looks at me carefully.

"Really." My heart sinks, but I look him straight in the eye. There is no way in hell I'm going to let him see how much those words have stunned me. "Married? To who?"

"A woman who works for the same company I do. That's why I'm going to India."

"You're getting married in India?" I don't want to ask if she is from India, but I'm curious. It would make sense, how he was intimidated by Bina and probably in love with her at the same time. Now he's going to marry someone from India. Isn't that a kick in the ass?

"No. In her hometown, outside of Chicago."

"She's from Chicago?" I ask stupidly. Of course she is. Why the hell would he get married near Chicago if she wasn't from near Chicago?

"Yeah, and we're going to India for our honeymoon."

"Oh."

"Don't you want to know when we're getting married?" Nate asks.

"No. Not really." Of course I do.

Nate accepts his fresh drink from the waiter. I pick at my dinner. I hate Latin-fusion cuisine, whatever the fuck that is. I hate LA. I hate Nate. I hate hometowns near Chicago.

"Are you OK, Jacqs?"

"I'm great. So is your fiancée so secure that she's cool with you going out with your ex-wife?"

"Uh." Nate squirms in his seat. "She doesn't know. She's back in Chicago taking care of last-minute details."

"How very convenient for you." So they're having a real wedding. With a real dress, real church and reception. My ex-husband is just fine without me. Better than fine, he's getting married.

"She has nothing to worry about," Nate says defensively. Yeah, I'm sure any woman, even this saint who he's fooled into marrying him would be OK with this. "You want to see a picture?"

I should say no, but of course I can't. Who wouldn't want to see? He pulls his wallet out of his pocket and fishes out a photo. It's a professional black-and-white posed shot. And speaking of which . . .

"She's white."

"Yeah. So? Her name is Bethany Michel, but she's taking *my* name. My last name. Hyphenated."

Toward the end of our relationship, when we had already started the divorce proceedings and we were getting along great in bed, Nate admitted that my not taking his name had hurt him very much. My name was on my diploma, for Christ's sake, the single-most important document, next to my unused passport, that I own. Nate, of course, didn't understand.

"At least it's good to know you don't stick to one type of girl." I start to hand back the picture to Nate.

"What do you mean?"

"I always thought you were more into, uh, brunettes . . . Latinas." I mean, he did fall head over heels for me. "You had that thing for Salma Hayek."

"Being with you wasn't so different from being with a regular woman."

"Gee, thanks." There's no point in trying to go deeper. To Nate, I was just his girlfriend and then his wife, who happened to be brunette and then some. The culture issue was never really an issue for him. He had the luxury of ignoring it and still does.

"She's pretty, huh?" he asks, slightly unsure.

I sigh and take the picture back and look more closely. She's OK-looking. Nothing special, not homely either. Blondish hair, chin length, good teeth, with her hand under her chin, and on her left hand, on her ring finger is *my* ring!

"Hey!" I yelp. People look up and over at our table. I lower my voice, trying not to hiss. "Nate, that's my ring! You gave her *my* ring?"

"It's not yours. You got the flat and I got the ring back," he says stupidly. As if this makes perfect sense.

"I got the *flat?* I got the mortgage is what I got." I feel tears well up in my eyes. I didn't even want the ring. It got caught in my hair and snagged my favorite sweater. It looked so lonely on my finger without a wedding band to anchor it and I was the one who filed for divorce. But it's my ring. My engagement-slash-wedding ring. And now he's given it to someone else! "Does she know it's been on my finger?"

"No. So what?"

Stupid Nate.

"So what! You gave your fiancée your ex-wife's ring, for God's sake. Why didn't you at least get a new one?" I don't know this woman, I don't want to know her (in person), but I feel personally insulted for her.

"She found it in my drawer and assumed it was for her. What was I supposed to do?"

"Why did you have it anyway? I thought you were going to pawn it?" That's what he told me, anyway. I thought he was just being petty. But when it came down to it, I knew the flat was sensible where the ring was merely sentimental. And in the San Francisco housing market, I couldn't afford to be sentimental.

"That ring cost me more than my first new car. I was never going to get back what I paid for it." Nate crosses his arms over his chest.

"So you thought the smart thing to do would be to recycle it? What is she, some militant ecologist? She can't bear to see a Tiffany diamond ring go to waste?"

"No. She's a lawyer. And she likes it, and that's what matters."

A lawyer. I was supposed to be a lawyer by now. I was all geared up to apply and then Nate moved in and my brain took a nosedive near the vicinity of his groin. But thanks to hours spent on Dr. N's squishy leather armchair, I know it's a choice I made and I can't blame Nate. OK, I can, but not much.

"And she doesn't know where it's been, right?" I don't know if you could find one woman on the planet who would accept a ring with that kind of history.

But for Nate it's like wearing the same underwear two days in a row or farting in front of friends and then rating it by sound and smell. Giving your girlfriend your ex-wife's ring is perfectly reasonable. To say otherwise is just nitpicking.

"Man, you have some balls, Nate. Giving a woman a *used* ring." I shake my head. "Maybe in India you could study up a bit on karma."

"So what's new with you?"

For Nate this is a natural progression to a conversation. Inform your ex-wife she was a bad wife, tell her you've found her replacement and *then* ask about her life.

"Oh. Me?" Me, what? He's getting married. He isn't emotionally destroyed. He's a normal person capable of having a normal adult relationship. He hasn't spent one minute in therapy. He got divorced, moved away, worked, dated and got engaged. To a lawyer. I feel my shoulders slump in my exquisite dress.

"Listen, just because we didn't work out . . ." Nate, bless his heart, can tell I'm a tad upset. "It doesn't mean we can't be friends. Right, Jacqs?"

We didn't work out, meaning me, I didn't work out. This much is obvious. But why should I care? I don't really, truly want Nate to marry me again, but it would be nice if he still liked me, or even loved me a little bit. Even though I don't want to have a relationship with him, I don't want him to have a relationship with anyone else either. At least not yet. Not until I find someone.

"Friends, Nate? What, are you going to have me over to a barbeque? Why didn't you tell me you were getting married? Better yet, why *did* you tell me?"

"I don't know. I mean, I know I should have called. Or dropped you an e-mail . . ." Nate looks off over my shoulder.

"So if we hadn't run into each other this morning, you'd have dropped me a postcard from your honeymoon?"

"No, of course not. I would have e-mailed you or something," he says, as if I've just suggested he'd eat the still-beating heart of a baby lamb and then ask for seconds.

"Well, of course you would have! Stupid me," I say, feeling the hurt thicken my tongue so it's hard to talk. He'd tell me, after the fact, from a nice, safe distance. Men have it so easy. "So why did you even bother to tell me? Here? Now?"

"I guess it's something I think you should know. I mean, you'd tell me if you were involved with somebody, right?"

"Maybe." Of course I would, if I was involved with somebody so freaking fantastic that I couldn't restrain myself from rubbing it in. But since I hadn't waved a 2-ton rock under his nose at the coffee shop (where I was sitting *alone*) he should have understood that I don't have anyone to mention and, therefore, he shouldn't either.

"Are you involved with somebody?" Nate asks, suddenly unsure.

"Why do you want to know?" I sit back and try to look relaxed. Now, this is the way I like things: with me on the offensive and Nate not.

"So you're not. I figured, since you asked me out," Nate says.

Our time apart has made me rusty.

"I didn't *ask you out.* My friend is sick. And we *used* to be friends so I thought we could have a friendly dinner. We haven't seen each other in a year, more than a year . . . And I was going to meet him, but he canceled—"

"But isn't it weird that your *friend* just happens to get coffee in the same place I do?"

"Weird? No." Obviously I am not showing enough cleavage to keep Nate from putting two and two together.

"All I'm saying is it's kind of odd that you show up here in LA, right before I leave for Chicago to get married."

"Are you suggesting that I'm *stalking* you or something?" I'm shocked, just shocked.

"I didn't say stalking; you did."

We stare at each other, silently. I know that he knows I've been visiting his blog and keeping up with his life. He probably thinks I've been sitting in our/my flat, pining away for him, scheming to get him back and tear him away from the loving, trusting arms of his precious and perfect Bethany. He probably thinks that's why I'm here tonight.

I'm wearing a beautiful (free) dress, a bracelet from Cartier (a gift from my boyfriend) and earrings from Tiffany's (which I purchased myself, thank you), but someone else is wearing my engagement-slash-wedding ring. And my ex-husband thinks I'm still hung up on him.

Where the hell would he get that idea?

"I have to go. It was . . . Thanks for coming to dinner with me." I signal the waiter and hand over my credit card without waiting for the bill. I'm expensing it anyway, so it doesn't matter. This whole night doesn't matter.

"Jacqs, wait. I didn't mean to—"

"Don't worry about it. It's really OK. Congratulations. From the bottom of my heart, I wish you all the luck in the world." I stand up and lean over to kiss him on the cheek. I feel his hand run down my back, and hover near the top of my hip. The place he always said was his favorite on my body.

"You mean happiness," Nate says, his eyes firmly on my breasts, "you wish us all the happiness in the world."

"Right." I straighten up quickly, begin to walk away and then turn around. "Can I ask you one thing, Nate?"

"Sure." He looks at me expectantly. He never did like to fight.

"If you're so into this Bethany, and she's everything I never was, what are you doing out with me tonight?"

He doesn't answer. He doesn't have to.

45

Nate and Bethany

When I get back to the hotel, I head directly for their business center, stake out a computer and open up a Web browser. From her picture I can tell his fiancée is totally conventional, modern and efficient. This means she has used the Internet to plan her wedding, which means I can find out every gory detail.

At 3 AM I get up and stretch. I have a sheaf of printouts that document the love story of Nate and Bethany. (Nate and Bethany, Bethany and Nate. How grossly sweet.) She's registered them at all the predictable places: Pottery Barn, Restoration Hardware, Williams Sonoma *and* Target; I guess she has a sense of humor.

It never occurred to me to check to see if he had registered with any of these places. I had kept an eye on his Amazon wish list and I thought that was enough to supplement the info I got from his blog and message-board postings. From those, I never gathered Nate was getting married, or even laid, and would need a ceramic fish platter.

What woman would be OK with her man going out with his ex-anything while she's stuffing Jordan Almonds into tiny plastic champagne glasses? The only answer is that he hasn't told her about me. I wouldn't put it past Nate to conveniently forget that little part of his life. *Oh, yeah, honey, by the way, I was married to this (nearly) perfectly proportioned Latina, and, oh, hee hee, that's her ring you're wearing.*

That's her problem, I guess.

I think I know Nate pretty well and I don't think it's my conceit that leads me to believe that the reason he hasn't mentioned her on his blog and hasn't mentioned me to her is that he still wants me, at least in a sexual way. I guess he thought that having sex with your ex-wife on the eve of your marriage isn't technically verboten; he is an Episcopalian, after all. And when I just happened to show up, maybe he even convinced himself that having sex with me would be more of an act of charity than cheating. After all, I have been a frequent visitor to his stupid blog and just happened to run into him, invited him out to dinner, dressed better than I did on our elopement day . . .

Poor Nate must have assumed he was going to have to do his all-American, former-frat-boy duty and put me out of my misery by putting out. God bless the USA.

I knew I had a sexual hold over Nate and, for a while, that was all that kept us together. I used it, and maybe even abused it, but I never thought it would come back and bite me in the butt. After a year apart, I guess I had hoped maybe he would have grown fond of me as a person, not just as a good lay.

And to come *this* close to cheating on his wife-to-be? What she doesn't know won't hurt her. Booyah!

Whatever. Not my problem.

I hope they find a good therapist and aren't naive enough to go into this thing without some sort of prenup. Marriage is hard enough without bringing a closet full of skeletons. I wish them all the luck in the world. I really do.

Still, maybe I shouldn't have sent them the George Foreman Grill with a note reading: "To Bethany and Nate, for when things need a little heating up. All the best, Jacqs."

46

Vivian

"Thanks, Jacqs." Vivian hugs me tight, her big American breasts pressing against my own not-too-shabby pair. "I really needed this."

"We should do it again, under different circumstances." I hug her back, ignoring the driver who's checking us out and his watch. He has just twenty-five minutes to get her to the airport for her flight back to San Francisco. "Promise me you'll check in on Natasha. She's being so cheery on the phone. I'm worried that she's killed Jesus and is marinating his body in the bathtub."

"Will do." Vivian holds me at arm's length. "I'm sorry about you and what's-his-name."

"Eh, no big deal." As far as Vivian knows, Nate and I had a pleasant but spark-free dinner and I came back to my hotel room well fed but unlaid. Thanks to Natasha's generosity with the pharmaceuticals, Vivian was sound asleep when I sneaked in. "Like I said, we parted on good terms. We're better friends than anything else."

"I wish I could be more like you, Jacqs." Vivian sighs, lets me go and steps into the car.

"I think one of me is all I can handle." I wave to her and watch her taxi pull away. "Barely."

47

Noel

On my way to Union Station I try Mrs. Mayor again. I haven't spoken to her since we left Carmel and I'm getting worried. After leaving another message with London I promise myself I won't call her again.

I called my mother and told her that the Santa Barbara train would arrive at 3 PM and let her know where to pick me up outside the station. I feel bad lying to her, but I'd feel worse if I had to admit I had spent almost three days in LA while pretending to be somewhere else because I didn't want to spend it with them.

My family is very reliable when it comes to pickups. Someone will always come—a cousin, aunt, or even (once) the whole family. Because of this, I know my ride will be from someone who remembers me from my pudgy pimply phase, and will bring it up, astonished that I'm not that girl anymore. And because of this, I always make sure to look as put-together as possible.

I arrive at 2:30, just in case my ride gets here early, and wait. At a little before 3, I start looking around for a familiar face.

"Hey, dorkolina, what's shaking?" From behind, my brother Noel puts a death grip on my shoulders.

"Hey! Rico Suave!" I turn around and give him a big hug. Noel is my favorite and, I think, the most heartbreaking of all my siblings and we're a pretty sorry lot. He's been arrested a few times (nothing serious, but seriously stupid) and has trouble holding down a job. He barely made it out of high school but has a few semesters of college under his belt.

He's the quintessential underachiever, but he's so charming that it's easy to overlook all his faults and just enjoy his company. He can do no wrong in my parents' eyes, which makes the rest of us resent him to varying degrees.

"So what are you doing in this dump?" he asks, cuffing the back of my head softly. Each time I see him, he seems better looking. He's one of those guys who get more handsome with age. Kind of like George.

"I'm here to mix with the natives. Hey, I thought your license was revoked," I say, punching him on the arm. Solid muscle and, thankfully, no tattoos.

"Just a little misunderstanding between me and the fine city of Glendale. I'm legit, don't worry, *hermanita*."

"So did they make you pick up trash by the side of the freeway again?" This actually happened right after Noel turned sixteen. To teach him (and us) a lesson, my father made us drive by and watch. It was one of the few times I saw my mother, father *and* Noel cry. "Sorry I missed it."

"I think I can make a real career of it," he says, as if it's no big deal.

"Our parents must be so proud." I point to my bags.

"Here, Jacqs, let me get those for you."

"Thanks, Noel! You're my favorite brother."

I watch him heave them up.

"You're looking fit." I don't want to make a crack about prison workouts, but I'm tempted.

"I'm working at a gym right now." He flexes his bicep so I can give it a squeeze.

"You are?" My mother hasn't mentioned this. Usually she fills me in on all the doings of my brothers and sisters. In detail. "Selling steroids?"

"Nah. I fix the machines and unclog toilets. Really thrilling.

Especially when I get to go into the women's locker room. I can get you a guest pass if you want."

"Thanks." My brother might not have much, but he's always been generous with what he does have. "How are *Mamá* and *Papá?*"

"Fighting. As usual."

Noel rolls his head back and forth, which causes his muscles to issue popping noises that he knows gross me out. He still lives at home, in his old room that he used to have to share. He doesn't pay rent, but does help around the house.

"I'm thinking of getting my own place."

"Are you sure you're ready? You're only, like, thirty?" We wait to cross the street into the parking lot. It's very warm and the air seems drier on this side of Los Angeles.

"Yeah. It's time for me to spread my wings and fly. Giselle is giving me a hard time."

Noel's girlfriend has been suffering for his full and undivided attention for about four years. I don't even want to know what keeps her coming back for more. My mother has made her an honorary daughter-in-law (for whatever that's worth), but still hasn't added her name to the family Bible. Nate's name wasn't recorded in ink, but hasn't been erased either. My mother said we'd have to get married in front of a priest first or have a kid (she'd kill me if I had a kid before getting married by priest) so I guess she's still holding out some hope.

"She wants to get married." He tosses my bags into the back of his car and has to slam the trunk twice, hard, before it catches.

"Don't do it!" I say a little too quickly. "I mean, that's a big step."

"Don't worry. I have no plans to get married. I might go back to school. This job is pretty flexible." He smiles, his brown eyes crinkling at the corners.

"That would be good." I try not to sound overly enthusiastic. Noel always has plans—big ones, little ones, and in the end very little to show for all his talk.

We pull up to the parking attendant. Noel digs out the parking ticket from his pocket. I casually hand over parking money. Noel doesn't refuse it, but he doesn't acknowledge it either.

After a brief car ride choreographed to the first couple of tracks of some Pink Floyd album, we come to a squeaky stop in front of my parents' house, with its neatly tended front yard and slightly dingy-looking paint job.

My heart gives a lurch, and I reach for the car door handle. The door doesn't budge. This is not a good sign.

"Hold on. It's sort of broken. I have to open it from the outside." Noel climbs out and comes around and opens my door. "I'll get your bags. Go on in. *Mamá* has been dying to see you."

"Are you sure?"

"Go on." I know he wants to smoke a cigarette, something my mother forbids in the house and my father envies since he had to quit. "They're all waiting for you."

"That's exactly what worries me."

48

Mamá

At the front door I stop and knock, like a stranger. From inside I hear muffled footsteps.

"Jacquelyn! *Mija!* Why do you knock? Come in! Where is your *hermano?*" My mother's eagle eyes, now permanently behind glasses, scan over my shoulder, looking out for Noel, as always.

"He's saying the rosary in his car." I briefly bury my face in her crinkly neck and inhale.

"*Grosera.*" My mother swats me gently on the butt and squeezes me tight. "I'm so glad you're here, Jacquelyn. You look so beautiful."

"Thank you, *Mamá*. You look good. I like your hair." I can tell she recently got her hair cut and colored, something she tends to let go. Since my father retired, my mother looks older and is more careless with her appearance.

"It was driving me crazy. I had to do something with it. Carmen did it."

"Oh. Her." My aunt, who owns a beauty salon, gave me a perm in the seventh grade that fried my hair to a crisp. When my mother mentioned it, she blamed me, saying I must have done something wrong.

"It still looks nice. None of those skunk streaks she calls highlights."

"Watch your mouth. Noel! *Apague ese* cigarette and get to work! Jacquelyn, go have a rest in your room."

Even though we've never taken a flight together, my mother knows I can never sleep on airplanes.

"OK, *Mamá*." Now that I'm home I can let my mother control my every thought and action because I know she won't let anything bad happen to me or let me be bad to anyone.

"Later we'll go out to the mall." She holds the door open so Noel can dump my bags on the living room floor. He dashes out before my mother has a chance to sniff him for telltale odors.

"Sounds like fun," I say as I sleepwalk to my old room. I collapse onto the bed, covered with the quilt my grandmother made me, and close my eyes. "I'm glad to be home, *Mamá*."

"We're glad to have you back. *Duérmase, mija*. I'll wake you in a few hours."

Behind my closed eyes, I can make out my mom moving around the room unpacking my suitcase. I've stowed anything incriminating in the tote George gave me, it's best to hide some crimes right out in the open. She stands over me. I try to keep very still. She reaches down and smoothes my hair out of my face. She tiptoes to the door and pauses.

"Oh, we're meeting Carmen and your cousin Lina there." She quickly steps out, and the door clicks closed.

"Oh, fuck, *Mamá*." I pull the pillow over my head and try to smother myself.

49

Mamá, Tía Carmen and Lina

Lunch out for my mom means the food court at the Glendale Galleria—my mother is addicted to Panda Express and she claims this particular Panda Express makes orange-flavored chicken like no other.

She escapes to the mall every chance she gets. When she retires (if Latina mothers ever do such a thing), I'm sure she'll get a place next to a mall the way some old people buy a condo on a golf course.

Shopping is her sport, her therapy, her salvation. With a life like hers, filled with the needs of others, shopping lets her indulge her basic need for something that is all her own—even though she mostly ends up buying stuff for other people, not herself.

"*Tu madre* says you were in New York?" my aunt asks casually, as if it's no big deal.

Tía Carmen once caught me making out with a boyfriend and since then I've been nothing short of a fallen woman in her eyes. The quickie marriage and divorce didn't do much for my image either. I'm sure she thinks her little Lina is as pure as the driven snow. Actually, as far as I know, Lina *is* a virgin. Poor thing.

"That was last month. We stayed at the Waldorf-Astoria," I say, knowing my family will not recognize the name. I also recognize how patronizing I sound. Who cares that I stayed at the Waldorf-Astoria? I care, but why should my family?

"Is that the place Donald Trump owns?" my mother asks politely.

"No, he owns the Plaza, I think." I knew that my family would have been more impressed if I had stayed in Donald Trump's hotel, not one they've never really heard about.

"He cheated on his wife, you know," my mother says, as if she's revealing a dirty secret about a neighbor. "*Con una mujer mucho más joven*. A teenager!"

"Men generally fool around with younger women, not just Donald Trump, *Mamá*." I was a little too involved in myself at the time to really pay attention, but I do remember studying Marla Maples's pictures and thinking that it was the tits that got his attention. Marla Maples had great boobs and big American teeth. Something Ivana was lacking because she grew up Communist.

"She got something like $25 million *en el divorcio*. Can you believe that?" my mother continues.

"Really?" Why does my mother know this? What is she trying to tell me about divorce? It's OK as long as you make him pay through the nose? My divorce was mutual. There was no honey on the side. There wasn't even a prenup. We sat down and put everything on the table and divided it all in a civil manner. "I feel stupid for settling for the flat. Maybe Nate had millions stashed away somewhere?"

"No. No. Just something a *mujer* must be aware of." My mother pats my hand.

"What? If her husband has a mistress or where he keeps his money, *Mamá?*"

"Both," my mother says, as if it's a normal part of marriage to monitor your husband's wallet and zipper.

"You're whacked, *Mamá*. No more orange chicken for you."

"Nothing could make up for a man cheating on his wife. *Nada*. Not money or an apology. If she took the money, shame on her." *Tía* Carmen sniffs. Her husband is a well-known womanizer. Something *Tía* Carmen aggressively ignores. She exacts her revenge not by the threat of divorce but by the finality of her commitment to never release him from the bonds of marriage. She's a good Catholic, that woman.

"So *Lina*, what's new in *your* life?" So far, my cousin Lina has had little to say. I've tried to engage her in conversation, but her mother cuts her off before she has a chance to answer.

Surprisingly, Lina doesn't live at home, but exactly twelve minutes away in a condo she purchased with a settlement from a malpractice suit. She lost one of her ovaries, but she gained a modicum of freedom from her mother.

"Lina just got a promotion at work." *Tía* Carmen gives me a smug look.

"That's great, Lina. Where's work again?" I ask and notice that Lina could use a facial and an upper-lip wax. I wonder if a long weekend is enough to give her a physical and emotional makeover? If I had it my way, by the end of my short, short stay, she'd look fabulous, have some good sex and tell her mother to go to hell.

"I'm the office manager now. With the sanitation department," Lina mumbles and looks over at her mom.

Since I don't have any plans for my visit, I'll stick close to Lina and turn her to the dark side with me. I'm lonely here all by myself.

"Oh, wow! That's cool." I'm not being condescending at all. I really like Lina. I just wish she'd stand up for herself.

"Lina also has a boyfriend. *Un médico*." My aunt looks at me pointedly as she says this.

"Who is he?" What kind of person would be able to get around *Tía* Carmen? She must have vetted the poor creature within an inch of his life.

"He's a dentist. I met him when I got my teeth fixed." Lina smiles. She has a mouth full of clear braces. Her mother refused to get them for her when she was growing up, but at the ripe old age of twenty-six, Lina finally took matters into her own hands.

"He's a real nice guy," my mother adds, as if to assure me that Lina hasn't ended up with a male version of her mother. "You should have seen him *para tus dientes*, Jacquelyn."

"Yeah. Too bad." I got my teeth fixed a few years ago, veneers, laser whitening, the whole bit. I had to do something useful with all the dot-com cash that was busting out of my wallet and distract myself from the fact that I was doing nothing useful with my life.

"Maybe we could go out to dinner together while you're here," Lina offers.

Next to her, my aunt stiffens. The last thing she wants me to do is to meet what might be her daughter's only hope at marriage. I am a slut, after all.

"Great. When?"

"Tonight? I don't know when—" Lina finally has some color in her face.

"Tonight is great!" I say before *Tía* Carmen gets a chance to unleash her forked tongue. I smile sweetly at my aunt. Surprisingly, she doesn't smile back.

50

Yolie

"What do you mean, *I'm* the troublemaker of the family?" I sputter, as I try to apply my lip liner in the cramped bathroom that, even when almost empty, seems too small. I can rattle off a list of all my accomplishments: I went to college and paid for it myself. I live in my own place, pay my own bills, have my own life. So I married a white guy. So I got divorced. Big freaking deal. (They don't know about my married boyfriend, George, so they can't hold it against me that he's white, too.)

"You've always been different, Jacqs. Look at that thing with Nate," says Yolie, the eldest and therefore most messed up of all my sisters and brothers.

Dr. N would say she never had a chance to be a kid, and was born to be the family nag. Whatever, get some therapy and get over it. Of course I could never tell her this because then she'd realize I was in therapy and all hell would break loose.

She's cornered me in the bathroom as I'm getting ready for dinner—which *Tía* Carmen, thanks to her machinations, has turned into a backyard family affair that my mother is currently cooking her ass off for in the kitchen. I guess *Tía* Carmen figures a buffer of about twenty people between me and Lina's Prince Charming will be enough to keep me from seducing him.

"That *thing* with Nate. What thing? The getting-married thing or the getting-divorced thing?" Or the almost-having-sex-with-him thing the week before he gets remarried? Or the sending-his-bride-to-be-a-gift thing?

I can't stand Yolie's superior, judgmental attitude on everything from the length of one's skirt to one's marital status. She's been an old lady her whole life. As stupid as it seems sometimes, I like my life. It's my life and I don't have to answer to anyone but me and sometimes Mrs. Mayor. Why can't Yolie just understand that?

"Both." Yolie says. Her husband is a lush who can't hold down a job. They've been married for years but don't have any kids, thank God. "You don't see me getting divorced even though I could."

"I'm sure God is overjoyed that you are so strong. I'm sure that'll earn you a gold star in heaven, Yolie."

"No one in our family is divorced," Yolie states proudly.

What about me? Have I been excommunicated from the family by Yolie because I'm divorced?

"I know of plenty who *should* be." I don't want to point out that our own mother is drowning in her marriage and that Yolie's husband would be better off if she showed him the door. He would probably stop drinking and become a CEO. Saying this would just cause a fight and Yolie likes to fight way more than I do.

"I'm just saying that you shouldn't put ideas into people's heads," Yolie says.

"What ideas? What people?" I love Yolie, I do, but I can't stand her.

"*Mamá*. You're always telling her how much happier you are after the divorce. It's all she talks about after she gets off the phone with you." Yolie sniffs at me.

"I am happy! I can't help it." Which is true and not true. I'm sad I got divorced but I'm glad I'm not married. This distinction would be lost on Yolie, who is a black-and-white person who dresses in primary colors.

"I'm just saying that *Mamá* doesn't need to hear things like that."

"Maybe she does. *Mamá* is a grown-up." I hate that Yolie thinks she can talk to me like this. I'm not a kid anymore.

"Have you ever considered what would happen to her if she did divorce *Papá?*"

Yolie's eyes rest on my makeup case, probably tallying what its contents have set me back. I won't enlighten her as to the fact that they're freebies from Natasha and my little trip through LaLa land with Myles.

"She's not going to divorce him!" Usually I think Yolie is talking out of her ass, but this time she might have a point. My mom does seem more subdued than usual and then there was the whole Ivana–Donald talk at lunch.

"You're so wrapped up in your own little world, Jacquelyn. With your house in San Francisco and your fancy job and clothes. Just remember, the rest of us have to deal with real life."

"Listen, Yolie, I'm sorry you're so fucking miserable that you have to come pick a fight with me while I'm putting on my mascara, but if our mother is talking about divorce, maybe you should listen to her instead of judging."

"You're a selfish bitch, Jacquelyn." Yolie slams the bathroom door closed.

"Coming from you, Yolie, I take that as a compliment," I call after her.

51

Mamá

After making sure Yolie isn't around, I head into the kitchen to help my mom and Noel. My father is outside firing up the barbeque. I've been here for hours but I've yet to say one word to him other than hello. I wonder if I can keep this up for the rest of my visit. It's not as if he's asking me to sit down and have a long-overdue father-daughter chat.

"Was Yolie here?" my mother asks as she chops tomatoes.

"She's damned me to hell, but she'll be back with the flan." Flan, of course, is my sister Yolie's signature dish.

"Jacquelyn, be nice. Yolie speaks her mind but she doesn't mean half of what she says. Too much stress *en el trabajo*."

My mother can never see the bad in her children, especially when they're at they're worst. And despite all his faults, my father also prefers to think of his children as works in progress. We can always do better, be better, but he'd never let us know when we got there.

It takes a lot and yet very little to disappoint them, though. They're as quick to defend us as they are quick to let us know how disappointed they are in us for having to defend us. They don't let us know this by directly confronting us; it's just insinuated and burned directly onto our souls for eternity.

My major transgressions started when I announced I was moving away to attend college. Since then I've done nothing but give them cause for worry and grief, though they would never tell me this to my face. I know they're disappointed in me and the way I'm living my life. My whole family has an issue with putting happiness first. Not that they've asked me if I'm happy; they just assume I am.

Not happy at home? Move away for college. Hate your job? Find another one. Fallen out of lust, er, love with your husband? Divorce him.

I, so far, am the anomaly—or flake—in the family because I'm vocal about how unnecessary it is to be unhappy and, if you are, about doing something to change your circumstances (thank you, Zoloft!). If I had it my way, my whole family would be comparing dosages at the dinner table the way some families talk about sports or politics.

Everyone has their role. My mother the martyr. My father the distant, unapproachable figure. Noel, with a few brief stints in jail, is considered misunderstood, not a handsome loser. Yolie is just outspoken, not a miserable, bitter shrew, which would be her clinical diagnosis in the "real" world. And the rest of my brothers and sisters have problems that my parents consider normal—like bad marriages, unruly children and too many bills.

So is it any surprise that I'm the troublemaker of the family?

52

Lina

I keep myself busy in the kitchen so I don't have to wander outside and not know who to talk to. Plus, Yolie is holding court at the picnic table, and I want to stay away from her as much as possible.

"Jacqs?" A nervous Lina hovers in the doorway.

"Lina? Where's your boyfriend? I'm dying to meet him." I wipe my hands on a dish towel and set the tortillas in the clay warmer.

"He's outside. Can I talk to you for a second?"

"Sure. Let's go to my room. I need to change my shoes." Maybe one of the reasons my family can't relate to me is because I'm standing over the stove heating corn tortillas in a pair of four-inch sling backs. "What's your boyfriend's name? I didn't get a chance to ask."

"Roberto." Lina looks behind her as if he'll materialize at the sound of his name.

I walk into my room and pull off my shoes and debate whether to change my whole outfit for something more casual. Lina clicks the door shut behind her.

"Jacqs?"

Something in her voice makes me turn around. "Are you OK, Lina?" My first thought is that this Roberto is a total asshole, beats her and she needs my help to escape. With a mother like Carmen I wouldn't expect her to end up with anything more.

"I'm so happy. That's the problem." Lina begins to cry.

This makes sense to me, and Lina knows I understand. Sometimes the worst thing you can do in this family is not be miserable. It makes for all sorts of complications.

"Sit down. Tell me." I hand her the box of tissue in its glittery crocheted cover. My mother knits them by the gross, and gross is the appropriate word for them.

"I'm pregnant." She looks up with an ashamed smile.

"Holy crap! Congratulations, Lina! I knew you and your one ovary could do it." I throw my arms around her and hug. She hugs me back, hard. She smells like Love's Baby Soft. I didn't even know they still made the stuff.

"Roberto wants to get married," she says miserably.

"That jerk?"

"He wants to elope," she says, still miserably, but with a tinge of excitement in her voice.

"Oh." I'm the elopement expert in the family and the divorce expert, too, according to my mother and Yolie, Carmen, my father . . . "What do you want to do?"

"My mother will kill me. Either way."

"Yeah, she will. But what do *you* want to do? That's what counts."

"I don't know." Lina twists the hem of her skirt in her hands. She used to do the same thing to her hair when we were kids. She would twirl it around her finger so tightly, her finger would turn white.

The first question I'd ask my friends would be, "Are you going to have the baby?" But Lina is my cousin and different rules apply for family. I put my hand on hers to stop her from mangling her skirt.

"Yes. I'm ready. Roberto is ready." She nods her head firmly.

"So?" I've been away from home long enough to get exasperated when my family doesn't see the obvious.

"I don't know if my *Mamá* is ready," Lina sighs and bunches up her shoulders.

"Fuck your mom, Lina." I love being blunt. It's my specialty.

"Jacquelyn!" Lina gasps. She looks around her as if her mom's going to spring out of thin air.

"Lina, you're an adult. You have the right to your own life. We all do. Your mom is just going to have to get over it." Easier said than done, but Lina doesn't need to be weighed down with small details right now.

Lina falls quiet, and I take the chance to change into my stalking Nate outfit. Dressed, I sit back down next to her and rub her back.

"I guess I have to do what's right for me. Right?" She smoothes the wrinkles in her skirt.

"There's nothing wrong with that, Lina."

For a minute we sit together enjoying our status of family outcasts.

"Are you happy, Jacqs?" Lina asks and stands up.

As I consider my answer, I watch her walk over to the door and open it, waiting beside it for us to walk back to our family.

"I'm not unhappy and isn't that almost the same thing?"

53

Mr. Mayor

I balance my plate of food—roasted corn on the cob, beans and chicken—and take the tiny phone from my nephew, who's fished it out of my bag. It's my dedicated Mrs. Mayor line. She calls only for emergencies, such as when she needs a new pair of tasteful fishnets or she's locked herself out of her car. Stuff like that.

"It's been ringing and ringing." He looks guilty. Going into someone's purse or pockets is a sure sign of much worse things to come in our family.

"Thanks!" As if on cue, my phone rings in my hand.

"See?" he says desperately.

"Thanks. Really, it's OK. Hold this for me, will you?" I hand him my plate and flip open the phone.

"Hello, this is Jacquelyn." I stiffen and wait for a Mrs. Mayor type of emergency.

"Jacquelyn?" It's *Mr.* Mayor! Well, hello!

"Mr. Mayor, is everything OK?" I stand up and fluff my hair. Mr. Mayor has *never* called me. Mrs. Mayor must be dead or something. I have to find a new job! I have to break up with George!

"Yes and no. It's Vivian."

"Oh, no! Is she dead?" I half-register my nephew setting my plate of food on the grass at my feet and darting back into the house to watch TV with the rest of the kids.

"No, no! She's fine, but . . . can you talk?" Mr. Mayor asks. "You sound as if you're at a party or something."

"No, it's fine. Go ahead," I say, trying not to squeak. Mrs. Mayor would never ask if it was a good time for me. She just talks into my ear and expects me to drop everything. Thing is, if I had an assistant, I'd sort of expect the same thing.

"Vivian and Curtis have, uh, broken up," Mr. Mayor says uncomfortably. I can imagine him running his hand through his thick hair.

"That's horrible." But not a surprise. "Where is she? At home? I should call her."

"That's the thing, Jacqs. Curtis has had her evicted from their place."

"Oh, no!" Vivian never liked living in Curtis's minimalist loft, but I'm sure she didn't want to get kicked out of it either.

"And he's talking about getting a restraining order against her," Mr. Mayor continues in a concerned tone.

"My God. What did she do?"

"She needs a place to stay. I would have her stay with us, but, you know . . . I was hoping . . . since you have that extra bedroom at your place . . ."

"Not to worry. She can stay with me. In my second bedroom. Not a problem."

How the hell does Mr. Mayor know how many bedrooms I have in my place? It's not as if we've talked square footage over morning coffee.

"Thank you, Jacqs. Really."

"Should I fly home? I can get a flight out tomorrow morning, tonight even." This offer goes both ways. I do suddenly feel the undeniable urge to get the hell out of here. I smile sheepishly at my cousin-in-law.

"No, no! Stay. Enjoy yourself. Lei mentioned she has a set of your keys. I'll make sure she's settled. Thanks, Jacqs. Thanks a million. You're saving my life. I don't know what I'd do without her. She runs my life."

"I'm sure she and Curtis will straighten this whole thing out. Mr. Mayor? Where is Vivian? Why didn't she call me herself?"

"She's sort of being detained by the police." Mr. Mayor sounds distracted. In the background, I hear Mrs. Mayor call out to him in a not-so-loving tone of voice. "I have to get off the phone. Thanks again, Jacqs. Don't worry about Vivian. I'll get it all straightened out. You're a lifesaver."

"Yeah, thanks. Bye-bye, Mr. Mayor." I can feel the eyes of my family on me, wanting to ask but not wanting to be the first. I pick my plate off the grass, take a huge bite of my corn, chew, smile, and pretend that I hadn't just taken a phone call from the mayor of San Francisco.

"So," I say, trying to get back into the groove of the conversation I was having before the mayor of San Francisco called and personally asked me for a lifesaving favor, "you were saying about getting a contractor out to install tile in your bathroom? I bet that was a total nightmare."

I can feel corn in my teeth. I immediately shut my mouth and try to work the corn out without making any obvious smacking sounds. As I'm performing this feat, I make an extra effort to show I'm attentive, but eventually she wanders off. Probably to talk about me and how stuck up I am.

54

Papá

I dump my plate into the garbage can set in the corner of the yard and grab a cold beer out of the humongous cooler. I need alcohol to get my nerve up. With my dad, things can go either surprisingly well or not. I always bank on not, so it makes being around him without my mother all the more awkward.

"Hey, *Papá*. Whatchya doing? Cooking steak?" Around my father, I become a huge, insecure dork.

"Yup," my father grunts. He's standing in front of the grill, jabbing a deadly looking two-pronged fork into cuts of beef. Since I moved away from my family, I've had beef only a handful of times. I can honestly say I had steak for dinner, maybe not very good steak, but steak nonetheless, most nights for the first eighteen years of my life.

"The yard is looking good." I rock back and forth from my heels to my toes, clutching the beer bottle behind my back, sort of hiding it from my father.

"Yup." A proud grunt and a nod. Can't ask for more than that.

"Well, I'll let you get back to your, um, OK. Have you seen *Mamá?*" I've done my duty as a daughter.

"*Cocina*."

"Bye, *Papá!*"

55

Mamá, Yolie, Tía Carmen

I fight my way into the kitchen—relatives seemed to have invited relatives—and find my mother sitting at the table with *Tía* Carmen and Yolie. Not good. I try to backtrack, but I'm caught.

"Jacquelyn, sit down. Did you ask your father about the grass?"

My mother knows that my father is a hard man to talk to. I don't think they've ever had a real conversation about anything except bills, their kids, their kid's kids and the state of the lawn.

"Yeah, he said it was great. OK. I think I'll go pee now."

"*Siéntese*, Jacqueline. We were just talking about you," Yolie enlightens me.

"I bet. I really have to pee. Don't want to get a UTI." They look at me blankly. "Bladder infection."

"You get those often?" *Tía* Carmen asks.

God, she really can't stand me. I can't imagine how she'll feel about me if Lina goes through with her elopement and fingers me as the one who encouraged her to do it.

"Only during Fleet Week." They look at me blankly. "I'm kidding."

I pull out a chair and sit gingerly on its edge, ready to make a quick exit when things go the way I know they'll be going.

"Your *tía* was telling us that she thinks Lina is very serious about Roberto."

My mother looks for drama where she can find it. She tries to re-create her telenovellas in real life, always suspecting someone is involved in a sordid love triangle or owes money to drug dealers. In my mom's mind, the idea that Roberto is cheating on Lina with me while selling kilos of cocaine between root canals isn't that far-fetched. Bless her heart, but the woman needs a life.

"Uh-huh." I nod. Someone must have seen us go into my room, and now my aunt wants to know if I corrupted her daughter. Too late! "Where *is* Lina?"

"She and Roberto had to leave. Has Lina said anything to you about Roberto, Jacqs?" Yolie asks.

"Like what, Yolie?" I can't help but sneer at her. She sounds just like our *Tía* Carmen. She's even starting to look like her.

"*Tía* Carmen thinks she's been acting funny."

Yolie takes a sip of her drink from a gummy plastic tumbler. My mother has tons of them. I've always hated them and refuse to drink out of them. You can never really get the smell of the last drink out no matter how hot and soapy the water. In my place, nothing is plastic.

"Lina is a funny person," I say to the air over Yolie's head.

"My daughter is a good girl," *Tía* Carmen states.

"Meaning what? That I'm not? If you want to know what's so *funny* about Lina, ask her yourself." They just stare at me, silent and damning. Even my own mother.

Without another word, I get up and walk away.

56

Noel

If I was still in my teens or hadn't been married, I would be in huge trouble. Now I'll just get some dirty looks, but they can't punish me since I'm officially an adult.

I sit on the couch with the kids and watch *Jurassic Park*. I thought I could make it for a few more days, but I know I'll be leaving as soon as possible. I'm tempted to pull out my cell phone and loudly make arrangements, but I don't. It would hurt my mom's feelings. After a few minutes, I notice that Noel is slumped in my dad's armchair.

"Hey, you passed out, Noel?" I nudge his foot with mine.

"Nope, not yet. Just riding out the storm." Noel is a big fan of the Doors. Everything he says has a forced lyrical bent to it. Especially when he's had a beer or three.

"Where's Giselle?" I ask. All Noel's girlfriends have had glamorous, romantic names. There was Roxanne in junior high; Karina, Dominique and Maxine during high school and some more after I left for school, and now it's Giselle.

I like Giselle well enough, but I wish she'd stop picking out the same chunky knit sweater for my brother to give me for Christmas. I haven't worn sweaters like that since I lost all my baby fat. Unfortunately, all the pictures my parents have on display are of me resplendent in a chunky sweater that I thought camouflaged my weight.

"She had to work. She'll be by later. Maybe." He takes a drink of his beer. "Hey! You want to go out for lunch tomorrow? Your favorite place. My treat."

"Are you sure it won't break the bank?" I've been waiting for him to ask. My brother knows I have a soft spot for Tommy's messy, and utterly delicious hamburgers, something I can't get in San Francisco.

"I think I can handle it." He digs into his pocket. "I got you that pass for the gym. Where I work. It's good for the whole week, but I know you won't be able to stand it here that long."

"Thanks. I'll go tomorrow. The more time I spend away from our family, the longer I can stand being around them."

"Tell me about it. Just come find me when you're ready for lunch," he says again happily.

"OK." Noel is drunk, but, as with everything bad Noel does, he's nice enough about it so that I or anyone else can't hold it against him. "Thanks for the pass."

Noel leans back with his eyes half-closed. I watch him carefully. It's not that I find him pathetic. He's too honest with himself and up-front with all his fuckups for anyone to feel sorry for him. But it's still hard not to root for him and hope that something, someday works out for him.

I remember vividly when I realized what a flawed and great person my brother was. He was in his second semester at Cal State LA and he was my hero. He had scrimped and saved and dug himself into debt so he could live near campus like a regular student. This devastated my mother, and my father said he wouldn't last a month. I was still in high school and the only kid left at home. My brother knew how hard it was for me to be at the center of the vortex of my parents' relationship and took pity on me. Every chance he got—when he wasn't goofing off, working or going to the odd class—he'd drive up from school in a friend's car, pick me up and take me back with him and we'd spend time touring the campus, hanging out and doing what college kids do: staying up late and eating junk food.

Toward the end of his second semester, I was walking home

from school, taking my time because I didn't want to get there, when I noticed my brother's current girlfriend crying her eyes out in a car. She lived a few blocks over and was going to the local beauty school, so we saw her a lot. She would drop by during the week to say hi to my parents and me.

I hid behind a tree and tried to get a better look. What I saw was my brother Noel, looking pale and tense, gripping the steering wheel while she cried and cried. I knew immediately that she was pregnant. I went home and threw up.

Two weeks later, my brother came home. He dropped out of school and got some dumb-ass job at Circuit City. He wouldn't tell my parents why and they never thought to ask me. He would come in and out of the house and not say a word to anyone. At night, I'd hear him pleading on the phone with her. He'd cry; she'd cry.

Then, one morning, he was gone before any of us woke up. His boss called looking for him, and when he showed up later that afternoon, he wouldn't tell anyone where he'd been. His girlfriend broke up with him shortly after whatever happened that day.

Noel had quit school, gotten a job and was prepared to do what was right and, even though he had, things still didn't work out for him. It made my decision to leave home for college all the easier. Why do the right thing? Chances are they won't work out anyway.

Noel starts to snore softly. The kids giggle. I get up and pick my way around the small bodies of my cousins and nieces and nephews, all transfixed by the television, and shut myself in my room.

No one comes looking for me.

57

Mamá and Papá

My mother makes a full breakfast in the morning, every freaking morning. When my brother has to be at work early, she wakes him up, irons his clothes (khaki Dockers and a red polo) and, while he's in the shower, cooks him breakfast. Creamy oatmeal made with whole milk, omelets with chorizo, pancakes. No hour is too early, no request too obnoxious.

She used to do the same thing for my dad before he "retired" from the company he and my other two brothers own together. Now that he is not working and doesn't get up at the crack of dawn, she has to do this routine twice: once for him and once for Noel, a couple hours apart. Incredibly this is the one thing she never complains about.

Noel has left for work and my father is already barricaded behind his morning paper.

"Good morning, Daddy!" I say brightly.

My mother gives me a warning look from the stove. My father grunts, turns the page and waits for the food to miraculously appear on a plate in front of him.

"Noel said you were going to his gym. You can borrow your father's car," my mother offers generously from her post at the stove.

"No." He doesn't lower the paper or acknowledge the fact that my mother has set his breakfast on the table: fried ham steak, eggs and more eggs. He's going to get ass cancer, and I'm not going to feel that bad about it. For my mom, yeah, since I know she'll have to deal with it, but for him, nope. He kind of deserves it, if you ask me. "*Yo lo necesito*."

"It's OK, *Mamá*. I'll *rent* a car." I can feel my upper lip curl. My dad works my last nerve almost as bad as Yolie does. But at least Yolie pretends to make conversation before she goes for the jugular. My dad doesn't waste any time.

"I—" My mother looks as if she's prepared to take one of her rare stands against my father.

"Really, *Mamá*. Trust me. It's OK." I smile at her and at my dad. I'll rent a big-ass car that uses lots of gas. Something foreign. Maybe a pink car, if I can find one in this town.

"I don't see why you should spend the money." My mother passes a stick of margarine.

"I'll expense it. No big deal. And, after I get back, we can go shopping. Just you and me, *Mamá*." I tilt my head and smile beatifically at my father. He digs into his ham steak and doesn't say another word.

Ass cancer, for sure.

58

Letti

After breakfast I take a cab to the closest Avis and rent a convertible. A red convertible, just to make sure my father and Yolie won't miss it. I was considering checking into a hotel later today, but now that I've been annoyed by them, I think I'll stay and flounce around the house and give them both heartburn.

Since it's too early to go to the gym—I can't possibly exercise for three hours—I drive by my old high school and the yogurt shop where I last worked before leaving for college. I swing by my high school boyfriend's house and have to speed away when his mother steps out to water her plants.

I drive by my high school best friend's house and get out. I haven't called to say I'm coming, and we haven't spoken for years, but this type of transgression isn't considered rude to most Latinos. What would be rude is if I didn't stop by at all.

I knock on the door and take a step back. Her mom, Keeka, comes to the door and peers out.

"Hello?" She sounds suspicious. I wonder if I look as if I'm selling bogus insurance policies or something.

"Hi! It's me. Jacquelyn. Letti's friend? From high school?"

"Oh, Jacquelyn! Come in! Letti will be so surprised. Let me go get her. She's in back with the baby."

"She's here?" I had assumed Letti would be at her own place, or even at work, not still living with her mom. And definitely not at her parents' with a kid.

"Sit down. Sit." Keeka moves a pile of fresh laundry off an armchair and physically takes me by the shoulders and lowers me onto it. "Letti! Letti! Guess who's here!"

From the kitchen, I hear some shuffling. Letti stops short and her mouth drops open. I get up, skip over and hug her tight.

"Oh, Jesus H. Christ. Jacqs! I must look a mess." And she does. My formerly trim friend has gained some weight, has let her hair get too long and shapeless, and is wearing saggy sweat pants and a tank top, with no boob support.

"Well, I assume it's because you just had a baby. I'll cut you some slack." I hug her tighter. "When did this happen?"

"Oh, about three years ago."

"Wow. Boy or girl?" I ask, hoping that Letti is so excited to see me that she doesn't notice I just agreed with her that she looks like crap.

"Girl. Her name is Brianna."

"Let me see her." Letti takes my arm and leads me back into her girlhood bedroom. She has the same nightstand and dresser, but has upgraded to a double bed, and wedged in the corner is a crib, complete with a sleeping toddler.

"She's asleep. She has a cold. Kept me up all night," Letti says as she takes a swipe at her hair and tucks it into an oversized clip.

"I can't believe you had a baby and didn't tell me!" I whisper. "This is so weird."

"Tell me about it." Letti sits on her bed. Her mom hovers in the kitchen. Letti kicks the door shut with her foot. "Christ. I can't wait to get out of here."

"What's going on?" I sit down next to her. I don't want to hear it. I've heard this story too often. I grew up hearing this story. So did Letti. I can't believe she didn't learn anything from it.

"Brianna's father is such a fuck. You wouldn't believe it. He won't pay child support. I had to move out of our apartment. He has a new girlfriend . . ." Letti rattles off her not-so-unique list of relationship complaints and, with each one, it feels as if another stone is settling on my shoulders. She seems resigned to her lot, though, and not looking for pity. "Same old shit."

"That sucks, Letti. Really." I feel like crying. I feel like getting on a plane and never, ever coming back. Ever.

"Whatever. So, tell me about you! I heard you got married. You bitch, why didn't you invite me?"

"Please, I eloped. I was temporarily insane. It's over and has been over for a while. Now I'm married to my vibrator."

Letti throws back her head and laughs and then springs up to see if she's woken up her kid. She pats Brianna on the back, makes soothing sounds and then settles down on the bed again.

"Man, same old Jacqs. Man . . . Remember we were going to be ZZ Top girls?"

"Don't remind me." We were obsessed with the women in the ZZ Top videos with their candy-colored pumps and ankle socks, short-short skirts and tank tops. They seemed to have the life of unbridled sexuality and a decidedly tacky but appealing fashion sense.

We look at each other and smile. Somewhere, buried underneath, I can still see the old Letti. I can't help but think that I look so much better than her. Her mother taps on the door.

"Yeah?" Letti calls out and rolls her eyes.

"Letti, you have to get to work. You can't be late."

"OK, Ma. Don't worry about it." Letti gets up and pulls out a waitress uniform from her closet.

I turn away and thumb through some magazine while she gets dressed, trying to stay out of my sight. When she's done, she leans over into the crib and kisses her sleeping daughter. I follow her out into the living room.

"Do you need a ride?" I offer before I realize how snobby this sounds. Just because she has a kid, no man and lives with her parents doesn't mean she doesn't have a car.

"Nah. The fucker kept the apartment, but I kept the car."

"Good for you, girl. Good for you."

59

Noel

After that dose of reality, I drive to my brother's gym and sit in the parking lot for forty-five minutes, crying. No one wants my pity, I'm sure of that, but all the same I feel so bad. I also realize that I could just as easily be living at home with a kid and a dead-end job, more dead-end than the one I have now.

I pat my face dry and look in the mirror. I look blotchy but not too bad. Who cares? I'm done showing off.

I show the receptionist my pass, put my stuff in a rental locker and head for the treadmills. With my earphones clapped on, I can space out for the next sixty minutes before exhaustion forces me to stop and stretch.

As I'm running, I catch sight of my brother meandering around equipment and people, carrying a stepladder and wearing a tool belt. Women stop to talk to him and he gives them an easy smile. I purse my lips like Yolie and keep running.

I take a shower, enjoying the fact that I don't have to ration my time or hot water as I have to at my parents', and spend a lot of time doing my hair and makeup so I don't look as if I've invested a lot of time on my hair and makeup. At exactly 12:30, I find my brother waiting for me by the front desk.

"Hey, Jacqs! Come meet my boss." Noel looks happy and relaxed. "This is my gorgeous little sister, Jacquelyn."

"Hi. Nice to meet you." I stick out my hand and it's crushed by a very muscled and tanned man in his early forties. Or maybe late thirties. The tan makes it hard to tell.

"How did a bum like your brother wind up with a sister like you?"

"Luck, I guess." I don't appreciate him calling my brother a bum, even if I'm almost sure he's just being affectionate.

"Going out to lunch. Back in a few days," Noel jokes and takes me by the scruff of the neck and leads me out.

"We can take my car," I say, not giving Noel a chance to protest.

"Oh, man, a convertible!" Noel has always had a thing for cars. His biggest aspiration has been to lease a new car every eighteen months.

"Here," I say, tossing him the keys. I didn't put him on the rental agreement, but I'm sure nothing will happen. "Just don't crash, kill us or dent the car in any way."

"Not to worry, *hermanita*. Top is coming down! Is that OK?" he asks.

"Sure." Actually, I hate riding around in convertibles with the top down, and it's about a hundred degrees, but Noel looks so happy, I think I can bear it for the ride to and from Tommy's.

Noel spends the next five minutes adjusting the seat, tilting the steering wheel and messing with the mirrors while I sit in the blazing sun trying not to complain. Just when I think I can't take it, he starts the car and hits the button to put the top back up.

"It's too hot to keep the top down," he says, and then punches me on the shoulder. "You're as pale as *Abuelita* Chela."

"I am not!" *Abuelita* Chela was my mother's mother. A bitter old woman who never wore anything but black and never went out in the sun without a hat. She powdered her face like a death mask and never wore lipstick—or rouge, as she called it—because she said only whores did.

"Just kidding. Come on, let's blow this joint and hit the road!" Noel says a little too happily. I become instantly suspicious.

"What's your problem?"

"Giselle broke up with me last night." He props his elbow out the window.

"She did not! Why? What did you do?" We stop at a red light behind a delivery truck.

"Nothing." Noel adjusts his seat yet again and runs his hand over the dashboard.

"Stop molesting my rental car. What do you mean *nothing?*"

"She wants to get married and I don't. So, nothing." Noel runs his hands along the steering wheel. I give him a hard look. "OK, man, you're just as bad as *Mamá*. Her sister is getting married and Giselle has marriage on the brain, but I told her I'm not ready yet."

"Are you not ready or do you not want to marry *her?*"

"What's the difference?" Noel expertly changes lanes and passes the truck. I relax a little. I haven't let anyone but Danny drive me around in a long time.

"Noel. You can't be that dense. There's a huge difference. Huge." I dig through my bag for some lip balm.

"I don't know," he says. But I know he does. He doesn't want to marry her and he has no way of telling her that without hurting her feelings and devastating both her and our parents, who have been hoping for something to come of the years they've been together. "Anyway, I'm sure once she cools off, we'll be cool again."

"You really should figure it out, Noel," I say, making a vow to stop counseling any more family members after this.

"I will. Don't worry about it."

He says this in a tone of voice I've heard him use with authority figures he's grown tired of. He pulls into the parking lot of the Eagle Rock Tommy's but doesn't get out. I can tell he's waiting for me to continue my mini-tirade. When I don't, he gets out and comes over to my side of the door and opens it.

"Man, I'm going to have one of everything," I say, and I'm pretty serious, too. It's been a long time since anyone has offered me something straight from the heart.

"Like I said, it's all on me, little sister." He smiles at me. "I always told you I'd take care of you. Only the best for my favorite sister."

"Thanks, Noel." I lean over and plant a kiss on his cheek. "For everything."

We get out of the car and line up on the pavement behind the construction workers, parents with grubby kids who are melting under the sun, and people who've driven over from the smattering of offices and stores in the area.

"So I'm supposed to ask you if you're seeing anyone," Noel says and takes a huge step back and hold his hands up defensively. "Don't hit me!"

"Fuck, can't Mom just leave me alone?" The woman in front of me shoots me a dirty look and peers down at her kid. She thinks she's Mother-of-the-Year material by feeding her child hamburgers, fries and soda. Gimme a break, lady.

"She's just worried, Jacqs. You know how she is." Noel stares off to the side.

"What? Are you worried about me, too? That I'm not married, pregnant and bitching in the kitchen about my lousy husband?" That's about the extent of marriage as far as she's taught me. I feel like a shit even thinking it. "Tell her that I'm fine."

"That's what I told her, but she doesn't believe me. She says . . . She says you look sad and sound sad on the phone." Noel shifts from foot to foot, a nervous habit of his, and mine.

"I'm happy. Perfectly happy," I lie.

"I ran into Nate." Noel looks at me over his sunglasses. We edge up a spot.

"Oh." My heart thumps in my chest. My brother has expanded his bubble a bit more than my family. "When?"

"A couple of months ago." Noel steps up to the window and orders for the both of us.

"That's nice." I grab a fistful of paper towels and fish some chili peppers out of the container near the ketchup dispenser, making sure to take only the fat ones. "Remember when Tommy's didn't serve fries? I was so surprised when we came and—"

"That's nice?" Noel steps off to the side to let the next person order. "That's all you can say?"

"OK, fine. Did he mention me?" Stupid question, of course he did.

"Nah, not really. He seemed a little busy . . . He was with someone."

Noel watches for my reaction. I already had it so he's not in luck.

"A woman?" I have to ask. What normal ex-wife wouldn't?

"Yeah. Nothing special." Noel turns around to collect our tray of food.

"Thanks." I can't help but smile. "I, uh . . ."

My brother has always been honest with me, to a fault. I've always kept secrets from him, from my whole family. I suppose Dr. N would say I do this because I'm afraid they won't like me if I let them see the real me, whoever that is. I lower my eyes, feeling icky. God, I'm a terrible person.

"What?" Noel sits down at a two-person picnic table under an awning.

"I'm seeing someone." I pick up my burger, peeling the paper away from the gloopy chili sauce. "You can tell Mom, but that's all I'm saying."

"He a nice guy?" Noel asks around a mouthful of food.

"Sure." It's usually all my family ever wants to know about my boyfriends since I left home and they finally realized they couldn't control who I consorted with. "Don't get her hopes up. I'm sure it won't work out, long-term, I mean."

"That's the spirit!" Noel salutes me with a ketchup-drenched fry.

"You should talk."

My mother, especially, has pressured all her children to marry. Especially Noel, who she thinks needs constant taking care of that only a mother or a mother-approved wife can provide. Poor Giselle, so close—but, unfortunately, she wasn't aiming to marry my mother, but her son.

"We just want you to be happy, Jacqs. All of us." Noel looks at me significantly. "You know in our own way, we all love you. Even Yolie."

I blink back tears and stare off into the busy street. Of course my family loves me, but I'm guessing they don't think I love them.

60

Passenger B6

On the plane back to San Francisco, I try not to think too much about home. My parents' home, that is. Time with my family always shows me the flip side of life.

Even though I was quick to run away from everything I knew growing up and use my past as a barometer for my present, I have the feeling life would have been much easier if I would have fallen in line like the rest of my siblings and cousins. Easier, yes, but better? I guess I'll never know.

I pretend to be absorbed in the in-flight magazine to avoid any chance of conversation with the woman sitting next to me. From her outfit—a tasteful black pantsuit and expensive shoes—I can tell she's a business type. Her carry-on is large and unfussy and she's wearing what looks like a Rolex, but it might be a good fake.

"I'm so excited. Do you have family in San Francisco or are you visiting?" she asks.

"Live there." I turn my head only slightly to face her. I don't want to be rude, but I'm not in a chatty mood at the moment.

"I'm going to get married in San Francisco! I am here to scout out some locations and meet with a planner."

"Oh. That's nice." Another bride I have to deal with.

"Our families are coming from all over the country. I haven't seen most of them in years. Years." She smoothes her expensively cut hair.

"Oh."

"My fiancé couldn't take time off work. Would you like to see a picture?" She pulls out a Coach leather photo book that matches her bag.

She makes sure to hand me the album with her left hand. I hadn't noticed her ring finger, hadn't actually looked for it, but now that she mentions she's engaged, I steal a glance at it. It's very modern, a thick band with a big stone set into it. Something I'd never pick.

"Sure." I flip it open to the first page and count five seconds before I turn to the next photo.

"We're both lawyers."

"That must be convenient." Her fiancé looks like a nice guy, if a little bland.

"The prenup was a snap. Not the nightmare our friends had predicted."

"Oh, that's nice." I turn back to the album and get to vacation photos. They're on some island beach, wearing linen shorts and shirts, with their feet in the water, a picture-perfect sunset behind them. He's sunburned.

"That's right after we got engaged. It was a total surprise. He whisked me off for a weekend in Cabo San Lucas."

"How romantic." Is it possible to whisk a lawyer off anywhere? I guess it's time to acknowledge the Ring. "That's a lovely ring. Tiffany's?"

"Etiole." She holds up her hand and the diamond catches the light and sparkles madly, just as a diamond should. "To tell you the truth"—she leans in closer to me—"I don't really like it. I would have preferred the traditional Tiffany setting. You know, the one with the round stone?"

"Yeah, I know that one." So does Bethany Michel.

"But, oh well!" She tucks the album back into her bag and sets it under the seat in front of her as we were instructed to do.

"Soon you won't even notice it's not the ring you always wanted." I smile at her hastily and she beams back. She's too happy to notice my sarcasm.

61

Dr. N

"And how did that make you feel?"

I stare at Dr. N. In all our sessions, she's never asked that, something I consider a pat shrink question. A TV-shrink question. It's not so much a question as an utterance resembling a sentence, a string of words masquerading as a question. It's the equivalent of asking a person how their day is going without the slightest interest in hearing anything other than "Fine."

I sit there debating whether I should ask her if she's bored with me or if I should try to really consider, for once, how all this stuff really makes me feel.

"Jacquelyn? How did your aunt insinuating that you might be a bad influence on her daughter make you feel?"

"A little bad, but at the same time, it was really, really satisfying." Mostly I felt like such an evil little snot, and a horrible person. This is way too personal to share with Dr. N. Especially after the "how did that make you feel" crap. "It made me feel like doing something you know is bad, but you don't care because it makes you feel good. You know?"

I have time to fill and Dr. N charges for a full hour no matter how little of it is taken up with actual therapy.

"Do you find that you go out of your way to shock your family? Your friends?" Dr. N asks, sounding only mildly interested.

I notice she said "shock," not "impress." Neither sounds too healthy, either way. I was only trying to show Lina that there is another way. There always is another way, no matter what they told us in Church.

"I don't know. Sure. Why would I want to do that? I just was playing, you know, devil's advocate. Or something like that."

This is my first session with Dr. N since I flirted with Mr. Mayor, found out my ex-husband is getting married, counseled my timid, pregnant cousin to give her mother the finger and got a new roommate in the despondent Vivian. We haven't even touched on the issues about my nonrelationship with my father, how my mother inspires equal amounts of love and frustration in me, and why it pains me to think of my brother stuck in a dead-end job that he obviously enjoys. So far, all we've talked about is how pissed off I am at everyone. Now I can add Dr. N to that list.

"So, how does that make you feel?" Dr. N asks as if she's on psychiatrist autopilot.

"It makes me want to shoplift," I lie.

"Really?" Now she's paying attention. "Shoplift?"

"Yeah, some trashy underwear. And then go out to a bar and pick up a guy. A couple of guys." This is less of a lie, more of a fantasy I know I'll never act upon.

"And what do you think that would accomplish?" Dr. N asks, sitting up straighter.

"Then, I guess, I'd be the bad girl everyone makes me out to be. Then they'd see what I'm capable of." I steal a glance at the timer; only a minute or so to go. "Maybe I'd even film it with Bina's camcorder. I could sell it on the Web. I've always wanted to be my own boss, have my own business, you know."

This is the juicy stuff Dr. N has probably been dying to hear. I'm sure her days are filled with boring people and their boring problems. This is the kind of stuff shrinks talk to other shrink friends about when they get together at the local cafe. ("A patient of mine is going off the deep end—is that my half-skim, no-foam latte?")

"Jacquelyn? Why do you think shoplifting and risky sex will

make you feel better?" Finally, she's really interested in what I have to say. "Don't you think you'd just be hurting yourself?"

"Hurting myself by having some sex? I'd use condoms. I'm not crazy, but I do feel like doing something . . ." I watch Dr. N's mouth part in anticipation. "Something *reckless*."

"I find this very interesting—" The timer chimes. Dr. N fumbles for it.

"That's all the time we have, huh? See you in a week or so. Thanks." I rush out, not giving her a chance to answer. I've never actually lied to Dr. N before. I'm guilty of the sin of omission, but this is different. This is outright lying.

Maybe I'll cancel my next appointment, with twenty-four hours' notice of course, to keep her in anticipation of my fictional downward spiral.

Whatever.

62

Megan

The Mayors are arriving in a couple of hours and I need to make sure the Mansion is ready for them. Fresh flowers, some food in the fridge and all the silverware accounted for.

Megan, from French Tulip, the Mayors's favorite florist, has promised the arrangements will be delivered by 4:30. I speed there, relieved to see the delivery van parked outside.

I love flowers. Just love them. They are so beautiful, varied and temporary. You have to enjoy them while you have them because, in a week or so, they'll be tossed out. I once toyed with the idea of getting a job as a florist, but when I found out I'd have to hit the flower mart at 4:00 AM, I quickly reconsidered my career choices.

"Hey, Jacquelyn!" Megan is plucking off stray leaves and dropping them and imperfect petals into a bucket at her feet. It's amazing how much of the actual flower never makes it into the final arrangement. "You like?"

"These look great, Megan."

I hang out, watching her, pretending to smell the flowers. It helps me postpone having to go pretend to supervise the cleaning. I don't like standing over Anita and Lei, making sure they aren't leaving streaks on windows or creases in the linen. That's Mrs. Mayor's forte. It just makes me uncomfortable.

The Mansion has been empty, except for Danny, so there isn't any heavy-duty cleaning to do. Anita and Lei get an unpaid vacation each time the Mayors go out of town. Danny gets to stay to keep an eye on things even though they have a security service. For some reason, the Mayors trust Danny more than they do their cleaning staff who washes their underwear and knows what kind of dental floss they use.

"Almost done," answers Megan. "Don't worry, we'll have plenty of time to put them in the perfect place."

"Thanks, Megan." Mrs. Mayor has designated spots for arrangements and they're all color-coded. Megan knows to stick with the color pallet, height requirements and all the other persnickety details Mrs. Mayor insists upon.

"So, did you like the flowers?" Megan asks.

"Flowers?"

"From . . ." Megan lowers her voice and looks around. In her business, she has to be discreet. "Your friend George? The Rustique roses? He mentioned you specifically, that you got all your flowers from us."

"Oh. Oh! Those. Yeah. Thanks, they were beautiful. Thanks." George couldn't have sent me flowers; he knew I was out of town.

"Not a problem." She goes back to fluffing flowers. "Special order, too. Lucky girl."

George told me his wife is allergic to roses and he knows I love Rustiques. I told him how elegant and unique they were, with their slight pink blush, compared with boring red roses. Red roses are so high school and, since I was miserable in high school, the last thing I'd ever want is a couple dozen long-stemmed reminders from a boyfriend. But, lucky for me, my boyfriend would never send me stupid red roses. In fact, he hasn't sent *me* any roses at all. Ever, in the whole six weeks we've known each other.

"Yes, I am. A very lucky girl."

63

Bina

I shut the door firmly behind me and pick up my phone and dial Bina's cell. She picks up on the first ring.

"Sanjay?" Bina asks. Crap. Sounds as if they've had a fight.

"Sorry, it's just me. Your best friend." I put my feet up on my desk. We are due for a long talk. I'd rather do this in person over cheesy nachos and boozy margaritas, but I'm not sure she has the time or emotional capacity to deal with me when her fiancé is obviously foremost in her thoughts. How selfish. "Is everything OK?"

"Yes. No. Sanjay is just being a dick. We had a fight," Bina admits.

Lately she's been more comfortable talking about Sanjay's faults and, lucky for her, I'm an eager audience.

"Wedding related?" I really don't have to ask; the wedding is all they talk about with each other. It's like they're two generals trying to strategize a very small military campaign.

Surprisingly, Sanjay has strong opinions on both their traditional Indian wedding in India and their traditional American wedding in Napa. Bina is as surprised as I am that Sanjay even cares. He's been nitpicking about everything from the choice of menu to the color scheme to the music selection. He's driving Bina batty. I feel for her, but what would you expect from a tax attorney? His life is all about tiny little details most people couldn't be bothered with until the IRS comes knocking at their door.

"He's complaining about the photographer! With such short notice, we're lucky to have gotten any photographer." Bina snorts.

"How about we get together for some nice midweek girl talk? Just you, me and some fattening food."

"Anything to get a break from Sanjay. Tomorrow night? Usual place?"

"See you there. Around 7:30. Bye!" I hang up and sit back, enjoying my last moments of peace and quiet.

I have to stick around until the Mayors come in, have dinner, wait for Anita and Lei to do the unpacking, check in one last time with Mrs. Mayor, and then finally I'll be free to go back to my flat . . . and Vivian.

64

Vivian

She keeps up a brave face, but I can tell Vivian is miserable. She tiptoes around the flat as if she's trying to be invisible, but it only makes me more aware that she's there.

It's been only a week, but each time we talk, she assures me that she'll find a new place and be out of my hair as soon as possible. Then I assure her not to stress, that I love having the company and for her to take her time. Then there's a brief silence and we move on to talk about work. Never about Curtis and never Nate.

I've even kept the fridge stocked with a couple of bottles of white wine, but Vivian's preferred mode of comfort turns out to be Chips Ahoy! dipped in Cool Whip. She carefully stacks a pile of about five cookies on a plate and then fills a small bowl with Cool Whip and dips and munches while she reads the morning paper and goes through her day planner. At night, it's almost the same routine: five cookies, small bowl of Cool Whip, magazine, day planner.

When I go to bed, she'll still be at the kitchen table, nibbling. Most mornings I find an empty cookie bag in the trash and the plastic container rinsed out and in the recycling bin. She's going through a bag of cookies and a tub of Cool Whip a day. Every day. But otherwise she seems perfectly normal, if a little sad.

We go out together, shop together, watch TV at night, eat dinner here and there. It's as if we're regular roommates, and I kind of like it. Even Bina is happy with it. She's been coming over and hiding out from Sanjay with us to eat take-out.

To deal with her Sanjay stress, Bina has stepped up her hair-removal regimen. It's become her obsession. The more difficult Sanjay becomes, the more hair Bina decides she has to remove. She's even talking about cutting her hair short.

My postrelationship neurosis was a little harder to keep private. I developed the incessant and irrepressible desire to yawn. No matter how rested I felt, I would break out into a yawn, a huge lioness-on-the-Serengeti yawn. I could be in the middle of an animated conversation with a guy I found attractive, and then all of a sudden—*bam!*—and the poor guy would sit there blinking while I resumed talking as if nothing had happened.

After a while, I realized that this was my brain's way of telling me not to date. So I stopped dating and almost instantly resumed a normal yawning pattern. This is why I think it's working out with George. Since there really is no chance for a long-term, committed relationship, I don't have the subconscious desire to signal my romantic apathy to him by yawning and making him think I find him incredibly boring.

I dial Vivian on my cell.

"Hey, Jacqs, what's their ETA?" At work, Vivian is all business. Though she told me people have been whispering behind her back, they've kept it pretty quiet, especially since the Mayor is backing her a hundred percent.

"About five, ten minutes. How's everything down there?"

"Chaotic, but nothing out of the ordinary. Mr. Mayor is going to have a very busy day tomorrow. You should let Mrs. Mayor know he won't be making it home for dinner. He's got a dinner thing."

Mr. Mayor has had a lot of these vague "dinner things" Mrs. Mayor hasn't been invited to. That's probably one of the reasons she might think that he's boinking someone else. It's what I would assume. But I know Mrs. Mayor has plans of her own for tomorrow, since she had me arrange an afternoon in-home colonic and delivery of organic wheatgrass and carrots, which Lei will prepare throughout the day to help the process along.

"She'll be fine."

"Don't make me laugh. I'm supposed to be the impassive public-relations person." Vivian sounds as if she hasn't laughed in a very long time.

"Speaking of which, Vivian, I was wondering if you want to come out tomorrow night with me and Bina?"

"Oh, what better way to spend an evening than with the doctor with incredible skin and hair?" Like most redheads, Vivian envies anyone with melanin that doesn't come from a bottle. "I don't know . . . Mr. Mayor might need something."

Vivian has been keeping close to work or my place in hopes that Curtis will come to his senses and beg for her forgiveness.

"What? He's going to need you to put out a press release that he farted at dinner? Come on, it'll be fun. I won't stop bugging you until you say yes."

"OK. Fine. Mr. Mayor can handle his own fart issues for one night."

"Amen, sister." I glance in my planner and see it's pretty light for the rest of the week. This is good and not good. Usually Mrs. Mayor has activities planned at least two weeks in advance. When she has a lot of time on her hands, she tends to get listless and mopes around their 5000-square-foot Mansion, which annoys Mr. Mayor, mostly because she always manages to do it in his vicinity.

Hopefully something will pop up to keep me busy and out of her way for a few days.

"You there, Jacqs?" Vivian sounds sad and vulnerable.

"Yeah." I wait. It's time for her to spill her guts.

"I . . . nothing. OK. See you later."

She clicks off, not giving me a chance to say good-bye.

65

The Mayors

The flower arrangements are in place, the Mansion is dust-free, the yard picture-perfect and dinner—sushi, per Mrs. Mayor's request from the car on their way from the airport—will be delivered shortly.

Now we wait.

I linger in the front hall, trying not to peek out the window. Lei and Anita have disappeared into the small room off the Kitchen that serves as their "office" where they're eating (in silence) dinner. Lei some noodle thing and Anita some rice thing that they heated up in the microwave. Their smallish TV is tuned to QVC, the only channel they can both agree upon.

I am debating giving my nails a quick file and buff when I see the car pull into the garage at a good clip. Danny must be in a hurry to get back to his porn.

I check my watch. The sushi won't be here for another 10 minutes or so. Hopefully Mrs. Mayor won't be expecting to sit down right away for her dinner.

The door opens and Mr. Mayor steps aside so Mrs. Mayor can step in before him. I try and gauge Mrs. Mayor's mood. Not easy, since she's wearing sunglasses.

"Welcome back. I hope you both had a nice trip," I say cheerily.

"Thanks, Jacquelyn. I'll be in my office." He kisses Mrs. Mayor on the cheek and grabs the cold beer from Anita who has materialized out of thin air.

"I'm famished, Jacquelyn. Is the sushi here?" Mrs. Mayor asks. It's obvious it isn't here, but I guess she can't keep herself from asking.

"Any second now."

"Will you have Lei and Anita do the unpacking? There are some things that need to be sent to the dry cleaner." Mrs. Mayor wanders into the living room, stopping to admire the flowers, still wearing her glasses, but that's not the reason she doesn't bother to address Lei and Anita directly, even though they are both helping Danny with the luggage and numerous shopping bags.

Lei gives me a curt nod and they head up the back stairs into the dressing area where they'll be busy for the next hour or so. I wonder if Mrs. Mayor will be nice enough to offer Danny's services to get them home. If not, I will.

"Jacquelyn, come in here and tell me how your family is? It feels like ages since I last saw you."

Is Mrs. Mayor drunk or on drugs? She's a bitch, yes, although she can be pleasant, but I've never known her to be this human.

"Sure. Let me get us something to drink." Hey, if she's going to be all chummy with me, I may as well get comfortable.

I grab a plastic bottle of water and two glasses and put them on a rattan tray. *So* not the Baxter way, but I doubt Mrs. Mayor will notice.

Mrs. Mayor is perched on one of the couches flipping through her mail.

"Oh, wonderful. Is the sushi here yet?"

"Any second now. Lei has set up the dining room. Would you care to eat somewhere else?"

"Hmmm. No. That will be fine." She lethargically flips through a magazine. "It's so good to be back."

"Did you have a nice time?" I try not to stare as I pour the water, but she's still wearing her sunglasses and it really is starting to bug me.

"Oh, it was wonderful." She makes a move to lift them up, but then the doorbell rings and she clamps them back firmly on the bridge of her nose.

"That'll be the sushi. Excuse me."

I rush to the door, pay the guy and as soon as I turn around Anita is there to take the food out of my hands. Without a word she heads into the dining room.

"Thanks, Anita."

"Jacquelyn, I'm going upstairs to change," Mrs. Mayor calls over her shoulder.

"Sure. I'll let you both know when everything is ready." I wander into the dining room and stand off to the side to make sure Anita doesn't set out my order of sushi with the Mayors's.

"Mrs. Mayor, she has a black eye," Anita states impassively. She and Lei call Mrs. Mayor "Mrs. Mayor" because that's what they think she should be called.

"Pardon me?" First of all, I'm floored that Anita actually spoke to me and, second, what the hell did she just say? "What did you just say?"

"A black eye. Danny told me." She doesn't look up from where she's refolding the napkins.

"One or two? Because if it's two maybe she had, I don't know, her eyes done. By a doctor." This is not out of the question, but unlikely since Mrs. Mayor would have been more than comfortable having me arrange it for her.

"No. One eye. The left." Anita is a fount of information.

"Does he know how this happened?"

"No. Dinner is ready." Anita leaves me gripping the back of a silk-upholstered dining room chair and with my chin on the floor.

Could Mr. Mayor have hit her? Could he have hit her so hard that she has brain damage and that's why she's being so weird? Not to be sexist, but what the hell could Mrs. Mayor have done that was so bad that he'd pop her in the eye?

I head over to Mr. Mayor's office door and knock. I can hear his muffled voice on the phone, most likely with Vivian. I knock again. After a few seconds the door opens.

"Hi. Jacquelyn. Come in." He looks tired but he manages to

give me a friendly smile. Come in! Have they both been inhabited by aliens?

"Actually, Mr. Mayor, I just came to tell you that dinner is ready."

"Oh. OK. Thanks." He sighs.

"I'll be right back. I just have to check on something downstairs, I mean, upstairs." I scamper toward the staircase and hope he doesn't say anything.

Upstairs the door is ajar to their bedroom. Anita and Lei are busy in the dressing room sorting and storing. Mrs. Mayor is nowhere in sight.

"Where is she?" I whisper to Anita and Lei. Anita shrugs and Lei gestures toward the closed bathroom door. "Is she OK?"

"She's in there with her cosmetic case," Lei says.

This whole thing doesn't seem to bother Anita. Maybe she's used to domestic abuse. I wouldn't be surprised. Though I've never met her family, or even heard her talk about a husband or anything, she seems like the downtrodden type. Kind of like my mom, though I know my dad would never hit my mom. If he did we'd kick his ass, at least I would.

I go to the door and knock softly. Out of the corner of my eye I catch sight of a pair of chocolate brown suede boots. They look like they feel like butter. They must be new, because they weren't here when we left for Carmel. I reach over—

"Yes?" Mrs. Mayor asks in a startled voice. I can hear the water running.

"Dinner is ready. The Mayor is down in the dining room," I say, not taking my eyes off the boots.

"Oh, thanks, Jacquelyn. I'll be down in a moment."

I turn around to look for some support, but Lei ducks her head and pretends to be absorbed in sorting the Mayor's dirty socks. Anita narrows her eyes and shrugs again. I guess they figure that since I get paid more I should deal with this on my own.

I hear Mrs. Mayor's heels clack on the marble floor and before the knob turns I bolt out of there and down the stairs and straight into my office.

Anita has set up my sushi on my desk, but I'm too weirded out to even think of eating.

I sit at my desk and rub my chopsticks against each other, even though they're silver-monogrammed chopsticks. Mrs. Mayor got a set of about 20 for a wedding gift and insists Anita and Lei set them on the table any time any vaguely chopsticky food is served. Along with the porcelain chopstick rests, of course.

I look at my place setting and it's all too perfect. A plain white china plate of the highest quality rests on a handwoven rattan place mat with a soy-sauce dish precisely at the one o'clock position, a linen napkin in its silver-monogrammed ring (Mrs. Mayor is big on monogramming—anything with a surface has their initials on it) on the left and my sushi set on a coordinating sushi plate anchoring it all at twelve o'clock.

This is Mrs. Mayor's life, the image of perfection. It's like living at a hotel 24 hours a day where everything runs smoothly and you never think about how your bed gets turned down, or how fresh fluffy towels appear in your bathroom each day. It's all very numbing and not at all unpleasant.

Why did she have to go and bring her black eye into the picture?

I expertly grab a roll—I used to use my fingers but when I got a load of the silver chopsticks I learned quickly—and pop it into my mouth and chew. And chew and chew.

66

Tía Carmen

My cell phone rings. It can't be Mrs. Mayor since she'd never do this while around Mr. Mayor. He would not approve of her speed dialing me when we are under the same roof. Sometimes when Mrs. Mayor wants something quick she uses the intercom and it never fails to scare the bejesus out of me to hear her voice echo throughout the Mansion. This is also frowned on by Mr. Mayor. (How he can overlook the fact that his own mother uses a buzzer to summon the help is beyond me.) If his wife wants to speak to me, she can very well have Anita or Lei fetch me.

I let it ring two more times. Rice is sticking to the roof of my mouth, but I'm not about to spit out an $8 piece of abalone.

"Hello, this is Jacquelyn." I wipe my face even though no one can see me.

"Jacqs, it's me, Noel."

"What's wrong? Is *Mamá* OK?" I ask, feeling panic rise in my throat. I don't know why, but I've been waiting for this call since I moved away. I guess I figured since I am not there, my mom would be bound to have some sort of accident or get sick and die with me not there to save her.

I secretly have an outfit picked out to wear: a black grosgrain knee-length pencil skirt and jacket with a notched collar and a ribbon-tie front. If she's in the hospital, I'll need something more casual and comfortable, since I'd expect to be there for a while, but not too casual. (One thing I've learned from my time with Mrs. Mayor is that people take you way more seriously if you're dressed well.) Dr. N says there is nothing really wrong with preselecting an outfit for your mother's funeral, even if she is still alive. She says it's a coping mechanism.

"No, Mom's OK. It's Carmen. She's had a stroke," Noel says in a flat voice.

He never liked *Tía* Carmen either. She was the one who ratted him out to our mom about his smoking. She reduced my mom to tears, granted not a hard thing to do, by going on about lung cancer and everything else that was going to happen to Noel if she didn't make him quit the instant he got home from his afterschool job at Burger King.

"A stroke? You're kidding me." I feel a tinge of, not concern necessarily, or even remorse, but fear for my soul. I don't know how many times I've wished something bad would happen to her because she's just so mean. Now that something *finally* has I have to assume I've had something to do with it.

"Does Lina know?" There are tons of hotels in Las Vegas and unless Lina was wishy-washy enough to tell them where she's staying, she could enjoy a relatively peaceful honeymoon.

"*Tía* Carmen was on the phone with Lina when it happened."

"Of course she was." What would be the purpose of having a stroke if you couldn't have it on the phone talking to your guilt-ridden daughter?

"How is Dad taking it?" For some reason our dad always deferred to her and expected us to treat this particular aunt with the utmost respect.

"He's upset, saying how she was a second mother to him," Noel says in a tight voice. Even though he still lives with my father he isn't any closer to him than I am.

"Well, that explains a lot of his problems." I hear Noel start to laugh and cover it up with a bout of fake coughing. "How about Mom?"

"You know Mom. Saying how terrible it is and how she'll be

next . . . Yolie wants to talk to you," Noel says quickly and next thing I know Yolie's voice is in my ear.

"Have you heard."

This is not a question, but a statement. Yolie obviously has her suspicions as to who is responsible for the stroke. And it's not *Tia* Carmen's fatty diet or that stick up her ass, it's me. Always me.

"Of course I did. Noel just told me. Is she OK?" I have to ask, I suppose.

"She's in the hospital. Did you know that Lina went to Las Vegas to get married?" Yolie asks, not accusingly, but she's ready to cast her stones.

"Married! Tell her congratulations from me and let me know where she registered. I can't make it for any party, I just got back. Really busy here at work." This should let Yolie know that if I won't come home for my favorite cousin, I sure as hell am not climbing on a plane to see *Tía* Carmen. The woman is Satan in stretch pants. Stroke or no stroke.

"And she's pregnant," Yolie says. I can almost see how saying it twists her mouth.

"Who is? *Tía* Carmen?" I ask stupidly. I enjoy jerking Yolie around and so does she. It gives her a concrete reason to dislike me and I am only too happy to oblige.

"You don't feel bad at all! Do you!" Yolie yells. I can see her working up into a fine tirade. I need to nip this in the bud. I don't need to hear what an awful, selfish person I am because I'm not prostrate with grief after hearing such unshocking news.

I clear my throat and say, as calmly and reasonably as possible without betraying the laughter building in my chest, "I didn't give her the stroke. God did."

Yolie slams down the phone in my ear and I go back to eating my sushi with a renewed appetite.

67

Terry

I've been in the Mansion all morning and have not once talked to Mrs. Mayor face-to-face. She has ensconced herself in a converted bedroom, as big as my living room, featuring a custom-built massage table and dubious therapeutic equipment, where the colonic technician has set up her butt-cleaning device.

When the butt tech, a supremely calm woman named Terry, comes out after giving Mrs. Mayor her flush, I can't help but ask if she noticed anything odd about Mrs. Mayor.

"Well, now that you mention it . . ." Terry looks around to make sure Mrs. Mayor isn't lurking around. "She seems to have had a lot of dairy. Much more than usual. It was all clotted—"

"OK! No, I mean about her . . . anything about her face?"

"Her skin is a bit congested, but I'm sure that'll clear up now that we got most of the cheese out of her."

"How about her eyes?" I ask before Terry goes any further. She can talk shit all day, but not the kind of shit I want to hear about. I know it from personal experience because she once, ONCE, gave me a colonic and she described in detail all the crap she was hosing out of my ass.

"Her eyes? She had a compress over her eyes. To help her relax her sphincter muscles. She tends to get a little tense when I'm inserting the hose. Oh, damn, look at the time. I have a client in Pacific Heights. Make sure to keep her hydrated and keep that wheatgrass and carrot juice flowing. Hee hee. Get it? Flowing," Terry snickers. Terry makes colonic jokes every chance she gets.

"Yeah, thanks, Terry."

"And you should really come back for another colonic." She gently takes my chin in her hand and inspects my skin. "You're building up lots of toxins again. We'll have to give you an intense cleanse again if you wait any longer."

"I wouldn't want that. I'll check my schedule and give you a call," I lie. There is no way in hell I'm subjecting myself to the hose again.

68

Cortez

My cell phone rings, my personal phone that only Bina, Vivian, Natasha and my family call me on. A 415 area code and number I've never seen before pops up.

I can't take any more bad news, but I can't resist my curiosity either. "Hello?"

"*Señorita* Jacquelyn, *cómo estas?*"

"Emilio?" I'm so surprised I drop my jam-smeared croissant. It hits my desk with a sugary splat.

"A breakthrough! You do love me. Now, quit that job of yours and run away with me."

I can imagine him sitting back at his desk with his feet up while one sexy assistant massages his shoulders and another pops peeled grapes into his mouth.

"What do you want?" He must want something. Something big, because he's never called me before.

"I just called to see how you are doing, *linda*," he says in his husky voice, both of his accents pitch-perfect. He'd be great at phone sex. "There is nothing wrong with that, is there? A chat amongst *amigos*."

"My mother taught me to watch out for *amigos* like you."

"Smart woman. I'll send her some flowers. I heard Rustiques are very popular now."

There is an edge to his voice. He has the upper hand and knows it.

"I wouldn't know." My heart beats in my chest and I squirm around in my seat, and not just because he's on to something about flowers. It's been how long since I've had sex? With another person?

"Jacquelyn, you know I have nothing but the utmost respect for you as a fellow Latino in the trenches." I look around my cushy office scented with burning $75 scented French candles. "And I thought I'd come to you first as a friend before I run my column."

"I'm not a source, Cortez. Just because you gave me a bite of your overpriced waffles in Santa Barbara doesn't make us friends. Especially friends who share information *anonymously*." This should cover my ass in case this conversation is being recorded.

"Don't you want to know what I'm going to write?" He sounds surprised. I guess this is a first for him, a woman playing hard to get and not kidding about it.

"No. I don't. I don't even want to have this conversation with you, Cortez." I really don't. The less I know the better. I'm sure the Mayors already suspect me of being in league with Cortez. How else could they explain the leaks?

"I admire your loyalty to your boss, Jacquelyn. But perhaps it's misplaced. *Comprendes*?"

"I understand more than you know, Cortez. Just please . . ."

Please what? He's doing his job and I'm doing mine. It's the person between us that's making things easier for him and harder for me.

"*Sí?*" He sounds almost gentle. I suppose in his own way he understands my situation, even if he doesn't agree with it.

"Please don't use that one picture of her where one eye looks bigger than the other. It drives her crazy."

69

Mrs. Mayor

I knock on the door and wait.

"Jacquelyn, is that you?" Mrs. Mayor sounds drowsy and relaxed.

"Yes, do you need anything?" I am dying to get in there and check out her eye for myself, but since she didn't say come in and doesn't sound like she's in danger of having a heart attack or anything, I stay behind the closed door.

"Oh, now, I'm fine. Just have Lei and Anita send up some juice to my room."

"OK. I'll be in my office." I wait a few seconds but she doesn't answer back.

Down in the Kitchen, Anita and Lei are fixing all sorts of concoctions, from recipes Terry has provided, that will help detoxify Mrs. Mayor from the inside out. Everything is ultranatural and therefore almost inedible.

"She's ready for some more juice," I say to both of them. They've been taking turns trekking up stairs and I've lost track of who is next. I watch Anita push some grass through the juicer until it fills up a water glass. She wrinkles her nose and holds it as far away from her as possible and marches out of the Kitchen.

Lei then cleans out the juicer and goes back to stirring a pot of something vile that constitutes Mrs. Mayor's dinner.

"OK. I'll be in my office." I haven't done much all day. I did some shopping over the Internet. Called some friends. Watched some TV, read a book Mrs. Mayor wants me to summarize for her, buffed my nails and picked at my skin. All in all, I've led Mrs. Mayor's life and I've found it very boring.

I'm about to sit down when my phone rings. The call is coming from the master bedroom.

"Hello?"

"Jacquelyn, I'm all set here for tonight. You can dismiss Anita and Lei for the day. I'll see you all tomorrow. Have a good night." She hangs up.

"OK. Hello? OK." I look at my watch. It's not even noon. I wonder if I should remind her that Mr. Mayor is out late tonight and Danny is with him. After Anita and Lei leave, and aside from the security team outside, Mrs. Mayor will be all by herself in the Mansion. Something I know she hates.

Either way, it means I have some free time to go to the movies. My finger is poised above the keyboard to check movie listings when the phone rings again.

"Oh, it's me again," she says. Who else would it be? "Please make sure the security system is on before you leave."

"OK. Of course." I'm tempted to invite her out to dinner with me, Bina and Vivian, but can't make myself take that leap from boss to friend. Plus, it's not like she could eat real food. Plus, it would eliminate about one-third of what we usually talk about: her.

"Have a good night, Jacquelyn. See you tomorrow," she says drowsily into the phone and has a bit of trouble replacing the receiver.

"Good night, Mrs. Mayor."

70

Bina and Vivian

I'm starting my second drink, this one with booze, when Bina lays her head on my shoulder.

"I need a hug," she says despondently over the buzz of hetero voices at Absinthe, a terminally hip and crowded bar in the equally hip Hayes Valley. Bina takes off her jacket and sits down next to me. "Sanjay is driving me crazy. He thought tonight was my bachelorette party."

"Your what?" I ask, alarmed. Bina hasn't said anything about a party. Bridal shower, yes, but nothing about a bunch of women carousing around town drinking and being obnoxious, it seems very un-Indian of her. Though I know for a fact that all her Indian relatives, the women at least, like to party when away from their husbands.

"Don't worry. I'm not having one. Too many parties. Too much family. Too much stress. This wedding will be the death of me," she sighs.

Even working with a professional wedding planner hasn't alleviated any of the stress on Bina. Sanjay's new hobby is finding fault with the wedding planner's ideas, which he relays to Bina on an hourly basis.

"Is there anything I can do?" I'm in charge of little things, nothing too important, since Sanjay doesn't trust me. Number one on my list is keeping Bina as stress-free as possible so that's why I take any and every opportunity to get her away from Sanjay. And I wonder why he doesn't like me? Who cares, the feeling is more than mutual.

"Yes, get me drunk and fat so I won't remember the last few weeks and won't fit into my dress. Take that, Sanjay!" Bina jabs the air, her engagement ring sparkling.

"What the hell is Sanjay's problem now?" Vivian asks as she takes a seat opposite us.

"He's crazy. My crazy fiancé," Bina answers. "I heard you've been having man troubles, too."

I can feel my face flame up. To Bina everything is one big pelvic exam where one doesn't mince words.

"You can say that. The bastard is going through with this divorce." Vivian desperately tries to flag down our waiter. "I've had to go see a lawyer."

"At least the tire slashing hasn't gotten out," I say, trying to keep the conversation going. The press finally picked up on the story and anyone who bothers to read the local papers knows that the Mayor's sexy press secretary has been kicked out of her million-dollar loft by her tragically hip, magazine-publishing husband.

"That's all I'd need. More innuendo, rumors, scandal. I'd have an easier time of it if I was a vegan transsexual suing my sexual surrogate for custody of my conjoined twins."

"True." Bina pats Vivian's hand, doctor style.

"I'll just have to be invisible." Vivian looks doubtful.

Part of the problem is she's so attractive. In a city where wearing makeup automatically pegs you either as a tourist, from the South Bay or a department-store drone, Vivian stands out too much to fade into the background. Vivian can wander most streets in relative obscurity even though her face has been on TV and in the papers as the official spokesperson for the Mayor of San Francisco. But that was before gossip, juicy gossip was attached to her heartbreakingly beautiful face.

"They'll lose interest soon enough," I add untruthfully, but hopefully. "You know how people are here."

Both Bina and Vivian nod and sip their drinks.

San Franciscans have a combination of tunnel vision, apathy and an obsession with alternative media. Most people concern themselves with mass transit issues, homeless problems and dog rights, but on a one-to-one and block-by-block level. When they do set their sights on City Hall it's to complain, then they all turn out in hordes.

It's a beautiful thing.

I've done it myself—bitched and moaned about something or another, done nothing, weeks later spotted a flyer and found myself marching in the streets on a Saturday morning. Surrounded by the true populace of San Francisco, light-headed from the stink of body odor and pot smoke I could almost feel what the sixties were like, except for the regular pit stops for lattes and iced coffee and people handing out product samples on corners.

Some scandal concerning a public servant and a magazine visionary will barely be a blip on the radar screen of most San Franciscans. They like to think they're above it all.

"I don't care. I came here to get drunk." Vivian takes a sip of my drink.

"And I came here to get fat!" Bina yells.

A table full of young women cheer her on. Bina stands up and bows.

"Well, let's get to it." I open the menu and decide now is not the time to bring up Mrs. Mayor's black eye.

Many, many hours later we emerge feeling a lot better. I've almost managed to forget about Mrs. Mayor, and Bina and Vivian are arm in arm, singing the praises of single life.

"Are you OK to drive, Bina?" They both drank way more than me and I already convinced Vivian to let me drive us both home. "I think, to be on the safe side, I should drop you off at home. You and Sanjay can pick your car up in the morning."

"Sanjay who!" Bina yells.

"Woohoo!" Vivian yells even louder.

"OK. Let's all quietly walk, if you can, to my car. Bina! Keep your top on!" I usher them toward the parking garage and stuff them both in the backseat.

"Put that CD on, Jacqs. The one by that cute teenager," Bina slurs.

"Which teenager?" Vivian is still clumsily trying to fasten her seat belt.

"He's not a teenager." I have a not-so-secret thing for Justin Timberlake. Last month it was a newscaster on CNN. I went as far as to TiVo his broadcasts.

Since I got divorced and stopped dating I've found myself careening from one junior-high crush to another. I'm starved for romance and affection. But junior high was many years ago and I know real life will never live up to my fantasies.

"What teenager?" Vivian gives up on the seat belt and sticks her head and most of her torso in between the front seats. "Jacqs, have you made a man out of some young lucky teenager?"

"It's Justin Timberlake. He's cute, admit it. And young, and very fit." Maybe that's what I need. To go on some sexual mercy mission for some young, young guy, over eighteen but under twenty-one. I would be doing good while getting done. And I could help him with his geometry homework. I was a whiz at geometry.

"Oh, he is. Nice hairless chest," Vivian moans.

"He probably waxes it," Bina says sensibly. "I wish Sanjay would wax his. Or at least his back."

"Sanjay has a hairy back?" This is something I should already know by now. I would never have allowed things to get this far between Bina and Sanjay if I'd known.

"No. Just so he can see what real pain is."

"You're mean. I like that in a woman." Vivian reaches over and gives Bina a sloppy pat on the head. "Why don't we go over to my place, sorry, my former place, and tie up my soon-to-be ex-husband and wax the hair off his balls."

"Maybe another night, girls." I double-park outside of Bina's flat and help her out. I look up and see Sanjay in the window. I give him a cheerful wave but he ignores me. I heave Bina out of the car and can tell she has put on a few pounds since the last time I did this. "OK. Up we go!"

"No! Let's go dancing." Bina leans into me, grabbing my shoulders for support. "Remember how we used to go dancing, Jacqs? You're the best dancer. Hey, Vivian, did you know Jacqs is the best dancer . . . Vivian?"

We look into the backseat and stare for a moment at Vivian's passed-out figure.

"Well! Let me walk you to your door, Bina, my pet. I'm sure Sanjay will be eager to see you. Kiss, kiss. I'll call you tomorrow."

"You're the best friend a girl can have, Jacqs. I don't care what the fuck Sanjay says. That asshole," Bina says as she stumbles inside. She shuts the door without saying good-bye.

I get in the car and even though I know I should get Vivian home (she has a press conference in the morning), I start toward George's.

He's left me a few messages, but I've been avoiding calling him back since I found out about the flowers. I don't know what to think, but it's a safe assumption to make that if he'd "cheat" on his wife with me, he'd cheat on me with someone else.

If this is the case, I'm not sure what I should do. We never came out and said we'd exclusively see each other, even though I haven't been seeing anyone else. And it's not because I love George. I like him, sure, but it's more laziness on my part. George satisfied just about every need, except the sexual aspect of a relationship. And the monogamous-commitment part, and the emergency-contact part, but otherwise I've been perfectly content with our arrangement.

And, up until now, I thought he was, too. I'm funny, smart, sexy, interesting and even though I never said sex was out of the question, he just had to ask and I'd consider it. I'd need to really be in the mood. Maybe we'd get a room at the Ritz. And there'd have to be lots of flowers and maybe a thoughtful gift or two.

I know I should feel slightly appalled at myself for even considering this, but I don't. Why should I? I'm an adult. So is he.

He's the one who is married and I don't expect him to leave his wife for me.

"Where are we?" Vivian mumbles from the backseat.

"Almost home, sweetie. You OK? Are you going to be sick?" I know from experience that vomit smells will linger for years in car upholstery, no matter how well you clean it up.

"No. No," Vivian says, sounding exactly like she's going to be sick.

I look behind me and see that Vivian is nodding off again. I hope she wakes up enough to make it up the thirty-six steps to my third-floor flat.

I double-park two mansions down from George's. Even though it's dark I don't want to take a chance of him seeing my car. Who knows if he's looking out his window at 1:30 in the morning? People do weird things. I peer out of my windshield and see the house is dark. Whoever is in there is asleep. In their separate bedrooms, I assume.

"Are we there yet? Jacqs?" Vivian shakes herself awake and leans forward, breathing into the back of my neck. "Hey! Where are we? We going someplace else for a drink?"

"Yes. No. We're going home. You just sit back and relax. Try not to get sick all over yourself or my car, Viv." I rub my eyes and feel pathetic. I'm spying on my married boyfriend. Look what spying got me the last time. A big kick in the ass. Still, I can't help it. I want to know but I can't even stomach the thought of asking George outright if he's seeing someone else.

"I promise not to barf, Jacqs. You're the best friend a drunk girl can ever have. You have it so together. I should be more like you. We all should."

"Yeah, it seems that way, doesn't it?" I put the car in DRIVE and force myself not to glance at his house as we pass it.

71

Mr. Mayor

"Jacquelyn, can I speak with you a moment?"

Instead of heading toward his office, Mr. Mayor makes a beeline for mine. I follow him, giving Lei and Anita a look of utmost confusion so they don't get any funny ideas.

"Did you see it?" His suit jacket is draped over his arm and he hasn't put on his tie, as if he had to leave the master suite in a hurry. He closes the door and leans against it.

"I saw it." What else can I say? I go over and stand behind my desk, to put some distance between us.

Emilio Cortez's column this morning is heavy on innuendo of mayoral marital strife, speculation on infidelities and the bad blood between Mrs. Mayor and Gail. Mrs. Mayor comes out looking like a victim of a joyless marriage who isn't accepted into her husband's blue-blood family. Vivian, though not named directly, has been fingered as the other woman. It's all very soap worthy.

"I can't stress how much Katherine and I value our privacy," he begins.

"Mr. Mayor, please." My hand flies up to stop him from continuing on and pissing me off. "I would never, ever speak to the press about your private life. Never, and I know Anita and Lei wouldn't either."

"I'm taking you at your word, Jacqs. What about Natasha?"

I had hoped he'd accuse Danny.

"Never." In her phone calls to me from New York she hasn't mentioned Mrs. Mayor once or coming back to work here. It's all "Jesus this, Jesus that." Distance, it seems, has only made Natasha's heart fonder for the man.

"Press like this makes it harder for me to do my job."

"I bet." I snort and don't bother to hide my annoyance. "I'm sure it's not a picnic for Vivian either."

He runs his hands through his hair. "Fuck. I don't need this right now."

I walk over to the door and reach around him for the knob. His eyes catch mine and he leans into me. I jerk the door open and step out.

"None of us do, Kit."

72

Mrs. Mayor

"I don't know why she doesn't like them. She didn't say, specifically, that she doesn't like them. All I know is she wants me to return them both and wants her account credited."

For the last twenty-five minutes I have spoken with four people regarding a pair of truly hideous hand-painted clown figures Mrs. Mayor must have purchased while in a delusional state.

"Is there something else the mayor and his wife are interested in?" The floor supervisor for Gumps, asks again.

"No, she just said to return them." I've told this to three other people. Each one has become more concerned and panicky.

"Was there anything wrong with them?" she persists.

"No." Other than that they're incredibly ugly? I don't care if they're $200 a pop. They're clowns, for Christ's sake. Pastel clowns hand-painted in the hills of Umbria. Who the hell has clowns in their house? Not even my mother had clowns. She was more into the musical instrument–playing frogs.

"Please make sure the mayor and his wife know they're always welcome at Gumps. And we hope in the future that they'll find everything to their liking."

"I will." She well knows that Mr. Mayor has never set foot in Gumps. It's Mrs. Mayor who handles the gift buying for Mr. Mayor and herself as well.

"I'm sure she'll be in sometime to do some shopping. It's just the clowns didn't quite go with her, uh . . . décor." I hand over Mrs. Mayor's platinum card and smile.

I'm done for the day. That's it. I've been going from store to store returning this and picking up that and none of it makes any sense. Return hideous clowns to Gumps, pick up scary Lalique birds at Saks. Return Jimmy Choo stilettos to Neimans, pick up two pairs of futuristic sneakers at Sketchers. Approve and, most importantly, messenger over to City Hall special-order manly purple tie from Hermès for Mr. Mayor for his dinner Friday night with the governor, which she won't be able to make because she'll be in LA.

She's decided to visit some friends to let the heat die down after Cortez's little story. She wasn't nearly as upset as I thought she would be. But she and Mr. Mayor had a long discussion after he was done with me and she called me right after, with a hiccup in her voice, to tell me she'd be going out of town and to not worry.

Since the whole "friend" remark and her coming back with a black eye, we really haven't spent any one-on-one time together. I am not sure if I'm supposed to pull up a chair and discuss menstrual cramps with her or ask her if she needs me to do anything for her, like have Anita and Lei alphabetize her shoe collection.

Lucky for me, Mrs. Mayor knows exactly where I stand at all times. A few minutes later she came downstairs with a bag full of expensive crap that needed to be exchanged or returned and a list of things she needed purchased while she's away.

Without so much as a please or thank you I was sent on my way with a reminder to keep my cell phone on.

After I sign Mrs. Mayor's name to the receipt I flee Gumps and retrieve my car from the overpriced parking lot, making sure to save my receipt. Mrs. Mayor didn't say anything about coming back to the Mansion after I was done so I have the unsettling feeling that I'm free for the rest of the day.

I could go to the movies.

It's something I like doing alone and got in the habit of when Bina was doing her grueling residency. Most of the appeal lies in that I smuggle in my own food and sit exactly in the middle of the theater and for the next couple hours I either enjoy myself or, if the movie fails to keep my attention, I balance my checkbook, pay bills, reconcile my expense reports or even read with a tiny light I keep in my bag for that purpose.

As far as I'm concerned, everything looks better in the dark. Even American Express bills.

73

George

I turn down on to Post Street and head toward another overpriced parking garage on 5th and Mission when my cell phone chirps. I pick it up and shove it between my ear and shoulder.

"Hello? This is Jacquelyn." I know it's not Mrs. Mayor because I have a special ring for her calls.

"You're not avoiding me, are you?" George's honey-smooth voice melts into my ear.

"Of course not. How are you?" I straighten up and am so surprised that I miss my chance to turn, causing a line of cars to honk their horns at me.

"How am I? So you are avoiding me. I knew it."

George sounds lazily distracted. I guess it's one of the perks of being an executive, along with calling your girlfriend in the middle of the afternoon.

"I was just about to call you," I lie easily. With George I have found that he's not so much interested in the truth as he is in the truth that suits him. This works for me, most of the time.

"I'm sure you were. How about dinner with my best girl?" George asks. "Somewhere new."

"Well . . ." I was really looking forward to the movies and I'm not dressed for dinner, at least dinner anywhere George would take me. "I'm not sure."

"Jacquelyn, I'm hurt. We haven't talked in days and days. Don't you miss me? Even a little bit?"

"No." Which isn't exactly a lie but not true either. I don't mean to hurt his feelings, but I don't like where I'm going with this relationship—the uncertainty, the suspicions. If that's what I wanted out of a relationship I'd get myself a real boyfriend. "Anyway, Georgie, I'm not at all dressed for dinner unless you want to go out for a slice of pizza."

"Pizza? I haven't been able to digest pizza since my late twenties. Meet at Jardinière at 6:30."

With that, George hangs up and literally leaves me at an intersection of decision.

The white calfskin Ferragamo wallet and purse distract me for a moment and I forget I'm sitting in the same restaurant where I had my last real meal with my then husband, who is getting married in two days.

After deciding what kind of girl I am, I rushed around the San Francisco Shopping Center assembling a complete outfit—from underwear and shoes, to a tortoiseshell hairclip to secure my chignon. I did my makeup at Sephora (thinking of Natasha the whole time) and made it to Jardinière fashionably late. And not on purpose, a first for me.

"George, this is too much!" Not even Mrs. Mayor has this bag. I'm sure she could buy it anytime, but mine is a gift, which makes it ten times better.

"Just a little something to make up for the short notice."

The wineglass in front of him has not been touched. I am guessing it's a pretty expensive bottle because the waiter's eyes bugged out when he ordered it.

"I'd hate to see what you'd give me if you stood me up."

George gives me a satisfied smile and leans back. Our table, by Jardinière standards is ideal. We are seated at the central table on the balcony overlooking the bar downstairs. This is a table that says "I'm not hiding from anyone. I want to be seen." I guess it's George's way of saying we've come out of the broom closet.

"I'm glad you like it. You don't own one, do you?"

"Not this one. I really love it!" I take a sip of my water and smile over my glass at him. I need to stop gushing now, George is enjoying it a tad too much.

"My wife is out of town," George says, straining a bit to sound casual. I notice he called her his wife and not his soon-to-be ex-wife. I guess that's too much of a mouthful.

"Oh."

Payback time. George is nice. I like George. I don't have much of a problem with George not being divorced yet. I obviously don't have a problem with him lavishing gifts on me. But what I don't want to know is that his wife is out of town. That could be a problem.

"Her sister is getting divorced. She was staying at our place for a bit. I sent her some roses. It didn't seem to cheer her up." George allows the waiter to refill his wineglass.

"Roses. How could a woman not like roses?" So that would tidily explain the delivery from French Tulip. I like the bag but I'm not stupid.

"I know one woman who loves roses," George says.

I smile. This is making me uncomfortable. This is outright flirting, which will lead to touching, which may lead to sex. This is wrong. I shouldn't feel obligated to have sex with George just because he's dropped some, OK, a lot of cash on me. Maybe I shouldn't have let him and kept things intellectual.

"George—"

"I was wondering what you're doing this weekend?" George and I have never met on a weekend. On those two days he has to play the dutiful husband for forty-eight hours straight, an exercise that leaves him too exhausted to meet me on Mondays.

"Not much." I did have tentative plans to throw a get-together to celebrate Nate's marriage. I was going to surround myself with people who think I'm the bee's knees and revel in all my glory. "Why? Are you going to whisk me off for a romantic weekend?"

"Maybe. Would you like that?" George asks a bit nervously.

I've never seen George nervous. He didn't even blink when he told me on our second lunch date that he was unhappily married.

"George, I do believe you are propositioning me," I tease.

"Such a technical word, Jacquelyn," he says, recovering his stride, but he doesn't say anything else.

If we were both honest with each other, that's what he's been doing all this time while I've been considering it. We both knew this day would come and now here it is and he's made his decision. Now it's up to me to stop pretending I haven't made mine. It's as good as done.

I'm finally going to see what the inside of George's house looks like.

"If you'd excuse me. I have to go to the ladies' room." I get up and smile. Just because we both know I'm going to give it up doesn't mean I have to be so hasty about it.

"Jacquelyn, you're not going to leave me here in suspense. Are you?" George asks, looking unsure.

"No. No, of course not. I just need to . . ." I glance over his shoulder at the bar below and freeze.

"Jacquelyn, are you all right?" George stands up and helps me sit down.

"George . . ." I cover my eyes with my hands. "Look over at the bar, near the door and tell me what you see . . ."

"Have a sip of water . . . Just people. Should I be looking for anyone in particular?" George hovers over me protectively.

"The couple by the hostess . . ." I lower my hands and look closely.

"The two men that are kissing? Jacquelyn, this is San Francisco, you should be used to that by now," George says in an amused voice and takes his seat.

"I'm used to it, of course, but I never expected to see my best friend's fiancé doing it."

74

Dr. N

"And how did this make you feel?" Dr. N asks.

She wants to play TV shrink again. I guess she had hoped I'd called because I'd pulled a threesome and was feeling all sorts of gooey Catholic guilt.

"I don't know. Confused. Happy. Shocked. Angry. All those things," I say to Dr. N as if she should know. I just finished recounting to her what I saw last night, leaving out crucial details of who I was with and what I was doing there.

After blood started flowing to my brain again, George arranged to have me smuggled through the kitchen of Jardinière while he casually went over to the hostess and asked to see the reservation book. Sure enough: Sanjay Gupta, party of two was listed for a 7:00 reservation.

George dropped me off at my car and asked me what I was going to do, and when I shrugged helplessly, he offered to come over to my place to keep me company. I declined, of course. Dealing with one sordid romance a night is my limit. As soon as I started my car, I speed dialed Dr. N and asked her for an emergency appointment. Lucky for me Dr. N is an early riser so here I am sitting in her office less than fourteen hours after I got the shock of my life.

"What I want to know is what I should do," I say. Dr. N is a mental doctor, she should know how to handle this kind of situation. I don't have time to write into Dear Abby so she's my next best thing—impartial, intelligent and in the position to have to give an answer.

"What do you think you should do?" she asks.

For this I woke up at 6 AM, lied to Mrs. Mayor about coming down with a raging UTI, avoided poor Vivian and will be shelling out a whole $150 for?

"I was kind of hoping you could tell me." I don't have time for this. I need to know what I should do now. I can't ask anyone else; she must know this or else I wouldn't have come to her. Why is she giving me a hard time?

"I can't tell you, Jacquelyn. We can discuss the situation, go over your options and then you have to come to a decision yourself."

"*Arggg!*" I pound my fists on the armchair. This gets Dr. N's attention. She looks at me like Miss Chavez (aspiring cruel nun and itinerate catechism teacher) used to look at me whenever I raised my hand in class to be excused for my umpteenth trip to the bathroom. "Sorry."

"You seem to be very angry lately, Jacquelyn," Dr. N observes.

"I am not!" I am now, though.

"And defensive." Dr. N flips through her notebook. I know this is where she has catalogued all my confessions from our very first meeting. I once got a quick peek at it when she had had some bad calamari and had to rush to the bathroom during a session. "How long has it been since you have been off Zoloft?"

"Months. I don't want Zoloft. I want someone to tell me what to do! Should I tell Bina? Or should I confront Sanjay?" I ask, feeling helpless.

"Why confront? A very angry word . . ."

"I am angry. Not that he's gay or bisexual. That's beside the point! He's cheating on her, it doesn't matter with who or what, it's cheating and that will devastate her."

"Yes. If she doesn't know already," Dr. N says with no hint of stupidity.

"Pardon me? Are you saying my best friend is in, like, cahoots with this whole thing?" I ask. "Next you'll say maybe Bina is also gay."

"It's a possibility. You've told me she comes from a very traditional family. This may be her way of saving face." Dr. N crosses her legs.

She's wearing new Birkenstocks. The price of my emergency session will cover the cost of them.

"That's impossible. Bina was a regular heterosexual slut during college. If she was a lesbian, she'd tell me." Or would she? She never let on that she was into this traditional, arranged-marriage thing and, before Sanjay, she hadn't had a serious boyfriend for a couple of years, but that was because she was too busy with, like, becoming a doctor, which is a totally plausible reason for not dating. She barely had time to shower, sleep or eat. Dating was the last thing on her mind.

Then again, there is her obsession with Emma Thompson. She owns every Emma movie and has even written to her for an autographed picture. I always thought it was because Bina admired her Englishness, now I'm not so sure.

"No, no, it's impossible. I know plenty of people who are gay or bi. She's not," I state firmly. Dr. N is just trying to get me to think "outside my comfort perimeter," something we've been working on since day one of my therapy.

"Why don't we go over your options?" Dr. N prods. I guess she wants to move this thing along and get to the real juicy stuff. "One option is to do nothing. Another is confronting her fiancé and the third is telling Bina yourself."

"I can't obviously do nothing. I couldn't live with myself, but I don't want Bina to think of me as the person who outed Sanjay to her. I guess . . . I guess I'll go to him and tell him what I know?" This is the last thing I want to do. There is no love lost between me and Sanjay and I doubt I'll endear myself to him by outing him a few weeks before his wedding.

"That seems like a good option, given the circumstances. How do you plan to do it?"

I can practically see her ticking off a mental checklist, but since I'm so desperate for a course of action, I'll let it slide.

"I'll call him up. Ask him out for coffee, somewhere neutral. I'll say it's about the wedding, which won't be entirely a lie. Then I'll just tell him what I saw and ask him if Bina knows. Then it's up to him to do the right thing." I sit back, feeling exhausted. There, I can wash my hands of the whole thing and just be there for Bina when it hits the fan.

"What if Sanjay doesn't say anything to Bina? What will you do then?" Dr. N intones.

How freaking annoying. I was done. I'd ventured "outside my comfort perimeter" and there she goes extending the boundaries. (God, I hate Birkenstocks.) Might as well cut to the chase. I know Dr. N wants to hear a firm, concrete, reasonable course of action. I take a deep breath and reflect her enthusiasm for the subject with my own flat reciting of words.

"If he doesn't fess up, I'll have to tell her myself. I owe it to her. She's my best friend. She'd do the same for me," I say in a rush.

Dr. N nods and purses her lips—her thinking face. I wait.

"How about your other issues, Jacquelyn?" Dr. N asks.

"Which one? There are so many this week, I get confused. Must be drinking too much . . . again." I smirk. I can't help it. For a whole year I've paid this woman to sit and listen to me and to help me figure out the mess that I'd made of my life. And she has helped me, as much as I've been willing to let her, but I realize she still doesn't have the slightest idea who I am. Especially if she buys this crap that I've been dishing out lately.

"Are you under stress? Depressed? Anxious?"

"Try all three. I just need some time away. From everyone and everything. Like a fresh start, you know?" Maybe that's what I do need. Maybe I just need to move away, get a new job, new haircut, sell my memory-haunted flat and start all over.

"It's understandable that you would feel this way. Being that you are so alienated from your family, don't have a serious relationship, and troubles with your job and friends. It's normal to feel like you want to escape or run away, but turning to controlled substances is not a healthy way to do that. Especially considering your family's background of alcoholism."

I squirm in my seat. Dr. N is being insightful and accurate and it's making me uncomfortable. I haven't had a drink to get drunk since my first semester of college, around the time my dad quit drinking. Unfortunately for my mother, most of his personality went by way of the bottle, down the drain.

"I don't see a problem with it, honestly. It's my life. I have a right to live it the way I want and if I don't want to deal with other people's problems . . ." I falter as Dr. N gives me a piercing look from her muddy brown eyes.

"Jacquelyn, you know and I know that you are not an ambivalent person by nature. You cannot force yourself to stop caring because things are difficult. That's what you did during your marriage."

"What's wrong with being ambivalent? Even clinically ambivalent? I think it's an underrated virtue." Really, if anything, Dr. N should be commending me on my ability to be selfish and not be the world's doormat. "You've always said I've had a problem with putting myself first."

"Yes, but this isn't the type of situation that you can put yourself first in. Is it?"

"No. I guess not." What good Catholic, even a superlapsed Catholic, could ever put herself first? It goes against our DNA. "I'll call Sanjay today. As soon as I get to my car, and ask to meet him for coffee. Might as well get it over with. Right?"

"If it feels right for you, I agree."

"Thanks." I gather up my bag, the first one George gave me. I wonder if I subconsciously brought it with me so Dr. N would ask me how on earth I could afford a $1,400 purse. She doesn't, the woman wears Birkenstocks for Christ's sake.

"About your next appointment . . ." Dr. N fiddles with her appointment book. I'm prebooked for two weeks from now. "I was thinking that perhaps you may want to come back next week? Usual time and day."

"Sure." I take the appointment card listlessly.

"And, Jacquelyn, it's not a personal failure if you do decide to go back on Zoloft. Think about it."

"OK. Thanks. See you next week."

"Good-bye, Jacquelyn, have a nice day."

"I will. You, too. Thanks again." I trudge out of her office, half-hoping she'll come after me, apologize and say she'll do the dirty work for me, but of course she doesn't. I bet she can't run in those shoes anyway.

75

Vivian

I get into my car and check my cell phone. Three messages, all from Vivian, and it's not even 8 o'clock in the morning. She's going insane. I speed dial her and lean my head on the steering wheel. I have a feeling I'll be here for a while, which is totally OK with me since I'm not too thrilled with the one humongous item on my to-do list.

"Hello?" Vivian sounds a tad on edge.

"Girl, put down that double latte. Are you OK?" I try to muster some energy and concern in my voice. It's not that I don't feel it, but right now I'm running dangerously low. "If you're calling about the Cortez situation, it wasn't me who blabbed, but I have my suspicions."

Mrs. Mayor has been walking around attempting to look innocent, a dead giveaway.

"Don't worry about it. Kit has agreed to the open forum interview on KQED. Just out of curiosity . . ."

"Do you really need to hear it?"

Mrs. Mayor comes off looking sympathetic while the rest of us have to deal with the consequences of her selective truths. Cortez, I can't blame him. Who could resist a gift straight from the horse's mouth? I'm not sure I wouldn't do the same thing if I was in her position, though, so I can't feel too betrayed by her attempts to influence her own PR.

"No, you're right. I don't need to know. Hey, I called the mansion looking for you and Lei told me that Anita told her that Mrs. Mayor said you were in the hospital. What's going on?"

"Hospital! I called Mrs. Mayor and lied to her about having a UTI. What a drama queen. Just for that I'm taking the rest of the day off to recover from my near-death experience."

"God, that woman. I don't know how he puts up with her. I was wondering if you had some time and a shoulder to spare tonight . . . He just served me," she says in a small voice.

"I'm sorry." There is no need to ask who the "he" is (Curtis) and what he served her (divorce papers).

"The one good thing is that only the incontinent security guard witnessed my shame." There are tears in her voice.

"Well, there's always a bright side." I'm beginning to realize she may have let him off easy by just slashing his tires.

"Yeah," she sniffled on the phone. I decide to wait her out. "Anyway, I'm ordering a large pizza and a case of three-ply tissues. Ice cream and movies will be in abundance, of course. Are you interested in joining me?" Her voice is small and needy.

"I may be bringing a guest. Is that OK?" Bina has always had an obsession with pizza and I hope it will offer her some comfort after Sanjay drops the gay bomb on her.

"The more, the merrier. See you tonight." Vivian clicks off and I keep the phone to my ear.

Maybe someone else will call. Behind me a woman double-parks and waits for my parking spot. Bitch. Can't she see I'm in the middle of a crisis?

I pull out carefully and head toward Sanjay's office. No phone call, no time to prepare an alibi, I figure I should catch him with his pants down. Again.

76

Sanjay

I sit with my knees pressed tightly together and clutch a Styrofoam cup of tepid coffee. Sanjay's assistant, a very good-looking and obviously very gay guy, gives me a smile as he pretends to type, his fingers dancing over the keys. He's actually bidding on something from eBay. I can see his screen reflected in the window behind him.

"Um . . ." I say. He looks up. His name is Liam or something. "How long have you worked for Sanjay?"

"For about two months. His last assistant quit to get married. Or was it to move to Minnesota? . . . Maybe it was both. Sanjay is great, a great boss."

I nod. Yes, I bet he is. I'm about to say so when I see Sanjay striding down the hall toward us. I have to admit, he's a gorgeous-looking man, dressed impeccably, flawless skin, perfect hair. It's so obvious he's gay. Why didn't I see it before? I always knew there was something off about him, but I thought it had to do with his moral character, not his sexuality. How can Bina possibly not know?

"Jacquelyn, this is a surprise." He gives me a stiff hug and I press my cheek to his.

"Thanks for seeing me, Sanjay. I know you're busy." I try not to betray anything with my voice. Not yet, he can still throw me out. Once inside his office, corner office, I take a seat and he closes the door behind him and sits on the edge of his desk near me.

"What's this about? I know I'm driving Bina crazy but I want to make sure our big day is perfect. Flawless. Both of them."

"Yeah. I understand. Completely." The more he talks the harder it's getting to come out and say what I came here to say.

"So? Is that why you're here?" he asks, arching a perfectly groomed brow.

Another obvious clue! No straight man, unless he's *really* open-minded or in show business, gets his brows waxed. Mrs. Mayor has to chase Mr. Mayor around the Mansion with her tweezers just to yank some hairs from between his brows. And he agrees to do it only before a photo shoot or TV appearance.

"Sort of. About the wedding, yeah, that's why I'm here." I take a deep breath and pray for an interruption. Maybe Liam can knock on the door and wiggle his fanny in here with a super-important fax. Nope. Nothing. See what praying gets you?

"I . . . I was at Jardinière last night. For dinner." I stop and swallow. Sanjay's pupils dilate. "I saw you. I saw you there with whomever it was you were there with."

I sit back and watch Sanjay turn from a light mocha brown to a ghastly shade of pale. I want to cry and it looks like he does, too.

"What do you want? Money?" Sanjay manages to rasp out.

"Money! No! I just wanted to know if Bina knows. I can tell from your face no." That much is pretty obvious. Also that Sanjay is an asshole. I can't believe he offered me money. I'd never take it, of course, but I wonder how much he'd be willing to pay.

Sanjay shakes his head and goes to sit behind his desk. He puts his head in his hands and moans.

"Are you OK?" I can't help but ask. He's taking this a lot harder than I thought.

"Are you going to tell her?" he asks in a watery voice.

"No! I'm not. You should. You have to." I feel bad for him but there is no way in hell I'm letting him off the hook.

"The wedding is set. Everything is paid for. Tickets to India. Family notified."

"Well, I'm really sorry it's inconvenient, but you can't honestly expect to marry Bina without telling her you're . . ."

"What? Gay?"

"I was holding out hope that you were at least bi." Bi I could understand. I have plenty of bi friends and even dated a bi guy in college. No problem there, except he wasn't monogamous.

"No, Jacquelyn, I'm 100 percent gay. All the way. Have been for years." Sanjay gives a bitter little laugh.

"So what the fuck are you doing proposing to my best friend?" I feel my face get red and hot like it does when I'm really pissed off.

"Jacquelyn, don't be naive. You know as well as I do—you come from a traditional family—the last thing you can be is who you really are."

"Why drag Bina into this? She deserves to know the truth. From you," I say. I understand what he's saying, but him tongue kissing another man while engaged to a woman who I know and love pretty much nulls any sympathy I have for him and the traditions that tie, bind and otherwise strangle.

"Bina deserves many things and I can provide her with a good lifestyle, children, even," Sanjay says, leaning back.

I can see the wheels spinning in his head. Somehow he thinks he can make this work. He's crazy.

"But you're gay, Sanjay." Enough said.

We sit there staring at each other. I can go on like this for hours. I was raised with brothers and sisters who regularly challenged me to staring contests. It's actually kind of relaxing, like meditating.

"Fine."

Sanjay sounds way too annoyed for a person in his position. He's wrong! I'm in the right here. For once.

"Huh?" I snap back to reality.

"I'll take care of it."

He stands up. I have no choice but to do the same. I half-wonder if he's going to offer to shake my hand. He doesn't.

"Well. Good-bye, Sanjay," I say. He nods and goes to stand by the window. "I'll see myself out."

I open the door, walk calmly past Liam and manage not to break into a run for the elevators.

77

Me

I get to the theater in time for the first movie of the day. I don't care what it is and I don't care if it's barely 10:30 in the morning and I'm having supernachos, a large root beer and gummy worms.

The ticket taker gives me a sympathetic look and I know I must seem pathetic, trying to balance all this food, carrying a really nice tote bag and wearing my favorite button-up coat that I bought with my first real paycheck out of college. If he only knew how pathetic I really am. And I'm not even talking about the impending trauma of my ex-husband's wedding tomorrow.

Things are crappy, very crappy, so I think I'm entitled to a few hours in the dark, and then back home for a long bath and sleep. Who needs Zoloft?

I do, that's who.

78

Vivian

At exactly 6:09 PM my phone rings. I've been waiting for this call all day. My eyes tear up in expectation of Bina's sad, if not hysterical, voice on the other end.

"Hello?" I say tentatively into the phone, expecting to hear great gobs of runny mucus being sucked up.

"Hey, Jacqs, it's me." Vivian, sounding very peppy.

"Hi." Damn, I don't know how much longer I can keep up this vigil. Maybe I should call Sanjay and remind him of our little talk this morning.

"Yeah, it's me . . ."

Vivian sounds distracted and giddy. I find this annoying. I should be the giddy one. I hardly have any problems. My fiancé isn't gay. My husband isn't suing me for divorce. Where's my fun?

"What's up, Vivian?" I have call waiting, but I still don't want to tie up the line.

"Yeah. I have to cancel tonight.. Just wanted to let you know . . . Are you OK? Feeling better?"

"I'm great. I wasn't sick, remember? I told you this morning when we talked," I sigh into the phone.

Vivian usually isn't this spacey. She must be getting slammed at work. How truly nice of her to call and let me know she won't make it to her own pity party tonight. My heart fills with love. No man, no matter how evolved, would do that. He'd just call up after he was supposed to be where he said he'd be and obviously wasn't and say he wasn't able to make it. Men suck.

"OK. Good to hear. Don't wait up. I'll be really late. Work crap," she says in a rush.

I completely forgot about the governor thing even though I spent most of yesterday taking care of last-minute details for Mrs. Mayor.

"OK. See you later, Vivian."

I hang up the phone and stare at the wall opposite my bed. I love my bed. When Nate moved out I got rid of our old bed, which had been my bed before Nate came along and camped out on it. But after we shared it, it ceased to be mine and I wasn't sorry at all to see it go. In fact I would have burned it if the City hadn't told me it was illegal when I called to ask.

I went down to a mattress superstore, tried out dozens of models, drove the clerk batty with all my questions and comparisons and finally settled on a medium-soft number that set me back almost $1400. I've never regretted the expense even though to date I've been the only one to sleep on it.

I reach for the phone and almost dial Bina before I realize that I can't call her until she calls me. I figure Sanjay will tell her sometime tonight. She gets off from the hospital at 7 and they usually spend Friday nights together.

I turn over onto my side and stare out the window into the neighbor's empty kitchen. I bet they're out having a great time. I once saw them having sex on the kitchen table. That was pretty interesting.

The only good thing about tonight is that I don't have to worry about food. Mrs. Mayor, still acting like a weirdo, sent over a smirking Danny with a jug of cranberry juice, chicken soup, a carton of raspberry frozen yogurt and a flower arrangement, with a note telling me to feel better and she would see me when she gets back from LA.

I drag myself out of bed and into the kitchen to heat up the soup and pour myself a chilled glass of cranberry juice. This is as close as I've gotten to mothering since I left home and it's by a woman without a maternal bone in her body. My life is so screwed up.

I settle on the couch and flip channels, go through a stack of magazines and eat at the same time; I'm a consummate multitasker.

79

Bethany

I startle awake to a ringing phone. I check my watch as I grope for the cordless in the living room. Vivian has a nasty habit of never putting it back on the base.

It's only a bit after 8. I feel like I've been sleeping for hours.

"Hello?" I say groggily into the phone. Now I won't be able to fall asleep until well after midnight and my internal clock will force me awake before 7 AM. I'll look like shit tomorrow.

"Yes, uh, may I speak to Jacquelyn? Please."

Oh, shit! Did I forget to cancel a hair appointment for myself? This means I'll either have to go or forfeit $50 on my credit card.

"Yeah, this is she. Me." I wait for her to give me the particulars. I reach for a pen and prepare to write over the smiling face of some model. "OK, shoot . . ."

"Uh. I'm . . . this is Bethany Michel . . . Nate's fiancée?"

"Oh, hello." Holy mother of God. Holy sweet Jesus. All of a sudden I remember the gift I sent off to them. I guess she was going through her haul and came upon mine and then hunted me down and now is going to give me a reaming over the phone. That's what I would do, after all.

"Do you know who I am?" she asks.

"You're Nate's fiancée." Smooth. We both don't seem to be at our sharpest. I know my excuse, but I don't even want to guess what hers is.

"Uh . . ." she says. And this woman is a lawyer? Puhleez!

"Is there something I can help you with?" I offer. Sister, if you only knew.

"Yes, I, uh, was wondering why you sent us a gift? Do I know you?"

"No, I just am one of those people who like to give random gifts. The Internet has made my hobby much easier." I wait. She can't possibly believe this.

"Oh . . . Do you know Nate?" The lawyer in her is coming out.

"Nate? Hmmm." I know it bends left, lady, that satisfy your question?

"I asked Nate's mother and she said to ask Nate. Nate's having his bachelor party and I can't reach him. We're getting married tomorrow," she adds unnecessarily.

"Listen, I'm sorry I sent you the gift. Really. It was a stupid joke. You get some sleep, and go get married tomorrow. Best of luck to you, really."

"Did you have a relationship with Nate?"

This bitch just won't let up. I'm trying to let her off easy for her own good and she keeps coming at me like a pit bull. I begin to feel unjustifiably angry.

"If I did it was a long, long time ago and is so over, you have nothing to worry about. I have this thing where I send my ex's presents on their special occasions. But I'm getting professional help so you don't have to worry." I've never felt so bad about something I've done in my whole life. And this includes the time I set my grandmother's house on fire when I was fourteen.

"Please, tell me the truth. I think I deserve that much," Bethany says, for the first time sounding like a woman. Not an unsure girl, not a detached lawyer but a woman who has the definite feeling she's been or is going to be screwed over.

"The truth . . . Are you sure? I . . . can't." Why should Bethany pay for my vindictiveness and Nate's stupidity and carelessness?

"Please, I'm begging you." Her voice catches in her throat.

I feel my own eyes tear up, like we're in this together.

"OK. But you have to promise me you won't do anything stupid. To yourself, at least." I wouldn't mind if she brandished a pair of rusty scissors near Nate's gonads. He deserves at least a scare.

"I promise. I won't. I just need to know," she sniffs, but sounds like she's bucking up for my bombshell.

"Nate and I were married." I hear her gasp and quickly add, "But we are beyond divorced."

"When? Why?" Bethany, I can tell, is a detail person.

"God, we weren't married that long. We lived together longer than we were married." This piece of information elicits another gasp from poor Bethany.

"You lived together?"

"Only for a while. Really. I mean who doesn't live together first these days? You can't really know a person unless you see them when their defenses are down. I mean, you'll never know if they keep the toilet seat up or if they take the time to completely shut their bureau drawers. Ha, I mean, I don't know about you, but I hate it when a guy leaves stuff just oozing out of the . . . drawers."

Freudian slip! I swear. It's not like I want to completely ruin Bethany Michel's life by hinting to her that she is wearing a tainted engagement ring she found in Nate's drawers. Or, maybe I do, I don't know. This is a question for Dr. N. Of course I can't tell her any of this. She would definitely think I'm a worse person than I have led her to believe, not counting my shoplifting and multiple-sex-partner lies of late.

"Drawers, Nate's drawers . . . The ring? My ring . . ." she says. I can almost see her holding it up to her face.

At this point it would be cruel to let her writhe around, I may as well confess for Nate. "It was mine. Nate kept it after the divorce, but I had no idea he'd ever give it to another woman. If I even had the slightest idea he'd do that I would have flushed it down the toilet. I swear." Not flushed it, but pawned it for sure.

"Don't worry, I'll take care of it. I've taken care of everything, every fucking detail up until now. I have to go now." Her voice sounds dead but determined.

If I still had any feelings for Nate I'd warn him to start running. Luckily, I don't. If she does kill him I'll feel partly responsible, but I doubt I'd get in any legal trouble. But this isn't about Nate or prison time for me. This is about poor, tragic Bethany.

"Wait! Wait! Please. What're you going to do?" I've ruined her wedding. A woman can never forgive (or forget) anyone who comes between her and her wedding.

"I have a house full of family," she says in a shell-shocked voice. I can only guess it must be pretty overwhelming to be on the phone with your fiancé's secret ex-wife on the eve of your fantasy wedding. "Everyone is here. Everyone."

"I know I shouldn't ask, but can you ever forgive me? It was beyond petty of me to send the gift. I just was so mad at Nate for springing it on me during dinner that he was getting married . . ." I trail off lamely. Why should she forgive me? I wouldn't. I have a list of people and what they did to derail my dream wedding. A list of names a mile long and whenever someone annoys me, it just reminds me about the wedding that never was—thereby keeping their name on the list just a little longer.

"You and Nate had dinner together? When? While I was in Chicago. That could be the only time. He said he was holed up at the office working. I was here running after the florist, making sure our cake is perfect, arranging every last fucking detail while he was out with his *ex-wife!* That goddamn motherfucker!" Her mind is like a steel trap. I'm glad the focus is on the truly guilty party: Nate, not me.

"We went to some fancy Mexican, sorry, Latin-fusion place. But nothing happened! I left him there." Why did I have to mention it was fancy? Now she'll hold that against me. I should have just said we met for coffee or something. Or ran into each other on a crowded street.

"He lied to me. His whole family has lied to me. He said he's never lived with anyone before. He's never felt as close to another woman. He asked me to marry him!" Her voice gets a bit shrill, something I know Nate doesn't like.

He always made remarks about "shrill women." Shrill women

at the office, shrill women waiting in long lines at the supermarket . . . If there was a shrill woman within half a mile of him, Nate would find her.

"What are you going to do?" I can't help it. I want to know. It's pretty obvious she isn't going to swallow a bottle of pills.

There is only silence on the other end of the phone. I can hear huffy breaths and her blowing her nose here and there, but otherwise nothing. I start to get nervous all over again. Maybe she's thinking of how to make my life a living hell. She'll have to stand in line.

"Uh, Bethany?"

"I'm going to take a pill. Just one. Get some sleep. Wake up. Get ready and go to the church," she says calmly, too calmly.

"Uh-huh." Not exactly what I would do, but it's her life.

"Then I'm going to have my father walk me down the aisle where I will take my place beside Nate . . ." she continues, her voice getting stronger.

I can visualize her standing up straighter, forming her left hand into a fist and raising it into the air.

"Uh-huh . . ." This is getting good. If I ever need a dramatic lawyer, she's my man.

"Where I will knee the motherfucker in the nuts and throw the ring in his face and say 'I don't do second-hand rings or men.'"

Triumph! There could be no better way to end it. No tears, no accusations. And for God's sake, no shrillness! Just quick, decisive and lethal action—just like in a movie. Myles would be proud. Dr. N would be proud. Maybe I should give Bethany their numbers?

"Wow! If you're ever in San Francisco—hello?" I stare at the phone. Oh, Nate is going to be in trouble! I have to call Bina.

Oh, wait, I can't call Bina, because I'm waiting for my little talk with Sanjay to ruin her wedding-marriage-relationship-whatever.

Two ruined relationships in one day. This has to be some sort of a record even for me.

80

Me

I borrow a little pill from Vivian who borrowed a whole bunch from Natasha. All the troubles of my day float past my eyes and out the window as I give into chemically induced relaxation and sleep.

81

Bina

I wake up with cotton mouth. I must have slept with my mouth hanging wide open for the last ten hours. Very attractive. I look at the clock as I tentatively sip water, spewing some over my duvet when I see it's past 11.

What the hell is in those pills? They're lethal. Next time I'll take only half.

I get up and pad to the bathroom and pee for what feels like an eternity. After I finally stop, I realize that the flat is too quiet, even for a Saturday.

Either Vivian is up and gone or passed out.

I brush my teeth, wash my face—twice—and pull my underwear out of my butt and make my way to the closed door of her room. I drum my fingers on the door and listen.

"Vivian? It's me. You up?" Nothing. I push open the door and her bed is in the same state it was the night before. Naughty, naughty. At least I hope that's what has kept her out all night and not some horrible car accident.

Speaking of which. I rush over to my machine to see if Bina called during my pharmaceutically induced coma. Nope.

This could be a good sign. He told her, she was totally cool with it, even sympathetic (she is a doctor, after all) and is now methodically canceling the flowers, caterers, reception venue . . .

As if on cue, Bina's number flashes on my caller ID. I pick up before the first ring is even finished.

"Hi, Bina! How are you? I was wondering if you were going to call." As when a nurse gives you a shot, I believe in distraction and a stealthy poke. None of that tapping of the fingernail against the syringe, rubbing the area and giving the person ample time to think about the needle and the pain. "Bina?"

"It's Sanjay."

"Oh." I feel as if I'm going to throw up. I sit down on the floor and wait for him to speak. He doesn't. "What's up?"

"I'd appreciate if you wouldn't mention anything. She's in the shower. She's going to call you when she gets out." Sanjay's voice is curt and flat. I can tell he's angry with me for making him tell his fiancée that he's gay.

"OK." There's not much else I can say. He clearly is telling me that he hasn't told her yet so I can't remind him to tell her because that would only make me look like a bitch and I don't need him feeling any more put upon than he already does.

"Oh! Here she is, Jacquelyn. See you soon!" Sanjay calls into the phone sounding cheery. That freak can turn on a dime, in more ways than one.

"Jacquelyn, sweets, I overslept. We can make the 12:45. I'll be by to pick you up in 20 minutes. Kiss, kiss." She hangs up.

Feeling slightly zombified, I head to the shower, hoping a blast of cold water will wake me up and that my Zoloft prescription hasn't expired.

I take more of a splash than a shower, and I don't even bother to shampoo or condition my hair, something I usually do religiously every day.

I like to take long showers, at least twenty minutes. It's one of the great things about living alone and having your own dedicated water heater. Long showers, sleeping right smack in the middle of the bed and peeing with the door open so you don't miss what's on TV are just some of the perks of living alone. I've had to adjust slightly with Vivian, but it's nothing compared to the sacrifices I had to make when I was with Nate.

I'm pulling on my shoes when the phone rings again. I look at it in horror. Maybe if I don't pick it up I can avert another disaster. I guess I can let it go to the machine, but what if it's my mom. This would be the third phone call in a row I've let my machine deal with. Three is usually my limit. It might just be a wrong number. I'm due for some luck. I pick it up, ready to toss it out the window if I don't like what I hear. "Hello?"

"Jacqs, it's me, Vivian." She sounds out of breath.

"Hey, where did you sleep last night? Wait! Don't tell me." I lean back and relax. At this point, I can handle anything Vivian throws at me with my eyes closed. "You pick up some young legislative aide and teach him the ways of the world the way only a true redheaded woman can?"

"I wish. Nothing like that, just work. Got held over with this dinner thing. With the governor, but . . ." This is a heavy but. I know this type of but. I brace myself. "But, um, I was wondering, if anyone asks, would you say I was at home? All night."

"Who would ask?" Besides me, of course.

"My almost ex-husband's jackal of a lawyer for one. We aren't officially divorced yet and there is a slight issue with the dividing of assets. Don't worry about it. I'm absolutely positive no one will ask, but just in case. I was home in bed and gone before you woke up, same old crap. Please?"

"Sure thing. Not a problem. I'm going to be out all afternoon, anyway. You want to meet me and Bina for lunch, shopping and a movie?"

"Really?" She covers the phone with her hand for a minute, and I can make out a mumbled conversation. "Oh, I can't. I'll see you when you get home. Ciao!"

"OK . . . Cheerio!" I hang up, feeling a little confused. Who knew that work could make a person sound so . . . exhilarated?

Bina double-parked right in front of my flat and the old lady neighbor has the towing company on speed dial.

I run down the stairs and take a quick peek at my mailbox. Bills. I'm not too eager to take a look at my American Express bill and be reminded just how stupid I can be. They can wait until I get back. I quickly walk toward Bina's Saab and see she has her ever-present cell phone pressed to her ear. I slide in next to her and give her what I hope is an innocent smile.

"Sanjay," she mouths and crosses her eyes. I settle down, feeling as if I'm about to get a tooth drilled at the dentist. "What is it with you today? Don't worry. Everything will be fine. I have Jacqs in the car . . . Yes, I'll put my phone on vibrate. See you tomorrow night!"

"Everything OK?" I ask.

"Sanjay has this big tax-fraud case. He's been asked to testify in New York. I told him to have someone else do it. He can't handle the stress. You should see how jumpy he's been. It's like he's the bride!"

"I can imagine that." What a weasel. He still has no plans to tell her. "What's going on tomorrow night?"

"Sanjay, he's an ass but can be such a sweetheart. Remember his friend Allen? He was at the barbeque Sanjay threw for his department in Golden Gate Park? Anyway, he just broke up with that bartender woman he was sleeping with. Or claimed he was sleeping with. I always get the feeling Allen is hiding something. You *know* what I'm talking about. Anyway, we are going for a little cruise on the bay."

"No, you're not!" I yelp.

"Yes, I am. Why shouldn't I? Allen's a safe sailor. Is that what you call someone who is a yuppie and took sailing lessons because he had to buy a boat for tax reasons?"

"It'll be dark and you'll be all alone. Don't you remember *Double Jeopardy? Sleeping with the Enemy? Dead Calm!* Remember *Dead Calm?* Nothing good happens on boats. Promise me you won't go!"

"Jacqs, don't be jealous. Once this wedding is over with, Sanjay and I will ignore each other and drift apart just as all married couples do. I promise. I'll be all yours." Bina pats my thigh and merges into the light Saturday traffic. "Anyway, you're due for a boyfriend. Any good prospects?"

"No. I'm done with men. All of them." I look out the window. I don't trust Sanjay, but I doubt he'd kill her. He doesn't seem that desperate. And I know Allen wouldn't have anything to do with a scheme that even has a whiff of being in the gray area. He's a lawyer and has grandiose ideas of running for office one day.

When he heard that I worked for the Mayor's wife, I became his new best friend until I let him know that if I was going to weasel a job on the Mayor's staff, it would be for me.

"So, how is Sanjay?" I ask, trying to sound extra casual. I've never inquired about his welfare until today and I don't want to make Bina suspicious.

"I told you, jumpy. On edge. Between this wedding thing and the lawyers keeping him late at work, he hasn't had a chance to relax. That's why we are going out on the boat, to get away from everything for a little while. You should come! I know you hate boats and you threw up the last time, but it might be better at night."

"OK," I say without hesitating. I don't just hate boats, I fear them. I was never so sick or scared in my life as I was in Allen's boat, which isn't small or rickety. Just the idea of being afloat in the middle of the bay, not being able to flee, can cause a panic attack. "I'll come. For you."

"Are you serious, Jacqs?" When I nod, she takes her hands off the wheel and tries to hug me. I bat her away to a chorus of car horns. "This is a miracle! This will be so fun. Who knows, maybe you can straighten Allen out once and for all. Invite Vivian! We'll have a party on the boat!"

"I think I'll pass on Allen. Vivian's husband served her with divorce papers on Friday."

"It's such a pity, but maybe for the best." Bina turns into the parking structure and heads for her usual floor. "They've been married only a little while and, thank goodness, there are no children."

"I guess she is lucky in a way. Right? She's young, attractive. She can find a new man, a better man, in no time," I chirp, hoping that subconsciously Bina takes this all in. We climb out of her Saab and head toward the elevators.

"Of course she can," Bina says as she links her arm through mine. "But we have to find one for you first."

"It can wait," I say, and lean my head on her shoulder. "I have a feeling I'm going to be busy in the near future."

I sit next to Bina and pretend I haven't seen this exact movie. The ticket taker recognized me and gave me a funny look, but I ignored him. Bina claimed I was flirting with him and I had no choice but to agree.

I can't concentrate, and I laugh in the wrong places or miss jokes entirely. I need someone to talk to, someone human, but not Dr. N. I need someone who can share the horror of my situation on a very basic level.

Vivian! She'll understand. Plus, she'll find out anyway when the wedding is cancelled. Bina extended a very heartfelt and drunken invitation to her the night we all went out together. Vivian accepted on the spot and has already purchased a gift for them.

I have to hold it all in for a few hours before I can ditch Bina and spill my guts to Vivian. They'll be the longest hours of my life.

82

Mrs. Mayor

After an hour of shopping and then eating a slice of Blondie's pizza standing up, I tell Bina (OK, lie) that I have cramps and I need to go home and rest.

She's very understanding and offers to sit with me and keep microwaving my gel pack. I feel extremely guilty telling her I'd rather be alone. Then, to make it worse, she tells me she'll use this time to work on wedding details.

By the time I get into my flat, all I really want to do is take another one of Vivian's magic pills and shut out the world for the rest of my life. I'll deal with all this stuff tomorrow. I'll go out to lunch with Vivian and have a nice long talk. I strip off my clothes and, wearing only a camisole and underpants, collapse on my couch and stare blankly at the wall.

After that gets too tiring, I let my body fall to the left and resume staring. That's when I notice the condom wrapper underneath my coffee table. One thing I'm absolutely sure of is that there hasn't been a condom opened in my flat for the last year (and counting), at least not by me.

All of a sudden, every nerve in my body goes into overdrive as I strain to sense if someone is having sex with someone in my near, too near, vicinity. I inhale deeply, trying to smell if this sex may have occurred on my Pottery Barn couch. I splurged and went for the linen/cotton blend and had to wait three extra weeks for it to be delivered. It's a virgin couch and I always thought I'd be the one to deflower it. I stand up and look closely around and see that things are moved around. There are two wineglasses on the side table, and a CD case (Marvin Gaye!) is open and empty on top of the stereo.

Her door is closed, but Vivian doesn't strike me as the quiet type in bed. I get up, tiptoe to her door and press my ear against it, trying to hear heavy breathing or, please no, moaning. Nothing but quiet. I tap on the door and then leap back. I lean forward and knock loudly but hopefully in a friendly manner. Nothing.

I gently crack open the door and peer inside without trying to look at the bed. "Vivian?" I say in a whisper so loud that even the neighbors in the next building should be able to hear through the window. Hearing nothing, I push the door all the way open.

Her bedsheets are all twisted up and there is *another* empty condom wrapper in the wastebasket by her bed. I rub my eyes and look again at her unmade bed. Buried in the sheets is a tie in a unique shade of lavender (purple, according to the Hermès salesperson) that I only just recently laid eyes on.

I go stand by the bed and hover closely over the tie, so close that the pattern blurs. For a second I don't really understand how Mr. Mayor's tie, the one Mrs. Mayor had me get him especially for his dinner with the governor of California, has gotten into Vivian's bed.

I'm about to gingerly pick it out of the tangle of sheets when someone pounds on my front door. I jump back, like a startled cat, and look for a way to escape, briefly entertaining the thought of heading out the window. It's the police! I just know it. Now I know what Monica Lewinsky felt like when the FBI came to her door looking for her blue dress. I'm fucked and I didn't even get laid!

I rush into the living room, peek through the peephole and get a fish-eyed view of a very upset-looking Mrs. Mayor.

"Open the door this instant!" She stops pounding on the door but is now yelling.

I snatch open the door before anyone sees her. Briefly I notice that her car, which she rarely drives herself, is double-parked outside.

"Hi. Katherine. What a surprise." I smooth down my hair. "I thought you were in LA."

"Where is he?" she asks hysterically, standing very close to me. I can see the faintest of smudges under her eye where it used to be bruised. "I know he's been here."

"Who? I'm here alone. Would you like something to drink?"

"Jacquelyn, don't fuck with me," Mrs. Mayor says in an icy-cold voice that scares me.

"OK." I take a step back.

"Where is that redheaded cunt? Tell me!" Mrs. Mayor spits.

I notice she's wearing pointy black Dior boots, sleek pants and a light cashmere sweater, and no jewelry except for her engagement ring—Mrs. Mayor's catfight outfit. That rock on her ring would do serious damage and turn a simple catfight into assault with a deadly weapon.

"You mean Vivian? She's not here. She's out. I mean, I guess she's out. I just got here. I was at the movies. You want to see my ticket stub?" I am totally innocent and Vivian obviously isn't. I still feel kind of bad even though technically I'm not selling her out. But, hey, she got laid in her bed, now she has to lie in it.

Mrs. Mayor gives me a disgusted look, pushes past me and stalks into my room. Sensing that there hasn't been any sex in there for a while, she beelines toward Vivian's room and her unmade bed with its flutter of lavender. She stops short, gives a pained gasp and then launches herself toward the bed. She grabs the tie and then crumples on the floor, crying, really crying. Soon the snot starts running down her nose, and she makes no move to wipe it.

I wince. This is getting messy. I grab a box of tissues and am about to go in when I realize I'm wearing only my underwear. I rush into my room, pull on a pair of pants and take the time to dig out a slightly wrinkled shirt out of my closet. I can face Mrs. Mayor without shoes, she seems practically harmless for now.

I lock the front door with the chain so Vivian will know something is up if she is so blinded by stupidity sex that she doesn't notice Mrs. Mayor's double-parked Mercedes in front of my flat.

I march into Vivian's room, shut the window so the neighbors don't hear any more than they already have and hunker down next to Mrs. Mayor with the box of tissues.

"Katherine? Do you want to go sit in the living room? I can make some tea." Tea seems like the thing to offer. It seems more medicinal than coffee, and there is no way I'm offering her anything stronger to drink.

"Why? Tell me, why?" she wails.

I dab her face with the tissue and notice she's taken the time to apply a full face of makeup. I'm careful not to smear her eye makeup. Her mascara is staying put, must be heavy-duty waterproof. I make a mental note to check her makeup case to see the brand.

"I don't know why, Katherine. Come on." I heave her up and she leans heavily on me. I deposit her on the couch, where she slumps and continues to cry. I watch her for a bit. "Oh, crap! I'll be right back."

I tear outside and pound on my old lady neighbor's door. She opens it holding her cordless phone.

"If you even think of calling a tow truck, you'll live in a world of hurt from this day forward." I jab my finger behind me. "That's the mayor's wife's car and, trust me, she can be a real bitch."

Without waiting to see if she has anything to say, I take off back toward my place and slam the door behind me.

"Now, what kind of tea would you like? I have green tea, of course, and chamomile and jasmine. Oh, and English breakfast, Irish breakfast. And orange spice, but it's in bags. I prefer loose tea. The orange spice is Vivian's . . . Let's have chamomile." I fill the kettle, set it on the stove, and go and sit next to Mrs. Mayor, who is now sniffling and staring at her engagement ring, the first and last Baxter heirloom she got her hands on. I pat her back lightly and realize that aside from shaking her hand the first day

I met her, this is probably only the second time I've touched her.

We sit in silence until the kettle gives off a shrill whistle. This seems to snap Mrs. Mayor out of her stupor.

"I knew he was cheating on me. This isn't the first time." She looks up at me with huge, sad eyes.

"I'm sorry. Let me get you some tea." Normally, I would try to keep the conversation going while in the kitchen but it seems kind of crass in this situation, especially since she is my boss.

I race through pouring tea into the pot and putting cups, milk and sugar on a tray. I empty a box of butter cookies onto a plate and carry everything to the coffee table.

"Are you sure? I mean . . . I mean, he could have lent her his tie for a tourniquet or something," I chatter while the tea steeps.

I love having tea. I have a huge collection of teapots, and the only thing I was really gunning for as a wedding present was a tea set from Tiffany's. I never got it, of course, because I didn't have a wedding and everyone assumed that since we were already living together, we had everything we needed.

My internal clock tells me the tea is just close to perfect. I pour it into a cup and offer it along with its dainty saucer to Mrs. Mayor, praying that her hands are steady and she won't drop it and break it. It's my best set. I got it on sale at Bed Bath & Beyond when I was supposed to be tracking down refrigerated, pure flaxseed oil for her.

"I'm sure." She takes the cup and blows. "I know. What more proof do I need?"

We sip in silence. Aside from the fact that Mrs. Mayor makes me uncomfortable, and there is a wrapper from a condom only a few feet away that was used by her husband and Vivian, this is actually pretty relaxing.

"I knew there were other women. I'm not stupid. He was practically engaged to that anorexic debutant when I met him. But no, I didn't listen to my agent and I went ahead and married the bastard." Mrs. Mayor snorts into her tea. "I'm surprised he hasn't tried to get into your pants."

"Thanks!" A compliment is a compliment, even a backhanded one, which are all Mrs. Mayor is capable of. "I mean . . . no. Never."

"Of course not," she says more to herself than me.

I'll let that one slide due to the circumstances.

"What are you going to do?" This seems like a reasonable question. If this isn't the first time he's cheated on her, it won't be the last, and she doesn't seem to be taking it too well.

"Nothing." She scoops in too much sugar into her cup. I can tell that Mrs. Mayor is not one for proper tea. She usually sticks to the iced kind.

"Pardon me?"

"What can I do, Jacquelyn?" The tears start flowing again. "Divorce him and go back to making horrible movies or being a supporting player on a bad sitcom?"

"No, I guess not. Especially if you don't want to." I could think of worse fates than being a working actress. Even a cheesy working actress. I hand her a tissue, but I'm not doing any more wiping. Mrs. Mayor gets very dependent when she's upset. "Have you guys considered going to a marriage counselor?"

"Of course." Mrs. Mayor nods as she dabs her eyes expertly. This was her signature move on her soap, *Love and Lies*. Watching her makes me feel nostalgic for those simple times when high drama was relegated to the family television set. "I've suggested it, but he says no one in his family has ever been to one and he isn't going to be the first."

I wonder if he either doesn't know she sees a shrink or doesn't consider her as part of his family.

"Do you love him?" Women have the immense and irrational ability to overlook the most horrendous of faults for love. I wouldn't hold this against her if she did, since I'd think twice about leaving Mr. Mayor and I only have a crush on him.

"Love? What is love, Jacquelyn?" This is Mrs. Mayor being philosophical.

I don't say anything and let the moment pass. I can see, now, that even a woman who seems so self-possessed as Mrs. Mayor is just as weak and insecure as a regular woman when it comes to her husband, or any man, for that matter. Mrs. Mayor, I can tell, probably has a lot of experience with cheating boyfriends and disastrous romances, but she's still holding on to hope that she'll find the right one. Someday.

I should say something supportive and understanding.

"Um." I start. I need to warm up.

"If that motherfucker thinks I'm going to divorce him, he's got another thing coming. I'm going to be First Lady if it kills him. The prick." She takes a butter cookie and dunks it and chews on it savagely.

I can see the wheels turning in her head. It's an awesome thing and not a little scary.

"OK. So what happens now?" Maybe she wants me to make a spa appointment. I'd like nothing better than to pass her on to a massage therapist.

"First, this doesn't leave this . . . place." Is she dissing my flat? "Second, we go on as normal. I'll take care of it."

She stands up and I automatically get up too. I guess teatime is over.

"If that's what you want to do." I walk behind her as she starts for the front door. She nods firmly and fumbles with my sticky front-door lock. I hadn't noticed, but all this time, she was clutching her car keys.

"I'll see you on Tuesday. Have a good day, Jacquelyn," she says as if we were standing in her multimillion dollar Mansion and it was the end of a typical working day.

"Yeah, uh, you, too. Bye! Thanks." I close the door and collapse against it.

I have to flee my own home. I dig out Natasha's key (I have to water her plants) and start toward my room to pack an overnight (or two) bag.

My phone rings and I pounce on it, assuming it's Bina.

83

Vivian

"Hello? Bina?"

"Sorry, it's me. Vivian. Remember me?"

She's calling me from her car. I can hear traffic noises.

"Where are you?" I ask. I almost wish she would have walked in while Mrs. Mayor was here. It's better for me if they go ahead and have their little showdown so I can get back to my life. The longer they put it off, the more awkward it's going to get for me.

"I'm driving around," she says, sounding lost.

"Another work thing? It's a good thing you're so flexible." I like Vivian, really I do, but she had sex with Mr. Mayor and he's married. And she did it in my flat at least twice. Never mind that I probably would have done the same thing, but she didn't have to deal with his wife's nervous breakdown and doesn't have to work with her either.

"I was just calling to say hi." She sounds small and insecure.

"Hi," I say. I know what's coming next. She's going to ask me to clean up her mess.

"Jacquelyn? I did something really stupid. Beyond stupid. Suicidal."

"Really." I wait. I can't act shocked and I won't pretend to. I'm angry and hurt, more than I'd ever admit to anyone. Especially myself.

"I . . . I slept with Kit." She lets the statement hang there. "Are you there, Jacquelyn?"

"Yeah, I'm here." I look down at my fingernails and see that they're chipped. I walk into the bathroom and gather up my manicure supplies and pack them along with my other stuff.

"I'm sorry," Vivian says.

No doubt she hopes this will mean something to me. She wants me to get mad.

"Why are you telling me you're sorry? I'm not his wife, Vivian," I snap. Gosh, I'm a bitch.

"See, I knew you'd be mad at me." She sounds almost relieved.

"I'm not mad. Just . . . This just makes my life all the more difficult. So . . . what? Is he leaving her for you? What happens now, Vivian? Did you ever consider that?" I ask, letting it all ooze out like pus.

"I don't know." She begins to cry. "Jacqs. Please tell me what to do."

I don't say anything. I don't think anything.

"Jacqs?"

"Come home. I'll pack you an overnight bag. We're spending the night at Natasha's."

I wake up like a shot at 5:30 the next morning, remembering Bina and the boat ride around the bay. I scramble toward my phone and find no messages on it.

I jump out of bed, and Vivian groggily pushes herself up on her elbows.

"What's wrong, Jacqs?" She looks beautiful. Even with the crusty things in the corners of her eyes.

"I was supposed to meet Bina last night! Sanjay is gay! He was supposed to tell her, but he hasn't." I scamper around the room like a chicken with its head up its ass. "And she hasn't called, and she doesn't know where I am, and—"

"Jacqs, calm down." She gets up and takes her shoes out of my hands. "I'll fix us some breakfast, coffee or something. You take a shower. We'll go over to her place and see what's up. No big deal."

"Yeah, no big deal. Should I call her? Why hasn't she called? Maybe they went on the boat and he's killed her!" I yell. "My aunt had a stroke and it's my fault. I told my cousin to elope and it's killed her mother. Or at least has made her a horrible cripple and I don't feel bad about it. And I ruined Nate's chances at true happiness. But he gave her my ring! What was I supposed to do? Maybe not send them a gift, but I couldn't help myself. And this is just the latest. I am truly an evil person and I'll burn in hell."

"Jacqs, you're not making any sense. I'll call Bina. You're in no state to talk to anyone. Take a shower. I'll take care of everything."

"OK. Yes. You can help me." She leads me by the hand into the bathroom and starts up the shower.

"You're not evil, honey, you're just complicated," she says in a soothing voice as she quickly strips off my clothes and settles me under the showerhead.

My heart is filled with real love for her. I forgive her for screwing Mr. Mayor, for screwing him in my flat and for probably screwing us both out of a job.

"Mrs. Mayor is feeding Emilio all the information, she's the link. Mr. Mayor knows it, but they're looking for someone else to scapegoat."

"I know, honey. You just relax. I'll take care of everything."

"Yes. Please." For once, I'll let someone else take care of me and I can just stand here and let life happen.

84

Bina

Vivian makes me have a cup of tea and an apple scone before we leave. She doesn't shower. She can't reach Bina by phone and is as worried as I am.

Without asking, she gets into the driver's seat and heads toward Bina's.

"So Sanjay is gay?" Vivian asks, more to herself. "That would explain why he's obsessing over every detail. You know, trying to make sure the façade was perfect to continue his lie."

"He promised me he'd tell her, but then he called and said he hadn't, and then she told me they had this boat cruise planned, and I promised to go with her but I totally forgot."

"That's my fault. I'm sorry." Vivian reaches over and pats my thigh. "I'm so sorry, Jacqs. Can you forgive me?"

I look down at my hands and realize it's not totally absurd that Vivian is asking for my forgiveness. She knew, though she never let on, that I had a raging crush on Mr. Mayor. "I . . . I guess I can understand why it happened. He cheats, and you were lonely and vulnerable."

"And a little drunk and desperate. I'm not totally innocent here. I feel bad for Mrs. Mayor, though. I'm going to resign today. It would be impossible for me to keep working for him. And he knows it," she says wryly. "How déclassé to sleep with your press secretary. The man will be president yet."

"What will you do?" It's nice to talk about someone else's problems for a bit.

"Deal with my divorce. Take some time off. Look for something new to do with my life." Vivian adjusts her sunglasses on her nose and looks over at me and smiles. "The world is my oyster, baby. Slurp, slurp."

I laugh for the first time in days.

I knock on the door and call out to Bina, being careful not to cause a scene in front of the early morning coffee junkies. She lives right next door to a very popular café, and her sidewalk is always clogged with people. No one seems to have a job in her neighborhood, so the café is always packed. How they pay for their $4 lattes is beyond me.

I wait for a moment before I use my key. I don't want to barge in on her, but she won't answer her phone or her door. I think this qualifies as an emergency.

I push open the door and feel Vivian's hand on my shoulder. "I'll be at the café. Call me if you need me."

I nod, thankful that Vivian has enough sense to understand that she's not close enough to Bina to be here for this. God, is anybody?

I walk up the steps and find Bina sitting at her kitchen table, wearing her windbreaker and sneakers. I feel myself begin to tear up.

"Are you OK?" I ask, taking a seat next to her.

"Hi, Jacqs. Tea, coffee? Waffles?"

She was raised, as I was, to offer a guest something to drink or eat no matter the circumstances. The worse the circumstance, the more elaborate the offer.

"I'll make some tea." I get up and try to be as quiet as possible as I brew the tea and set out some of her favorite shortbread cookies. She doesn't move or say a word. Doesn't even cry. I could understand crying, or even laughing, but not silence.

I sit down next to her and pour her a cup of tea, using the hodgepodge of cups and saucers I've given her over the years.

She takes a sip and puts down the cup. I reach over and run my hand through her hair. Her head bobs down and I can see the tears start.

"He's left me," she says simply.

"When?"

"Yesterday. He said this wedding, getting married . . . It wasn't right." She cries harder. I fold her into my arms until she's practically on my lap. "He said he wasn't ready to get married."

"Wait. What?" I ask, trying to keep the rage out of my voice. "That's the reason he gave you?"

"I said the same thing! I said we could postpone. We could wait, but he said he was leaving for New York and it was over. That he loved me, but he wasn't ready to get married."

"That asshole! That complete bastard!" I yelp. How dare he put it all on her shoulders? What a pathetic, cowardly copout!

Bina nods soggily against my chest and cries. I cry with her while formulating revenge plans. If Sanjay thinks I'll let him get away with this, he doesn't know me very well.

Sometime later, long after our tea has gone cold, we hear tentative knocking on the front door. Bina looks up at me.

"It's Vivian. She's got issues of her own. She slept with Mr. Mayor."

"Oh, God, let her in. I'll make us some fresh tea." Bina gets up without her usual bustle and trudges over to the stove.

I scamper downstairs and open the door for Vivian to slip in.

"How is she?" Vivian whispers, looking concerned, but surprisingly well rested considering she was in a chemically induced coma for the last fifteen hours.

"Devastated. Practically catatonic." This is true, if a little dramatic. Bina has always been on the dramatic side but not necessarily a drama queen. "How are you?"

"I just talked to Mr. Mayor," she says nonchalantly. I keep myself from pointing out that she called the man she just slept with *Mr.* "Things are a little more complicated than I thought. She knows."

"I'm sorry, Vivian." And I am, too, but I'm also sorry that Mrs. Mayor found out, and not only found out, but found out it happened in my flat with someone she knows I consider a friend. A good-enough friend to let live in my flat, where she, my friend, had sex with her husband.

"I hope Mrs. Mayor doesn't take it out on you. Kit won't stand for it," Vivian says, but we both know my job security took a downward spiral the second Vivian's panties did. "I'll talk to him."

I'm about to tell her not to bother when Bina calls down to us.

"What are you girls whispering about down there?" Her voice sounds stronger but full of sadness. "It better be about me."

"Of course it is, sweetheart. We'll be right up." I grab Vivian and move her hair out of the way to whisper in her ear. "Sanjay, that prick, left town. Told her he wasn't ready to get married."

"That asshole!" Vivian whispers furiously. "He can't think he'll get away with this!"

"For now, that's the story. I don't know if it's better for Bina to think he didn't love her enough to marry her, or that she came this close to marrying a gay man."

"OK! That's enough time! I'm coming down!" Bina yells.

We head upstairs and try not to look guilty. Bina is sitting at the table, a romantic spread of fresh sliced fruits, scones, strawberry jam, orange juice and a bottle of personalized champagne in front of her. I realize this is probably what she had planned on feeding Sanjay this morning. What better way to send off the man you love to work than with some homemade jam, scones and a mimosa? The prick.

"Champagne, anyone?" Bina asks with a hiccup. "I have tons. It was Sanjay's idea for the wedding favors. We were going to hand them out at the reception, after, the, the, the wed—"

Vivian rushes over to Bina and enfolds her in an embrace and begins to cry. This sets Bina off, and since I'm not into three-way hugs, I hang back and sniffle, feeling a little left out. They hang on to each other while I clumsily think about the multitude of problems I have that would normally warrant attention and sympathy. Getting a little impatient I pop the cork on the bottle and pour the fizzy drink, sans orange juice, into the crystal flutes.

"At least now I can eat like a normal person. Sanjay had this thing with my weight. An unhealthy obsession," Bina says as she spreads a thick layer of strawberry jam on a scone. She stops and turns the bottle so the label, with their names in elaborate script and wedding date on it, faces away from her.

"A woman's weight is never a man's business," Vivian adds, downing her glass and holding it out for a refill. "Curtis had this thing with my boobs. He wanted me to get a reduction."

"He did not!" I check out Vivian's chest. She has the kind of boobs that are a cup size too big to be anything but sexy knockers. Usually she hides them behind demure suits, but she always wears high-quality lingerie.

Even though I already ate, I take a scone and load it up with jam and butter. After all, it's never a good idea to drink on an empty stomach. Especially when you're drinking champagne before seven in the morning.

"He said they made me look common." She grunts and opens her shirt and puts them on display for us. Bina reaches over and gives one a gentle poke, like testing the softness of a ball of dough.

"Common! They're fantastic. I'd kill for breasts like that." Bina is a small B cup and has always had boob envy. She takes a healthy sip out of her flute. Vivian refills it before she has a chance to put it down. "I think I'll use the wedding-deposit money and buy me some."

"You should." And I really mean it. She needs boobs. She needs something to totally distract her from the fact that her secretly gay fiancé just dumped her without telling her the real reason why. "Couldn't one of your doctor friends give you a good deal?"

I'm pandering to her vices, but she needs distraction. Second on Bina's list of favorite things to do is bargain hunting. First is watching movies, with matinees being the pinnacle of both favorites.

"I don't know what I'm going to tell my family," Bina says quietly. She finishes off her glass and tips it toward me for a refill.

"I'm sure they won't notice unless you get really big implants," Vivian says, taking another scone off the plate.

"Not about my breasts. Sanjay. What should I tell them? They'll be so disappointed in me," Bina whispers.

I reach over and take her hand before Vivian butts in. "You didn't do anything wrong. He's crazy. This is his . . . failure to live up to his promise."

"Jacqs is right. Men are weak and we women spend way too much time compensating for them while never letting on we know. It's a vicious pattern. I'm glad that my husband has put me out of my misery by suing me for divorce. He's doing me a favor." Vivian pours the last of the champagne into our glasses.

"Maybe you're right. Right? I mean, I would have gone through with the wedding even though I've been having my doubts," Bina says, sounding a little stronger.

"What doubts?" Vivian and I ask simultaneously. Bina gets up and pulls another bottle from her stash and expertly pops the cork. It's warm so I get up and get a bowl of ice from the freezer and plunk cubes into the glasses. Bina tops them off.

"He was so fastidious about his clothes and grooming. He spent more time getting ready than I did. And he always had something to say about my appearance, tips on how I could look better." Bina reaches up to finger her necklace. She does this when she's nervous. "It drove me crazy. I could never find my favorite tweezers."

"He was very stylish," I offer up cautiously. The guy left clues like breadcrumbs and eventually Bina has to figure out where they lead to. "He also had that thing with your magazines."

"What thing? What magazines?" Vivian asks. She picks at her fruit plate as she sips.

"Oh, he would always read my *Vogue* before I did and he made me subscribe to *Harper's Bazaar* and *W* magazine even though I told him I barely had time to read *Vogue*," Bina says with a slight slur.

"Oh," Vivian says. And looks over at me and widens her eyes. It couldn't be plainer than day to the both of us that Bina should at least have some inkling as to what her doubts were really about.

"But enough about that snake, Sanjay. So you actually slept with the Mayor, Vivian?" Bina, back in her straightforward-business mode. "Not smart."

"Tell me about it." Vivian puts her chin in her hand. "Now I'll have to find a new job, and you didn't hear it from me as the official spokesperson for the Mayor of San Francisco, but the economy is in the toilet."

"Vivian is going to resign," I explain to Bina. "When will you do it?"

"Today. I'm going into the office later today and telling the staff. Might as well get it over with."

"What will you tell them?" Bina asks Vivian.

"Some bullshit story about sick parents back in Ohio?" Bina and I shake our heads. "A juicy job offer in Borneo? Half those Ivy Leaguers will think I mean Bora Bora because they have fond memories of spending a carefree summer there after college, all of twelve months ago."

"This is terrible. To have to leave your job! He should . . ." Bina trails off.

"Do what? I had sex with my boss. My married boss who happens to be a rising politician. I'm a casualty of my own making." Vivian shrugs.

"How can you be so matter-of-fact about it?" Something like this would take me another year in therapy to figure out. I'd keep Dr. N in Birkenstocks for life.

"I don't love him, Jacqs. It was sex. Stupid sex. I knew what I was doing when I did it. I didn't have any illusions."

"Speak for yourself," I say jokingly and take a pass on a refill. One of us should be halfway sober to face the rest of the day.

My whole life is built on illusions. My illusions of a long-lasting connection with my ex-husband, that my mother would be happy if she just completely changed her life, that my brother Noel could be a great person if he just got off his ass, that Mrs. Mayor is a nice person who really likes me and when she gives me her castoffs she's not doing it out of charity but because every woman should have some Gucci in her life, that my married boyfriend is really a boyfriend, that my best friend isn't so blinded by love that she refuses to see that her fiancé is so gay and that's why he left her and, mostly, that my therapist thinks I am the single-most normal and together person she knows and only continues to see me (and take my money) because she likes my company.

I watch Bina and Vivian polish off the second bottle between them, not bothering with ice.

"I should go shower and change." Vivian gets up. "I'll catch a cab. I really shouldn't drive in my condition, but I sure as shit ain't showing up at work sober. Maybe they'll give me a random sobriety test and fire me on the spot. It'll save me the embarrassment of having to resign."

"If you wait for a few minutes I can drop you off and come right back," I say, looking at Bina to make sure it's OK.

"No, you stay here with Bina. I've caused you enough trouble." She reaches down and gives Bina a hug. Bina hugs her back. Vivian gestures toward the crystal flutes. "And by the way, you can keep my gift. I'm glad they came in handy, but not this way."

"Thank you, Vivian. Good luck." Bina walks her to the door and I follow and hug her. We stand there and watch her hail a cab and climb in. She's a bit unsteady on her feet but I'm sure a shower will sober her up enough to face the Ivy League barracudas that Mr. Mayor calls his staff and friends.

"What are you going to do with the rest of the booze?" I ask.

"I don't know," she says as we go back up the stairs. "I wonder if I can write it off on my taxes?"

"You can always donate it to a homeless shelter, I guess." I'm a bit drunk so this doesn't seem like such a stupid suggestion.

We sit back down on the couch, huddled together and enjoying our buzz.

"There is another thing that always worried me about Sanjay," Bina muses as we stare out the window a little glassy-eyed.

"What's that?" I ask, my heart skipping a beat.

"His politics. You think he was a closet Republican?" she asks, holding out her glass for refill.

"Sanjay?" I pour for us both, filling her glass to the rim. Fuck being sober. "Nope, Bina. I can assure you Sanjay was liberal, very liberal when it came to his politics."

85

Emilio

"Why don't you ever return my calls?"

Cortez corners me next to a huge plate glass window as people mill around during intermission at the ballet. The Mayors have decided not to mingle, but have the chosen few come to their private box for an audience. I've been sent away to make room for the important people.

"I don't return anyone's calls. Hasn't my mother told you?" I accept a quick sip from his drink. It's a very intimate gesture and I want to show him I am not at all flustered by it. "Is that your girlfriend over there? The one shooting knives with her eyes?"

Emilio takes his time turning around. "Her? We work together. We're just friends. I bet you know all about getting friendly with people you work with? *Qué dices,* Jacquelyn?"

"*Yo digo nada.* I think that's something a man in your position should be able to appreciate, a woman keeping quiet." I raise a brow archly and his blink confirms what's been lurking in the back of my mind about him and Vivian in Santa Barbara.

"How is the lovely Vivian?" He takes back his drink.

"How do you think she is? She's out of work and hiding out in my flat. Her husband is threatening to accuse her of adultery if she doesn't null their prenup. She couldn't be better."

"Should I call her? . . . I mean, as a friend?" Cortez looks pained, genuinely troubled by what he's done. "Is she mad at me?"

"For writing a column based on information from a decidedly biased source about her relationship with her now ex-boss? Or for sleeping with her when she was confused, vulnerable and probably drunk?" Emilio flinches, making me smile. So the man does have a conscience. Interesting. "Leave her alone. She has enough troubles."

He leans in, embraces me, his lips against my ear. "I'm sorry."

"What for?" I lean back and before he can answer, I lightly cover his mouth with my hand. The stubble feels so good against my palm, I tingle all over. "Don't answer that."

86

Jesus

"Jesus Christ!" I'm standing in Natasha's kitchen clutching a sticky plastic watering can, my heart in my throat. "You fucking scared me!"

"I'm sorry. I need to talk to Natasha." Jesus isn't looking so hot. He has circles under his eyes, he needs a haircut and a shave. He doesn't look so much dangerous as just merely desperate. "Please. Please, Jacquelyn."

"Does Natasha know you're here?" I commence with the watering of the plants.

"No, the landlord let me in. He knows we are together." He begins to cry.

"Is that what you call it?" I can't hold back the sneer in my voice. He really hurt Natasha, drove her away from her home and me. For that I can't forgive him, even though I know Natasha will.

"I love her! I do, you have to believe me." His slim shoulders heave under his wrinkled button-down.

"I don't know what you want me to do, Jesus. I can't work miracles," I snicker.

"Just please, call her for me. Tell her to call me. That's all I want. I promise, I've changed. I love her." More crying.

"Fine. Shut up. I'll tell her I ran into you and the rest is up to her." I shrug off his hugs.

"Thank you! Thank you!"

"You thank me now," I say as I pat him on the back, "but just wait. I don't have the best track record when it comes to relationships."

87

Vivian

"Are you sure you want to do this?" I ask her as I pull my car up to the airport curb.

Vivian looks tired but as if a huge weight has been lifted off her shoulders. She smiles at me. "Like you said to me once, sometimes family are the only people you can turn to when you've made a mess of your life."

"I said that?"

"OK, you were drunk from celebrating your first official month as a divorcee, but still you said it."

"By family, I meant you guys." That's unfair. My family was really supportive, mostly by never bringing it up.

"I just need to get out of here, to clear my head." She pulls her hair into a messy ponytail.

"And then what?" I'm afraid to ask. I've already lost Natasha, she's not coming back. I don't blame her; it was time for a change. Maybe Jesus will find temptation a lot less tempting in New York. Doubt it.

"I don't know. I liked LA. Maybe I'll peddle my talents there?" She starts to cry a little.

"I know a great guy there. He'll show you a good time, no pressure." Wouldn't it make Mrs. Mayor happy for me to pimp out her producer friend to the woman who slept with her husband? I laugh despite how awful the whole thing is.

"Love, love, love you, Jacqs," she says giving me a kiss full on the lips.

"I love you, Vivian."

We hugged a long time until some cop taps on my window and tells us to move along. For once, I don't mention who I work for.

88

Anita and Lei

I've never seen Anita and Lei work harder. If they didn't exchange more than two words before, now they communicate solely through telepathy. They are avoiding me like the plague and I think this is really unfair. I didn't do anything. Much.

They're just covering their asses. The Mayors haven't broken out the lie detector to find out who leaked to Cortez, but the Mayor has been making noises about having us sign a confidentiality agreement.

I wonder if he'll make his wife sign one as well as the help.

They leave shortly after I do, climb on the bus together but sit in different seats. We never talk about what we see and hear. Not that we did before, but now I feel even more isolated than I did before.

I can't blame them, much. They've been here a lot longer than I have and I guess they want to keep it that way.

89

Danny

"Whatcha doing, Jacqs?" Danny drawls as he leans up the balustrade in the foyer.

"What does it look like I'm doing?" He's caught me bending over, trying to retrieve all the slippery mail that's pooled at my feet.

"You've been quiet as a mouse lately. Wonder why?"

Danny is as slimy as ever. I find it kind of comforting to see that some things stay the same.

"Shut up, Danny." I look around and lean toward him to whisper, "Mrs. Mayor had me order some of those tiny listening devices off the Internet. I don't know where she put them."

"She did?" His eyes dart around frantically. "You're lying."

I scoop up the last of the mail and push past him to proceed upstairs before heading back down. I step in close to him and hold a finger to his lips.

"Yeah, Danny, I'm lying. Say whatever you want. Just be careful where and to whom you say it to."

Danny flushes. I turn around and head up the stairs, taking my time.

I'm so mean, but a girl's got to throw a boy a bone once in a while. It's the polite thing to do, after all.

90

Nate

"Hello?" I squeeze my phone between my chin and shoulder.

I'm killing time organizing Mrs. Mayor's workouts and regular spa appointments for the next two months. I seem to have her booked for a full leg wax and facial at the same time. This just won't do.

"Jacqs? It's me."

I drop my cell and scramble to pick it up. "Nate? Hi!"

"I just called to tell you the wedding went great!"

"It did?" I stand up and sit back down again. My hands start to shake. "Congratulations." I guess.

"Thanks. Really. I was having major second thoughts and seeing you just confirmed that I was doing the right thing by marrying Bethany."

"Gee, thanks, Nate. Really." What an ass. The thing is he thinks he's being an enlightened male by telling me this. "So are you calling me from India?"

"No, we cancelled India. We're coming out to San Francisco for our honeymoon Isn't that funny?"

"No." I'm not surprised to hear India is out and San Francisco is in. Nate is too dense to realize he's walking into a trap.

"But, hey, India will always be there."

"Yes, it will, Nate." But I won't. "When are you coming?"

"In a couple of weeks. We had to turn our plans upside down. I was really touched when Bethany suggested San Francisco. She knows how much I loved living there. I would love for you to meet Bethany."

"Would you, now." Why do this to yourself, Nate? Why do this to me and Bethany? There is nothing worse than meeting your ex's new partner. That is, unless you're the new partner who has to deal with a reunion between two ex's.

"We'll go out to dinner. To that place where I had that great fish," he says, as oblivious as ever. I can imagine him with his feet up on his desk tossing one of those ever-present stress balls he always used to clutch at. "Man, that was one good meal. Is it still open?"

Yes, and so is my mouth. I can think of so many things I want to say. All of which will only make me look bad, worse than I already do.

"Jacqs, you there?" Nate asks.

"Yeah. Sure. Call me when you guys get in. I'd love to meet your Bethany," I lie.

"Cool. Cool. Talk to you soon, babe." Nate clicks off and I toss my phone into the garbage can.

91

George

I arrive at our usual dinner place right on time, and George is nowhere to be found. After hanging around outside for ten minutes, I go in and pretend to read the framed restaurant reviews, hoping the new hostess doesn't come over and ask me if I'm waiting for someone. What would I say? I'm waiting for an older gentleman, nudge, nudge, wink, wink.

Another five excruciating minutes, the door swings open and I see George's familiar figure in the doorway. I feel a surge of love. Not necessarily for him, but for the fact that he's here and hasn't stood me up.

"Sorry I'm late. I got held up with a board meeting." George takes my elbow and follows the hostess, who shows us to our usual table.

"Board meeting? Can't you just send some lackey in your place? Don't they know you have a golf game to get to?" I tease. I'm not sure exactly what George does at the company he works for, only that he makes a lot of money, *a lot* of money, and doesn't seem to do much real work. It's mostly telling other people what to do, who tell other people what to do. And having those people write up reports, which then get rewritten by the second tier and then presented to George, who then has his assistant rewrite them so he can present them to his vice presidents and board members.

It sounds horribly boring. Almost as boring as listening to Mrs. Mayor talk about her chakras.

"You would think so, but sometimes you have to pay the piper, my dear," George says, pulling out my seat for me.

As soon as he sits, the wine is poured, as always. I take a sip of mine and enjoy the taste of it. It took me a while to get used to drinking wine, especially wine that was $75 a bottle, but it's grown on me. Lots of things have grown on me.

George watches me drink, and I start to think about what it would be like to sleep with him. I mean, sure, it would be kind of gross, but not as repulsive as it used to seem to me. And now that I know George is interested, why not? He's not happy in his marriage and I have my flat all to myself. I think I have all the bases covered to take this relationship to the next level.

"The reason I asked you here, Jacquelyn, is because I have something to tell you."

George reaches across and takes my free hand. I immediately know this isn't good. I put down my glass and lean forward. I'm Catholic and one thing I know is true is that the Lord giveth and the Lord taketh away, and it's never truer for a bad Catholic like me.

"OK." I half-hope he stops there. "Really."

"I think we should stop seeing each other," he says firmly but kindly, looking straight into my eyes.

"For a while or for good?" I ask stupidly, already knowing the answer.

"My wife and I've reconnected. I think I should give my marriage another shot. I'm sorry. I hope you understand."

He squeezes my hand. It feels warm and soft and I see his cuticles are immaculate, as if he's recently had a manicure.

"Of course," I say numbly, not wanting to remember the thoughts I was entertaining a few seconds ago. "Of course. It's totally understandable."

George sits back, looking relieved. I blink rapidly. Seeing my face, he leans forward, frowning. "Are you OK, Jacquelyn?"

"Yes. Just a little taken by surprise. But it's a good surprise. For you. And your wife."

I feel so stupid. So young and immature, but not used. George never promised me anything, and I came into this thing with eyes wide-open. It still hurts, though, to be set aside, even if it is in the nicest of ways.

"I'm an old man, Jacquelyn. You are a young and vibrant woman. It would be selfish of me to keep you from finding a young man who can do you justice. Who could make you happy and be there for you all the time," he says kindly. As if he's offering me a new lease on life by removing the burden of himself.

"Yes. Thanks." I push back my chair. I can't stay here one more second. I stand up, walk over to him and press a kiss on his cheek. "Good-bye, George."

I walk quickly out of the restaurant, and am halfway down the block when I hear the hostess's spike heels clicking after me in an awkward jog.

"Wait! Miss? Wait!" She calls, sounding winded. She must not eat to stay that skinny because she's obviously not an exerciser. I turn around. "Thanks. I can't run in these shoes but my boss likes me to wear them."

"I know the feeling." I feel crushed inside.

"Here. He asked me to give you this."

She hands me a carefully wrapped box from Tiffany's. It's heavy, too deep and big for jewelry, but I doubt George would give me flatware or china. I automatically scan through my mental inventory of Tiffany stuff, but can't call up what might be inside.

"Thanks," I say, and take it without even considering what it means to be accepting it. I just want to get back to my car and cry in privacy. And open the box when I'm done.

"Who would have thought, huh?" she asks.

For the first time, I see her in natural light and see she has smoker's skin and wears too much foundation. For months, I've been slightly intimidated by her, but now I see she's not as imposing when she's not standing behind her ornate podium.

"Thought what?" I ask, ready to start walking again.

"That a guy that old could move so quick. Just last night he asked out Kim, she's the hostess who usually works days. You know, the cute Asian girl? He asked her out for a date," she says, pulling out a cigarette and lighting it quickly. "Men are pigs, even the ones who smell good and look like your grandpa. Sorry."

"Yes." A new girlfriend. A new exotic girlfriend. Of course there is a new girlfriend. Why wouldn't there be? "Well, thanks for this, and don't take it personally if I never eat at your restaurant again."

"Honey, I don't blame you. But at least you got some good gifts out of it." She looks at my bracelet and inhales deeply on her cigarette. "Kim told me."

"Yes, at least I can take comfort in that. And that I didn't sleep with him," I add quickly. I desperately want the Globe hostess to know I have some self-respect.

"Sure. I've got to get back to work. You take care." She clicks back, smoking, and then flicks her cigarette into the street before disappearing inside.

When I get to my car, I open the box. Inside is a velvet case with a sterling silver pen. Beneath that, wrapped in tissue paper, are five banded stacks of crisp $100s.

92

Me

I spend most of my days half-heartedly checking out job boards on the Internet and helping Bina with the logistics of canceling a 336-person wedding and reception in Napa, as well as her village-sized reception in India.

Mr. Mayor has been a good boy. Coming home every night for dinner and asking Mrs. Mayor about her day, which she offers only terse tidbits about. He assiduously avoids me, as if I had something to do with him porking his press secretary. If he has to be in a room with me, he makes sure at least one other person is there, too. I don't know if he doesn't trust me or himself. Either way, I'm a bit flattered and grossed out. My crush is a thing of the past. Near past, but I'm over it.

I've been making an effort to call home every couple of days to check on my aunt's status. It turned out her stroke was not a stroke at all but a massive panic attack. Yolie is still mad at me, especially after I sent a huge flower arrangement. She claims I was showing off and that I must have plenty of money to spare if I could afford to throw away $100 on flowers. I found this out through Noel, who got a good chuckle out of it and told me our lovely aunt was milking her "stroke" for all she could.

Lina is back home. After her mother's "stroke" the doctor assured her that sharing her good news would not give her mother a real stroke. Lina announced she was happily married *and* pregnant and now a combination wedding reception and baby shower are in the works. Of course, I'm expected to attend. Of course, I'm looking for a way to get out of it.

93

Bina

"You swear you're coming." Bina had blocked out a whole month for her traditional wedding and honeymoon in India and was on the verge of canceling her trip when somehow I convinced her she owed it to herself to go. Now she's convinced that I need to go as much as she does. "Swear to me, Jacqs."

"Bina, relax. Everything is going to be OK." I'm in such a funk, I don't know which way is up. Lucky for me, she's also a little distracted and doesn't notice I'm not saying yes, but not saying no either.

"I can't do this by myself. I need you."

"I'll ask for the time off. I'm sure it will be OK." I try to make my voice sound more interested than I feel.

"At least two weeks. There's no point in going to India if you don't have at least two weeks," she tells me, for what feels like the hundredth time.

I doubt Mrs. Mayor will give me one week; two are out of the question, but I have nothing to lose by asking.

"I promise. I'll ask today." Maybe I will, maybe I won't. Bina doesn't have to know how pathetically lethargic I've become about making decisions.

A couple of weeks ago Mr. Mayor, with a beaming Mrs. Mayor at his side, announced his intention to run for governor next year and unleashed a media feeding frenzy. If he ever needed Vivian it's now.

Mrs. Mayor even had me hire a PR firm, saying she didn't want to burden me with the extra duties. I guess she figures I'll be too busy picking up dry cleaning to sit down and write a press release on what she'll be wearing on the campaign trail.

I'm ready to give my notice and, with my tax-free, strings-free gift from George, I have enough to survive in style for a few months. But quitting and changing my life just seems like so much work. Things are comfy here. Why rock the boat any more than I already have. Right?

"It will be so fun. Just the two of us!" Bina says, trying to rally the troops. "I've got to go, I'm being paged. Kiss, kiss."

"Yeah." I hang up the phone and resume staring at my nails.

94

Mr. Mayor

I'm sitting at my desk in self-imposed exile while Anita, Lei and Danny have lunch and watch CNN in the Kitchen. Mrs. Mayor is having lunch with some of her "business" friends who are visiting from LA, so I'm eating her Zone meal and my own as well.

"Jacquelyn?" Lei knocks softly on the doorframe and peeks in. I sit up straight and try to look busy.

"Hi, Lei. What's up?" I ask, shuffling papers with one hand and holding a fork in the other.

"Mr. Mayor wants to speak to you in his office," Lei says impassively.

"Mr. Mayor? In his office?" First of all, what's he doing home in the middle of the day and, second, why is he asking me to see him?

"Yes. He says please hurry." Lei ducks out before I can get any more information from her.

I quickly touch up my makeup and smooth out my skirt. This is so wrong, I think, but it doesn't stop me from primping before I step out of my office.

The Kitchen is deserted and it looks as if they've all cleared out to another end of the Mansion. How discreet.

I get to the huge double doors and knock assertively. A few seconds later, Mr. Mayor opens one door and stands aside to let me in. I notice he leaves it open.

"Jacquelyn, thank you for seeing me on such short notice," he says, sounding vaguely like George.

I nod and sit down in one of the stiff leather seats in front of his desk.

"I hope I didn't interrupt your lunch." He sits behind his desk and presses his hands into a little pyramid, another of his signature looks.

I shake my head and keep my mouth shut. He smiles at me. I manage to lift up one side of my mouth, the side without the dimple. His smile gets wider and then disappears completely. This is his serious and torn-up press-conference look: good for apartment fires, budget crises or the gang shooting of a bad boy turned high-school basketball star.

"As you know, I've announced my intention to run for governor."

"Congratulations," I say, not sure if I should be wishing him luck instead.

Bosomy pictures of Mrs. Mayor from her acting days have already showed up in both *The Los Angeles Times* and the *Sacramento Bee*. Yesterday, *Newsweek* called me by mistake. I guess they didn't get the memo that I'm merely her personal assistant; I can't be trusted to talk about the important stuff.

"This is very difficult for me . . . and Katherine, too, of course . . ." He trails off with a huge sigh and slumps slightly in his chair.

I'm getting fired. Hallelujah! My pulse picks up and the fog that's been clouding my eyes seems to lift.

"Katherine has nothing but the highest praise for your work, Jacquelyn, but she feels . . . we both feel that perhaps it's time for her to reevaluate her needs." He presses his lips together and tilts his head. The words change but the actions are all preprogrammed. He's going to make a great governor and maybe even president. "Perhaps it's also time you consider your options."

"Why didn't she fire me herself?" I don't blink. I don't smile.

He shifts around in his seat. I'm going off script and he doesn't know what to do. What a lame way to fire a person. Why doesn't he just come out and say it? I know way too much and I make them both uncomfortable. Never mind that Danny, Anita and Lei know as much if not more than I do. To the Mayors, they aren't real people, just shadows. After all, how threatening are the people who sort your dirty socks and drive you around all day? Plenty, but Mr. and Mrs. Mayor don't think this way. Rich people can afford to be dense.

"Not fire, Jacquelyn. Let's just call this a mutual termination of employment." Harvard Law School wasn't wasted on him. "Katherine just didn't have the heart to do it herself."

Doesn't have a heart, is more like it, but great fucking taste in clothes and accessories.

"I'm sorry, Jacqs," he says and pushes an envelope toward me and a document to sign.

Do I look so malleable that a chunk of change can buy my silence? I look inside the envelope. It's a cashier's check for $500,000 from a New York bank. Seems Gail is, as always, watching over the Baxter family. She can't have me killed but at least she put a fair price on my silence.

"Well," is all I can think to say as I discreetly tuck the flap back into the envelope and place it on my lap. It's all turned out rather profitably. Money-wise, at least.

I reach over pick to up a pen and sign the document.

"I wish things could be different," he says, his eyes dipping to my boobs, knees and then legs.

I'm wearing Mrs. Mayor's chocolate-brown boots. I had only borrowed them for kicks but am now going to keep them for an extra kickback.

"Don't we all, Kit . . . Later!" I get up and stride to the door and turn around before I close it. I grip the doorknob and feel weak with an overwhelming sense of relief that I'm getting off so lightly and richly. "There is one question I do have."

"Yes?" He stands up and smoothes his suit jacket.

"Did you give her that black-eye?" I ask point-blank.

"No, Jacqs, my mother has the dubious honor of that," he replies with a smile, a real smile for once.

"Do me a favor and thank her for me. Bye now! And thanks." I wave the check at him and close the door with a firm thud.

95

Dr. N

"So there you have it." I lean back after a solid forty minutes of talking. I take a sip of water. "All the little secrets I've been hording."

She clears her throat and adjusts her glasses, clears her throat again. "And how does this make you feel?"

I stand up, holding a check to close my bill for our sessions. I hand it to her, smile and ask her the question I should have asked at our first meeting.

"I was wondering, Helen, are you married?"

She takes the check with a confused expression as she watches me make my way to the door. "No. I've never been married, Jacquelyn."

"It's probably for the best."

96

Emilio

"*Hola,* Jacquelyn." He took my call right away, a sign, a good one for once. "The *chisme* is you're back on the market."

He called me a couple of weeks ago with an offer to work for his newly formed Citizens for the City, a grassroots organization he hopes will get him elected to the mayor's office, once Kit officially vacates his seat in September.

"And so are you, or so I read." He and some rich chick from a wine family recently went kaput. I haven't completely broken myself of reading the society page in the *Chronicle.* I knew it would never last.

"I just haven't found a woman who can keep up with me."

"I'm not surprised," I say and cringe. Flirting is OK, but I want this guy to give me a job, a real job, when I get back from wherever I wind up.

"I've got big plans. I need good people with me. From *la raza.*"

"Fresh meat?"

"A little less white meat, you could say. Brown meat has more *sabor*. You're not going to sue me for harassment?"

I can tell he's joking, but a guy in his position needs to cover his ass. It's one thing to be a playboy columnist but quite another to be a philandering mayoral contender.

"No." I have more than enough ill-gotten money to last me a lifetime. "I'm not the suing type."

"Are you ready to put your education to good use?"

"I'd like to interview for a staff position, if you can wait a few months." The prudent thing would be to lie low for only a couple weeks and then hit him up for a job, but I've never been prudent when it comes to job hopping and other endeavors.

"For you, Jacquelyn, I'd wait an eternity."

"Not an eternity, but a little while. And, Emilio, call me Jacqs."

97

Noel

"The mortgage is automatically deducted from my bank account, so you don't have to worry about it," I tell Noel as we go over last-minute details. It didn't take much to convince him to come up to San Francisco and "watch" my flat while I'm gone.

I put all my jewelry in a safe deposit box and put a lock on my closet, just in case my family comes to visit and Noel isn't around to guard my stuff. Last thing I want is them tallying up the contents of my wardrobe and then wondering where I got the money to shop at Gucci and to, oh, take a little trip around the world. They'll assume I was either selling drugs or a hooker. A busy hooker who sells drugs.

Marrying a white guy, getting a divorce, having a platonic affair with a married man, seeing a shrink, almost sleeping with your ex-husband before his wedding—*pfft.* All small beans compared to the stigma of being branded the family whore. Even a successful one.

"Are you paying attention? You do need to pay the PG&E and phone bills. I've left my checkbook here, but don't go crazy turning on lights and making phone calls or I'll kill you when I get back."

"Uh-huh." He's distracted, as always, surveying the place as if he is imagining all the changes he can make.

"I've set up a system for you to sort the mail. Magazines go here. See? The label says magazines." I had to do something with all my organizational skills and energy now that Katherine what's-her-name doesn't want them.

"How many fucking magazines do you get, Jacqs?" Noel asks, hoisting up the three oversized boxes I picked up from the Container Store especially for this purpose.

"A lot." I made sure to renew all Mrs. Mayor's magazine subscriptions a week before I was let go to roam greener pastures. "Bills here in the red bin." I hold the red bin up and wave it under Noel's nose. He bats it away. "Letters and invites, here. Whatever you aren't sure of throw into the junk-mail bin. DO NOT throw anything away."

"Relax, Jacqs." Noel plops down on the couch and puts his feet up on the coffee table. Instead of scolding him I do the same.

"My friend Vivian will be back in two weeks. She's staying in the second bedroom so you can sleep in mine." I grab his chin and point his head in the direction of the proper room. "This one: yes. That one: no."

"Is she cute?" He and Giselle got back together for a while, but she finally has had the good sense to dump him for good. It's one of the big reasons he's eager to clear out of our parents' house for a while.

"Noel, she is beyond cute. She's radioactive." By the look on his face, this got his attention. I think this will make up for the lack of cable. And, lucky for me, she's also going to be working with Citizens of the City, thanks to a very generous consultant package finagled by Emilio Cortez.

"You're shitting me?"

"I'm sure the two of you will hit it off. Just not on my couch, please." I've slipcovered it, just in case.

"You got it, *hermanita*. Send me lots of postcards and buy me some hash if you make it to Amsterdam . . . I'll miss you." He folds me into his arms and squeezes me hard.

"I'll miss you, too." My eyes water from the pressure and the sentimentality of the moment. "I love you, Noel."

"I love you, too, Jacqs." He kisses the top of my head. "Hope you don't spend most of your trip on the shitter."

98

Nate and Bethany

I took the easy way out and left a message at Nate and Bethany's hotel, just hours before they're supposed to check in. I apologized, of course, that I wouldn't be able to make dinner since I'm on my way to India and to give me a call the next time they find themselves in San Francisco. A beautiful arrangement of Rustique roses from French Tulip will greet them in their room and set the mood for the rest of their married lives. Together.

I doubt Bethany would have married him if she didn't really love him. Why would she? She had a good-enough reason to call it off, but she didn't.

Maybe Nate has really changed and his being my former husband isn't a handicap after all. Maybe he is truly capable of having a fulfilling adult relationship with the woman he has kept the truth from, convinced his whole family to lie to and presented with a used diamond engagement ring. You never know. It is a very nice ring, after all.

Either way, I truly wish them the best of luck.

99

Mamá

"Did you get the money *tu papá* sent *con* Noel?" These are my mother's first words to me when I call her to tell her good-bye. "He sent *cien dólares*."

"*Sí, lo tengo*." I pressed the crisp $100 bill between the pages of the Bible my mother gave me when I first left home, the first time I've ever cracked it open. I never plan to spend it. I can imagine my father driving to the bank and requesting the crisp new bill and maybe even bragging to the teller that his daughter was leaving for an adventure of a lifetime. More likely it's all my mother's doing. But I'll let myself pretend it's my father's way of saying he loves me. "Tell Dad *gracias*. Really, it means a lot."

My mother, instead of lamenting my lack of husband, lack of job, lack of direction, merely asks, "*¿Qué buscas?*"

What can I say? I didn't have a good answer for her almost a decade ago and I don't have a good one now.

"I don't know, Mom . . . Maybe I'll finally find out if I'm looking for anything at all."

100

Me

By hour nineteen, and still a few thousand miles from Bombay, or Mumbai, as Bina insists on calling it, I finally feel it's safe to just let go of everything I've left behind in San Francisco. I cry and laugh in the cramped bathroom, bouncing up and down with the turbulence.

I wash my face, trying not to get any of the funky airplane water in my mouth and head back to my seat, relaxed and excited at the same time. Myra is meeting us at the airport, along with a throng of Bina's relatives, and I'm looking forward to having a long talk with someone who understands what I've been through, at least the Mrs. Mayor part.

The plane gives a jolt and Bina startles awake and looks over at me with a scared smile. I take her hand, lean my head back and close my eyes. I have my best friend at my side, a fanny pack stuffed with traveler's checks, comfortable but stylish walking shoes and a whole continent full of people who know nothing about me to look forward to discovering.

What more could I want? What more is out there? I don't know and I can't wait to find out.

A READING GROUP GUIDE

UNDERNEATH IT ALL

MARGO CANDELA

ABOUT THIS GUIDE

The suggested questions are intended to enhance your group's reading of this book.

DISCUSSION QUESTIONS

1. In the opening chapter, Jacqs is at her parents' home in Los Angeles trying to figure out a way to tell them she's divorced. Instead of telling them she is, she hedges and announces she's going to get a divorce. Is her reluctance to be straightforward with her parents a sign of her immaturity or that she herself isn't used to the idea that her marriage is over?

2. Jacqs and Mrs. Mayor have a difficult relationship. On the one hand, Jacqs covets Mrs. Mayor's life (and her husband). On the other, Jacqs is aware how desperately unhappy Mrs. Mayor is. Why would Jacqs fantasize about taking Mrs. Mayor's place when she knows what her life is really like?

3. When Jacqs's best friend, Bina, announces her plans to marry Sanjay, Jacqs is flabbergasted and subtly, and not so subtly, tries to undermine Bina and Sanjay's relationship. Even after Jacqs's suspicions about Sanjay turn out to be far worse, is Jacqs still motivated by selfishness to keep her friend close? Or do the new circumstances justify Jacqs's initial feelings and actions?

4. Jacqs allows herself to be swept off her feet by George, a married man, with flattery, gifts and fancy meals. She also assumes a persona not unlike Mrs. Mayor's. Even though they never consummate their affair, is Jacqs's behavior morally reprehensible or is she just playacting? Who is more culpable in the whole charade?

5. Vivian (Mr. Mayor's sexy press secretary) and Natasha (Mrs. Mayor's makeup artist) are on a downward spiral and

both grab on to Jacqs for dear life. She is unable to help them as she's facing her own relationship issues on all fronts. But she tries. Is this just another sign that Jacqs can't stop meddling or that she finds it easier to live through others than to face the reality of her own life?

6. Reporter Emilio Cortez is a constant thorn in Jacqs's side, reminding her that he knows the game she's playing. At one point she realizes that Emilio has slept with Vivian, thereby dashing all hopes she had of having a relationship with him. Instead she asks him for a job in his campaign to be the next mayor of San Francisco. Is this just another version of her other relationships with unattainable men or is Jacqs really interested in making a difference in the political landscape?

7. Jacqs has a complicated relationship with her family. Her mother hopes she will settle down close to home and marry. Her brother Noel is in need of saving, and she can barely say two words to her father and older sister. Is Jacqs's distance from her family her own doing? Have her choices (leaving home for college, eloping, divorcing, staying in San Francisco instead of going back home) led to her sense of alienation when she's home with her family or is she just different from them?

8. A year after her divorce from Nate, Jacqs still keeps tabs on him and goes as far as to run into him accidentally on purpose when she's in Los Angeles. When she finds out Nate has moved on, she's devastated. Does this mean she is still in love with him? And when Nate expresses his attraction for her, why is she so offended? Isn't that what she wanted? Or did she expect something more?

9. Jacqs makes out quite well financially, even though she loses her job and rich boyfriend. When George and Mr.

Mayor offer her money, not only does she accept the payoffs, she never considers not taking them. Is she just being pragmatic or is this more evidence as to how misguided Jacqs is about life and love? Does it make it any better that she uses the money to help Bina escape her own heartbreak and to give her brother Noel the little push he needs to start living his own life?

10. At the very end of the book Jacqs decides to be honest with everyone and then, conveniently, goes on an adventure of a lifetime, finally using her treasured passport. But along with her passport, she's carrying many secrets with her. Does this mean Jacqs is doomed to repeat history once she gets back to San Francisco or even as she travels around with Bina? Has she learned anything? And if so, will it make a difference as she goes forward with her life?

A CONVERSATION WITH MARGO CANDELA

Q. What's your background and how did it lead you to becoming a writer?

A. I'm first generation Mexican-American. My mom has a goofy, almost dorky sense of humor and my dad is a great storyteller with a slightly caustic wit. I like to think I've inherited the best of both and turned it into an honest profession. I became a writer because my mom suggested it. (Kids, listen to your mother!) I was a little lost and she said, "Why don't you do something with writing? You seem to like it." At the time I had purchased a manual typewriter that had script lettering and I was typing on a comic story for my own amusement. But I'm a practical person and I went the journalism route and eventually I started writing fiction. I don't think I've properly thanked my mother for the little push she gave me. I'd buy her a mink coat, but she's just not that kind of person. Maybe a rubber chicken.

Q. How much of you is there in Jacqs?

A. A little here and there, but mostly I envisioned Jacqs as the woman I could be if I had taken a different path in life. A radically different path, as in imaginary and not even remotely possible. It was such fun to write about someone who really only had to care about herself, what kind of choices she could make, but at the same time have a sense of all-encompassing guilt over living only for herself. This I could relate to easily, as any Latina Catholic daughter can. I wanted Jacqs to be a flawed but essentially good person who is a little lost and looking for her own place in the world.

Q. Who was the inspiration for Mrs. Mayor?

A. No one in particular. I just imagined what it would be like to be an incredibly beautiful woman who was completely selfish, self-centered, insecure and in way over her head. How awful and fabulous would a life like that be? To never have to worry about a bad-hair day but to know that the only thing that matters is how you look. She was a lot of fun to write and I think readers will find she's not a horrible person. She's kind of sad and lonely, but you're not quite sure you'd want her as a friend, much less as a boss.

Q. How about George? Is there a George in your life?

A. George was a devil, if not the Devil. A hot, romantic one with great taste and time to spare. I have no George in my life, but that's because I don't get out much. For me George represented the ultimate temptation for Jacqs to completely reinvent herself and throw away her values, and morals, and truly compromise her self-worth. It was very important for me to tempt her this way and I considered letting her go through with it, but it would have been a very different book. I think at one time or another we all face a George in life; the seemingly easy way out, the path of least resistance. But I wanted to show that there is a hidden price for making that kind of choice. I'm not a moralist or trying to steer people away from the allure of emotional adultery, fabulous lunches and dinners, and expensive gifts. I just wanted to show that Jacqs was aware of the price she was paying and what she'd do when faced with the choice to go all the way.

Q. How about Jacqs's brother Noel?

A. He's the person we all want to save and protect in our lives but who we ultimately have to let go. These were the most emotional passages for me to write because I really thought about all my loved ones and how I want to make them happy, make everything right, but I can't and shouldn't. Sometimes you have to let people be who they are, appreciate them for what they can give and do, and leave it at that.

Q. There's a lot of tension, sexual and otherwise, between Jacqs and Emilio Cortez, the newspaper reporter.

A. He's a melding of all the men in Jacqs's life—from Mr. Mayor and George to Nate and her brother Noel. Jacqs is attracted to him for all the right and wrong reasons, and this is why she automatically rejects any idea of having a real relationship with him. Imagine how much work it would be! Plus, he's a little too much like her, though she gets around emotionally where Emilio just gets around. In life it's always interesting to have that one person who makes you stand up straighter, makes you take your game up a notch and who you know won't let you get away with fooling yourself. This is what Emilio does for Jacqs. He pokes holes in her façade. And who can't use a good poke now and then?

Q. What would be your ideal reader's reaction after they close the book on the last page of *Underneath It All*?

A. Reading a book is such an intimate and personal experience, but I hope a reader would have a sense of having taken a satisfying journey and would have a reaction to Jacqs. Some people may love her, others may find her selfish. And they could talk about her and the other characters in the book as real people, because that's what they were to me—real people. Not caricatures or stereotypes or convenient foils to advance the plot. I have more respect for the people I'm writing about (even though they are entirely fictitious) and the people who I'm writing for to do that.

Q. What are you working on now?

A. My wonderful editor, Sulay Hernandez, is putting me through my paces for my second novel. It's about a tightly wound caterer who realizes she's fallen short of her own potential after her boyfriend leaves her. This story was a little more risky for me because it deals with love in the romantic sense, and nothing makes me more uncomfortable than squishy love stories. Being who I am I dealt with it the only way I could, through humor. Wanting to be loved and cherished is universal, but I believe you have to know yourself to truly appreciate it, and this novel follows her journey to finding that place in herself. Along the way there are a few detours that were fun to explore and in the end she comes full circle with a twist.

Q. Why don't your books have happy endings?

A. Because I believe there are no happy endings. All endings are ambiguous to me, the start of a new story. But there is closure and the infinite possibilities for another chapter, just like in life.

We hope you enjoyed
UNDERNEATH IT ALL
as much as we enjoyed
working with this talented author.
And now please turn the page for
an exclusive first look at
Margo Candela's next novel
coming in October 2007 from Kensington.

When You're Unhappy and You Don't Know It

"Natalya, we need to talk."

"Talk?" I barely bother to look up from the list I'm making. This is my first Saturday off in months. No brunches, wedding receptions or engagement parties to cater. Rick knows or should know by now t hat when I have time to myself I like to sit around in a comfy pair of sweats and plan out my week, my month, my year in my planner. But still, duty calls. "Talk about what, babe?"

"I don't know how to say this, but . . ."

When my boyfriend, my very nearly fiancé, tells me that he's moving out after living together for almost three years, the thing that pops into my head isn't "Oh my God, he's breaking up with me . . . Maybe I should pay attention to what he's saying."

Nope.

What I'm thinking is "I really need to redecorate this place." Mentally, I begin to rearrange my furniture. I have already rid myself of the beat-up Pier One white wicker from my girlhood bedroom and family hand-me-downs (particle board does not an heirloom make) for real grown-up gal décor. I have it all nicely put together—home, career and personal life, all in order.

"This is really hard for me . . ."

When Rick moved in, after four months of serious dating, all he brought with him were a cardboard box of clothes, a vast collection of cult movies and related paraphernalia, and one beat-up medium-sized saucepan and wooden spoon that made up all his cooking and eating utensils. At the time I admired that he traveled so light.

"You know I care for you. A lot . . ."

I've always been the practical one in my family, especially when things are falling apart. And I've never been one to let things fall apart, no, never completely. I've mastered the art of rearranging, reorganizing, and reconceptualizing. (Is that a word?)

"It's not you, it's me, Natalya." Rick looks into my eyes. He knows I have a soft spot for his. Despite the fact that he's grown doughy around the middle, he still has huge hazel eyes with long dark brown lashes that melt my heart, most times. "It's me, please believe me."

That snaps me back into reality. I don't believe him; of course he thinks it's me. And it's not just because I'm Catholic and think everything is my fault. The fact is, Rick has never been one to take full responsibility for anything. Forgive me for finding it surprising that he's going to start now.

"It's you?" *He* wants to break up with *me*. I always thought it would be the other way around. And so did most of his friends, all my friends and both our families. I must have misheard him. "Exactly what are you telling me?"

"I don't know how to say this, but . . ."

Rick is now twenty-nine, we both are. According to my planner we should be announcing our engagement in the very, *very* near future and be married two months after my thirtieth birthday next year. I hate it when special occasions and holidays are bunched together.

"This is really hard for me . . ."

How many times after seeing the disappointment in my parents' faces had I reassured myself there's nothing, *nothing* unusual about two adults living together and not being married in San Francisco—it's even expected. Who in their right mind would get married without living together first? Who's that crazy? Not me, that's for sure.

"You know I care for you. A lot . . ."

I told my parents we were going to get married, just as soon as Rick finishes his master's. Of course I didn't tell Rick this. Who needs that kind of pressure? I also haven't gotten around to telling my folks that Rick dropped out of grad school two years ago.

"It's not you, it's me, Natalya."

"Is this about your parents and what happened the last time we went over?" I interrupt him, choosing to ignore that he seems to have just repeated himself, and I sat through the whole thing again and still didn't pay complete attention to what he was saying.

"No. No. It's not at all about them," he says which, of course, leads me to believe that it's a little bit about them. "It's not about anything like that."

Though it never came up directly, we both knew that his parents weren't thrilled with the fact that I'm not white. His father's only topics of oration ranged from anti-Castro tirades to bitching about NAFTA. His mother's dinner table chitchat was limited to which of Rick's old girlfriends was still single or newly divorced. I'd manage to endure in silence—I was raised Catholic, after all—but this last time we had to have dinner with his parents, I snapped. When his mom brought up Heather/Crystal/Tiffany, I innocently asked Rick if she was the one who gave him crabs in his senior year. They didn't even offer us leftovers when we left shortly thereafter. We both know the race, cultural, whatever thing has always mattered and, I know if I'm willing to commit the next twelve hours, I can make Rick admit it, too.

"Are you sure?" Desperation begins to creep into my voice. I clear my throat and blink back tears.

"It's entirely my fault, Natalya." Rick does the leg jiggle thing that drives me crazy. I put my hand down, hard, on his knee to get him to stop or at least slow it down.

"Entirely your fault? Not mine? You're saying this is all about you?" I sputter, feeling like a fool.

"No, no. It's me. I just need . . . space."

"Space? Space? You want to break off an almost four-year relationship because of space?" I ask incredulously. Men never need "space." If they want some time apart, they watch endless reruns of *Knight Rider*, play computer games, or, if they're not Rick, start putting in extra hours at work. They do anything except think about the need to articulate their desire for space. "That's what you need? Space?"

"Yeah," Rick says sheepishly.

"Space for what?" In my opinion this is a valid question. It is, after all, his reason or at least the reason he's giving me for this breakup.

"I don't know, space. Just space," he says turning defensive. What, am I making him uncomfortable? Too friggin' bad!

"You already said that. Explain it to me because I would really love to hear what you mean by *space.* Really, tell me! Do you want more room in the bathroom medicine cabinet or do you want to date other women? Space means a lot of things, Rick."

He flinches. He's not used to me losing my temper. I'm not used to me losing my temper. It's something I make a point of not doing. Until now. Three years and four months and five days of being levelheaded, being the grown-up and the responsible one in our relationship is coming to an end and I don't care if he finds it unattractive or scary.

"I don't know . . . I just feel I need more space." Rick says digging his hands into his ratty jean pockets. I hate those jeans, always have. I even tried to toss them out once, but he fished them out of the trash bin and put them on. Without washing them.

"I thought we made a point of giving each other plenty of space? How much more space could you want? Especially considering the space you've been occupying for the past few years is technically *my* space but I've never, ever held it against you. Wasn't it part of our *agreement*? You do your thing and I do mine and each of us is happy and fulfilled and, how did you put it? Oh, yeah, we both enjoy an autonomous, yet *committed* relationship."

Rick shrugs. Obviously he thought his needing space would

settle the issue for both of us. He wisely keeps silent because I'm on a roll.

"What is it that you told me last week? How cool it was that each of us was so OK with our agreement, our commitment to each other. And how it was so cool that we could live the way we wanted to and not have to worry about what anyone thought. Isn't that what you told me?" I say, trying not to whine or rant or rage, but I can feel the effort making my eyes bug out.

"That wasn't last week, Natalya, it was last year," Rick says in a voice that makes me think he may have been thinking about space for a while.

"Yeah, well, you still said it." I sit back and cross my arms over myself. Was it that long ago that I last checked into the state of things between us? I know I've been busy, but it's his fault, too. He's so laid back about things like who makes more money, who's on top, I just thought he was going with the flow as usual.

"We're just different, Natalya," Rick says. I guess he's through explaining things to me.

"Different? Like I'm an adult and you're . . . you're . . ." I could go many different ways here, but why make myself look petty and bitter? Even though that's the way I feel. ". . . you're you?"

"You know what I mean." Rick is starting to look exasperated and annoyed with me. He has some balls. "Natalya. We want different things out of life. I want different things."

"What different things?"

"I don't know, Natalya. What do you want me to say? It's just not me. This is just not me," Rick says, continuing to be abstract.

"It was you for years and now it's not? Now all of a sudden you gotta be you and you can't do that with me?" If I phrase my question the right way, Rick may spit forth some nugget that will explain this, and I can then go live the rest of my life in peace. Is that too much to ask him to do?

"Natalya, it's been happening for a while." Rick shuffles over to stand by the window.

"Oh," is all I can say. That's pretty concrete. Well, of course I knew things weren't perfect between us, but I never expected it this. I'm usually so organized, so perceptive. I always know what's going on in my life and Rick, like it or not, *is* a part of my life, an important part. And I thought I was an important part of his.

"Look, Natalya this is hard for me, too, but I have to leave. It's just not . . . me. I mean, it's me, not you." Rick wrings his hands and gives me a pleading look. He wants me to be nice. Yeah, right, and maybe he wants me to fix him a sandwich and then rub his feet while he finishes breaking up with me.

"So when are you planning on leaving?" If he says he needs a couple of weeks to get things together I'll throw him and his videos out the window. But if he needs a couple of weeks, maybe there's some hope of working something out. If I move some commitments around, I could block out an hour a week for couple's therapy.

"Uh . . ." Just then the doorbell rings. "Uh . . ." Rick sprints for it. He opens it a crack and whispers urgently. He closes it and gives me a pained puppy look.

"Oh, Jesus Christ, you're telling me you're moving out like five minutes before you actually move out! This is so . . . so . . . *like you!*"

"I understand if you don't want to be here for this." He says hopefully.

"How damn generous of you, Rick. Spare me. Just get your crap and go!"

I sit on the couch and clutch a pillow to my chest while he lets in a couple of geeky friends from the video store. They don't even say hi or acknowledge that I'm even in the room.

They start with Rick's prized possessions—a rickety put-it-together-yourself unpainted shelf unit for his massive TV, state-of-the-art entertainment equipment and his beloved video collection. The unit takes up an entire wall but I tolerated it because adults in adult relationships make compromises for the sake of the relationship. His clothes are carted out in garbage bags, two of them.

"OK. So, well, I'm going now?" Rick shuffles his feet. Put some music on and it's pretty close to his attempt at dancing.

"Are you asking me a question or stating the obvious?" I watch as Rick wanders into the kitchen. I get up and walk to the door and hold it open for him. "Your TV is out there and I know how much it hurts for you to be parted from it."

"I guess this is good-bye." He steps toward me like he actually thinks he can give me a good-bye kiss. I turn my face away. He steps into the doorway and looks at me. "Natalya, please—"

I slam the door in his face and go put my head down on the kitchen counter. I open my eyes and catch site of his beat-up saucepan, pathetic among my gleaming copper pots hanging off my stainless steel Williams-Sonoma ceiling rack.